Seductive

THEA DEVINE

Seductive

BRAVA

KENSINGTON BOOKS
http://www.kensingtonbooks.com

KENSINGTON BOOKS are published by

Kensington Publishing Corp.
850 Third Avenue
New York, NY 10022

All Kensington titles, imprints and distributed lines are available at special quantity discounts for bulk purchases for sales promotion, premiums, fund raising, educational or institutional use.

Special book excerpts or customized printings can also be created to fit specific needs. For details, write or phone the office of the Kensington Special Sales Manager: Kensington Publishing Corp., 850 Third Avenue, New York, NY, 10022. Attn. Special Sales Department. Phone: 1-800-221-2647.

ISBN 1-57566-798-3

First Kensington Trade Paperback Printing: April, 2001
10 9 8 7 6 5 4 3 2 1

Printed in the United States of America

Prologue

London, England
Winter 1896

He sat hunched in a corner out of the rain, picking at a loaf of moldy bread, a ragged peasant with no home, no life, nowhere to go—the consummate actor so in tune with his character that not a single passerby, on that rain-fogged night, gave him a second glance.

The moment was at hand. Everything ended here. It had been a long road, but he was finally ready to give it all up, ready to walk into the light after having spent most of his life in the dark, edging into the unknown.

He waited, his patience deep as a well. He'd learned the hard way: he never took chances and he always plotted everything out so that he had some control. As recklessly as he had lived, he still was ruled by that caution. He always had been.

Tonight was the culmination of a career lived in secret, in the shadows, and on the run. A few more moments—he merely awaited the sign, the signal, already prearranged—and it would be over.

Over . . . A chilling thought. An idea to embrace. *No, no— this is just the beginning, his mother had whispered on her deathbed. Claim your inheritance. Don't deny that which is rightfully yours.*

But nothing was his. He'd lived a life devoid of anything that could have a claim on him. He'd needed freedom, detachment, ease of movement, and those things he *had* claimed, at the ongoing risk of his life.

And so he waited, wallowing in a muddy corner just out of the rain, waiting, waiting, waiting, with the seemingly infinite patience of the bone-weary derelict who knows life will never be fair.

He lifted his head every five minutes or so, as if he were praying for the rain to stop, seeking through the sheets of pouring water, the one inimitable sign that his contact was near.

Shadows, as eerie as ghosts, moved through the downpour, bent double by the rain, darting in and out of doorways seeking shelter. Light punctuated the dark as a door opened or a lantern flashed on a carriage pushing through the muck and mayhem of the storm.

Soon, soon . . . nothing to fear—all under control. Mere moments until . . . until—

Now . . . ?

He breathed deep, inhaling the scent of rain, mud, dirt, horse . . . there—*that* . . . He waited that additional moment longer, always cautious . . .

And then he moved into a crouch—scent of unwashed man, rotting bread, faintest whiff of incense perfuming the air—

—he peered around the corner—long shadow coming closer, closer, swinging the thurible, the scent stronger and stronger—

. . . the sign, the signal—

Now—

He levered himself upward to a howl of pure terror . . .

NOOOOO . . . !

An ominous thud. Footsteps running, receding . . .

Body in the street, drowning in blood, the embers from the thurible spread all over the road hissing wildly, rain drowning the scent of incense . . .

—no time no time to stop, to make sure—

—*bloody damn hell* . . . a knife . . . grab it—*shit*—drop it . . . get out!

Pounding footsteps—voices: "There—the vagrant—after him . . ."

Bloody, bloody hell . . . the Yard—

"There—" A whistle blew; more men, streaming out from corners, from houses, from who knew where. Pounding feet, bodies angling off in four directions to corner him . . .

Shouts in the night—"Stop . . . ! *You*—halt!"

Shots in the night, cracking one two three . . . swallowed by the fog and the rain as two dozen constables converged under the street lamp where he was last seen, and where *he* watched triumphantly from afar.

As if mere mortals could stop him.

Nothing had ever stopped him.

He was the man they called Vapor, because he was known for disappearing into thin air.

And this time, he was taking thousands of pounds' worth of Russian imperial jewels with him.

Chapter 1

Shenstone House
Exbury, England
One week later

Never come at night.

That was the first thing. She was to be utterly circum-
spect—and she must come by day, because no one ever knew
who might be prowling around at night.

And second, food was not that important. Security was.

And—*she would have to take everything on faith.*

She balked at that, but she had no choice. Nor did she
question; there was no point.

She felt like the most Gothic of heroines as she crept down
the steps to the secret underground room every afternoon
with a sack of food in hand.

"Are you there?" she whispered, groping for the door to
what had been the wood trough years ago.

And as it had for the past four days, a shadow emerged
from one of the dark corners. "*Shhh* . . . not a whisper, dear
girl."

The sack was taken from her outstretched hands.

"A small candle—today surely it's safe . . . " she ventured.

"No, no. This will do for now. Another day or two, I
think, and then I'll be able to leave, and everything will be as
it was before."

"Will it?" she murmured.

"My dear Elizabeth—"

The chiding tone set her back for a moment. Things *would* be the same. Things would be better, even, now that her husband was dead, because the waiting was over.

But that was neither here nor there at the moment.

"This changes nothing. No one knows I'm here. Everything will be the same as before."

"I believe you," she whispered. She did. This was the one person she *could* believe, the one person she trusted.

And that was the first time this promise had been spoken. And that meant something too.

"A little more time, Elizabeth, and all will be well."

But *she* was the one who must still wait, she thought mordantly. She was so very good at waiting—and always for *everyone else's* plans and schemes to come to fruition.

But she had made her own bed, she would never deny it. At seventeen, she had purposefully become the bride of the widowed William Massey, Earl of Shenstone, solely to gain entrée into those rarefied circles in which royalty moved.

She had walked into that marriage with her eyes wide open, knowing that William Massey wanted a son, and that she was exactly what an aging bull needed for that purpose: a beautiful, young, untried, uncritical virgin.

She had thought William would pass away sooner than later, but it was seven long unendurable years until he finally died of a heart attack during yet another futile attempt to get her with child.

And still she was waiting.

"I'm so tired of waiting," she murmured.

"It won't be long. This was just a slight detour . . ."

Among so many other detours, she thought stringently, but why go over things that were past? There was no going back. She, of anyone, knew that. And besides, the promise had been made.

She changed the subject. "And I'm to just leave you again?"

"You are." The tone was implacable now, just as it had been for the last four days, warning her that questions and sympathy were not welcome, and that answers might never be forthcoming.

Women must wait . . .

"So you're set for tonight then."

"Perfectly. But I'll be with you soon."

Another promise?

"Very well." She kept her tone cool. The answers would come eventually. She paused at the door for a moment, but she could see nothing in the dark.

"Elizabeth—?"

It was like talking to a ghost. "Yes?"

"There's been nothing from the solicitors?"

"Nothing," she whispered.

Good . . .

Did she hear that, or did she imagine it? The darkness was impenetrable behind her.

Everything was impenetrable at the moment; nothing in her life had made sense since her capricious royal lover abandoned her that unspeakable last time because he would not, *could not*, marry a commoner.

Ah, so be it, she thought grimly, as she picked her way through the long black tunnel and out of the cellar. No use repining about *that*. And certainly not about her marriage to William.

She pushed against the metal doors at the cellar entrance that gave into the gardens. No one knew of this secret entry, except she; the doors were flush to the ground, and she always covered them over with vines and branches, so no one could ever tell anything was there.

"Mum—"

The rusty voice of the elderly gardener caught her by surprise, and she whirled on him. "Watton! You scared me half to death."

"Didn't mean nothing, mum." He ducked his grizzled head, as if he couldn't—or shouldn't—look at her directly. "Just saw you walking and thought you might need something."

"Nothing. I need nothing, Watton. I was just out for a walk." Why was she explaining to him? *Stop it now.* "Thank you."

He nodded his head, an odd bent-up old man her husband had taken on some five or six years ago, who knew how to grow things and spent hours on his knees digging in the soil. And that made him invaluable despite his infirmities and quirks.

Unless, this afternoon, he had been skulking around. And that made him a nuisance. But surely not a threat.

He hadn't been prowling: she was just overwrought and not thinking clearly. *All those promises . . .*

She waited impatiently, mistress of the manor now. "Is there anything else, Watton?"

"No, mum." He ducked his head again and shuffled off in the opposite direction, as slow moving as an elephant.

It meant nothing. No one could tell there was anything beneath that pile of vines and branches. She would leave it at that. He had just unfortunately come upon her at the wrong place and time. There was nothing more to it.

And besides, soon everything would be as it had been, and none of this ridiculous secrecy would matter.

It had been promised. And she was counting on it.

Know your enemy. It was the first lesson Nicholas had ever learned and he lived by it.

You never know who your enemy might be.

It might even be his own father, whose death became a betrayal when his mother revealed on her deathbed that his father had been the younger brother of an earl, had had an affair with the Earl's wife, and thus had been banished to the far reaches of Russia.

It turned everything upside down for Nicholas: his sense of himself and his family; the idea that things could have been so different, and that he could have been raised in another place and lived an entirely different life, if his father had not succumbed to temptation. And worst of all, it made his father too human, and too fallible, when before Nicholas had idolized him.

And all the titles in the world could never make up for it.

That was the hardest lesson, and it had taken root like a weed, growing, gnawing at the bedrock of his being, tangling him up for years so that all he could do was run from it.

But a man never escaped his past.

It haunted him like a spectre, it pursued him with promises, and branded him with a birthright he never wanted.

A man like him only inherited trouble anyway.

There was always an enemy, known or unknown.

This was the second hard lesson that ruled his life.

Even now, he felt that sense of foreboding hovering like sin, defining a world where he had taken too many risks, seen too much danger, caused too many deaths—a half dozen this last mission alone, with him the sole survivor.

But he wasn't even sure of that.

Yet walking that edge, in and of itself, had been the lure of the cat-and-mouse life he'd led all these years. He'd loved manipulating the chess game; being three jumps ahead, slipping two behind; confounding the enemy, and making him sweat.

He missed it. He loathed it.

He wanted to be back in control. A man in hiding, a man chasing shadows, a man wanted for murder, was not in control.

If only he could be sure about the one he called the Unseen Hand.

But even that could be his mind playing tricks on him.

Perhaps it would never be over, he thought warily, and he would die alone, and at the mercy of the shadows.

The choices a man made . . . the things a man did . . .

And someone knew. Knew everything.

And someone had killed.

And that someone was still out there, waiting to steal a fortune in royal jewels; waiting for *him* to make the next move.

* * *

There had been four murders in as many months, in towns from Exbury to London, and there was no doubt in the savage editorials in the London tabloids that there was a maniac on the loose.

Her friends were troubled that Elizabeth lived so far in the country and so all alone, and they were all grateful she was in London this week on the news of the fourth body having been found.

"Oh, nonsense." She brushed away their concern. Her stay in London had been part of the plan, a plan that had backfired, but her guests didn't have to know that. "I have the servants, and the groom and stable boys. And if worse comes to worse, Watton can defend me."

Everyone laughed. Everyone knew that Watton couldn't defend a dandelion let alone a damsel in distress.

Her father protested. "Truly, Elizabeth, until this thing is over, one or the other of us ought to come stay with you."

"Or I can stay on at the townhouse," she offered, more to make peace with him than from any desire to stay in London. And besides, this talk of the murders was putting a damper on her father's dinner party, and she wanted to remedy that as quickly as possible and get everyone focused on the purpose of the gathering: business.

"And how safe is London? What about that child thrown over the cliffs at Tyne?" her father murmured. "And the body they found in the churchyard at St. Clare."

"And then the one out at Montmorency," Elizabeth put in. "So there's hardly a way to predict where this lunatic might next strike. Surely I'm safer at Shenstone than anywhere else."

"Well, here's what we'll do," her father decreed. "We all like a weekend in the country. We'll just all come out and stay with you. Remain in London till Friday and then we'll all go to Exbury—if you must."

Elizabeth closed her eyes in resignation. There was no *must* about anything. She could stay in London for months, or immure herself at Shenstone forever. There was no difference in

that respect. Her friends would come to either place and remain so long as they continued to be amused, and when they
got bored, off they went to the next house party, the next
hostess, the next round of fun and games.

But something *was* different now—something not even her
father knew yet: Nicholas Massey, the long-lost, presumed-
dead son of her husband's only brother was, in fact, alive.

Alive, and on his way to claim everything she had thought
was hers.

How could this have happened? It still wasn't real to her.

She opened her eyes and smiled at them all down the long
glittering damask-covered table. Her father. His three business
associates and their wives. Yolanda, the actress, mistress of
kings. Grigori Krasnov and his wife Marie. Victor Illyev, ever
rebellious, even as he scraped his plate down to the bone
china pattern. The Grand Duchess Mena, daintily dipping her
fingers in the plate-side cut glass bowl. And Giles, her butler,
standing impassively to one side.

She couldn't tell them yet, not yet, not until she had come
to terms with the news herself. *Dear God. How? . . . How,
when agents on two continents had not been able to track him
down?*

Never . . .

"There's an open invitation even if my father issued it," she
murmured. "Please, all of you, come for the weekend as well,
lest Father bore me to tears." And lest *that man* show up and
try to remove her from *her* house.

"My dear," her father said reproachfully. "You're feeling
constrained again. But take heart, your time of mourning will
be soon up, and you can begin to go out and about even more.
But not—please, humor me—while there's a murderer prowling around."

"We will come," Victor said.

And why not? Elizabeth thought trenchantly. Victor lived
to sample the luxuries of English country life, while being al-
ternately contemptuous and covetous of them. He was the
revolutionary of the moment, handsome, tortured, soulful,

spouting rhetoric which never made sense when probed deeper.

But he was amusing, and he was so magnetic that people followed his lead, hoping they would be the first to be counted the friend of a man who might topple an empire. And he was a resource for her father, who was navigating the treacherous waters of financial speculation in Russia.

But more so was Grigori Krasnov, who was so loyal to the new Tsar, and a repository of the underutilized resources ripe for investment by foreign banks in his vast homeland.

A weekend with them would involve business talk unending, but it was better than being alone. And there was always that odd nugget of information that might prove useful later.

But that was something else her father didn't need to know, how she mined every dinner, every contact, every conversation for possibilities, even as she burnished her reputation as the perfect hostess: elegant, beautiful, tragic, discreet.

And destitute. No. She just wouldn't think about that.

She stood, signaling that the gentlemen were free to retire. "It's settled then." And anyway, she didn't know what else to do. "We'll stay in town till Friday, and then you'll all come back to Shenstone with me."

Nicholas didn't know when it occurred to him that there was a pattern to the killings, because at first glance, they seemed so random, and because no one had linked the death of the priest at Bengate to what came after.

But the priest *was* the first, and five more had followed: the woman in the churchyard; the child dashed on the rocks at Tyne; the elderly woman strangled at Montmorency; and the attack on a young mother and her child in Lytton Wood that took both lives.

Brutal murders, all of them, and different enough to send the Yard scrambling after four different killers.

But the killer was one and the same: the one he called the Unseen Hand, taunting him, knowing he would deduce who it was from the clues, and daring him to put a name to the evil, and stop the murders.

So simple, my worthy opponent—I want YOU.

It was that simple. He had merely to show his face publicly and the killings would stop.

And meanwhile, he must live with the possibility of another death.

Ingenious. The cat toying with the mouse, presenting the one thing that would draw it out of hiding.

Goading *him* with the one thing for which he would willingly become the pawn: to save the families of the men in his charge who had been murdered.

All those so-called unrelated killings, all members of his hired mercenaries' families. A sister. A child. A mother. A wife.

Blood on *his* hands . . . not the Unseen Hand.

The killer didn't care.

Come to me. We have much to discuss, much to decide.

The message was as clear as if it were written in stone.

The Unseen Hand was waiting.

And just as he always had thought, there was always an enemy, and he had never been alone.

Shenstone House—One Week Later

"Victor . . . you drink too much." Deftly, Elizabeth lifted his glass and held it away from his grasping hand.

"I drink not enough." He reached up to grab it, and she caught a whiff of ripe male scent and a blast of vodka fumes. "Besides, we have come to play. And how can one play without liquid sustenance."

"Oh, please—" She backed away determinedly. She could have written the script for this scene: it was the same every time, and she should have considered that before issuing her open-ended invitation to Shenstone. Perhaps the *last* invitation to Shenstone.

She shuddered at the thought. "Enough of this." She threw the glass against the wall; the shattering sound halted conversation, and then: "Oh, it's just Victor," someone murmured, and the voices rose again.

"It's just Victor," Victor mimicked. "That is what I do. I drink. I give a voice to the part of the English soul that lives so comfortably and feels so guilty. There is a purpose here, Elizabeth, deeper, higher, and more moral than even you can know. I need to drink because, with alcohol, there comes clarity and direction and . . . and the *words* to encompass the work that still must be done . . ."

Elizabeth clapped. "Oh, bravo, Victor. You've never been so *eloquent* . . . it's a shame you play to an audience of one . . ."

He made a sound. "You have no idea what you mock. Change is coming, Elizabeth. They all are blind. They go their heedless way down the long corridor toward death . . ." He wobbled toward her, and then collapsed at her feet.

"Oh, put him away," Elizabeth begged, as her father wandered into the foyer. "He's babbling again."

"My dear, he's serious as aces."

"I should know better than to invite him anyway," Elizabeth muttered. "Take him up to one of the guest bedrooms, Father, do. And perhaps get him a bath. There's a revolutionary idea."

"Don't be snobbish, my dear. He's a great help to all of us."

"When he's quiet, he is," Elizabeth retorted. "Ah, here comes Giles. Take him away, will you?"

"As you wish, my lady."

Two footmen magically appeared and immediately and efficiently lifted Victor and carried him up the steps.

"There now, Father. Now he is most useful—*not* disrupting the house party."

"You're too cruel, Elizabeth. You know what that man has suffered."

"Yes, and despite all his protestations, his pamphlets, his lectures, and his *philosophy*, here he is, coddled by you—us—and selling himself for a morsel of caviar. Really."

"*He,* at least, is honest," her father said pointedly.

Elizabeth stiffened. *This on top of everything else, and she hadn't yet said one word about the other. God.* "We weren't to talk about Peter ever again. That episode is over."

"Nonsense. You'd take him back quicker than I could snap my fingers."

"He made his choice. He went back to Moscow seven years ago to give his allegiance to his family. There is truly nothing more to be said."

Only there were volumes to be said, and no one to confide in, so she had submerged it all for these seven years And she thought she had held together so well after all this time. One mention of his name and—what? Her knees went weak? Her resolve buckled?

It was too unkind of her father to flick the whip now. He had been the only one to talk to during those heady months when it seemed that Peter would come to the point and ask her to marry him.

Until that painful letter had come, handwritten by Nicholas Romanov, Emperor-to-be and Peter's nephew, laying out for Peter exactly what marriage to her would mean and precisely what he would give up and what he would lose.

She could not compete with that. Back Peter went to Russia and that had been been the end. Except for her broken heart. And her ill-considered marriage, which threw her, as she had hoped, into the elevated social circles in which Peter traveled because she had thought, if she could just *see* him once in a while—

But no. Even seeing him . . . no—she heaved a deep breath. That had been futile too.

Her father looked at her oddly. "He never married, of course."

"No."

"And now that another of Nicholas's uncles has paved the way . . ."

"The grand love affair of Peter's brother that produced a child? No. How could any woman settle for that?" *Her free-*

dom for an illegitimate child and the bottomless monetary gain? Never. Never?

Even if he walked in the front door right *now* . . . ?

"So happy to hear that—" her father began approvingly, only to be interrupted.

"My lady?" Giles, silent as smoke. "Another guest, my lady."

"I'm expecting no one else," she murmured, frowning. "Who would be so rude, so late? Who is it, Giles?"

"My lady." He handed her a card; she scanned it and her breath caught.

Her father read it over her shoulder. "Oh, dear God— Peter . . ." And Elizabeth glanced up at her father.

. . . Everything will be as it was . . .

The promise and prophecy—surely the complications didn't matter—and all her good intentions evaporated.

And then Peter was there, tall, incredibly handsome, perfectly dressed, reaching out to take her hands, and seven years' separation vanished on a sigh, and it was as if he'd never gone away.

Mornings, the rare times when there was company, were the best. Everyone slept in, and would take breakfast *en buffet* at eleven.

Today, however, Elizabeth chose to have breakfast at seven o'clock, on the terrace outside the library, long before her guests would join her. Long before she had to face her father.

She needed to think. She needed to plan. And on top of all of that, *Peter* . . . She hadn't expected to see him again—not soon, not ever.

Not after the last time—two years ago, was it? Across a hot, crowded room, buffeted by the dainty fluttering social butterflies on the hunt, who were in the midst of their first Season.

God, it had been ghastly sitting there with William by her side, watching them preen and parade by, open to every chance and choice, watching Peter eye them all speculatively until he had seen her, made a move toward her, and then veered away.

She didn't think her heart could break a second time. She had thought she was over him. And the worse part had been that he hadn't yet married. And that he was going back to Moscow one more time.

She'd had two years to harden her heart.

And the minute he walked in the door, it had burst open again, and she felt as violently happy as if she were seventeen again.

She had almost forgotten what it was like to be in love. And it didn't matter that mourning must still be observed. Peter was finally here and all things were possible.

Everything will be as it was . . .

The thought of the promise stopped her cold.

She had to tell her father about Nicholas Massey. There was no time, no time at all. And Peter's arrival muddled everything . . .

"Elizabeth—" Her father came up behind her, and pulled out a chair.

She glanced at her watch. It was ten o'clock.

"Good morning, Father." *She could tell him now— Maybe—*

He poured his own tea. "So he's finally here. He didn't have much to say, did he?"

"He speaks volumes by his presence," she murmured. That sounded good. Royalty should be that charismatic, she thought, and Peter *was*. They hadn't needed words. They had joined her guests, and she had spent the entire evening just *looking* at him.

He wasn't a day older, it seemed. And he'd captivated everyone with his interest in every topic they discussed. And everyone pretended not to notice that he'd spent a good part of the evening staring at *her*.

She would not let her father deflate her happiness. The explanations would come later, she was sure of it. And ultimately, Peter's proposal.

"True—you couldn't hear a word he said, his voice was pitched so low," her father said.

"Stop it. *I* am happy to see him, if you're not."

"He won't marry you, Elizabeth."

"Nor do I want to hear any doom-and-gloom predictions."

"You're still a naif, even if you've been keeping such sophisticated company."

"Then let me not remind you, Father, that all your good fortune stems from the Masseys."

"Indeed, do not. I've spun gold from such hay as William cared to toss me, Elizabeth, but all my success is not pinioned on what little he chose to send my way."

Elizabeth stiffened. How the story changed as the years went on. In point of fact, *every* success her father enjoyed had come from William and his connections, and lately from her, as she gutted her income to keep him in business.

But while they had each made their own bargains with the devil, only she had been the one to pay. Surely with Peter's arrival, she would finally have her reward. The rest didn't—shouldn't—matter.

"Come back to London with us tomorrow," her father said.

"But I won't be alone here, Father. I'm sure Peter is planning to stay."

"Until he tells you his plans, you can't be sure of anything."

"You really are determined to spoil my day."

"I'm determined to get you to think clearly about Peter. There's no future there for you."

"I think I will let Peter tell me that."

"And trample your heart all over again?" her father asked. "*I* can't go through that again."

"Well, then, you won't. I won't tell you a thing."

Not a thing. About anything.

Dear God, what was she going to do?

She picked up a piece of cold toast and bit into it hard, angry again at how adamant he was about Peter when he'd never even tried to dissuade her from marrying William at all.

How was she going to tell him about William's heir?

"Well, now you've put a damper on everything," her father muttered. "And here come your guests. Not a moment too soon, my girl, or we'd have been in the midst of something very unpleasant. I'd better ring for Giles."

But Giles followed hard behind the sweeping morning dresses of Yolanda and Krasnov's wife, and was pulling out chairs for the ladies just as the footmen entered with trays of food and fresh tea, and Peter stepped onto the terrace behind them.

He was a sun god, tall and golden in the late morning light, and dressed to perfection in a light summer suit.

Elizabeth watched hungrily as he greeted every guest as if they were all the best of friends before he came to sit beside her. His manners were faultless, his English perfect from all those years spent at British boarding schools.

"My dear Elizabeth," he murmured, and grasped her hand meaningfully under the table.

This, this made everything worthwhile. And anything else was meaningless.

The moment was perfect: a confluence of the luxuries of a country house weekend, the warmth of the sun, the light cool breeze, the footmen moving silently around the table offering breakfast choices, the sense of ineffable well-being among friends.

I won't think about the rest . . .

Not a word was said as Elizabeth poured the tea and passed the cups. But nothing had to be said. Peter had said everything, with his eyes and with the grasp of his hand.

"What a pretty scene." A new voice intruded and every head popped up to see a stranger pause on the threshold as Giles tried to detain him.

He limped onto the terrace, a black-clad presence both mesmerizing and a little threatening with his height, his hawkish nose, and the sharp hard look in his eyes.

Elizabeth bolted to her feet. *No . . . no—oh dear God— Not now. Not yet. Oh, God—the solicitor had said he was on his way.* On his way . . . *not here, not in Exbury. This was too quick, too soon . . .*

She felt frozen in place. She was certain her shock showed on her face. And her knowledge. She had to get control. *Fast.* She had to act like the outraged widow. She couldn't let this— this . . . pirate—upend everything, not now, not today . . .

Not on the heels of Peter's return . . .

Oh, God—no one could ever know she had been told about this in London.

Her father pushed her aside; Peter put a hand on his arm and murmured, "Let me take care of this . . ." just as her father demanded, "Giles, who is this interloper?"

"I'm delighted you all are enjoying the hospitality of Shenstone," the intruder went on. "Please, do go on—don't let me interrupt. Giles—" He snapped his fingers, and the butler stepped back, startled. "Find me a chair, will you?"

"And who *are* you?" Peter, this time, moving out from behind the table to confront the intruder, while everyone just stared.

"Oh, I know who *I* am. Who are *you?*" the stranger said easily. "Ah, thank you, Giles, put it right there—" He pointed to Elizabeth, and then proceeded to seat himself next to her. "Oh, sit down everyone, please. I'm delighted to be able to join you this morning."

"Are you?" Elizabeth snapped. *Act like you know nothing.* "Who *are* you?" She already knew what he was: a rock, immovable, immutable, wholly there to stay. "Who invited you?"

"Oh, the question isn't who invited *me;* it's who invited *you,*" the stranger said. "But I won't quibble, it's too lovely a day, and truly, I don't mind unexpected company."

"This man is insane." Her father, making a totally useless pronouncement. "Giles—"

"Call the constable," the stranger finished for him cheerfully. "Call the doctor. Call the local barrister. Line them all up and let them have a go at me. I don't mind. I could do with a cup of tea before the storm, however. Elizabeth, would you do me the honor . . . ?"

I know nothing. She sent him a skewering look. "You are too familiar, sir, and I want you to leave."

"Who the devil *are* you?" Her father again, trying to sound reasonable in the face of this irrationality.

The stranger looked up at him. "Why, I thought you knew. Elizabeth—surely you got the solicitor's letter?"

He looked around at them, noting with interest their shock and expressions of denial. Excellent . . . so much better than he ever could have planned.

"No?" He reached for his cup and took a little sip to prolong the moment. "Oh. Well. Let me introduce myself then. I'm Nicholas Massey. Richard's son. William's *heir.*"

Chapter 2

Elizabeth! She was everything he expected, all blond hauteur and those knowing, intelligent eyes.

She was cool as the earth, hot as the sun, passionate, burning, all consuming—and too beautiful, too contained and too ripe for seduction.

Nicholas wanted her. Instantly. Ferociously. Appropriately, he thought. On any terms. Where the father had taken the wife, the son would ravish the widow, and vengeance would come full circle.

He would make sure of it, he thought, he would take such pleasure in it, as he watched her gracefully and efficiently dispatch all those guests who absolutely had to leave by the four o'clock train to London.

Good. The less interference the better.

But still, her bulldog of a father remained, as well as the noxious Victor. And the dumpling, the so-called Grand Duchess, Mena. And the elegant Peter, scion of royalty.

All those people to get in the way.

Nothing would get in the way of his fucking her.

The thing was so simple: he was the new Earl of Shenstone and they were all trespassing on his hospitality.

Only Elizabeth would have leave to stay.

It was time for some plain speaking; he waited until the carriages had gone to the station before seeking her out.

"Elizabeth." He limped through the library doors, startling her at William's desk.

"Nicholas." Her voice was like ice. "Do sit down."

"I believe I'll stand."

No, he looms. "As you will." She shuffled the papers in her hand, one of them the letter from William's London solicitor, and skimmed them for a distancing moment before she put them down.

Not her problem anymore. Not her house, her space, or her land.

And one last trump card to play. "What have you come to say, Nicholas?"

"I want the others to leave. You can stay."

She bent her head. "Thank you for your concern, but I will leave as well."

"My dear Elizabeth. Where can you go? There is no dower house; the London townhouse is mine and I will not relinquish that pleasure. And my uncle made no provision for the folly of your looting your income to assist your father. So all your resources are practically gone. You have nothing left but my good will, and I offer it to you freely."

She felt the shock down to her toes that he knew so much about her financial drain. "You?" She arched an eyebrow; her tone was frosty as a queen's. "Who are *you?* There's nothing to say you are Nicholas Massey. There has always been a rumor *he* might not be the legitimate son of Richard and Irena Kaza-kovna."

His expression, so openly genial before, turned hard, purposeful. Threatening. Here, now, *this* Nicholas was not the same man who had disrupted her breakfast party.

Here was a contradiction, a lie.

He caught himself and shrugged. "It is no concern of mine."

"The rumor says he *might* be the love-child of Richard and his brother's wife . . ."

He went very still.

"And if that were so, if it could be proved, where would your good will and generosity be then?"

"You tell me, Elizabeth. *If* it could be proved . . ."

"Face down in the mud, Nicholas. And I would grind you down in it with no remorse whatsoever."

He didn't answer; the image was too powerful, and he was that much stronger. He'd take her down into the mud with him. And do things with her and to her she wouldn't want to know . . .

He turned and limped to the window to stare out at the terrace. A lovely thing, a terrace, built high up over the grounds of the house so that when a man looked out over the edge, he felt like a king.

"You want the Russian."

"Don't change the subject."

"This is now the subject. The other is closed, though it was an excellent, albeit risky, bluff. You have no proof, there is no proof, there will never be any proof. So, we now turn to what you want: you want the Russian. You'll never have him, and it is pure vanity on your part to even try. What can you offer him, that he cannot command from any woman?"

She didn't want to get into this; she didn't want this intruder, this stranger, to know any part of what her heart's desire might be. But the unbidden thought reared up: *He wants me.*

And she didn't know which *he* she meant.

"He wants me."

He fixed his hard gaze on her. "You have nothing to give him but your body and your innocence. And he can have that from any woman, any time."

Innocence?! She stood up abruptly. "I will not listen to another word."

"But you will listen. You have no choice."

"There are always choices." She slammed the papers down on the desk and stalked toward the door.

He followed, unperturbed. "Then make the right one now. I offer a bargain."

"Truly, Nicholas. A bargain? What have I got to barter, I who have nothing to offer anyone?" Rage, there, fury at him trapping her like that.

"Rumor. Supposition. Things people gossip about, things I don't want dredged up, even if they can't be substantia ed."

"Things William knew," she threw back bitterly.

"William knew nothing, least of all how to break a virgin."
She swung at him. "You bastard."

He caught her hand and his touch was so shattering, she
was conscious of nothing else but his power for a full heart-
stopping moment.

"You're still a virgin, in every way that counts," he told her.
"And if you want the Russian, you need me. What I can give
you. What I can teach you. What I can make you feel."

"No. No. *No!*" She wrenched away from him. "No. What
do you think I am? *Who* do you think I am?"

"What you are is a young, beautiful widow who has never
been fucked properly and who may well have to sell her body
anyway to make ends meet. I suggest you think about that,
Elizabeth. Envision these two scenarios: your stubborn way,
you go to London and plunge headlong into dire straits and
the brothels on Meet Street. My way, you stay at Shenstone
with all its luxurious comforts, and you have two desirable
men at your beck and call: one to educate you and one to
make love to you. And further to that, I will give you a
stipend, to waste as you will on your father. Or—let him stay
here and keep out of trouble. Either way, your problem is
solved. You cannot ask for more than that."

"So *you* would set me up as the mistress to two men, all for
the price of never mentioning *the rumor* again," Elizabeth
sneered. "The wonder is, I don't jump at the offer."

"You ought to jump through hoops at the offer," he said
coldly. "The Russian *will* leave you if you don't have the expertise to hold him. Did he not, once before? Think about
what a man like that expects. He's had everything the royal
court can provide. Money. Leisure. Notoriety. Travel to exotic
places. Women panting to spread their legs for him from the
time he understood where to poke his penis. Every princess in
Europe scheming to land him as a husband. Every daughter of
every duke and earl plotting to pin the uncle of an emperor
onto her family tree. A harem of naked willing women if he

wants them, one after the other. So what can an English rose give him that a harem woman can't?"

Love seemed too puny a word. And all her dreams and desires just so much air in the face of that kind of reality. "I *hate* you."

He shrugged. "I don't particularly care if you hate me. I don't even care if you accept the offer. But know this: I *am* going to fuck you, if you accept my not-so-onerous terms, and I will teach you the secrets of owning a man."

And so this was what seven years with William came down to: his heir wanted to *educate* her, fuck her, and then, for some preverse reason, watch her work her wiles on the jaded womanizing son of a royal family.

The man she loved.

Dear heaven. How could she even listen to such vulgarity? *Yet ... yet ...*

... two desirable men at your beck and call ...

Dear heaven, never had she thought that way—

Her body tensed, twinged. *Mistress to two men ... TWO men at her beck and call ...*

And comfort—and money ...

Things she would learn, things he *would show her ... things she didn't know. Things made from the fantasies of men. Secrets. Pleasure. A thousand and one nights to give her naked body over to a naked humping stranger to do whatever he wanted with her ...*

How different was that from marriage?

But at the end of it all, there would be Peter—

Desiring her. Making love to her. Begging her to stay with him for always ...

Because she knew all the ways of owning a man.

And all that knowledge, comfort, and money at the puny price of never mentioning the rumor *ever again ...*

Not so onerous at all, to make Peter just a little jealous. A little unsure. Especially when she was not as fresh, not so ripe as she had been.

Was she seriously thinking about this?

. . . two men possessing her . . . after all this barren time . . . ?

And the wonder was, she hadn't slapped him, hadn't screamed, hadn't stormed out of the room; she was standing there and listening to a one-eyed pirate calmly talk about *fucking* her. *She* was crazy. Or desperate. Or something.

"Elizabeth . . ." Nicholas was amused. She hadn't fainted at his crudeness. She hadn't jumped out the window. She looked like a woman who needed a good fucking. And a lot more. She actually looked as if she were considering his outrageous proposal.

But then, he knew women. No woman could resist the idea of two men slavering over her naked body. Any women would love the idea of two virile men competing to give her the the longest, hardest ride of her life.

She turned to him. "What exactly do you mean by—*fuck me?*"

"I mean, if you stay, we fuck. Hot, wet, anywhere-I-choose naked-and-ready-when-I-want-you fucking. Make no mistake. I'd fuck you right now, right on this desk, I'm so hard for you. But there is no bargain yet, is there? So you will learn no secrets today. And if you go, there won't be another offer. And you can tell the world whatever you want, I truly don't care."

And so he had diffused *that* threat as well, and probably thought he was doing the noble thing, offering to *educate* her, offering her everything she now couldn't otherwise have.

Peter . . .

She was trembling like a leaf, from excitement or disgust, she didn't know. Did the idea of learning the sexual secrets to attract Peter resonate so deeply with her?

Or was it because he had not touched the root of what *she* wanted, and she needed to make clear exactly what she would get out of this bargain that put her so firmly and completely in *his* power.

"I want to make Peter jealous," she said suddenly, "so jealous he'll go down on his knees begging me to take him."

A faint smile played across his mouth. "We'll have him crawling on his knees naked, his penis at full staff, desperate to attraction your attention. Caress him or ignore him, whatever you feel like *that* day. As opposed to any *other* day, of course, when you *might* feel like fondling his penis and doing obscene things with it."

"Of course," she whispered. *Of course.*

What obscene things?

"Do know, Elizabeth, that a man and his penis do not like to be ignored."

There was a lesson, she thought, snapping back to reality. And he meant himself, not Peter. *And she was ignoring his penis now by not having decided to take the bargain, to take him.*

What was she thinking?

She shook herself mentally and looked up at him from beneath her lashes. He was not a handsome man: his features, apart from that aquiline nose, were unremarkable. And the look in his eye. And he was tall, where William had not been, his lean body accentuated the more by the severe black suit he wore. And he was long and thick and hard, where William had not been—

Stop it!

But look at how it moves against the fabric ... how it would move inside me ...

She felt a tremor go through her.

She was thinking of doing it, she really was. Really?

"How—?" she whispered; she had to know.

"There are so many lessons, so many ways. So much skill involved to teach a woman hunger for the penetration of a man's penis. And I promise, you will crave it, you will beg for it. I will teach you how to kiss a man; how to dress for him; how to tease and excite him; how much to give him, and when to make him plead ..."

Yes, yes, yes ... all that, all that ... she felt feverish, powerful.

Was she CRAZY?

"Everything you must know to make the Russian mad with jealousy. Everything to captivate and hold him . . ."

Yes yes yes . . . she wanted Peter rabid with jealousy . . .

". . . all the while you are fucking me."

And down to earth with a bang.

Nicholas noticed. "My dear girl, how else can you learn all this except by spreading your legs for me?"

She felt as if she had been dashed with cold water.

"I see. And tell me again, what am I going to learn?"

"You have no idea the power of your body, of your sex . . . I will tell you this and no more until you reckon whether you will accept my terms: I am a man of many parts; I've had more women than I can count; more varieties of sex in more countries than are on the map. And just looking at you, I am hard as iron and primed as a gun. I want to grind my penis into you so hard and tight, you couldn't move for five days; and you still wouldn't be able to because I'd still be inside you, hard as a poker and pumping away. You are so seductive, Elizabeth, your sex is as alluring as any courtesan.

"Can you take it? Can your cunt take the length, the thickness, the hardness of my penis? Can *you* take two men in sexual thrall to you? Two men bursting to penetrate you? Two men competing for your naked body and your hot wet cunt? Two men fighting to sink themselves into you as deep and hard as they can go? Answer those questions and come to me then. Or leave. Whatever you will . . . But make up your mind today."

He left her then, limping out onto the terrace and disappearing behind the potted bushes. Left her with her body burning with the images he had conjured, and the sensuous words that still hung in the air enticing her, seducing her.

Two men . . . lusting for what was between her legs . . . one of them Peter, crawling, begging, her supplicant, on his knees . . .

*   *   *

"This is intolerable," her father barked, stomping into the library fifteen minutes later. "He barges in, makes claims, presents nothing to authenticate who he is, and takes over the house. The heir, indeed. The heir is dead, everyone agrees, or he would have come forward a year ago when he was notified of his father's death."

Elizabeth jerked her attention back to her father with the greatest of difficulty. "I'm sorry, Father?"

"Who *is* this man? He could be a thief, a murderer; he could steal us blind, rob us in our beds. We shouldn't even have left him alone with the silver."

She watched him pace agitatedly around the room, the man with whom she had been at odds most of her life, the man to whom she owed her loyalty, her life. Her money.

"The solicitors notified me when we were in London, Father. He came to them with all satisfactory credentials, everything in order, nothing to impair his taking the title and all that goes with it."

That stopped him cold. "*What?!* You *knew?* And you didn't tell *me?*"

"I couldn't tell you—not there, not with Victor and Peter and the rest of our guests. Think clearly, Father. There wasn't a moment . . ."

"I cannot believe this. You *knew* and you couldn't find a minute—no, five *seconds* to tell me? Not even on the train . . . ?"

He *would* argue with her. "There wasn't a moment when someone couldn't overhear us. And that holds true here as well."

Heat swamped her whole body. *Too late for that concern now . . .*

"Damn and bloody blast it!"

Ah, the prelude. Elizabeth knew it well. He needed money, ever more money for that sinkhole of an oil company he had funded in Siberia.

"I suppose you're going to tell me that William meant to make another will."

Elizabeth sighed. "No, he thought by the time he died he would get at least one son from my body. He saw no reason to change that stance. So Nicholas wins the prize."

"Bloody damn hell."

"What now?" she asked resignedly.

"Krasnov's connections don't feel secure enough to finance more drilling. And they are so close, so close. Enough oil to fuel the world, I tell you. I must keep the company going. I have floated too much credit, sold too many shares to just walk away. Elizabeth—perhaps Nicholas . . . ?"

"We don't know if he has access to any assets yet, Father. And he may not be a gambling man." She tasted the lie before the words were out of her mouth. *He was a gambler to the soul, that man. Just threw the dice at her and walked away, knowing before she did what was the outcome of the roll.*

"Ask him, Elizabeth. We'll be face-up down in the Thames if you don't, and our closest friends could lose thousands of pounds . . . Elizabeth . . . ?"

Or maybe his subtle blackmail had roots in a reality he had known long before he set foot in Shenstone. Things he had found out. Things he knew he could use to manipulate her, her father, and the merest evidence of the rumor.

She had no choices now. If she'd ever had any . . .

"Yes, Father. I'll ask him if you wish."

A stipend for her father to waste as he would, Nicholas had said . . . and two potent virile men to service her.

Save his soul and lose her own.

And the price, in the end, wasn't all that high . . .

Dinner. Early. Her stomach churning, Elizabeth moved to the head of the table, and motioned Peter to the opposite end.

"Big mistake, my dear," her father whispered as he held her chair. "You should be playing up to Nicholas."

"You think everything is a mistake. There is nothing I can do that isn't a mistake. And anyway, Nicholas isn't here. Yet."

"As you will," he muttered, taking his place opposite Mena.

"But you know what's at stake. Damn it . . . damn that William—"

Victor seated himself across the table from Nicholas's empty chair, eyed it dispassionately, and spat, "Peasant manners," just as Nicholas sauntered in the door.

"I know this man," Mena said suddenly, abruptly, and Nicholas stopped dead in his tracks. *The one thing he didn't need, the one thing he could not plan for: someone recognizing him. Or thinking they did.*

And Elizabeth would pick right up on it.

She did. "Do you?" Elizabeth murmured. "Do tell us, Mena dear."

Mena furrowed her brow. "I don't remember. But I will. It's just at the edge of my memory . . ." She looked up at Nicholas as he seated himself.

"The Grand Duchess and I have never met," he said coolly, whipping out his napkin. "But if she wishes to claim the acquaintance, I have no problem with that." Hell, it wasn't just a problem, it was a complication, and not one he needed right now.

He held the Grand Duchess's gaze, and hers wavered first. Good. There would be no more of that just yet. Mena wasn't sure. And the more he denied it, the more unsure she would become.

He glanced at Elizabeth. Her face was impassive as she picked up the small crystal bell by the side of her plate to signal that service should begin. Immediately two footmen appeared to present the first course.

Nothing about that had changed: William had been a man who loved his food, and she had continued his custom of always having a bountiful table.

Tonight the menu consisted of oysters on the half shell to start, followed by a clear light bouillion. The fish course was boiled salmon with green peas, removed by a fillet of beef in mushroom sauce accompanied by olives, pickles, potatoes, and asparagus. And to finish, assorted fruits, nut cake, two choices of sherbet, lemon pie, and vanilla ice cream, all served with coffee and cordials.

No one spoke as the first course was plated. Everyone watched Nicholas covertly, wondering, Elizabeth thought, what he was going to do.

She wondered how much, if anything, *he* had overheard of her conversation with her father, or any conversation for that matter.

The reality hadn't set in yet. She was presiding over this table as if she were mistress of the house, when all she would ever be after this night was some man's mistress.

No, the mistress of two men, TWO . . . lusty . . . men each craving the same thing, the one thing that only a woman could give . . .

She felt a throb deep in her vitals, and a stab of excitement. She had nothing to lose if it came to that. Nothing. She would be a widow forever, no matter what happened; she had no reputation at stake, nothing on which leading a life of purity and virtue depended. In truth, she could do whatever she wanted behind the walls of Shenstone, with whomever she wanted, and no one would ever have to know.

. . . two vigorous men in their prime . . .

Behind the curtains where no one could see . . .

. . . and comfort and luxury and a stipend forever—

And Peter . . .

And no one would ever know—

She looked up and found Nicholas's hard, disquieting gaze pinned on her. He knew what she was thinking; he was watching every calculation, knowing that she would add the sum properly and make the decision he wanted, the only decision possible.

Her expression turned to stone. She didn't want to be that easily readable, not by him. She would be a convenience for him, and one less complication as he took over the reins of Shenstone. He had known her threat was an empty one; no one could prove the rumor. At best, it would cost him some months of litigation, which he would win, and by which time she and her father would be bankrupt and ruined.

This was the way. She just didn't want it to be so easy for him.

But . . . she wanted it. Everything he said, she wanted. With everything it entailed.

She was shocked by the thought. She wasn't thinking it through clearly, because it really meant wholly surrendering herself to *him*. Naked in every way possible, for *him*. It meant she was willing to spread her legs for him. To willingly take every long hard inch of him deep into her naked core.

Her breath caught. *What would that feel like? All that muscle, and heat and power, thrusting into her? As opposed to William's . . . no no no . . . no, she didn't have to endure that ever again . . .*

She chanced another look at Nicholas. He had taken a helping of sherbert, and licked it from the bowl of his spoon.

She almost couldn't stand watching him, thinking about all the places on a woman's body a man could swirl his tongue. And then his lips clamped over the spoon, and a little whorl of pure pleasure darted between her legs.

There . . . oh there . . . NOW—this minute . . .

She had to get out of there. Dinner, thank heaven, was done. She rose. "Gentlemen . . ."

It was like sending Nicholas into a den of lions. Her father alone would try to eat him alive, and Victor and his tiresome rhetoric would bore him to tears.

No, maybe not. Nicholas could take care of himself. After this afternoon, she didn't doubt it; he was three steps ahead of all them already.

Way ahead of her, knowing what she wanted before she did.

. . . two men—it was too fantastical, too indecent, so enflaming she almost couldn't contain herself . . .

And he knew it. He knew once he offered her two strapping men at her feet, she would hunger for it, burn for it . . .

She felt the heat seep into her cheeks, and she sank into a chair beside Mena. She had to stop thinking it about it. Had to stop squirming and yearning and imagining all the forbidden things that two demanding lovers could do *with* her, and *to* her.

"Who is he, Mena? Why do you think you know him?"

Mena shook her head. "I can't pinpoint it."

"If only you could." *If only she would. Just to have something to give her some leverage. Some little thing that only she knew about Nicholas.*

"I'll think of it," Mena said. "I promise. It would be a good thing to know, don't you think? Oh, here they come . . ."

"Good news, Mena." This from Elizabeth's father. "The Earl has invited all of us to stay on at Shenstone as long as we want. Even Victor, who'd much rather sleep on a mattress, in spite of what he says."

"How lovely," Elizabeth murmured. "How lovely, Nicholas."

"Isn't it?" he answered in kind.

The tension between them was almost palpable, but no one seemed to notice except Elizabeth. He wanted her answer, and it wasn't enough for him to have surmised it.

"Perhaps it is time to retire," Elizabeth said, determinedly keeping her eyes away from Nicholas. "I, for one, have had a long exhausting day."

"Oh, yes."

"Certainly."

"Good night, my dear." Her father.

Mena, taking her hands, whispering, "Everything will work out."

Peter, following, placing a light kiss on her cheek. "I need to see you alone in the morning. I want . . . to tell you . . . what I need."

"I want to hear," she whispered. "I wish you could . . ."

Victor elbowed him aside. "Tomorrow, after the mattress, the revolution."

"Good *night*, Victor."

One by one, they filed out until only she and Nicholas were left, and he looked so formidable, she felt stone cold and just a little deflated.

"Well, I've made my gesture of good faith," he said. "I can rescind it at any moment, of course. Do you have something to tell me?"

"I—" The words stuck in her throat.

He moved closer to her. "You want it, don't you? I saw it in your eyes, in your body." He grasped her arm. "But more than that, you want *him*, any way you can get him. You'll do whatever you have to, won't you? Even fuck me. Yes. I see it. But *you* must say it."

She wrenched her arm away. There was no way out, then. But what were words, after all? He'd thrown them around like ha'pennies this morning.

"That's right. I want him. I . . . want . . . *him*. I'll do whatever I must to get him and hold his interest, *even* giving *you* my naked body. I'll fuck you wherever you want, whenever you want. Is that what you want to hear? That I *love* the idea of having two forceful men at my feet? That I want to make Peter so jealous, he won't know what to do about it. Well, I do. Two hard throbbing penises lusting after me? What woman wouldn't want all that mighty male muscle craving her sex? I can't *wait* to start those lessons you promised."

Her defiant gaze traveled from his implacable face down his body and farther down to the huge, obvious bulge between his legs.

Did she thrill, just a little, to the sight? He was hard for her still. All that power and muscle, almost bursting through his clothes, and all for want of rooting in her. The power of it was undeniable.

"An excellent decision, Elizabeth. Fifteen minutes, my room. Naked and on my bed, with your legs spread and your body open to me."

She shuddered with excitement at his demand. He wanted her naked. Waiting.

"I've been hard for you since the minute I walked into this

house," he said dispassionately. "A man's penis can only take so much arousal. It's time to embed myself in you. Time to flood your hole with all that cream."

Her breath caught. All *that cream* . . .

His penis throbbed visibly against his trousers, elongating still more at his hot words.

"You made your decision, Elizabeth. Go get ready. Tonight, we fuck."

He poured himself a brandy. *Damn,* he needed it. What a day. What a night. And more to come.

So much for his evening. In peace. Rest in peace, more likely after he was done with Elizabeth.

That one part of him wouldn't rest at all.

Hell.

Well, he was here.

Jesus.

What the hell had gotten into him?

Elizabeth, he supposed. Another detour on the way to clearing out the debris in his life.

He'd hadn't been so hot for any woman in years. And that haughty icy way she'd taken his challenge—she'd take his penis in just the same ferocious way. And he couldn't wait.

His penis couldn't wait. Five more minutes and he'd be between her legs, pumping himself to oblivion.

Thank God, she wanted that inbred insipid Russian. He didn't have time to fall in love with her. But he had time enough to use her and to stoke her to a fever pitch to service some other bastard's penis.

It would do for entertainment for the moment.

He got up and walked to the stone parapet that edged the terrace; below him lay the tiered gardens that stepped precisely down to the drive, and beyond that the undulating countryside now shrouded in the oncoming darkness.

Mine . . .

Jesus.

Shenstone. All tangled up in vengeance and despair.

He couldn't afford to let himself be led around by his penis; he couldn't forget for a moment that somewhere farther out there, watching his every move, was the Unseen Hand.

He'd wager his life on it. He *had* wagered his life on it.

. . . Elizabeth . . .

He couldn't let anything distract him from that.

Well, you bastard, I'm here. I know you're out there. I've made my claim. Now come and get me.

Chapter 3

And now it was time to play the game. She could not back down now. He would call her to account for all her bold brazen words, and if she reneged, she would lose everything.

In this room, she had nothing to lose. If he took her, if he discarded her, she lost nothing. She was still the mistress of the manor this night, and soon to be mistress of two potent men who would vie to possess her naked body.

That was power. Pure arousing power. Her body liquefied just thinking of it. If he would just come, *now* . . . it would be easier . . . fast . . . and over . . .

Whatever happened, however it happened, she had to remain strong and in control. She had to forget about her fumbling husband, his flaccid member, the endless pushing and shoving and eventual gratification for him.

All of that was in the past, never to be thought of again. She must act now as if she were the most desirable woman in the world, and that *he* was so enflamed, he had created this bargain for sole purpose of possessing her.

Maybe he had. Whatever happened in this room, no one would ever know. She could play the virgin or the wanton. It was up to her, and in which scenario the power lay.

She hoisted herself onto the massive tester bed, and dropped her wrapper onto the floor. Naked in his bed, in his room, in the farthest corner of the house. Such an appropriate place to commence the life of a voluptuary.

It was an opulent room, and wholly male, the walls painted a deep claret color, which was echoed in the thick

Persian carpet and the gilt-framed paintings on the wall. Matching velvet curtains swagged the windows and draped from the bed. A heavy ornately carved armoire was tucked into a corner, and an upholstered chair and small table placed by the window.

And over the marble mantel, a round beveled mirror reflected the light of a half-dozen candles on the dresser on the far wall—and Nicholas, finally, as he eased in the door, already divested of his frock coat, and unbuttoning his shirt.

"So . . ." he murmured, "the bargain is met."

This was harder than she'd thought, to recline naked on his bed, and watch him examine every inch of her body by merely looking at her.

She wanted to bolt; she wanted to stay.

It was a moment of high tension. It was the first time in her life she was utterly exposed to a man. The first time a man had ever looked at her. The first time she was wholly naked to a man's gaze.

She didn't think it was possible, but she was loving the way he looked at her. *Loving it.* Loving that his penis looked full to bursting against his trousers. Loving how it seemed to keep elongating as he looked her over. Loving, loving, *loving* it.

She didn't think she would love it. She didn't think the words she had flung at him might really be true.

She arched her back to push out her breasts and her rigid pointed nipples. She parted her legs to reveal the tuft between and returned his impassive gaze with all the insolence she could muster.

"I have kept my end of the bargain," she said finally, her voice husky. "I'm waiting for you to keep yours."

"Oh that." He tossed his coat onto the bed. "I've changed my mind about that."

"*What!?*" She bolted into a sitting position.

"No, I've decided my penis can wait. The pleasure is so much more intense when it's honed to a fine pitch. Know this: I'm ready to erupt all over your naked body right this minute, but I have something else in mind for tonight, so I'll save my cream for another night."

He held out his hand. "Come."

She *wanted* to come, *damn him.* She didn't want this voluptuous arousal to dissipate. But she didn't resist when he pulled her toward him, into the chair, onto his lap, onto the bulge of his jutting erection, settling the curve of her buttocks against all that power and heat, and spreading her legs over his thighs.

Seated this way, she arched back against him naturally, so that her breasts, her nipples were thrust forward, and his penis just nestled in her buttocks' crease.

"Put your hands on my hips and *don't* move them."

She did as he told her, savoring the fact she was wholly nakedly open to him, and he could do whatever he wanted to do to her.

Her excitement escalated. He didn't have to do a thing. Her body shuddered with anticipation just straddling him; her breasts quivered, her juices were already dripping from between her legs.

And the thing he did that was so arousing was, he *didn't* touch her. He let her *feel*—her body, her nakedness, her wetness, her tingling nipples; he let her *imagine* what he would do to her, with her; he let her simmer in a voluptuous excitement that made her squirm impatiently against the jut of his penis, mutely begging for release.

And even then he didn't touch her.

"Close your eyes." The demand was barely a breath in her ear.

Her head fell back as she obeyed. And waited. And waited as she writhed against his thick root, waiting, her body molten, wet, wild, waiting . . . and then—and then . . .

A touch—smooth, cool, rounded, sliding against the tip of her stiff nipple, and then around the aureole, and back and forth, back and forth, over the nipple, back and forth, over and over until she almost couldn't bear it, back and forth, back and forth on and on—

And then, and then . . . his fingers, oh, just his fingers compressing the other nipple, lightly, firmly, perfectly, just, just—*right* . . . and her body contracted, and her bottom ground on him hard, as she spiraled downward into a long, lush, shimmering orgasm.

Everything stopped. She felt hot, cold, used, finished. She felt like she wanted to get away, but he held her tightly. She felt, she felt, she felt . . .

Something between her wide open legs. No, no, not yet—. . . not yet . . .

. . . something he manipulated, something very round, oh so smooth, moving in a tight thrusting motion just inside her labia, oh yes, in and out, tight, hard, rhythmic . . . she wanted to enclose it, keep it inside her, to feel it more keenly, to rub her nakedness against it as hard as she could . . .

She drew a sharp hissing breath as she canted her body to come down on it more firmly. And suddenly it was inside, hard up against her pleasure nub, enfolded in her sex.

Her breath caught. *This* was pleasure.

"You can wear it," he whispered in her ear. "But only for me."

Her body writhed all over it. "For you . . ."

"There's more."

She could barely whisper, barely concentrate, she was in such a haze of voluptuous euphoria. "Do it."

Now she felt his fingers, parting her cunt lips and feeling for her hole. And then the pressure of his fingers pushing pushing, filling her, filling her . . . until something pulled at the round object and almost dislodged it.

He saved it, pushing back in voluptuous little circles until it nestled tight against her nub. And then her vulva enclosed everything, and as she comprehended it, she felt her labia convulse and convulse, and she rocked and spasmed ferociously around the fullness deep inside.

There were no words for this overpowering carnal volcano.

Everything went still. Neither of them moved. He didn't

speak; he let her feel the fullness of possession, of orgiastic sensation.

And then he pulled slow slow slow, and she felt little round droplets of pleasure cascading deep in her vagina. *Perfect. Perfect.*

Perfect . . .

And then he stopped. "Stand up; I want to look at you."

She didn't want to move; she wanted to straddle his legs like that forever, but he lifted her off of his lap. "Lift your leg onto my knee and look."

She looked. Dangling from her most private place was a strand of pearls, still partially enclosed by her vaginal lips. And the other end was attached to . . . attached to—whatever it was nestling at her pleasure point.

It was the most arousing sight. Little round droplets of pearls giving her that much pleasure. He cupped her mound with his hand, his fingers working into her vagina, wriggling and pushing against the pearls until her knees went weak.

"Give me your nipples." He guided her back over him, and pushed her forward so that her breasts were even with his mouth. "So stiff. So hard. Perfect for sucking."

He licked the tip of the closest nipple, and the heat of his tongue and the feeling of his fingers and the way his lips closed over that hard hot nipple tip almost made her faint. And then he pulled on it, sucking it so hard, so wet, so tight, so rhythmically . . . that she convulsed all over his fingers, and sank onto his knees.

Stillness again. And the sense that she still enfolded all those pleasure toys. Such power. Such pleasure . . .

His engorged penis throbbed against her bottom, hot, ferocious, demanding.

"Not yet for him," he murmured. "We must first play the game."

"Pearls," she whispered in wonderment. "Pearls?"

"Look." Softly, he removed the object at her pleasure point and held it up for her to see: a round, smooth, slick pearl attached to the necklace that slipped so easily from her soaking vagina. "Yours." The strand was long, lustrous, even coated with her juices, and the bigger rounder pearl dangled from one end. "You can have this much, for now. It will fit around your hips, and you can tuck that wherever it will give you the most pleasure. You can wear it like a piece of jewelry between your legs. But only for me, only to arouse yourself to prepare for me."

He handed her the necklace. "And with it goes this condition: if you wear it as a necklace, it tells me you want to be fucked—*now*. This is our talisman, our signal that you lust for *my* penis to service you. If you wear it for anyone else, ever, the bargain is over, I take back the necklace, and you leave Shenstone. Do you agree?"

"Yesss . . ." she whispered.

He lifted her up from his lap and rose from the chair. She sank right back down into it, snuggling into the residual heat from his body, and watched as he picked up her wrapper and draped it over her.

"You have seen tonight what your body is capable of. Now I will keep the rest of my promise. I will tell you what you must do to attract and hold the Russian.

"The first thing is, you must make him believe you might be interested in me. I will aid and abet you in that, and we will start tomorrow.

"The second thing is, be submissive. Whatever he says, whatever he wants, except sex, agree to it. He'll want you that much more.

"Third. You can let him fondle and feel you all he wants. Don't wear your drawers and make him believe the suggestion didn't come from you. It will whet his appetite to taste bare flesh. But be careful: don't fuck him because once he has you, he won't want you.

"Fourth. If you think he's losing interest, slip your hand between his legs and fondle his penis and his balls. That will engage his interest immediately. Do it as often as you think is necessary, but don't arouse him unnecessarily. The more you are interested in his penis, the more engaged in desiring you he'll be, so don't ignore his penis."

"I wouldn't dream of it," she murmured. This was too strange. After fucking her with everything *but* his penis, he was sending her off with advice on how to handle Peter and how to get Peter to handle her.

It was crazy. She felt the heat, the pleasure dissipating like smoke.

Shivering, she slipped on her robe and wrapped it tightly around her. And then she picked up the pearl necklace, put it on, and gazed up at him mutinously.

"Yes, I thought you'd want more. Give a virgin a taste of pleasure and she'll lie down for you anywhere. Believe me, I'm not done with you yet. Not with that voracious body and those hard responsive nipples. So go back to your bedroom, Elizabeth. Play with your pearls. Let me imagine that smooth hard ball nestling against your clit as you go about your day. And have no fear, I will give you all you can take of my penis, and I will drown you in my cream. But there's time, Elizabeth. A lot of time. I'm not nearly done fucking you."

Blessed morning. Early, on the terrace with her tea, and no one about. Her body still resonating from everything he had done to her last night. Feeling a buoyant sense of release and well-being.

And in the cards, all the tricks she would ever need to captivate Peter.

It was a beautiful morning, no less so because the heir had come. Everything would be as it was. The promise kept. She would have money, her father could implement his plans and schemes, she would have no responsibilities, and Peter was there . . .

"Elizabeth!"

Her heart stopped. No—it wasn't *him*, not this early . . . It was Peter. *Peter* . . . *!*

"Elizabeth . . ." Peter's tone was softer now, and she felt his hands grip her shoulders as he came up behind her. She leaned into him as he turned her around, and when he saw her face, he pulled her hard against his chest.

She had longed for this moment since he had walked out the door of her father's house all those years ago.

"God, Elizabeth. This is awful, that man just walking in and taking over."

"Yes, it is." Her voice was muffled. He didn't have to know that she had known for a week before they'd come back.

"God, we haven't had one minute to talk since this happened. How you must feel!"

She melted into him again. Dear God, how good he felt, how strong, how solid. *Peter* . . . "Let's talk then."

He brushed her lips with the airiest of kisses. "Perhaps not *talk* . . ."

A little pleasure dart punched her vitals. Was this too soon? And after she had swooned, naked, in Nicholas's arms last night? "Peter . . ."

"I know. Too public. And that damned *man* could be prowling around anywhere . . . Come for a walk, Elizabeth. It's a beautiful morning."

"Beautiful because you're finally here," she whispered, taking his arm. A walk was perfect, together, private, behind trees and hedges where only the sun bore witness to whatever folly she chose to commit.

She felt a sense of urgency after last night. She let him lead her from the terrace down the shallow stone staircase to the gardens.

"Elizabeth—"

"Shhh . . ." She didn't want him to say a thing. The moment was too perfect, too long yearned for to have anything spoil it.

She turned to look at him as he paused to pluck a flower from one of the raised garden beds. "For you." He handed it to her. "I never saw a rose but that I thought of you."

Really? All those years . . . ? She brushed the petals against her cheek. *He had thought of her.*

"Elizabeth—" He took a step toward her and she leaned in toward him.

"Peter . . ." She stroked his lips with the rose. She felt his arms come around her.

"I want you," he whispered. "I can't wait to have you, Elizabeth. All those years. It will be that much more perfect for the wait. Tell me you want me, Elizabeth. Tell me what you want . . ."

"A kiss," she breathed, and he settled his mouth gently on hers. Such a sweet kiss, sending those melting little darts downward.

A promise, she thought, but she couldn't ask for that, not yet.

He pulled away first. "Give me some sign, my darling Elizabeth, that's ours alone; I need to know how much you want me."

"I do. I want you." She crushed her lips against his again and he wrapped his arms more tightly around her so that they were whispering breath to breath and kiss to kiss.

"Then let me . . ."

"But Peter . . ."

"Some way I can know . . ."

This soon? To have him at her feet? A tremor went through her. *Two men . . .*

"Peter . . . I can't tell you how much I want you. How can I show you?"

"You know how . . ."

"If you want," she whispered. "I need . . ."

"Tell me . . ."

". . . you . . ." she sighed against his lips. "Hold me tighter."

"Always."

"Oh yes. Now I feel you. *Peter. . . !*"

He ground his hips against her. "Like that?"

"Ummm . . ." She sucked his lower lip. *Don't ignore his penis.* "Hard . . ."

"For you." A growl against her mouth.

"I'm glad."

"And you?" He nipped *her* lower lip.

She gasped. "Wet . . ."

He groaned. "Dear Elizabeth. I need to feel your wet."

Her breath caught. *Two men . . .* ". . . yes—"

He ground his tongue into her mouth. *"Now . . ."*

"Whatever you want, Peter . . ." She clung to him, she felt him working the back of her dress, cursing its length, its cut, her underclothes . . . She couldn't wait to feel his hands on her . . .

"Elizabeth—" They jumped apart guiltily as a new voice— the dreaded voice—interrupted the perfect moment of discovery, and Nicholas limped toward them from behind a nearby stone wall. "Oh."

Elizabeth stared him down. "Nicholas."

"Fast work," he murmured, *sotto voce.* "Lovely view." He turned away from them to give her a chance to right herself. "Lovely gardens. My people do wonderful work."

"You'll have to talk to Watton, my—the head gardener," Elizabeth said frigidly, "and express your appreciation."

My *head gardener . . .* she'd almost said. *His people, he'd said. Oh damn damn damn . . .* The ramifications of his existence were never ending over and above the bargain. She had to stop thinking that everything was hers. Nothing would be hers ever again, except perhaps Peter.

"I need a moment of your time," Nicholas said calmly.

"Certainly. Excuse me, Peter?"

"I need to feel you," he whispered for her ears only; heat washed her cheeks as she followed Nicholas to the stone wall where they would not be overheard.

"You're good," he murmured. "Sleeping Beauty was thoroughly awakened last night and it didn't even take a kiss."

"*Something* kissed me," she said acidly. "Oh, it was Peter. Why did you interrupt us? What do you want?"

"Just didn't want to see things get too critical too soon," he said. "When is dinner by the way?"

"At six," she said through gritted teeth. "We dine early, as you probably already knew. But you might want to change that."

"I might."

"Is that all?"

"Peter is steaming. Give him nothing else today. Although you might fondle his balls, if you feel like it."

She closed her eyes and exhaled a long weary breath. Would he *never* go away?

Nicholas slanted a glance at Peter. "Did he used to come to Shenstone often?"

Elizabeth could barely contain her temper. "*Will* you go away?"

"That is intensely rude, Elizabeth," Nicholas said gently.

"It was meant to be," she snapped.

"I'm certain it wasn't, especially after last night, and when you collect yourself, I'll accept your apology. Meantime," he turned to include Peter, "I'll see you at dinner. Peter . . ." He bowed and limped off again as Elizabeth watched, seething in quiet fury.

"That man . . ." she muttered, and then drew in a deep deep breath. This was the bargain. To make Peter jealous. He had said he would start today. But *this* soon?

Damn him damn him damn him.

"He is rather infuriating," Peter said.

"Yes he is, but he's not taking over *your* life," Elizabeth retorted, trying to keep her irritation under control. "Do you wonder I'm angry?" But she was even more furious that the sweet petal-soft moment when Peter might have declared himself was utterly shattered.

Damn damn damn damn . . .

This was not how the afternoon should have gone. Peter should have kissed her again, and then taken her into his arms and told her that after all this time, he couldn't forget her, he didn't want to live without her, and now she was free, unencumbered, and willing . . .

. . . so willing . . .

Damn it. He might have *said* something, *done* something if Nicholas had not interfered.

Peter took her hand and pulled her into the shadow of the stone wall. And then he took her in his arms again with an urgency that surprised her. "You must tell me, did you mean it?"

She had to make herself focus on him. "Mean what?"

"That I could . . ." His lips grazed hers.

Oh yes, he could.

"Are you still . . . ?" she whispered.

"It takes but an instant when I'm with you."

She sighed. Yes. Nicholas didn't matter. However Peter had occupied himself in the intervening years didn't matter. He wanted her now. He was erect and all there for her, showing her that she still aroused and attracted him. And he kissed like an angel, and his hands were soft and gentle as he moved them rhythmically down her back, the curve of her hips and her buttocks.

"I love knowing that."

"I love knowing your body reacts to it." Another kiss, harder this time, longer. Yes. "You'll let me . . ."

She pulled away slowly, slowly, and just far enough from his lips to whisper, "I want you to . . ."

"We could go to my room . . ."

Forget the rules; don't make him wait or he might leave . . .

"I'll turn my back to the wall. No one can see us . . ."

"Ah, Elizabeth, if only I'd known . . ." His hands worked her gown up and up.

"You know now." On a breath as he cupped her buttocks.

"So firm . . . God, I wish I could tear these clothes from your body . . ."

"E-*liz*abeth . . ."

She wrenched away. "Oh dear God, my father."

"Don't leave me like this, Elizabeth."

"What can I do?" she said helplessly.

"Do *something*."

A man and his penis do not like to be ignored.

"I must go." She touched his cheek, his lips . . . *slip your hand* . . . She ran her hand down his chest, down still farther, and cupped his protuberant member.

"Oh, *Peter* . . . !" she murmured.

And then, she ran.

"I want to know what this all means," her father said, storming after Elizabeth into the morning room an hour later. "What's left, what do you get, where is the solicitor, and why don't we know *anything?*"

"I told you, I have all the papers, Father. Everything is signed, sealed, and legal. Nicholas gets it all, apart from my possessions, my jewelry, and my income, and that will be paid until I remarry or die."

"Nice motive for murder."

"Dear God, Father. Can you give over? No one is more shocked than I at this turn of events. And yet we need change nothing. We can stay here as long as we like—or take lodgings in London, whatever you prefer. And do not worry, there will be enough to see you through this next crisis—which is truly your concern."

"You want to stay here, with *that* man eyeing your income, and possibly bringing home a bride someday?"

Murder, brides, and surrender to Peter, all in one morning. It was enough to make any other woman faint.

"I want to stay here for the moment, Father, to adjust, to make plans, to give you what help I can."

"Fine words," her father muttered. "You never give any but the most grudging help."

Time to bluff. "Well, here it is." She went to her desk and brought out her checkbook. "I can write the check whenever you wish." But the truth was, she had no inkling when or if Nicholas might fund that account, let alone if there was enough in it for her to give her father what he needed.

"Oh. Well. That's better. As long as the money is *there.* We have to protect our interests, my girl. If you won't, well, thank heavens you have me. I'll take the check—oh, Friday will be soon enough."

"Fine." She closed the checkbook. One bluff off the table.

Where was Peter? Or had she disgusted him? No. No man could ever be shocked by a woman's interest in his penis.

An expert had told her so.

"Are we done?"

"I hope you're done," Peter said from the doorway. "I want some time with Elizabeth."

"Do you?" her father said. "Well, well. Let me leave you to it then."

He edged his way past Peter, and shook his head meaningfully at Elizabeth. She ignored him, and stood, holding out her hands as Peter closed the door behind him.

"My dear Elizabeth, I could hardly—"

"I know, me too . . ."

She was in his arms again, the door closed, privacy assured—except, oh, if only she'd thought to tell him to lock the door . . . But she wouldn't move now for a fortune in jewels. Peter was holding her; heaven was in his arms.

They spoke in breathless whispers.

"Do you feel it?"

"Can I feel it?" Was she being too coy?

He folded her more tightly against him, his lips again just barely hovering above hers. "I couldn't believe you touched . . ."

How much to reveal? "I . . . it's different now . . ."

"Oh God, yes—you want . . ." A kiss here, brief, thrusting.

"I know . . ."

"Yes, you know. You feel . . ."

"I can't tell you . . ."

"There's time now. Come to my room . . ."

. . . Anything he wants—but don't let him fuck you . . .

Too soon. Too soon.

"I can't wait a minute longer . . ." she whispered. She would do it, lift her dress, give him whatever he could feel of her body. Or would she seem too eager? Perhaps all that underclothing was a *good* thing—a proper thing, but she couldn't even think straight about that: he was kissing her, soundly, thoroughly, his hands rooting in her clothes.

Good. She wouldn't have to . . .

Oh! His hands on her buttocks again, centering her body against his shaft. "We fit," he muttered, his tongue grinding into her wildly, his fingers flexing against the soft cushion of her bottom.

Oh, yes. That felt good, right, slow, perfect, as he held her buttocks and undulated his hips against her.

"I want more . . ." He pulled at her undergarments. "So much more . . . Do you want me, Elizabeth?"

"Yes . . ."

"Then let me . . ."

"Too risky . . . didn't lock the door . . ."

"My room . . ."

"Now?"

"If you want *this*—" He pushed his erection hard against her belly.

Uh oh, dangerous territory here. No fucking. Distract him.
She feigned a gasp. "Your hands feel so good down there."

"Tell me how good . . ."

"I love it when you fondle me that way."

"Your bottom is so arousing."

"I feel how aroused you are."

"Good. Feel more." He wriggled against her.

Time to pay attention to his penis.

"I know how to feel more." Coy again. *She had to stop that.* She inserted her hand between his legs and squeezed him. "Definitely more."

"*Elizabeth*—" Urgent now.

Maybe not the wisest thing to have done?

"Not here. Peter, *not* here."

"When? Where? I need you *now* . . ."

"We can't . . ."

"You get me that hard, that aroused, and we *can't?*"

"We will," she promised.

"When? Where?"

BAM BAM BAM—the door swung open followed by a dramatic pause in which time Elizabeth wrenched away from

Peter and went to stand by the window, just waiting for Nicholas to enter the room.

"Oh, I'm so sorry. I didn't know anyone was in here."

"Nobody is *in* here," Peter said caustically. "Elizabeth and I were just catching up on old times. I think I'll go for a ride. Elizabeth. Nicholas." He stalked out of the room.

"Oh dear dear," Nicholas murmured. "My best mare just got that pony in a lather, and now he's going to take it out on one of my fillies."

My . . .

Mare—

"I did what you said," Elizabeth said defensively.

"I didn't think you'd try to bed him twice in one day," Nicholas said chidingly. "You have to save some of that for me, Elizabeth. Not that I see any signal of your desire this morning. But I suppose it was too much to hope for when it's only the first day. Nevertheless, it has come about as I told you: you have two desirable men hot and bothered, and begging to fuck you."

"I don't see *two* men begging."

"I'm always at your service, Elizabeth."

Well, she could *see* that. "That's hardly begging, Nicholas."

"No, it isn't. You should be naked and on your back already, begging *me*, after last night."

"Is this one of those anywhere, anytime you want it times?" she asked nastily.

"I do believe it is. Lock the door, Elizabeth."

She stared at him.

"I thought for sure after last night . . . but—well. Man lives in hope, as does man's penis. Go on. Lock the door."

"Just like that?"

"Just like that. Do it."

There was no brooking that tone. And she could always jump out the window if things got too difficult.

Nicholas did not sound pleased. "What you *can't* give to the Russian, you will give to me."

She hated him for mocking her. And herself for letting his

strictures dictate how and when she would make love with Peter. She ought to just bolt from the room, find Peter, and throw herself on him.

A luscious thought. Why not? What difference was there between them? A hard penis was a hard penis, after all. Peter could bring her to completion just as easily as Nicholas had done. More so, because she *loved* Peter. And she had no evidence at all of Nicholas's prowess in bed.

"Oh, aren't you the fickle one—thinking about the Russian after last night."

"I shouldn't have listened to you. I should have let him take me this morning."

"You have me for that." He had worked himself out of his trousers. "Him, you save for marriage."

And there was his cock, massive, hard, jutting, the tip thick and bulbous, long and strong, everything he promised, everything he said he was.

She reached out to touch him, and he pushed her hand away.

"Don't touch me. I'll blow if you touch me."

"Would that be a bad thing?"

"I don't waste my cream. I blow it in your cunt or I save it." He flexed it and she felt her body tighten. "It makes no difference to me." He stroked his pulsating shaft. "I'm ready to service you now."

Her throat went dry; she felt her body contract, her juices flow. She couldn't take her eyes off his long strong fingers manipulating his penis.

"You said you wanted it. You said you wanted two men lusting after you. Well, you've got two men panting to fuck you, but *I'm* the one here, and I'm the one hard to go."

He waited another beat, waiting for her as he kept stroking himself.

"What about the money?"

He stopped the movement of his fingers, and then slowly and deliberately he began tucking himself away. "Ah yes, the money. The payment for services rendered. Give the man a

58 / *Thea Devine*

taste of your sex, just a taste. Goddamn, you *are* an apt student. And the hell of it is, I recommended the strategy myself.

"Well. This is the last time you will refuse me on that account, Elizabeth. These are the particulars: a sum equivalent to a quarter of your income will be deposited in your account monthly, starting next week, to use at your discretion. We will sign the papers; I've already sent for the solicitor. He should come in a day or two. I don't want to know what you do with it. I only know you will never mention it again.

"And now—I will join you in your bedroom in five minutes and I will fuck you. That's what I bought—my money for your body. This time."

Chapter Four

Two men . . .

And learning the stuff of men's fantasies. It did come down to that. Winning Peter. And the money. She would have Peter, her income preserved, and her father would have the money he needed, and that was all that mattered.

She held up the strand of pearls and the round pearl pendant against her naked body.

Unspeakable pleasure.

That was the bargain. He would service her. Peter would marry her. *If* she could entice him and keep him.

Peter knew about things like this; things worldly women knew and she didn't. She needed Nicholas. She knew nothing about luring a man.

And yet, Nicholas had been hard for her, he had said, from the first moment he saw her.

And Peter was hard for her. This morning, this afternoon . . . tonight? Yes, he would be hard for her tonight.

Two men hot and avid to possess what was between her legs.

But Nicholas had paid for it. Paid her to stay. Paid to take her whenever he wanted. Did that mean he wanted her more?

Her body surged. *She* wanted . . .

Where *was* he?

She rubbed the round pearl against her nipple.

Not the same when she did it. But her nipple tingled and

stiffened. She could just . . . stop thinking about his penis and how that iron length would feel stuffed inside her.

She could just . . . insert the pearl . . . just for a minute, just to see . . . just to feel—

She pushed it against her tuft, experimenting, that was all, just the gentlest push against her slit, and her body unexpectedly took it and enclosed it tightly against her clit.

Ohhhhh . . . This was pleasure. This was primitive, simmering, unbelievable pleasure. And he had inserted it, knowing what it would do to her. This was a woman's secret, deep, moist, hidden, euphoric.

She gave herself up to it, shimmying into her bed and just lying there, feeling it, moving against it, rocking her hips into it.

Wear it only . . . to prepare yourself for me.

She could stay like this forever, in this constant haze of arousal. She would wear the pearl forever, naked forever, giving herself to any man who was hard for her. *Any* man.

This she could bring to Peter . . .

She shivered with excitement. *All this carnal knowledge for Peter—*

She cupped her breasts and bore down on the pearl. Oh there, right there . . . She shimmied, she writhed, her body curled around it—*there* . . . and she went slowly, deliciously, unerringly over the edge.

"And *now*," Nicholas said, and she opened her eyes to find him, stark naked and his penis at point, standing at the foot of her bed, "now, you're ready for me."

She inched herself up into a sitting position and muttered crossly, "Now, I don't think I need you."

"Oh, so true. Give a virgin a pearl and she thinks she can dispense with a good fucking. Not today, my lady cherry ripe, now that you are satisfied, you will be well paid for your body. Not after you almost let the Russian get cocked up on you. You are dangerous. And the only thing to do is keep you locked in your room, naked in your bed, and whop you day and night."

He grasped her ankles and pulled her toward him. "And so that is what I'll do. Turn over, and on your knees. Now. Raise your bottom up higher."

"I don't like this . . ." She wasn't ready, not after that shimmering culmination. She didn't want him, not now.

But he had her just where he wanted her: at edge of the bed, on her knees, where he could caress and feel her freely between her legs.

"I don't care. I want those cunt lips. Like that—" He slid two fingers between her delicate folds, feeling her soaking heat as he slipped out the erotic pearl, and she groaned.

"You don't need that, you have *me* . . ." Sliding his fingers up and down her slit, up and down, up and down, lulling her with a drugging pleasure she didn't expect from just that light rubbing of her pubis.

"No talk." He thrust his fingers suddenly, four deep into her hot drenched hole. Her body contracted, and he thrust deeper. "You hide nothing from me." He rammed his fingers tighter. "Tell me to give you more." Ramming tighter still, twisting his fingers inside her, as she moaned at the unremitting pleasure of his penetrating fingers.

"*More* . . ." she panted, grinding her hips wildly. "Fill me . . ."

"My fingers don't fill you?" He twisted them again and she bore down on them hard, her body undulating like a belly dancer.

"Ummmm . . . more . . ."

"There's much much more . . ." He slipped out his fingers as he worked the thick ridge tip of his penis just inside her labia.

Her body jolted as he breached her, and she arched up to accommodate his length, but he didn't move to push himself into her. Instead, he held himself poised, just at the brink, letting her feel just that much of him sheathed in her wet heat.

She moaned, pushing and gyrating to try to pull him deeper.

"Oh no, my lady, oh no. This much you get . . ." He contracted his hips so that she felt his bulbus penis head with-draw. "And this much you get . . ." He pushed into her again, just to the ridge, and undulated his hips so that she could feel the length and the power of him that was not enveloped by her body. "This much . . ." He withdrew again, caressing her nether lips with the hard ridged edge. "And this . . ." Into her again, just within, just the thick shaft head. In and out, in and out, in and out . . .

"More . . ." she whispered. "I need more . . ."

"You need no more than this one inch of my penis to plea-sure you, my lady ripe and ready. And this is all I will do until you come."

And that was all: just in and out, in and out. In and out.

She couldn't bear it. She could feel all of his long strong penis behind the controlled pumping of his hips. And she wanted it desperately and he wouldn't root himself in her.

"Give it to me."

"You can't get enough of my penis head, can you, my lady?" In and out, in and out. Bulbous inch in, bulbous inch out. Thick ridge in, thick ridge out. Hot hard in, hot hard out.

She writhed against his tip, seeking his length desperately. He was a piston—in and out, in and out, just so much, no more—in and out, centering her hips, in and out, in and out . . .

"*Ohhhhhhhhhh* . . ." And *in* it came, slowly, insidiously, in a long, lavish swirl around her sensitized labia before it un-furled— "Oh!"—and exploded rhythmically into a thousand points of pleasure.

And there he stayed, rooted in her just that one inch, his hands grasping her hips firmly and holding her firmly in that reverse position.

"Don't move your penis," she groaned.

"It's perfectly happy where it is."

"I thought we were done."

"We're just starting, my lady muck and fuck, especially since you can't get enough of my penis." He wriggled his hips so that another inch of him breached her. "The Russian can wait. I can't."

"The Russian isn't the only one who can't wait," she muttered.

"Oh, so give my lady an inch," he wriggled another inch inside her, "and now she wants"—another inch—"she wants"—pushing and pumping still deeper—"and she will get"—so deep that his pubic hair scraped against her buttocks' crease—"what she's begging for . . ."—centering her again with his strong grasp on her hips and pulling her body more tightly against him as he poled himself still deeper inside her.

God, she was so hot, so ripe, a bitch in heat. And no one had fucked her up in years. She was too tight, too untried. She enveloped him like a hot moist glove, the fit so snug, so encompassing, he couldn't cram himself in deep enough.

And every movement made her gasp and catch her breath, as if she couldn't believe how big he was, and how much and how fully her body could take him.

And then silence. A long thick silence coupled with their erotic carnal intimacy. He could have stayed that way for hours. Days. Months. Years.

Who *was* this woman whose sensual hunger was beyond knowing?

He didn't care; he was naked and stuffed into her, never to move again, and the world, and his duty, and his enemies, could all go to hell.

But his penis had another idea. It wanted pulse, push, thrust, completion, urgent, hot . . . *now*.

He bucked wildly against her, spurting suddenly and uncontrollably.

"Bloody damn hell . . ." He pulled back with an effort. *Not yet not yet not yet.* He held himself tightly, erect, held that firm writhing bottom beneath his hands with just the iron length of him connected to her by that one luscious inch of his penis.

Under control.

Listening to her erotic whimpering begging him to ram himself home.

Hard and contained . . .

Pushing . . . just a little, testing—
Man of iron . . .
". . . *can't* . . ."
"*Now* . . ." He drove into her, embedding himself in her so
tightly he could feel his pubic hair rubbing against her crease.
"*Now* . . ."
Thrusting like a piston . . . *Nownownownownownownownow-
nownow* . . . bringing her up relentlessly, hard, hot, insatiable,
until he felt her yield, contract, shatter . . . her fisted hands
pounding on the mattress in rhythm with her come.
His body seized and stiffened on the edge; one move . . .
one draw—one breath . . . and—*and*—he erupted, spewing,
spewing, spewing from the unending source of his power until
he was wrung to the bone, and collapsed and covered her, paid
in full . . .

What an insidious thing pleasure was. Society negated it.
Men killed for it. And women lied about it, lied because they
loved it, wanted it, yearned for it.
And it took nothing more than relinquishing fear, nothing
more than girding yourself to go after what you wanted. Why
didn't she know this, all those years ago? She never would
have married William; she would have pursued Peter until he
capitulated and damned the consequences.
*The stuff of men's fantasies . . . She understood now: a naked
body willing and open to anything a man might devise and desire . . .*
*A woman was a toy, a sated man was damned heavy, and
pleasure was an evanescent thing.*
And if she wriggled and writhed too hard in an attempt to
get away, she would rouse him up all over again.
"Aren't *you* eager to get away," he murmured, winding himself around her still tighter. "Not a pretty compliment after
what just happened."
"I'm just eager to get fifteen stone of man *off* me," she retorted.
"Of course, quite ungentlemanly of me, but then I've been

away from the more civilized aspects of copulation for a while."
He rolled off her and on to his back, his arms under his head,
while she gingerly climbed to her knees and propped herself
up against a pillow.

Now for the first time, she could really see him, and she
was awed by his body, its sinew, its muscle, its strength, and
amazed by its fragility. A man without clothes, even a man as
beautifully made as Nicholas, was as vulnerable as a newborn
baby.

"Have you?" she said tartly. "And where have you been,
Nicholas, that the solicitors couldn't find you?"

"Ah, here and there." He stared at the ceiling. "Over and
yon, and nowhere you need concern yourself about since the
solicitors are satisfied. As will you be, when Mr. Giddons arrives with the papers for you to sign that ensure your father
will be able to mine your income on an ongoing basis. Thank
God, *you* will have no expenses to speak of."

No expenses? Did he mean she might just as well hand her
widow's portion over to her father and have done with it?

No, no. It wasn't going to work like that. There would be
an end to it somewhere down the road. She would put conditions on it; her father would not drain her only resource forever.

She made a restless movement to get out of bed. "I need to
tend to things, Nicholas."

"You need to tend to *me*." He nodded at his rampaging
erection.

"I thought we had done with that. Aren't you . . . *sapped?*"

"You obviously aren't. And I presume the things you want
to attend to are the Russian's hurt feelings. I don't think so,
Elizabeth. Not at *my* expense."

"And yet—and yet, *your* house does not run by itself. *Your*
servants need guidance and supervision, and *my* guests need a
hostess. And I don't need any gossip spread about *me*."

"My dear Elizabeth, those three or four guests who went
back to London spread the news of my arrival like galloping

horses. Have no fear. The rumor mills are cranked up to full speed. Thank heaven you have the protection of the Russian. Oh, and your father. And me."

"And we see what good all that protection has done me."

"A world of good, did you but comprehend it. You will want for nothing, even the Russian, eventually. And concurrent with that, you have the pleasure of me."

"That indeed was what I was yearning for," she said acidly.

"I think it's pretty clear you were, Elizabeth. I think it's easy to assess what your marriage was like and what you gave up and what you got."

"I will not listen to this. I have kept my end of the bargain, and now I must keep *your* house since all you are willing to do is lay about and plug yourself into whatever socket you find handy."

"Surely not whatever socket," he drawled as she swung off her side of the bed.

"You've made your point, Nicholas."

"Let me make it again."

"Let me make sure there will be dinner on the table." She began grabbing up her clothes.

"I'm always hungry," Nicholas murmured. "It is an ongoing chore."

"Yes, indeed it would be," Elizabeth said furiously, ducking into her sitting room. "A chore."

Nicholas levered himself out of bed and followed her, pacing slowly toward her from the threshold. "Only if the persons involved weren't"—he came closer, too close—"ravenous all the time"—and backed her against the wall. "Some people crave what they can't have. Others feed where they can . . . and still others come to the banquet to feast—"

Too close, too too—she hadn't yet put on a stitch of clothes and he was rubbing his penis against her belly suggestively.

"And *you*, my lady cherry ripe, are the feast . . ." He covered her mouth, the first time he'd kissed her, he opened her mouth and took her tongue; he nudged her between her legs, and he savagely stove his hips upward to prong her hard against the wall.

It was the kiss that destroyed her; never had she been kissed like this, with this wet violent possessiveness, as if he were feeding on her tongue, on her mouth, on her lips, her naked body. He filled her in every way, pinned her tightly, roughly to the wall, and pounded into her ferociously, oblivious to anything but engulfing her in his cream.

And still it wasn't enough for him. She felt impaled by him, crowded by him, her body overloaded by his size, his power, his force.

And it was all for him this time. All for him, and she was the vessel. All that vigor and virility to sate his senses . . . This, *this*, was familar to her. Another few moments to endure, and he would be done.

It was coming, everything tense, stiff, hot, ready to blow . . .

"And this," he whispered against her lips, "is exactly how I like to spend my cream," and he poured the last spuming blast of his seed into her.

The kiss.

That kiss utterly unnerved her. She had never been kissed like that in her life. Not even by Peter.

William . . . ? Oh, no—that had been horrible . . . slimy poking kisses hard, wet, and noisy, and oh, so disgusting . . .

What to make of that kiss? She had to stop thinking about it was what. It was a thing apart, just like the bargain, and the only thing it had to do with her life was to equip her with expertise to ensnare Peter.

"And where have *you* been?" Her father, as she entered the library, seated at a table with Mena in a desultory card game.

Damn. Her father was the last person she wanted to see after the last two hours she had spent. She *was* spent, her body boneless and languid, and she would rather have just fallen asleep, if only Nicholas would have gone.

But no, *he* was asleep in her bed, and she needed find Peter, even if she just collapsed in his arms. After she had sunk herself into another lie.

"I was with Nicholas." Well, that was the truth as far as it went. "Estate matters, you know."

"Oh, yes, estate matters. *His* estate, *his* charity dispensed to the indigent widow. Damn it all. I still can't come to grips with this stranger taking over everything. Are you sure he's entitled?"

"Well, we'll find out soon enough. Mr. Giddons, the solicitor, is coming in a day or so with papers for me to sign. He'll either be delighted to see Nicholas or he'll call the constable, and then we'll know."

"Maybe we can know sooner," her father said.

Elizabeth sank wearily into a chair. "I don't understand your problem. I was properly notified. I can't inherit the title; I have sufficient income. You'll have all the money you need for business, and you may stay at Shenstone as long as you like. Exactly what do you need to know further?"

Her father waved off her enumeration of his entitlements. "We—we need to know who this man is, where he came from, and why it took him a year to claim the estate."

"Have you asked him?"

"Did we not try yesterday morning? He shrugged us off, made light of our concerns, showed us no papers to prove his birthright."

"Giddons sent *me* the papers in London. Nicholas brought a copy of the letter."

"Blast it, Elizabeth. He didn't send you the man's baptism certificiate. He could be an imposter. What does anyone know of Nicholas Massey? This man who *calls* himself Nicholas Massey—don't answer. No one in *England* knows anything."

"And so therefore . . . ?"

"It is up to you to find out *something*."

"I see."

"Well, search his room or something. A man has to have papers, for God's sake."

"Where's Peter?"

"Out riding with Victor. Lovely trails on this estate. Excellent horseflesh. All *his*. Do you hear me, Elizabeth? *All* his, and after you served seven years penance in that marriage."

Another flick of the whip. Her misbegotten marriage was *her* fault.

"I am so delighted you think so," Elizabeth said stonily. *Maybe it was.*

"If only you'd borne a son . . ."

"Dear God . . ."

"Now, Frederick." This from Mena, who *never* interfered. "That's too harsh, by half. And William could have been the one at fault."

"Well, if there'd been a son, there wouldn't be an heir. I mean, the *child* would have been the heir, and no questions asked. And now we're stuck. Unless Elizabeth takes some action, that is."

"Search his room," she interpolated.

"At least."

"You could have done it these last two hours," she pointed out.

"It's *your* house . . . or rather, you at least could find some reason to *be* there if he caught you."

"Could I?" she murmured ironically. "I suppose I could . . . I could tell him I've come to bed him—"

"Elizabeth!" Peter, horrified, in the doorway. "What on earth?" He strode in and knelt by her chair. "Where have you been?"

"Estate matters," she said, thankful those two little words said it all.

"*Estate* matters," Peter huffed. "My dear Elizabeth. We're all talking about the ramifications of this . . . this *interloper* . . ."

"I'm so tired of repeating this. I was properly notified. I just chose not to notify *you*."

"But *who* is he? Where has he been? How do we know?"

She held up her hand. "Peter—"

He took it and kissed it. "I'm sorry. I'm so sorry. I have no business interfering. None. I want only what's best for you."

"I know, I know." She gave up under the pressure of his fingers entwined with hers. She wanted that more than anything—*don't let him fuck you yet*—and some answers about Nicholas Massey and his specious bargains suddenly didn't seem too high a price to pay.

If only she could share with him what she knew now . . .

"Come," Peter said, almost as if he read her mind. "We'll go for a ride. We'll walk in the garden. We've put too much strain on you. This is harder for you than any of us. We only want to help."

She allowed him to pull her from the chair, to lead her down the hall, down the stairs, and out the front door. He always seemed to be leading her away from something, rather than toward it, she thought.

"This is a beautiful park," Peter said as they strolled down the drive.

"*This* I have loved these last seven years." And she had loved it, the long sweeping vista from the house rising upward and away to the road to London a mile beyond. The landscape was dotted with trees, and hedges, and banks of flowers in unexpected places. Even now in the distance, she could make out the bent form of Watton digging in the soil.

"Poor Elizabeth. But you see—all those years invested in Shenstone—to what end?"

Waiting for you . . . Words she could never say. "My youth," she said finally. "An income. Sufficient funds that my father may speculate on oil wells in Siberia. A morsel of freedom. What more do I need?"

"Ah. What more indeed?" He took her hand and kissed it. "You need to know if this is the man to whom you will give up your legacy." He took her in his arms. "*We* need to know . . ."

We . . . There was a we . . .

She tilted her chin up; she would chance saying the words. "That sounds so lovely, Peter. *We . . .*"

His lips brushed hers. "So much we need to share . . ."

Not that *kiss.* "Yes," she whispered. *A better kiss, a sweeter kiss. Peter's kiss.*

"So you have to know . . ."

"Yes." She would do it then. Peter thought it was the right thing to do, and her instructions had been to submit to him in everything. Almost everything.

"Really, Elizabeth. It's utterly unseemly for you to be in someone's arms so soon after your husband's death."

Nicholas, striding up the drive from—well, who knew where? Somewhere that made it very uncomfortable for her, knowing where he had been and who had been with him up until a half hour ago.

"So. What do you think of my stable?" he asked Peter, and not waiting for answer: "Elizabeth. I still have some questions . . ."

She shot Peter a look. "Do you? Can't they wait?"

He looked at them, one to the other. "Oh, I suppose. You can't do much harm to my reputation just standing outside and talking."

He strode off and Elizabeth turned to see Peter staring after Nicholas.

"I *loathe* that man."

"I think we're all coming to dislike him," Elizabeth said. "And it didn't take two days. I'll do what you advise. You're right, Peter. We have to know."

He swept her into his arms again and kissed her, and she was absolutely certain that Nicholas was watching.

It was time to go on the offensive, time to find the answers. Her father was right: the place to start was where a man was most himself—in his bedroom. There, she would find out all his secrets and run him to the ground.

But there were no secrets to be found. The man who had no past had brought nothing to his present. She discovered nothing that spoke of any kind of life this man had led before he limped through the terrace doors yesterday morning.

All she found was one leather bag, worn and torn, on the

armoire shelf, along with three serviceable black suits hanging precisely apart, two fresh white cotton shirts, and an extra pair of well-worn boots placed on the armoire floor.

There was nothing extravagant about the cut and style of his clothes. He had no jewelry, rings or watch fobs, no silk cravats, no fancy nightwear.

There were no pictures, books, notes, letters of credit, or money lying around. There was nothing under the carpet, under the mattress, behind the chest of drawers—or in them.

Nothing in the pockets of the suits, or tucked into the boots, nothing in the suitcase, not even anything slipped into the cracked leather covering.

Nothing but three suits, two shirts, one pair of boots, and one battered suitcase.

How did a man exist with nothing personal to identify him?

The man was a cipher, she thought in frustration. He could have come from anywhere—or nowhere. He could be anyone, and there wasn't a scrap of anything to identify him, let alone identify him as Nicholas Massey, in that room. And she hadn't much more time to search either: she had been there too long already.

Damn him.

The door creaked open and she jumped, her heart skittering wildly.

"*. . . there you are . . .*" Her father, on the breath of whisper, edged into the room. "Peter told me. Did you find anything?"

She shook her head.

"Damn. I was hoping . . ."

She raised her hand, and he lowered his voice still more. "Let me try. Two heads and all that . . ."

She was finished. For now. "As you wish . . ."

"Keep watch . . ."

Easy to say when Nicholas might return at any moment and find *her* on the threshold of his room while her father had ample time to hide.

Nevertheless, she took up her position by the door and let him try his luck.

"Not a bloody thing," he whispered in her ear a good ten minutes later.

"Then go. He mustn't catch us here."

"You first."

"You go—I can fabricate a reason for being here." Oh, absolutely, she could invent at least one good reason for being there. "Go, now." He didn't argue—he went. Her father was very good at going, she thought acidly. It was one of the things he did best.

She took one last look around the room to make sure that nothing had been moved, and then she turned and there was Nicholas, and she thought her heart would fall right out of her chest.

She lifted her chin, ready for combat.

"Ready for more so soon, Elizabeth?" he drawled.

Remember Peter's kiss. Remember what's at stake. Don't think about the bargain. You have every right to be in this room.

"Just what I would expect you to say, Nicholas," she said tartly. "I have found it is always wise to make sure that there are fresh linens on the bed, particularly when the guest wing has been so rarely occupied." *Talking too much. This is more than any guest needs to know, let alone him.*

"Your attention to detail is most gratifying."

"So my husband taught me."

"And your *very* individual attention to your guests," Nicholas murmured, moving toward her. "I'm quite impressed. Did your husband teach you that? I mean, as opposed to what you have learned from *me*."

There ought to be a law against tall *looming* predatory men, she thought furiously as she backed away. There ought to be a law against *bargains*.

In his room, clothed and civilized, he once again became the man she had seen behind the mask of the glad-handing host; there was nothing amiable about him now. There was only the faint aura of danger that surrounded him. And that look in his eyes, as if he knew everything *she* was trying to hide.

"I expect you will find out," she answered in kind.

"Absolutely I will," he agreed, and she didn't doubt it.

"As will I," she muttered, not meaning him to hear—or perhaps she did, because he caught her words and understood them, completely.

"You might not like what you find, Elizabeth."

She stiffened. "I don't like it now, Nicholas."

"Or you like it too much."

She eyed him warily. The mask was back in place. No threat now, just a cosmic amusement at her expense. "Women do fall all over you, don't they?" *Now why did she say that?*

"Do they?" he murmured, slanting her a knowing look as he deliberately moved to the walnut side table by his bed.

"*I* won't." She watched in dismay as he pulled a leather billfold out from under the marble top of the table, the *removable* marble top that she hadn't even thought to look under. But who would have?

"Really? But you're here, aren't you?" He examined the contents and then looked up at her as if he knew all her secrets.

But she had no secrets. Only one.

No, only two. And he was one of them, and that he knew.

"Can't get enough, can you?"

"Oh, I've had enough of you, Nicholas. I'm filled to the brim with you."

"Yes, you are, my lady. Utterly clotted with my cream. And ripe and ready for more, even if you won't admit it. You loved every minute this morning, and quite obviously, you're willing and available to give this guest even more of your individual *attention*, if he so desires. And that's why you're in my room, isn't it?"

Trapped.

She looked at the billfold in his hand. He knew she was planning to go to Peter. He knew.

How did they get from her implausible presence in his room to his taking her to his bed again?

Or had her unconscious plan been to distract him, should he catch her skulking?

She felt a tingling in her breasts. *Hard for her, paid for her.* "Do you desire me, Nicholas?"

"I'm always ready to fuck you." He locked the door and turned to face her. "Do you doubt it?"

Her gazed swerved to his groin. His penis was rock hard and at the ready, nothing less than she had expected. But then he had trained her already to anticipate it.

Was she wet already? No, not for him, never for him. It was because Peter was waiting. Peter's arms. Peter's kisses.

"Come and get me, my lady cherry ready. Show me how much you want what you see."

She wet her lips. Even she didn't know how much, or *if*, she wanted *him*. But the bargain was the bargain: she'd just get it done and get out of there fast.

She sauntered up to him and cupped him with a brazenness that caught him by surprise. That was good. An excellent lesson, in fact: *a man and his penis do not like to be ignored.* All she had to do was take his penis out and play with it. Make him erupt. Cover *him* with his everlasting cream.

An amazing thing, a penis: a body part with a mind of its own, ready to capitulate to all the cooing and petting and stroking a woman wanted to give. And more.

She pushed him back against the wall, took his manhood naked in her hands, jutting, full-blown, granite hard, spurting to further life even as she slid her hands all over it, stroked it, fondled the underside, rubbed the tender head, sought his taut scrotum, and tickled that sweet patch of bare skin beneath.

She had him all in her hands, and in her caressing fingers she held all that power. He was utterly hers that moment as she wrapped both her hands around his bone-hard shaft and stoked him.

. . . fast fast fast . . .

She squeezed him, she pumped him, she primed him . . .

until she wondered just how much a man's penis needed to be cocked. But she would win. She would make him come, she would make him spew to the ceiling, he would come so hard and so violently. The maids would be cleaning his cream off the walls for days, there would be so much of it.

"Down . . ."

She felt his hands firmly on her head guiding her to her knees, and down to his penis head. "Take him in your mouth . . ."

"I—"

"Do it. I told you—I don't waste my cream . . ."

His hands pushed, and her lips brushed the delicate and delicious opening where just a pearl of his ejaculate glistened. He pushed again, and she parted her lips and took his penis head into the heat of her mouth.

His groan told her everything. She lapped at the ridge, pulling on the head with her lips and tongue.

Just an inch. Why not punish him, too?

She pulled back, compressing the very tip between her lips, and then sucked him back into her mouth. Just like that. *Compress, suck, compress, suck.* Just an inch. *Torture him.*

Torture me . . .

In and out, compress and suck, compress and suck . . .

In and out. Compress . . .

She felt his whole body seize up and she kept her lips tight around the tip, growling like a puppy with a bone, refusing to give up that luscious tip to his orgasm.

"Open up . . ."

She shook her head, pulling more firmly on the tip.

"Open up . . ."

Oh, he was delightfully desperate now. She waited to see what he would do, the man who wouldn't waste his cream. She had him good and tight and hard at her mercy, the whole long luscious bone-stiff length of him by the very tip, and it was a powerful and sensual thing.

"O-pen *up* . . ."

But a person did get tired, she thought with some compassion. It took a lot of energy, a lot of resolve to keep on sucking him like that. And he was getting really annoyed. He wanted his come, and she supposed, now that she understood where the power lay, she could grant it to him.

More power. *Her power.*

She took a deep breath, rounded her mouth slightly, and let him come in. More than an inch now, more than she could ever encompass that he seemed determined to thrust into her mouth.

"My lady *bitch* . . ." he hissed, and then he reared back, and she opened her mouth, and he exploded his cream into her.

She couldn't take it fast enough; it dripped from her mouth, thick luscious cream, onto her chin, her breast, her bodice. There was so much of it, all over her, all over him. And he kept coming and coming and coming, as if he couldn't stop, and she didn't want him to stop.

And then, suddenly, he stopped. Completely stopped.

"My cream becomes you," he murmured, lifting her head and rubbing it into her cheek. "Lie down."

"Surely . . ."

His expression was implacable. "Lie down. Believe me, I have enough left to service you, my lady suck and fuck."

He followed her down, lifting her dress and tearing apart her drawers so he could get at her, and spreading her vaginal lips with his fingers before he forcefully swooped into her, and jammed himself tightly against her, his pubic hair scraping against her tender womanflesh.

"*This* is where a man wants to shoot his cream." He undulated his hips. "*Here.*" He pressed deeper. "You couldn't wring me dry, could you?" Embedded in her. "You thought you knew what a man wants, what a man needs . . ." Rooted. ". . . but you didn't . . ." Oh, he was losing it. ". . . know this . . ." She was too hot, too tight, too willing. ". . . did you . . ." Too good with her mouth. ". . . my la—"

He lost it right then; he blew it all like a volcano, all that was left, and shot his wad into her deep and hard and helplessly in one ball-wrenching blast.

Chapter 5

"Elizabeth!!"

She froze. She was barely down the hallway from Nicholas's room, barely decent, barely dry, her mouth still full of the taste of him, her body still reverberating from his ferocious orgasm.

And here came Peter, exactly in a place she didn't want anyone to see her, a place she wasn't supposed to be.

She turned slowly, trying to get herself in hand. "Peter, thank goodness, Peter . . . !"

He clasped her arm and pulled her out to the stairwell. "Did I just see you come from *that man's* room? *Did* you?"

Oh yes, I did, I did that and more, and I left my torn undergarments there to prove it. Ah! I have to stop this. All I did was service that man's penis. And that was all.

But then, thank heaven, Peter had no idea that Nicholas was even in the room.

"Yes." It was better to be brief: obviously Peter was under the impression that she had followed *his* advice. That was good. Then she wouldn't have to explain anything more.

"Come to my room. Tell me what you found. *Shhh*—don't talk here." He took her hand and they tiptoed down the stairs and through the corridor to the family wing.

The gong sounded for lunch.

"So we'll be late," Peter said in an undertone. "Let them make whatever they want of it. Come—" He opened his bedroom door and pulled her inside and into his arms.

Comfort once again. She let him hold her, support her, she

let him stroke her back, and she refused to think about what she had been doing not twenty minutes before, or to consider what Nicholas would think if either of them were late to lunch.

And anyway, these were supposed to be lessons she could use to attract and hold *Peter.*

"So . . . tell me . . ." Peter whispered.

"I wish there were something to tell. I found nothing. My father found nothing." *And now the lie.* "If there's anything in that room, it's hidden too cleverly to be found."

"I knew it. I knew it. The man is devious and he's hiding something. There's the proof. And I'm thinking very strongly that we need to keep guard outside his room until your solicitor arrives tomorrow."

"Peter—must we?"

"Elizabeth, *think*—who *is* this man?"

Her heart started pounding. It was too late for that. He had had a letter of introduction from Mr. Giddons.

"Anyone could have papers. Anyone could forge an identity," Peter went on. "Anyone could walk into this house and *say* he was Nicholas Massey."

Truly? Then she had made a bargain with the devil, if this man was *not* Nicholas Massey.

And he was part of some masterful conspiracy.

It did not bear thinking about, not right at this minute.

"Peter . . . can we *not* talk about that man?"

He rubbed her back again. "Of course we can. None of this needs to be talked about *now.* Do you realize we are alone—and *no one* knows where we are?"

"Oh yes . . ." She lifted her face to his, inviting one of his petal-soft kisses. "Oh yes . . ." As he obliged her, dropping featherlight kisses all over her mouth. The mouth that had just . . .

She turned her head away, and he murmured, "Don't be afraid, don't be shy. I'd never hurt you."

"I want to stay like this in your arms forever," she whispered.

"I want to keep you here." He smoothed his hands down her back, over her hips, questing, questioning, as he sought to take liberties with her body.

This, this was the way things should be, she thought, laying her head against his chest as he felt for her buttocks. Soft, sweet, respectful, a seeking and a response.

Except what would he think when he found her naked beneath her clothes?

He would think she was naked for him. She would convince him she was naked for him. If the circumstances were different, she would *be naked for him . . .*

"Sweet Elizabeth—we've waited so long."

Too long, she thought, but she would come to him now a woman who had known secrets and sorrow. A different woman, really, who had instantly fallen in love with him all over again, and the intervening years didn't matter.

Everything will be as it was. The promise not to be broken.

"Elizabeth . . ." he murmured, seeking her lips.

But she couldn't quite bring herself to kiss him, not after . . . "Peter—" She did love saying his name, loved being in his arms, adored the sweet veneration of his hands as he pulled up her gown.

"I have you now, sweet Elizabeth. And nothing will make me let go."

He had her skirt now, bunched up under his arms. He could just reach her over that layer material. Just touch her. "Oh lord, Elizabeth . . ." Just shape the rounded curve of her bottom with his palm. Her naked bottom. "Eliza-*beth* . . . For me?"

"All for you," she whispered. He held her so tightly against him, she felt a part of him. Such a light touch he had, such adoration of her body.

Let him feel and fondle. Don't let him fuck you.

If he was really Nicholas Massey . . . oh damn, she hated to have these doubts after the shock of receiving Mr. Giddons's news in London.

But she didn't have doubts: her father did, and Peter. And so let them do what they must to quell those doubts.

Her job right now was to concentrate on Peter. A man and his penis did not like to be ignored. And Peter was all man, all hard.

"Oh God, Elizabeth . . ." He was feeling for her now, wanting to take as much as he could get in this rare moment of privacy. "Would you . . . ?"

"Anything—"

Anything he wanted—

—except that brisk rapping at the bedroom door.

"God-*dammit* . . ." Peter cursed as the door was opened; he instantly relinquished his hold on her skirt. "Giles! What the *hell* is it?"

"The master sent me, my lord."

Elizabeth's ears pricked up. *The master?*

"Indeed, sir, he wanted to make certain nothing was amiss and to remind you luncheon is being served. And perhaps to tempt you with this afternoon's menu. Yes. Let me see: melon in white wine; leek soup; shirred eggs; a choice of herring or roast beef sandwiches; a choice of prawn or cheddar cheese salad. And for dessert—"

Peter slammed his hand down. "Jesus!"

". . . almond pudding with vanilla sauce," Giles finished, ignoring his outburst. "I think that's all, sir."

"Thank you, Giles," Peter said, barely holding his temper in check, and pinning the butler with a meaningful look until Giles took the hint and withdrew. "Goddammit to hell." He turned to Elizabeth. "I swear, I believe that man wants you. Now he's sending Giles to be his mouthpiece. Can you remember one time that we've had a private moment that he hasn't interrupted us?"

"Not a one," Elizabeth said staunchly. No, because Nicholas was hewing to the plan: to make Peter believe she might be interested in him. And how interesting that Peter perceived it in just the opposite way.

"He is determined we will have no time together for some nefarious purpose of his own. On the surface, you see what it appears to be. He can't stand it if another man even *talks* to you. And it makes me all the more determined to get to the bottom of this question of his identity. You do agree, Elizabeth?"

"Oh, absolutely." Anything he wanted, anything he said.

"Then I suppose, since I'm in no mood for lovemaking now, blast him, we should go to lunch, and make plans to keep an eye on him until your solicitor arrives."

Be submissive. Whatever he says, whatever he wants, agree to it.

"Whatever you think is best," Elizabeth murmured and he smiled and dropped a kiss on her cheek.

"My lovely Elizabeth. When this is all settled, we'll have all the time in the world."

She debated slipping her hand between his legs, just to juice things up a bit. But no—he was in no mood for lovemaking.

"I can't wait for that moment," she murmured, and she wondered if she wasn't a little thankful that Giles had interrupted? *Could* she have given herself to him with Nicholas's juices still on her lips?

She didn't want to think of it, and she didn't have to make that decision. *Thank heaven.*

Docilely, she followed him out of the room.

"We're letting him ride us to hounds."

Elizabeth looked up at her father and put down her teacup. He just never stopped. Apparently, she couldn't get one moment of peace with Nicholas in the house. "He's more like a runaway horse, Father."

"So we're just to carry on until that solicitor comes," her father grumbled.

"There isn't anything else to do. And frankly, it hardly concerns you. You'll have whatever you need. It's my future at stake."

And besides, it had always galled her that while she had married the title, it was her father who'd reaped the vast rewards by extension.

Although he had never hesitated to point out that, by that union, she had accumulated everything a woman could ever want: the most expensive clothes; a beautifully furnished country estate; a London townhouse; social status.

Misery.

And then a man died, and in the end, it all came down to his blood line. Damn damn damn . . .

And there was still one more dinner to get through until Mr. Giddons would arrive.

Tonight it was just as abundant a table: oxtail soup, broiled skewered oysters, roast pork with mustard crust, fillet of sole in sauce, scalloped potatoes, a cucumber salad, assorted cheeses, sherbet, and pie.

No one spoke as the first course was served. Everyone watched Nicholas covertly, almost as if they all thought he would scavenge the silver if they didn't keep their eyes on him.

He stroked his fork and knife deliberately, maliciously; it was lovely silver, at that, heavy, ornate, monogrammed.

Mine.

He felt the hostility like a wall. They were all thinking the exact same thing as he.

All of it, *his.*

And they wanted to prove it wasn't somehow.

There was only one way.

He scanned the table. They were all busy with dessert, with coffee, with little side murmurings that deliberately excluded him. Counting the minutes, the hours, until bedtime. Wondering how they were going to contain him.

They couldn't.

There was always an enemy . . .

A nest of vipers, ready to strike.

Who had the most to lose?

The answer was too clear: Elizabeth. Lovely, luscious, ripe-for-the-taking Elizabeth. Or had that been part of *her* plan?

You never know who your enemy might be . . .

He took a helping of sherbet; it was tart on his tongue. He

took a sip of coffee, the heat contrasting with the edge of iciness as he swallowed.

They all watched him, the tension escalating.

Waiting . . . for what?

They looked around at each other, as if they had discussed something and no one wanted to be the first to broach it.

And finally: "I will say it," Victor pronounced suddenly from across the table. "We need to protect ourselves. We know nothing about this man. Or if he is who he says he is. He could kill us in our sleep."

Ah, the hard truth—the glare of suspicion. And only the revolutionary bold enough—or foolhardy enough—to voice it.

"Now why would I want to do that?" Nicholas asked. "What could I possibly gain that I don't have already?"

"Time to loot the house and disappear," Victor retorted. "We could wake up tomorrow and everything could be gone, and poor Elizabeth will find out that you *were* setting her up to steal everything from her. Ah, but never fear, Elizabeth. I"—he thumped his chest—"*I* will watch him night and day, as of this moment. He will never make a move that I am not aware . . ."

"And I," Peter said suddenly. "I'm not comfortable with this situation either. I think we should take shifts watching him until your solicitor arrives and we know for sure if his claim is legitimate."

"An excellent plan, gentlemen," Nicholas said heartily. "By all means, post watch by my door. I have no objection whatsoever."

They all stared at him.

He slanted a long look at Elizabeth. "I have nothing to hide. I am who I say I am. Elizabeth has the solicitor's letter of introduction. But if you all feel so strongly about it, I'm agreeable to whatever makes you more comfortable. Will this make *you* more comfortable, Elizabeth?"

She broke her gaze away first. "I don't . . ." she bit out and stopped. She wasn't so sure about this plan, except that it would put Nicholas out of commission for the night. And maybe that was a good thing. ". . . have an opinion one way or another."

"You know I'm Nicholas Massey."

"I took it on faith that you were because of Mr. Giddons's letter, but everyone else seems to think there is some doubt."

"You take too much on faith, my dear Elizabeth," Peter muttered. "You know nothing about the world, and certainly nothing about this man that isn't written on a piece of paper anyone could falsify."

The problem was, she knew too much, Elizabeth thought acidly. Things she could never excise from her mind and imagination. But it didn't do to dwell on that either. Mr. Giddons would arrive tomorrow with all the answers, and meantime, Nicholas would be guarded and contained.

She wasn't so sure she could handle any more of this covert suspicion—and of finding Nicholas on top of her every living minute.

She rose. "Gentlemen . . ." Time for cordials among not-so-cordial acquaintances.

And tonight, her father, Victor, and Peter would have him hemmed in as tightly as a straitjacket. She might be able to do something, find something, maybe Mena would remember something, tonight.

The fools. He had never felt such contempt for anyone. Not that they knew whom they were dealing with. Or as if any of this meant anything.

Didn't it? No. From the moment he'd first stepped foot on Shenstone, the thing became to take it away from them.

From her. Her?

No. To have the satisfaction of knowing he had triumphed and William Massey had lost. To vindicate his father, even in death.

And to smoke out the Unseen Hand.

But he hadn't known what he'd wanted until he'd seen it.

He wanted Shenstone.

He hadn't thought he would feel that way. It was momentous and totally unexpected: he felt as if he were coming home.

And so he had to give up the lie; there was no going back now.

Shenstone was not the enemy.

Elizabeth?

But he hadn't known how much he wanted her either until he'd had her . . .

But that wasn't the point anymore. The point was *them.* He needed to focus on *them,* out there in the long broad hallway, stretched against the wall, thinking they were all so clever.

And the Unseen Hand out there somewhere in the darkness, waiting, watching, and poised to strike.

The house was like a tomb, the darkness eerie and otherwordly, not a light anywhere, and not a breath, or a step marring the thick matte silence.

They were all watching *him.*

Who is watching me?

She was crazy to leave her room, crazier still to think there was anything to be discovered about Nicholas Massey in the dark that couldn't be found in broad daylight.

But how could she sit still, waiting, wondering?

. . . waiting . . . God, she hated waiting.

The dark blotted out everything. There were no boundaries; it was as if she had dropped off the earth and into a void.

She stretched out her arms tentatively; she could feel nothing, and nothing was the scariest thing of all.

Stupid not to have taken a candle.

She'd be better off crawling back to her bed than to step into the black nothingness that surrounded her.

Her father, Victor, Peter—they would take care of everything. Why couldn't she trust that? She'd make things worse if they had to worry about her creeping around the house like a ghost.

But she felt like one, like she didn't exist anymore, now that this *presence*, this *other* had disrupted her life.

... *William's brother's son. That whole tangled family history that was supposed to have been resolved by* her *conceiving William's child* ...

It was a nightmare pure and simple.

And it was so dark. A darkness where nothing existed: it was like death, surrounding you, blinding you, enfolding you.

Holding you.

Holding her ...

She was imagining it. Anyone's imagination would run riot in the dark. She took a step backward, her heart pounding, but it was like backing into emptiness.

There was someone in the hallway with her ...

Oh God ...

She reached out—and touched nothing, not even the door.

Oh God, now what?

She twisted her body—and touched *him*.

She jumped and shrieked, and he clamped his hand over her mouth and pulled her roughly against his chest.

"Did you think," a voice whispered in her ear—*who?*—"anything or anyone on this earth could keep me from you?"

Terror, quick, abject.

She was wholly immobilized by his arm around her midriff constraining her arms, and his hand flat against her mouth. He was too strong. He pulled her back into the bedroom, inch by painful inch, moving backward with the certainty of a cat. Moving inexorably toward her bed. Dumping her onto it like a sack of flour, and then climbing after her to cage her with his body.

She felt his heat, his strength, his fury, his molten desire to consume her ...

... *Always in the dark, where a woman felt helpless, hopeless* ... *and a man always knew what he was doing* ...

And now she knew exactly what a man could do—

But wait—

Was it—him?

She was sure of nothing at that moment except the rock-hard solidity of that body above her.

And his scent—

And his touch . . .

She knew. She knew.

It was him . . . it was HIM—

How—?

HOW?

In her room, how long now, since they had settled themselves outside his door to watch him?

Did they know?

How long? How long was a kiss? A long hard penetrating kiss—*his kiss*—she knew that kiss; her whole body melted into that kiss.

He kissed her to arouse her, to distract her, to forestall her questions . . . He kissed her like that in the dark, where nothing was forbidden and he knew she would forbid him nothing.

In the dark, he could do anything to her that he wanted, and she wanted him to do everything he could think of, in a place where no one could see, no one would care.

In the dark . . .

"Don't ask," he whispered, taking her mouth violently again and again. "Just feel."

He eased himself down onto her body as he deepened the kiss. She felt him pull at her nightdress, felt him delving for her vulva. Felt him slip something tight and hard against her clit, something familiar, something her body instantly enfolded.

The pearl!

Immediately, she felt erect, aware, aroused . . . she wanted to keep it *there* forever; it was so smooth, so tight, so perfectly positioned where she could move against it . . . arching and writhing into his hands, his questing fingers, his ferocious tongue.

"Tonight, for you," he murmured against her lips. "Tonight, this is *my* pleasure . . ."

She made a sound.

"Yes, you want more. That elegant little pearl arouses the deepest need for more. It doesn't fill you, does it? And you have learned, my lady of the erotic pearl, that the filling is as important as the feeling . . ."

He nudged her legs apart. "And so, tonight you will have both. The pearl and the filling . . ." He penetrated her slowly, oh so slowly, rocking his hips against her, rooting his penis in her hole inch by filling inch.

"Like that, my lady cherry ripe. And that. And that. Squeeze yourself around my penis," he whispered against her mouth. "Like that . . . now you feel it, now . . . my penis, the pearl— both so hard, one so deep, one so tight . . ." He licked at her lips, murmuring between kisses as he gyrated his hips against her shuddering, undulating body. "Like that. And like that. I want more. Give me more. You feel it, you want it, give it to my penis"—as her body quickened, and escalated into a frenzied pumping— "fuck me"—as all the molten feeling skeined downward, gathering, coming to a head, coming, coming, *coming*—

"NOW—"

And erupting, inundating her, as she rode the cascading waves of sensation that crested in spangling bursts of pleasure that slowly tailed off and eddied away.

In the dark.

No one had to know anything—in the dark.

Even that he had been with her—

Her breath caught.

Pleasure was too insidious; it made you completely relinquish your sanity . . . she was not supposed to be on his side—

He knew exactly what she was thinking, now that sanity had returned.

"For the Russian," he murmured, giving her a quick deep hard kiss as he withdrew his penis and the pearl. "For me . . ."

And gone.

No. At the door. The window? Somewhere in the room.

"Catch me—if you can," he called out mockingly, and then—silence.

A deathless silence, full of images of all she had done with him in the dark.

Damn damn damn . . . she could barely move, she was so sapped.

Damn that insidious pearl; damn her treacherous body.

He was damned right it was for the Russian. All, everything he was teaching her, all for Peter.

Peter!

They had to catch him—Nicholas—out of his room . . .

She swung her legs to the floor, pulled down her nightdress, and groped for her robe and that misbegotten candle.

Matches, then, God, her hands were shaking like she had palsy, and finally—light. And shadows, long and eerie, pointing the way.

And Nicholas, abroad in her house—*his* house?—making fools of them all.

Damn and damn. She raced down the hallway and up the steps to the guest wing by guttering candlelight, pursued by the shadows.

She found them still there, all of them: her father sound asleep in one of the hallway chairs, Victor and Peter half-awake on the floor, Peter coming instantly alert and to his feet as she came running down the hall.

"Is he there?" she demanded breathlessly.

Peter held his finger to his lips and whispered, "Of course, he's there. What a question. That was the point, Elizabeth."

Making a fool of her too. "How do you know?"

"We've been right here the entire night. Now what on earth is this about?"

"Check and see if he's in the room."

"Why would you want to wake him up?"

Why? Because he walked in the night and nothing could

contain him. Why? Because he was too agreeable and then he'd come to her, a ghost in the night, and she was the biggest fool of them all.

"Just to—just to . . ." *See.* "I just think we should check that he's there."

Peter looked at her uncertainly. "All right, wake him, then."

Victor came awake. "What is this?"

"Elizabeth apparently questions the whereabouts of the putative heir tonight."

Victor looked at her closely. "You have reasons."

Victor at least understood. "I have reasons," she said gratefully.

"We will do. We cannot trust this man, not for a minute. Come—"

He knocked briskly on the door, the sound awakening Elizabeth's father from his deep sleep. "Elizabeth?"

The door opened; Nicholas appeared, dressed in little more than his trousers and an unbuttoned shirt, and looking more than ever like a pirate with his touseled hair and the stubble on his chin.

"What's to do, my gatekeepers? And Elizabeth? Oh my, the whole contingent come to wake me up in the middle of the night. And why is that, I wonder?"

Victor bluffed it through. "To see if you were there, of course."

"Am I?"

"Don't be boorish, Nicholas." This from Peter.

"I think I am being amazingly good-natured about this," Nicholas said. "Are we done now? Elizabeth"—he trained his quizzical gaze on her—"are you satisfied?"

She cringed inwardly. *Too satisfied, blast his smugness.*

"For now," she murmured.

"There is nothing more convincing than a man roused from a sound sleep," Nicholas said chidingly. "Look at me, for heaven's sake."

"Let's not." Peter, this time. "Whatever you thought, Elizabeth, he could not have left the room and one of us not be aware of it."

"Exactly," Nicholas said. "So you see . . ."

"The problem was, I couldn't see . . ." Elizabeth muttered, and then caught back the rest of what she had been going to say.

Too late. Peter caught her words.

"See what, Elizabeth?"

She swallowed back the explanation. "I was jittery tonight, that was all. I was imagining things."

"There is nothing like a dark silent house to make you imagine things," Nicholas said.

"You shouldn't have been alone," Peter put in. "Especially with a stranger in the house."

"Absolutely, you should not be alone," Nicholas echoed.

"No—" Victor stepped forward. "We must take this more seriously. This man is not to be trusted. Therefore, someone will stay in his room altogether for the rest of the night."

"And who will volunteer?" Nicholas asked, not bothering to hide his amusement. "Elizabeth? Yes, Elizabeth would like to sleep with me. That way we'll know for sure if I am in my room. Come, Elizabeth, what do you say?"

She flushed.

"For God's sake—" Elizabeth's father now, finally outraged by all the insinuations, and Victor stepped in front of him before he tried to attack Nicholas. "I say, we have wasted enough time on this . . . this—"

"Now, now," Nicholas said. "Let's not resort to name-calling."

"But you're right," Peter said, "someone should be in the room with him for the rest of the night—perhaps *all* of us . . ."

Nicholas shrugged. "I think Elizabeth could keep me suitably occupied, but"—as he saw Peter's hands curve into firsts—"of course, I bow to your superior wisdom."

"Dear me . . . dear me—" Mena's agitated voice floated

down the hallway a moment before she scurried into sight, her kerosene lamp held high. "What's happened? What's *happened?*"

"Nothing, nothing," Elizabeth told her. "We were just checking to make sure Nicholas was in his room." And it sounded like a fool's errand at best when it was spoken out loud like that: where else would he be?

. . . *in my room, haunting me, taunting me, making me come—*

. . . *did you think anyone or anything could hold me—?*

"Well, where else would he be?" Mena asked, the voice of reason.

"I think Elizabeth should spend the rest of tonight in Mena's room," her father said.

"An excellent idea," Nicholas said. "Really, this has all been a lot of sound and fury over nothing. I'm here." His gaze touched Elizabeth again, who felt like skewering him. "We're all here, for that matter, and now it's time to get some sleep."

"Do go with Mena," Peter murmured. "I'll see you in the morning and you'll tell me just what this was all about."

She nodded her head. . . . *nothing and no one can hold me—*

Peter grasped her hand reassuringly. "We'll all be with him tonight. Nothing more can happen."

Give me more . . .

Nicholas watched her, a glittering light in his eyes.

And more . . .

There was nothing else to do. She sent him a scathing backward glance . . . *for the Russian* . . . and followed Mena down the hall.

Chapter 6

It was time to stop playing games.

The fools.

Locking him up, thinking they could confine him. Thinking he couldn't outlast them and outwit them altogether.

Well, it was four in the morning, and here he was in the library, rummaging through William's desk, and *they* were all sound asleep on the floor of his room.

So much for them. So much for his uncle as well. There was nothing worth looking at among William's papers. Nothing that would disprove his birthright. And with Giddons's arrival later this afternoon, all their doubts would be laid to rest, and everything would be finally, irrefutably his.

Mine.

Elizabeth—?

Mine.

No. He couldn't think like that. She was a diversion. An amusement.

A disturbance.

No. She hadn't gotten *that* far under his skin.

He couldn't afford the luxury anyway.

It was enough he had claimed Shenstone, and put his life in further danger. And his mission wasn't over yet: there was still the package, the imperial jewels, the Empress Alexandra's insurance policy should the Russian royal family ever need to seek asylum, that had yet to be delivered to her sister in London.

And for that, five men had died, five innocent people had been murdered, and he had put his life in the public domain, an open invitation for the Unseen Hand to strike.

And he'd thought he could close that book.

Well, he'd thought a lot of things before he'd come to England, and all his caution, all his planning, had proved to be so much dust in the wind.

There was always an enemy, known or unknown . . .

The clock in the entrance hall chimed five. He heard the subtle movements of the servants beginning their morning rounds, saw the first gray-blue swath of the morning sky as he leaned back in William's chair.

No. His chair. *His* desk.

His house.

"Where *is* he? Dammit . . ." Noise in *his* house. Boots thundering down the staircase. Garbled voices and then Victor, bursting into the library, wild-eyed, "Everyone—here he is . . ."—and then Peter, and Elizabeth's father, following one after the other.

"I'll be damned." Elizabeth's father. "We thought you'd gone."

"I hope you checked the silver," Nicholas said helpfully.

Victor, then: "But *how*—"

And Peter, putting out a cautioning hand. "It doesn't matter *how*. Nicholas has been having us on obviously. You look too damned smug. So perhaps we all ought to just go in to breakfast."

"We planned a breakfast party, did we?" Nicholas murmured, swiveling his chair around. *His chair* . . . "Rather like a scavenger hunt. Find the real Nicholas Massey and win the prize. What *is* the prize anyway, gentlemen? Thruppence in your porridge? Does Giles know he's feeding a horde of hungry hunters?"

"Very glib," Elizabeth's father said acidly. "It happens we don't quite see it that way; we're protecting Elizabeth's interests, that's all. And I'm hungry. And stiff from sleeping on the floor, and I goddamned *do* want to know how you got out, with Peter at the window, and myself and Victor at the door."

"Trade secrets, gentlemen." *Hell. That slipped out. Time for distraction. He was getting too damned good at distraction.* "Where is Elizabeth anyway?"

"Calling for tea and *porridge,* of course," her father said coldly. "What else would she be doing?"

Nicholas could think of at least a half-dozen other things, but all he did was motion them to the door. "Please—to the dining room then. I like nothing better than to discuss the failure of a good night's surveillance over a cup of morning tea."

Elizabeth's father glared at him.

Nicholas ignored him, so easy to do, he thought, as he followed slowly behind them. "Ah, Elizabeth. Good morning. You're up early this morning. Didn't you sleep well?"

"As it happens, no. I had a nightmare."

"Really? And I had the most interesting *dream* in which I *rode* a mare." He moved to the head of the table as did Elizabeth, their hands touching as they each reached for the chair.

Nicholas gave her a benign look. "Do sit down everyone. Elizabeth?" She reluctantly took the chair to his right, and he eased himself into his seat and surveyed the table.

"Well, Cook seems to have outdone herself on such short notice. Eggs with chicken livers. Cold ham. Smoked salmon. Oatmeal. Fruit compote. Hot chocolate. Tea. Everyone, by all means, help yourselves."

They stared at him.

The mask of the genial host was back again, Elizabeth thought resentfully, acting like he owned the place. Well, he *did* own the place, or he would when it was confirmed by Mr. Giddons.

She made the first move, picking up her cup and deferring to her father. "Tea, Father? Or chocolate?"

"Tea will do," her father muttered, reaching for the eggs and the oatmeal.

And thus breakfast commenced, Nicholas thought cynically. They all loved the bountiful table, the elegant surroundings, the unstinting service. And they would all pretend they hadn't tried to hold him hostage last night.

Let them enjoy it then. There was time enough to shake up their complacency today. After the meal should do it, when they were stuffed, contented and *fat* with condescension.

Nobody spoke. Everyone was busy eating, gluttony rampant even that early in the morning.

Even Victor, for all his radical protestations, ate like a peasant, shoveling food into his mouth as if he thought someone would take it away if he even paused to chew it.

And Mena had yet to make her appearance.

"I'll have a tray taken up to Mena," Elizabeth said at one point.

No one cared. Mena could have gone back to London for all they paid attention to that comment. All the better, Nicholas thought, to have just those four at his table, under his thumb.

. . . always an enemy . . .

He hadn't really given a thought to the coincidences. But they were inescapable: Elizabeth's family ties to his motherland were jarring. That Elizabeth's father was heavily invested there and seeking business advice from Grigori Krasnov, a staunch supporter of the Tsar; that Elizabeth was in love with a royal; that they had taken a known revolutionary to their bosom; that a Grand Duchess was a permanent houseguest . . .

. . . I know you . . .

None of it boded well.

The clock struck seven. Nicholas threw down his napkin.

"My compliments to Cook. Most excellent. Has everyone had their fill? Would anyone care to go for an early morning ride? No? Well, let me tell you my plans for this morning. It's time for Elizabeth to give me a full tour and report about everything concerning the house and gardens. I'd like to do that this morning, before Mr. Giddons's arrival. Say around nine o'clock, after we've all had a rest and changed? Will that suit your schedule, Elizabeth?"

"I'm at your disposal," she said grimly. She wasn't looking forward to this, handing the house over to him and whomever he would hire to run things.

It was a godawful thought. She loved Shenstone. She had assumed she would remain here forward, surrounded by all that William had provided. At least there had been that comfort. And now there was almost nothing, except the increase in her income to support her father, and the tenuous possibility of marrying Peter.

Or remaining at Shenstone, at Nicholas's *disposal* until he might tire of her.

Everything will be as it was.

"Good," Nicholas said, rising, signaling the meal was at an end.

But her duties were over, her job was done; the promise was broken and nothing would ever be the same.

"Nine o'clock then." He limped out of the room without looking back.

Peter turned to her, took her arm, and led her to the opposite side of the room, where neither her father nor Victor could hear them.

"We searched his room, you know. You were right. There's nothing. Not a thing. He's damned clever, Elizabeth, damned clever; three men couldn't contain him; three men couldn't find so much as a coin in that room. So this visit from the solicitor is of paramount importance. We don't want him to see Giddons until the man steps foot over the threshold of Shenstone.

"So you must keep him occupied until Giddons comes. I'll make sure to meet the train and escort him here. And then— then, my darling Elizabeth, you'll know the truth and we'll know what must be done."

. . . keep him occupied . . .

She didn't want to face Nicholas at all later, let alone escort him through the house and keep him *occupied*. She didn't want to spend another minute in his company after last night. Last night was the limit, in the dark, and shrouded in the forbidden.

She could still feel the smoothness of the pearl, tucked hard up inside her; could still feel him, hot, explosive . . . as dark as the night . . . and fleeting as a dream, an episode laced with memory, desire, and evanescent pleasure.

The stuff of men's fantasies coming up hard and fast against reality.

She knew enough, now. Surely *he* had had enough now. There didn't need to be any more "lessons."

Maybe, after Mr. Giddons came and the papers were signed, she could just go away, go to London, and cut a wide swath through society. She and Peter together, the golden couple, star-crossed and destined for each other, coming together finally after all those long years.

There was a dream. The fulfillment of all her fantasies that had nothing to do with her life at Shenstone and the changes to come.

Still, there were things she needed to do. She ordered up the tray to be delivered to Mena's room at nine. She consulted Cook over the dinner menu, and about replenishing the food stores; she checked the housekeeping chores that needed to be done in the coming week: polishing the brass, the silver, and the bedroom furniture. The washing of the cut glass chandeliers that hung in the entry hall, the ball room, and the formal dining room. There was laundry to be supervised: the bedclothes changed and washed, the covers aired out, the pillows restuffed; things that would be done one day at a time, one hour at a time when there were guests at Shenstone.

Soon, the rugs would have to be taken out to be aired and beaten; the floors scraped and polished; the marble fireplaces given a thorough cleaning; the upholstered furniture gone over and stains and dirt treated and cleaned.

All the things she used to do would be Nicholas's responsibility as of this afternoon, and she wouldn't have to know whether any of it got done ever again.

Oh damn. She hadn't thought she even cared that much about it. But she cared about Shenstone. In the seven long awful years of her marriage, Shenstone had sheltered her, enveloped her and comforted her, the work of being its mistress had kept her busy and sane.

How could she lose it now?

"Are you ready for our tour?"

His voice shocked her, and Elizabeth recoiled as Nicholas limped up unexpectedly behind her.

"You are too excitable by half," he murmured, and the timbre of his voice gave the words another meaning, another level.

Scotch that. "Nonsense," she said briskly. "I was deep in thought, considering all those things I must tell you about everything that needs to be done."

"I can't wait to hear. Do let's start right from the entrance foyer. I don't feel I have *really* had a chance to truly appreciate *my* house."

"As you say," Elizabeth said stiffly. His house. Shenstone, *his . . .*

She led the way from the dining room and into the hall which ran the length of the house to the staircase. It was a formal entry, set off by a long Persian runner, two gilt-framed paintings on opposite walls, the beautiful chandelier, and the grandfather clock tucked into the curve of the stairwell, its steady ticking, Elizabeth had always felt, like a heartbeat.

From there to the drawing room, a long rectangular room the full width of the house, and furnished in the French style, with small couches and *bergères* forming intimate groupings for conversation or cards; the formal dining room with its frescoed walls and highly polished mahogany furniture and the matching breakfront housing dinner service for fifty. The library, with its deep green walls and floor-to-ceiling bookcases, that massive desk, and the French doors that opened onto the terrace. The family dining room, from which they'd come, smaller, more intimate, with paintings suspended from the moldings and wainscoting. The morning room, with its paneled fireplace and walls, comfortable sofas and small desk by the window that was perfect for writing letters and doing the accounts.

Up the steps to peer into each of the bedrooms, and then farther down the hall and up another set of steps to the guest wing, and across another hallway, down still more steps to the ballrom, sparsely furnished with gilt chairs, a marble fireplace, with its ceiling-height breastplate, the dais on the far end for the orchestra, and the anteroom with the small tables and chairs set out for refreshments.

And over and above this, the servants' quarters, and the attics, which were filled to the brim with still more furniture, trunks, paintings, and boxes of papers, all of which had to be catalogued sometime.

From there, Elizabeth took him to the kitchen, in the ell, which was five deep in helpers dicing, slicing vegetables and washing up pots as Cook began to put together the luncheon menu and plan for dinner.

Nicholas said a kind word to her and they proceeded to the vegetable garden, just outside, and then they stepped into the brilliant glare of the sun, and a beautiful late-morning day.

"You see the number of workers for the house alone," Elizabeth said, continuing her bone-dry narrative of the necessaries to run the household. "And of course, there is the gardener and his underlings. The stable hands. The drivers: we keep two on staff, as well as a farrier and a blacksmith, who also helps out with repairs on the estate. But there are able-bodied workers in Exbury should you need them. And then of course—"

"Are there cellars?" Nicholas interrupted her.

"I'm sorry?"

"Cellars."

"Oh. Cellars. Yes. Yes, there are cellars, but they're never used."

"Nevertheless, I should like to see the cellars."

Elizabeth shook herself. She'd girded herself for a strenuous walk around the estate and here he wanted to bury them both in the cellars. In the dark. The forbidden dark.

Nonsense. He just wanted to see the cellars.

"Come." She strode toward the front of the house, and they entered through the colonaded doorway into the front hall. At the far end, built into the stairwell wall just by the grandfather clock, there was a door that gave entrance into the cellars. "I believe there's a way through the butler's pantry too, but this will do. We'll need some light."

She sounded braver than she felt; she hated the cellars. They were damp, cold, dark; they reminded her of the promise broken. And she had to be certain she kept him from going too far, too deep into the darkness, to keep him away from *there.*

Nicholas limped off and returned a few mintues later with several tapers and some matches he'd filched from the family dining room. "There. Enough light?"

"Enough for you to see there's nothing to see," she said tartly. "This way." She opened the door and held high her candle which shot her shadow down the steps and into the gloom. "It's narrow here. There's a flimsy railing, so be careful. Can you see?"

"Well enough," he murmured. It was something out of a Gothic novel: the eerie light, the rough stone walls, the winding staircase going downward to oblivion. There was nothing romantic about it either.

"Watch the ceiling," Elizabeth cautioned as she felt for the next step. "Watch your candle wax . . ." She felt a drop drip onto her hair; she pulled it out. "I think we're there." She straightened up, and turned to give him more light. "There are sconces down here, but I don't know how long it's been since anyone has used them."

Liar.

She waved her candle ahead of her. "The passageway leads to a set of storage areas, if you wish to see them."

"I do."

"Why?"

"To see what I might be able to store down here, of course."

I . . .

I might . . .

She drew a deep breath. "Then on we go."

The passageway widened out after a moment, shored up by thick timbering along the wallways and dividing out the passage into individual storage areas.

"There were no windows here, no chute of any kind, no way to gain entry any other way but by the stairwell. You couldn't get, oh, firewood or hay or even household items in here," Nicholas said. "What on God's earth could be stored down here but wine?"

"William never used it even for that," Elizabeth said. "But then, he had no palate for it, no interest. I assure you, there's nothing more to be seen."

"But the cellars underpin the entire house, do they not?"

"I suppose so."

"Let's keep walking. I have another couple of candles."

She swallowed hard. "As you wish." She didn't suppose he would do as she would wish, and that was to leave things as they were, including that one small tight contained place that she hadn't even thought to clear of the debris of its former occupant.

In that small room, there was a cot, a table, a wash basin, candles, a kettle of water, and in all probability, some remnants of a presence there.

And she didn't know how she was going to prevent Nicholas from pressing on and, in the end, discovering her secret.

Which you will deny. Because there is no way for him to know you had any complicity in there being a presence in the cellars.

Of course. Of course . . .

Everything will be as it was.

But who could have predicted that Nicholas would wish to explore the nether regions of the house.

On the other hand, it was one way to keep him "occupied."

They pressed on, slowly because of the unevenness of the dirt floor and Nicholas's limp. "I've never seen so much barren unused space," he commented, holding his candle high as they proceeded.

Soon enough, they saw intermittant doors niched into the wall opposite the storage bins. "And these open to what?"

Elizabeth took a deep breath. "I have no idea." *Step up to the lie.* "I don't believe I've ever come this far."

"Let's see." He grabbed the small knob on the first of the doors and pulled. "Hmm. Locked. Or stuck. Or . . ." And the next, with the same result. And the next, as Elizabeth looked on with an awful sense of foreboding. He had only to keep going, straight down the line, and soon enough he would find it.

Her heart jumped into her throat; her hand quivered and the candle flame wavered. She had to stop him from going further.

"Hold steady," Nicholas cautioned her, as he continued pulling on the knobs with great effort and no effect.

"It's cold down here."

"Is it?" On he went. She counted: he had tried ten doors, and there were five more visible in the candlelight, and at least ten more beyond it as they moved toward the rear of the house.

"Nicholas, this is ridiculous. These things don't open, there's nothing here to be seen, one can only conclude the other doors, if indeed these are doors to anything, will not open either, and what's to be made of us wasting all this time trying?"

"Satisfy my curiosity?" He stopped his exploration and turned to face her. "Satisfy me?"

Distract him. "I think, I hope we can say that has been done already, Nicholas."

"I think we can say there's a long way to go, my lady, contingent on the arrangements we will make today."

She felt a twinge in her vitals. It was never far from the surface, this unholy yearning of her body.

Or was it the fact that she would be signing away her body for a thousand pieces of gold?

"I will keep my end of the bargain," Nicholas said, "provided you keep yours." He limped around her, back toward the staircase. "By the way, I do mean Mr. Giddons as well, Elizabeth. You know exactly what I mean. Everything ends—and begins—right now, right here. Your choice. Your money. Your life. And now, I think we're finished. I know we're finished for today—down here."

The hem of her skirt was filthy from the dirt floor.

Her nerves were close to shot. And Nicholas acted as if trudging around the cellars was just a day in the park.

Nothing would ever be as it was—and Mr. Giddons already on his way, Giles told them. Peter had gone to the station to meet his train.

She ran upstairs to effect a quick change. She doused cold water on her flushed cheeks, she brushed out her hair and piled it in a topknot. She changed her shirtwaist and skirt and added a matching jacket to look more businesslike.

Exactly what kind of business do you represent? Ladies who sell their bodies to men who will finance their father's debt. Some modern monetary sleight—of—hand and Cinderella gets the prince.

Or, rather, the uncle.

Why was she thinking this way?

She composed herself and made her way down to the library, where Nicholas and her father were already waiting. A bad sign. Her father looked out of temper, and Nicholas stood by the terrace doors, looking out at the sky.

She sank into one of the wing chairs by the desk.

Waiting . . . always waiting. It was enough to wrack the nerves of a tightrope walker. And wasn't she doing just that . . .

walking a thin line between morality and greed? One stroke of the pen and money and every comfort would be hers.

Just don't mention "the rumor." Even to Mr. Giddons— that was what he'd meant before they left the cellars. Perhaps, especially to Mr. Giddons?

Such emphasis begged the question that there might be more to it than just idle gossip, she thought, eying Nicholas's back. So the devil's choice had to be made: the money or her life. But he'd been bargaining with a winning hand; she had the distinct feeling now that he had known every financial permutation with regard to William's estate, and there was nothing left for her to do but sign the papers.

The sound of the front door slamming and Giles's plummy tones signaled that Mr. Giddons had arrived. A moment later, Giles appeared to announce him, and Peter followed behind, watching Mr. Giddon's expression, watching Nicholas's response as he turned his gaze from the window.

"Ah, Nicholas, there you are. So good to see you." They shook hands, Mr. Giddons being a full foot shorter than Nicholas, and looking as if Nicholas's grip could fracture every bone in his hand. "And Elizabeth, how are you? And Frederick, too. Everyone is here. Excellent." He put his leather case on the desk and turned to Nicholas. "We don't have that much time till the outbound train. So, shall we get down to business?"

Nicholas bowed to Elizabeth's father and Peter. "Gentlemen? Are you satisfied?"

"You probably paid some actor to come and vet you," Elizabeth's father said snidely. "But I suppose we must give in."

Peter shot a long meaningful look at Elizabeth. "We'll let you get on with it. Come to me later, Elizabeth?"

"I will," she said fervently. But she watched with mixed emotions as they withdrew.

"And now," Nicholas said to Mr. Giddons, "we come to the purpose of your visit. Elizabeth? Do we continue—or do you wish to withdraw as well?"

"So gallant of you," she murmured. He was every bit the gambler, she had known it in her bones, calling her bluff, offering the dare.

"We all know what's at stake," he said cryptically. "It's still your choice."

But she had gone too far, given *him* too much to cry off now. "I made my choice three days ago," she said stiffly. "I'll keep the bargain."

"Wise choice," Nicholas murmured, limping over to the desk and pulling up a chair. "Then let us proceed."

"Something just occurred to me," Elizabeth's father said as he and Peter conferred in the morning room. "We don't know precisely why Mr. Giddons came here this morning. I mean, Elizabeth had no doubts about Nicholas, so surely she didn't summon him, more's the pity. Really, my daughter is too gullible. But still, what could Nicholas be about with the solicitor so soon after he claims the title?"

"I'm sure she'll tell us," Peter said. "I know this was a shock to her, his coming out of nowhere. And obviously he has proven his birthright to Mr. Giddons's satisfaction. So we have no just cause to doubt him anymore."

"I still doubt him," Elizabeth's father said. "More so since Mr. Giddons's arrival. After all, a man like that, with *nothing* of relevance on his person. *Who* is he, really? I tell you, Peter, Elizabeth must find out."

They stared at each other for a long moment.

"You know, that might be the very thing. She's a beautiful woman. Men tell secrets to beautiful women, we all know that."

Elizabeth's father shot him an inquiring look. "What exactly are you saying?"

"Well, look, we both want what's best for Elizabeth. So doesn't it seem reasonable that since she will be staying on at Shenstone with you, she could—get to know him a little better. Perhaps discover something about him she might use—you understand—to her advantage?"

"Exactly my thinking," Elizabeth's father said. "Something to—disprove his claim."

"Exactly."

"Without fault," Elizabeth's father added.

"Oh absolutely. She *has* to know. And she is in the best position to find out. There *will* be times neither of us will be here to intercede, after all."

"Indeed. Sometimes there are things a gentleman doesn't need to know."

"Yes. You're absolutely right, Frederick, And I'm thinking that we could persuade Mena to stay on as chaperone. For the look of it."

"Excellent idea," Elizabeth's father said. "And if all that falls into place, things should start to happen. And then, it shouldn't be too long after that you—"

"I could feel confident then," Peter said. "It's all a matter of degree."

"Quite," Elizabeth's father agreed. "Such a little thing. Such large consequences. Well, you must speak to Elizabeth now, and then we'll just wait and see."

Chapter Seven

"Psst . . . Elizabeth! *Elizabeth!"*

"Father?" It was late afternoon; Nicholas had just gone to drive Mr. Giddons to catch the four o'clock train to London after several hours of complicated legalities and signing of papers. She was exhausted, and not prone to be put upon by her father on top of everything else.

Yet here he was, jumping out at her like a ghost, hoping to scare information out of her. Or money.

Yes, he would want to know all about the purpose of Mr. Giddon's visit.

"Shhhh—" Her father pulled her into his bedroom and quietly closed the door. "I swear—those servants . . . no loyalty whatsoever. They'll just report anything to Nicholas and that will be the end of it. Sit down, my dear girl. Tell me everything."

"Everything? There's no everything, Father."

"Then why was Giddons even sent for?"

"Estate business that couldn't be taken care of before Nicholas came out to Shenstone." Glib; she was so facile with the lies. And now, some hard truth. "Oh. And a small matter concerning my portion."

His ear pricked up, but then she had expected that.

"Really? I thought that was untouchable."

"It is, in a sense. But it can be manipulated, and so, given that I have promised you the money you need, an amount has been set aside in your name to do with what you will. You will have complete control . . ."

Oh yes, he did like that, her father. Control was important.

". . . but it will not be a bottomless well. When it is used up, there will be no more. I will not fund another cent."

"I see."

She could see him parsing it out. So much here, so much there. Some return on investments that he could disburse over there.

"How much?" he asked finally.

She named a figure, and he looked affronted. She didn't particularly care. That money, Nicholas's money, the money promised in the bargain, was separate from her income, and that was the only thing that was important. And that it would put an end to his ceaseless importuning, preserve her principle, and force him to put parameters on his speculative spending.

"It's not enough."

"It's all there will be. It's all I can afford." *Lies and more lies.* "So I suggest you think before you spend, Father, and let those phantom Siberian oil wells dry up."

"No. I have an obligation, a duty . . ."

"Ask Peter then. He'll know if this is in indeed way a wise investment."

"No. It's already done. I'm going to need more."

"Father, listen to me. There can be no more. The interest on what's left of the principle can barely support me, and that is only because we will be staying on at Shenstone for the foreseeable future. Do you understand? The money was never limitless. And from what little remains, I've carved out a portion for your needs, and you must be responsible for it.

"William never could have predicted that the sole surviving male of his line would be his estranged brother's son. So everything I expected to inherit, I will never have.

"But none of that enters into the calculations. And that is what you refuse to recognize. There is no getting around it. Shenstone and everything that derives from it belong to Nicholas, and I am but a young widow with little money and virtually nowhere to go."

"But your personal things, your jewels . . ."

"Mine. Locked up. And I won't touch them, ever. Even for you."

She watched her father pace the room angrily.

"I don't like it."

"It doesn't matter."

"I won't stand for it."

"The estate doesn't care."

"You care."

"Not to the extent of putting myself in the poorhouse," Elizabeth said acidly. "Nicholas is not going to throw us out; we can stay as long as we need and want to. And perhaps that is the best we can hope for."

But her father did not see the positive aspect of his new-found financial autonomy. Not yet, anyway.

"Still, he's a mystery."

"He may be whatever he wishes."

"But what if there were something—something that could overset his right of inheritance."

You know something . . . a niggling little voice inside her.

"I can't imagine what that might be." *Yes, you can. The problem is proving it. How could you prove it? If you could, you could have Shenstone and all the money too* . . .

Dear heaven—she fought off the insidious thought. Her father always could make her crazy that way, trying to convince her that things were not irrevocable.

But not this time. She'd struck the bargain. There was no going back.

Except—except . . . that one little tenuous might-be-true fact that only she knew . . .

"I don't either. I think you need to figure it out."

"I think I need to take a nap. I'm tired of everyone questioning Nicholas's veracity. And I'm tired of being pulled down into dark places where I don't want to go."

She turned to leave, and her father grasped her arm just as she opened the door.

"Why are you defending him?" he demanded. "Listen to me. If we can find that one thing that will disprove his claim, we can have everything. Again. You can have everything. It will all fall into place. You, Peter, the future . . ."

Oh, dear lord, she was listening to him. How could she help but listen to him? It was so exactly the truth, the truth Nicholas did not want her to know: she could have everything, if she could just find the proof.

And meanwhile, she could have Nicholas—

. . . and Peter too . . .

"So here we all are," Nicholas said expansively as he surveyed the faces around the dinner table. "One happy family. I trust you will all sleep in your own rooms tonight?"

"It was a necessary precaution," Elizabeth's father muttered. "Anyone would have done the same." He looked over at Elizabeth and she turned her head away.

"Perfectly understandable," Nicholas agreed heartily—too heartily, Elizabeth thought—"but now you are *my* guests, and we'll just forget all of that ever happened."

"Too kind," Elizabeth murmured.

"I do so enjoy having guests. I'd forgotten the joys of entertaining one's good friends."

"Really?" This from Peter. "How long *has* it been since you've been socialized, Nicholas?"

"Oh, I'm not a socialist at all, Peter. Are you?"

Peter bristled. "I assure you . . ."

"No, no." Nicholas held up his hand. "Just dinner table conversation. No offense meant. With your connections, you must be a welcome guest wherever you go, and your friendship with Elizabeth will always make you welcome here."

"Thank you." Stiff as a board. No one missed Peter's little flare of anger in those two words—except perhaps Nicholas. Or had he deliberately goaded Peter?

Elizabeth jabbed at the meat on her plate. A galantine of veal tonight, stuffed with all good things: sausage, walnuts, bacon, hard-boiled eggs, and served with a choice of salads, boiled potatoes, rolls, and meringue cake for dessert, and she could barely work up an appetite.

Victor, however, tackled the meal like it was his last, and everyone but she was on at least one second helping.

Well, she had too much to think about. This whole episode had turned from solving problems to creating new ones, and she needed an ally.

She eyed Mena, who was pushing some potato around on her plate. Mena had spent most of the day in her room, not unusual for her to do by any means, but still, with all the undercurrents swirling around, and Mena's own statement that she knew Nicholas from somewhere, she ought to have *helped* somehow, or at least been around when Mr. Giddons had come.

But Mena was the only person among them who did not want something from her except a comfortable room and some companionship, and that was what she needed most herself right now.

She leaned over and touched Mena's arm. "Mena, dear. You must stay for as long as you can."

Mena smiled up at her. "I'd be happy to stay, however long you like."

"Good."

Good? They were all looking at her, suddenly, as if someone had spoken and she hadn't heard.

"Gentlemen." She rose, from habit, to signify they were free to leave. Nicholas looked amused as he limped out of the room followed by Victor, her father, and Peter, who mouthed, *"Don't leave."*

She leaned over to Mena. "Mena dear, can you at all remember from where you know Nicholas?"

"Well, I've been trying to remember. Probably from home somehow. Not that he frequented the same social circles . . . and of course, I've been out of the country for several years . . . I just can't connect the circumstances. But it will come to me. I'm sure it will. And meantime, I won't let him or your father bully you."

"Bully me? Oh truly, do you think it's that bad?"

"Dear girl, your father has been manipulating you since

I've known you. It is kind of Nicholas to let us all stay on. And I'll do everything in my power to help with Peter, if he's the one you want."

"Thank you, Mena dear. I knew I could count on you."

"And me, can you count on me?"

"Peter!" Mena cried. "Oh, now I must leave you two alone. Do excuse me, both of you. Good night, Peter." And she exited the room in a flurry.

Peter sank down into her chair and took Elizabeth's hands.

"What a day, dear Elizabeth. Between guard duty . . . and Nicholas's hostility—how are you holding up?"

"Tired," she said succinctly, grateful for his presence, his touch. But then he always had the right touch. "I took Nicholas all around the house today, and down the cellars even before the solicitor arrived."

"You did? Oh, my poor darling. The time you spent with Mr. Giddons cannot have been easy. And walking Nicholas around—it must have been a terrible reminder of everything you had to relinquish."

"And yet, here I am," she said lightly, "so all is not lost."

"I hope not, dear girl. I still don't believe a word *that man* says. I wish there were some way . . . for your sake, I mean . . . some means of . . ."

"So do we all," she murmured. "But all his bona fides were approved by the solicitors."

"Still, such a man of mystery. Are we supposed to infer he was injured during some romantic adventure? It makes me so angry to think of all that he's taken from you."

And all he's given me—but Peter couldn't know that, not yet.

"You mustn't stop trying to disprove his claims."

"Peter!" Hadn't her father said almost the exact same thing?

"Something will turn up, I'm sure of it."

"What are you saying?"

Peter squeezed her hands tighter. "I'm saying, dear girl, that there's so much at stake, you ought to use any means at your disposal to get at the truth."

"*Any* means?" She felt just a little disingenuous. Surely he wasn't suggesting . . . ?

"You're a beautiful woman . . ."

"I'd hoped *you* noticed," Elizabeth interpolated with a touch of irritation.

"Elizabeth. I'm certain you understand. You are the only one who has the—means to get at the truth, the only one—well, you'll be here for the most part, where your father and I may be going back and forth to London to take care of business. I told you, *that man* wants you . . . There will be opportunities—just use them wisely, and everything you ever desired can be yours."

"Peter?!" *But all she had ever wanted was him. He couldn't be saying what she thought he was saying. Or could he?*

"My dear Elizabeth," he murmured. "You know what you have to do."

Oh, she knew, she knew. And what would he think if he knew she'd already done it?

"Let's not talk about it anymore. Let me kiss you instead."

"I like that idea a lot better," she whispered, as he leaned into her, cupped her face, and pressed his lips on hers gently. Sweet sweet kisses, light at first, and then demanding, almost as if a switch had been thrown, or his desire had been kept in such rigid check and unleashed only when he tasted her.

This was the promise and the passion she had waited for. This was worth everything. Just everything. She wound her arms around him and pulled him closer. He shifted his chair; she moved hers. She wanted closer still, and that solidity of him that she had so yearned for.

Her heart pounded wildly as he thrust his tongue into her mouth. He pulled her one arm from around his neck, and pushed her hand between his legs.

And there he was, all man, all there for her. She grasped him hard at the tip and reacted. "Ohhhh, Eliza—beth . . ."

"Yes-s-s-s . . ."

"Come to my room."

"I want to. I can't."

"Don't play with me, Elizabeth. You use a man too indiscriminately and you will lose him."

That was too harsh a warning. "Will I lose you?" she whispered against his lips as she stroked him and heard his responsive sigh.

"Not yet. Not if you keep doing that."

"I could . . ." she murmured, and squeezed him. "I will . . ." She slid her hand down his shaft. "I can . . ." She cupped his balls.

Nicholas's rules of procedure; they always worked—

"Kiss me."

"Ummm."

"Ahhhh . . ."

"Is there more dessert?" Nicholas, hovering at the door. "Oh, oh, forgive me. I heard such moans of ecstasy coming from in here, I supposed Cook had set out another helping of dessert. Don't mind me. Go on with what you were doing."

"I think I'm done," Peter said through gritted teeth. "I don't know about you, Elizabeth, but—if you'll excuse me . . ." He leaned in toward Elizabeth to whisper, "Stay, it's an opportunity."

"For heaven's sake . . ." she hissed back.

He brushed her away. "No. Stay."

She pressed her lips together as he left the room. This was what she wanted, to rouse him and bring him to point, and she'd done a damned admirable job of it until Nicholas entered the room.

"What do you want?" she asked grumpily.

"You."

"Oh dear heaven, Nicholas. Must you? Tonight?"

"You tell me."

She didn't even have to look. She wondered if Peter had even noticed Nicholas's bulging member. She thought not.

"I'm paid in full, Elizabeth. That was the bargain."

Lord, the everlasting bargain. "I'm sure I'm quite educated enough by now," she muttered.

"I see. It's Peter. Our strategy isn't working?"

"It's working too well, Nicholas. What can he think about this interruption but the same thing he assumed before: that for some insane reason, you want me."

"Peter is very astute. I would take you here, but I think your father wouldn't react very well to finding us naked on the dining room table."

He glanced at the table and then at the door. But on second thought, it wasn't likely anyone would return to the dining room at this hour. "I just rethought that—"

"No, you didn't. No. Nicholas—"

"We won't get naked, Elizabeth. We'll just . . . have dessert."

She protested again. "Anyone could walk in on us."

"That just makes it more exciting, don't you think? No one will interrupt; theyll probably skulk outside the dining room and watch. You're wearing the perfect skirt, Elizabeth, easy for a man to burrow under. And probably those everlasting combination things underneath. Just balance yourself on the edge of the table, and believe me, my penis will find you."

She rose slowly, reluctantly. This was insane, for him to try to breach her here. There wasn't a door they could lock. Anywhere to hide. Anyone had access.

Peter . . . Oh Peter—what if Peter saw them?

He'd probably encourage her to use this opportunity, she thought acidly.

Except it was Nicholas using her, using their bargain and his money as leverage to take her wherever he wanted just because he could. He was already undressed, his penis jutting up at her, and whatever she thought, whatever she felt, was of no importance to him right now. All he cared about was getting her up his stick; lifting her so that she was poised at the edge of the table, her body angled slightly below the thrust of his hips.

"Perfect," he murmured. "Pull up your skirt. Spread your

legs." He grasped her thighs and inched her closer to his penis. "Now . . ."

Someone would come, she was certain of it, and he didn't seem to care. He nudged himself at her frillies, pushing through the material to her cleft, thrusting as he felt her pubic hair, and driving himself home.

She gasped.

"Wet, tight . . . don't move—"

She couldn't; her body was canted at an awkward angle, her legs splayed and wrapped around his thighs. She felt him throbbing inside her, felt his rigid attempt to get himself under control, and she felt an unexpected rill of excitement at capitulating to him in such a public place.

Did she want someone to see them?

"Look at you . . ."

He withdrew his penis just to the ridge and she shifted so she could see his elongated shaft partially embedded in her, connected to her in the most primitive, erotic way.

He rotated his hips, shoving his penis a fraction deeper. And just a little deeper, so that his formidable length seemed to be enveloped by her body, engorging her as he pushed himself deep and hard within until he was crammed tight against her cleft.

And then he just undulated against her, working himself deeper, tighter, closer, his penis surging with every incremental movement, swelling, throbbing, reaching—and blasting into her with his seed.

"Whip't cream for my lady's cake," he murmured, rocking hard against her. "And the dessert course isn't over yet."

He ate her.

He pushed her flat on her back on the table, tore away her underclothes, and just buried his face in her muff and ate her.

Naked on the dining room table, where anyone could see.

And after that first stormy moment, as his tongue burrowed into her, she ceased to care.

He licked at her, sipped and sucked at her, and buried his

tongue as deep into her jamhole as it could go. And then he expertly lapped the juices from her cream-engorged slit, sliding his tongue up and down her cunt lips, seeking her, sapping her, and finally driving his tongue hot and tight against her quivering pleasure point.

. . . there—there . . . and there . . . he knew just how to eat her, how much, how hard, how tight—ahhhhh . . .

Her body rippled and writhed against the point of his tongue; she bore down on him, hard hard hard . . .

—like that . . . like that . . . like that—

. . . her body melting around his taut pointed tongue . . .

. . . and there . . . dissolving, fusing, bursting bursting, bursting . . .

. . . riding his tongue, riding, convulsing to completion on the very tip of his tongue . . .

Naked on the dining room table, with him lapping between her legs.

This late at night, Shenstone was eerie. Everyone was in his room, behind closed doors and drawn curtains, hiding secrets, immersed in dreams.

The last two hours had been an erotic dream. Now she knew how nights should be spent: in a lover's arms, and drowning in his cream.

Peter's arms, Peter's cream.

Her body twinged thinking of it, grew languid with longing, hot with need; she shimmied her cunt down into the upholstered bench on which she sat brushing her hair. She was insatiable, she thought. Two hours of flat-backing wasn't enough for her. She wanted more.

No, she wanted Peter.

Her nipples grew hard beneath the thin silk of her dressing gown. She pulled away the skirt of the gown and straddled the bench so that her nakedness was canted against the upholstery. She felt a quickening inside, as she softened and unfurled.

Her body wanted it; she was ready for it, something hard and hot and filling, and spilling over with cream.

Someone could just sneak into her room, get down on his knees, and lop that thick hard something right up inside her and give her another good hard mount and ride.

If only he would come . . .

She drew a deep sizzling breath. It was the night and the dark that made her feel like this, and thinking about all the erotic things she'd done, last night, in the dark.

And on the dining room table.

And with the pearl.

And with *him.*

Not Peter.

His hard hot penis, not Peter's . . .

She made a sensual little sound, and ground her hips downward.

Her body was ripe for the taking, her movements languid, heavy, aware of her sex, her wet, the weight of her breasts, the brush of silk against her stiff-pointed nipples.

All she wanted was a man's hot hands fondling her nipples, and a jutting penis to take her hard and hot between her legs.

And if that man would not come to her, she thought, she would go to him. And she would come for him the minute he penetrated her.

It made sense. How could Peter know she was yearning for him when she'd turned him off once this evening already?

His room was directly down the hall. She could just go to him, naked, and give herself to him, and let him mount her and ride her to oblivion.

Peter's penis—her breath caught at the thought of it. She had fondled it and felt it up often enough. It would take but two minutes to slip down the hall and beg him to stuff it up inside her.

Oh yes. No one would have to know.

Finally, Peter's penis . . . she squirmed, envisioning it. She would knock on his door, and he would grab her, knowing exactly why she'd come. He'd tear off her flimsy gown because

he'd want to look at her body, and she wanted to display herself for him. To offer her taut nipples and her moist receptive
cunt for his eyes only. She didn't need his kisses; she only
needed his penis, rock-hard and lusting for her . . .

She leapt for her door, certain that Peter was waiting . . .

. . . *and she would climb into the bed, and he would climb
over her, and mount her, and*—

And a hard hot hand stopped her, pulled her back roughly,
and pushed her onto her bed.

Nicholas.

"Not tonight, my lady sticklicker. The only balls you'll be
tossing tonight are *mine*."

She made an outraged sound. "Where *were* you?"

"Where I needed to be, obviously. And by the way, my
jockey stick is bigger than his."

"Spying on me," she muttered resentfully, as she inched her
way to the edge of the bed.

"Can't trust a virgin who's discovered sex."

"The whole point was for you to *educate* me. For Peter."

"Was it? I tend to forget after I blow off my cream. I seem
to want to poke and pole even more afterward. And you, my
lady stiff nipples—"

"Don't"—as he moved toward her—"come near"—he was
climbing on the bed—"me . . ."

"I'm here. And you know what else is here." He slipped his
hands under her heaving breasts. "I want those nipples. Un-
dress them for me."

"No."

"I'll take them anyway." He thumbed one stiff peak and she
writhed against him. "That hot . . ." He compressed the second pointed nipple, and she moaned. "That ready . . ."

He fingered both together and she convulsed in long hard
spasms, melting down into the coverlet like hot wax.

He leaned over her curled-up body, and whispered succinctly in her ear: "You will not go to him when your nipples
need fucking. You come to me. And if you crave a good stiff
penis, you fuck my bangstick. And if you come twice in a day

or ten times in a day, and you still hunger for a stiff thick penis in your blowhole, you come to me. That's the bargain. Remember the bargain? And in return, you get the money, you get the . . . education, you get all the fucking you can handle, and you get to marry him later."

"Quite generous of you," she muttered.

"It is," Nicholas said complacently. "Very generous . . . what's that?"

Elizabeth wriggled out from under him and swung her feet to the floor.

Voices, in the hallway. Banging on doors. Her father's voice—and Giles—

"Fire! Fire! Everyone, up and out, up and out . . . !"

Nicholas swore. "Go on, get on some shoes and a thicker robe and get out of here . . ."

"But they're not going to find you in your—"

"Don't worry about me. Get your things and go—"

A bell started ringing somewhere in the distance.

Fire—fire—fire!

She grabbed a robe from her closet and shrugged into it, shoved her feet into a pair of shoes, and pulled open the door. "Nicholas—I can't leave you here—"

"Yes, you can. Do as I say—Go . . ."

"Oh God—"

She hesitated another minute, read the impatience in his expression for her to be gone, and she dashed into the hallway and into a thick billowing cloud of smoke.

Chapter 8

She fought the smoke, the hands grabbing at her, the voices—
her father, Victor, Mena . . . someone bashed a chair through
the hallway window, the smoke billowed out, and they raced
in the opposite direction, in a body, for the stairs.

They pounded down the steps, coughing, and grabbing for
each other, and tumbled out the front door and into the cool
night air.

"Oh, my God, oh, my God . . ." Mena, holding herself
around her midriff and moaning in a dispair.

"Where's Peter?" Elizabeth cried. "Where's Victor?
Someone, did anyone get to Nicholas? Mena? Where's Peter?"

She whirled around and into a sea of servants running every
which way.

"It's coming from the cellars," her father wheezed. "Tell
the servants. Get some water. There's entry through a wood
trough somewhere in the lower field. Giles!" He ran after the
butler. "Victor—help me!"

Everything was in chaos, the servants scrambling everywhere, for water, for sand, to do something, anything to help.

In the distance, a bell clanged.

"Where's Nicholas? Where *is* he?"

"Dear God, Elizabeth." Her father, coming up behind her.
"Who cares about him? Help me get these buckets on the cart.
We're going to try to find that old entrance, and get to the fire
that way."

Elizabeth raked her hand through her hair, a tremor of terror coursing through her body. "Omigod . . ." *The secret en-*

trance . . . *the vines and branches so carefully laid* . . .
"Omigod . . . where's Nicholas?"

"Elizabeth, stop nattering and help me."

She couldn't see what else to do: she started heaving buckets onto the cart.

Peter came running up to them. "Oh God, Elizabeth, are you all right? Listen, the servants started hoisting dirt buckets through the hallway entrance, but the smoke is blowing through. And we're not even sure if the fire is centered there."

"Then get a brigade of servants to line up with lights out to the field so we can find this other way in," Elizabeth's father commanded. "If any townspeople get up here, get them on the line. We need light more than we need anything right now, except water and dirt. Elizabeth—?"

"Yes. Yes." She swiped her hair out of her face. "God, I wish we knew if Nicholas was all right."

Her father straightened up for a moment. "And if he wasn't?"

"What do you mean?"

"I mean . . . if something happened to him? What would that mean?"

"I don't think I want to know."

"Maybe you do."

"Maybe we won't talk about this ever again," Elizabeth said, swinging a bucket onto the cart emphatically. "No one wants him . . . wants anything to happen to him. *No one.*"

"Whatever you say."

"Where's Victor? He can help with these buckets; they're too heavy for me. And I want to find Nicholas."

Her father grasped her arm. "Are you sure, Elizabeth?"

She wasn't sure of anything, except a feeling of foreboding. Shenstone could burn to the ground; her secrets could be revealed, if she kept insisting she must find Nicholas, and if that secret entry way were found.

She should be with Peter, directing the servants who were marching across the field with lighted spills in hand. She should tell them she knew about the secret entrance and where to find it. She should be the one to save Shenstone.

"Look—help is on the way . . ." She pointed in the distance where lights and movement were coming toward them from the town. "I'm going to Peter."

"You do that, my girl. And think about when Shenstone was wholly yours—three days ago, was it?—and how alluring that was to some interested parties."

"Father!" What a time for him to do this to her. He couldn't be suggesting what she thought she heard. She wouldn't listen, she wouldn't.

"Go to Peter, my dear. Don't worry about Nicholas. I have a feeling he'll turn up."

Or something else will turn up, she thought mordantly as she hurried toward Peter, and past some two dozen townspeople who were taking directions from Giles, and two carts with water tanks that were being driven out to the field by the light of the long line of flaming spills.

They were counting on finding the secret entrance, dear Lord, or Shenstone might burn.

"Peter!"

"We haven't found it yet," he called back. "We're beating every bush, pulling up every branch and vine."

"Have you seen Nicholas?"

"Who cares about him? We've got to find the fire." He waved at a dark figure who was just crossing the light line. "Here, you—take four or five men and keep on picking up the brush. Oh, shit. Nicholas."

"I'm heartily reassured to know you're in command," Nicholas said coolly. "Elizabeth."

She expelled a long breath. Apart from smudges on his face and arms, he seemed perfectly fine. "I'm all right."

"Good. Now what about this supposed entrance from the lower field?"

She turned and looked back at the house. In the dim flaring firelight of the spills, it seemed hunkered into the ground, as immutable as time, and as solid and real as if it were alive.

She looked at Nicholas. "There supposedly was a secret tunnel that gave out there. Or perhaps in the gardens. That much I can tell you. I must assume it's in some proximity to the house. But that's just . . ." She'd been about to say a guess.

Oh, the lies.

"All right," Nicholas said. "Get those men with the torches in a circle around the field closest to the gardens. Now, Peter. I don't want my house to burn down."

"Your house," Peter muttered. "All right then, this is what we'll do. We'll make a semicircle and walk in toward the house. You'll need a couple dozen men to beat up undergrowth and see what they can find."

"I'll do that," Nicholas agreed. "Let's get going."

"I'm going too," Elizabeth said.

Nicholas looked at her, hard. "Fine."

In ten minutes, it was organized, the lights sweeping in a forward motion around the field, and a line of men and women with shovels, hoes, brooms, and knives hacking up anything that looked like ground cover.

Elizabeth positioned herself on the long side of the field, her heart pounding. This was it. She was the one who had to *find* the entrance, and she had to make it look as if she had just stumbled on it.

There were three or four men behind her with lighted spills, and a cart wheeling up and down the line replenishing the slats of wood as they burned down.

They marched slowly, an eerie army lit by flame, searching for flame, sweeping through the undergrowth like fire.

The air was permeated with the faint smell of smoke. They wet down shirts and handkerchiefs from the tanks of water on the carts and wrapped them around their faces as they paced slowly toward the house in an ever-narrowing semicircle with Nicholas at the lead.

They were coming closer, and closer. Nearer to the house,

the land undulated into rises and berms that were dense with trees and bushes and pathways to the terraced gardens.

She would be the one . . . they were that close now—

She pushed her shovel into a thicket of vines and branches, and pitched over as she struck metal.

"Nicholas!" And her voice was that frantic, even knowing what she knew, and what lay beneath.

Everyone crowded around and began pulling up the debris, ignoring the smokiness.

"Don't touch those doors," Nicholas ordered. "The metal is hot. Someone, get a pitchfork, or something we can use to pry open the doors."

Someone on the line had a pitchfork, and Nicholas grabbed it, motioned several of the torch-bearers closer, and began working the tines into one of the metal doors to the sound of coughing behind him.

"Goddammit . . ."

Someone else came forward with another pitchfork, and Peter took it and began trying to move the other door.

Behind them, the torchbearers started to alternate holding the light, a half dozen at a time moving away from the semi-circle to clear their lungs, with Elizabeth wetting them down as fast as they changed places.

Nicholas swore as time after time the tines caught, but didn't hold.

He motioned Peter to come to his side, and together, they dug the two sets of tines into the metal, and this time, this time the tines caught and held.

"Goddamn . . . all right—push . . . *push* . . ."

Now the tines were under the metal plate of the door, and now, slowly, carefully, they levered it up.

Smoke and heat swirled out of the tunnel.

"Holy . . . Elizabeth, get back—everyone—back . . ." Nicholas now, accepting another soaking rag to tie around his nose and mouth, and on his knees at the entrance to the tunnel. "Jesus . . ."

It was black hell down those steps, with the smoke eddying out, and he didn't know what the hell to do. "Let's get those pumps in here. We'll wet it down, and then I'm going in."

"You can't do that," Elizabeth protested.

"It's my house and I'm going in. Get those carts over here. Let's go, let's go . . ."

They pushed the carts closer, ran the hose down the stone steps as far as it would go into the tunnel, and then two of the torch beareres manned the pump, with two more lined up to relieve them, and in two minutes more, a blast of water gushed into the tunnel.

A cheer went up. The smoke receded.

"This is the other end of the cellars we visited yesterday?" Nicholas asked Elizabeth. She nodded. "And you didn't think to tell me they tunneled all the way out to here?"

She felt cold in spite of the roaring heat. "I didn't know for sure. I never thought—"

He cut her off abruptly. "Right. Who could have known there would be a fire in an empty cellar? . . . How much water is in that tank?"

"The tank is almost empty," one of the men reported.

"All right—start the next one, and get that one filled. Ah, Giles—you see to it. And bring everyone back here who isn't working on the inside cellar entrance. Oh, and look—" Nicholas said to Elizabeth, "Here come Victor and your father—and Mena, for God's sake."

"My God, Elizabeth." Her father grabbed her hands.

"Plots," Victor pronounced. "Enemies, they are all around you. They will stop at nothing to kill. This is but a warning, Nicholas. Heed it well."

"From which revolutionary faction?" Nicholas asked dryly. "I've had enough of this. Elizabeth—wet down my shirt. Peter, get me a fresh spill. I'm going down."

"Not alone you're not," Peter said.

"I'm coming too," Elizabeth's father put in.

"And I—" Victor.

"Not without me," Elizabeth said, and they all turned as if they were one man and said, *"No!"*

She handed Nicholas his shirt, and a handkerchief to tie around his face.

"Give me a couple of buckets too. I can try to suffocate whatever's still burning."

"Or get killed yourself," Elizabeth said. "If we all come, we can help. I'll stay back and carry the torch. Mena—you can direct the pump and make sure there's plenty of light at the entrance. Father—you, Peter, Victor, and Nicholas can start hauling down the dirt. Everyone else can line up and start passing buckets. At least we'll know how far gone things are down there."

"And at most we'll all suffocate," Nicholas added. "Not a good plan, Elizabeth. My property, *I* go. Get everything ready, if you must, and keep that water pumping down there. The smoke has abated but it's still dangerous."

"All right," Elizabeth's father said resentfully. "Play the hero if you must. Let him go, Elizabeth. We'll know soon enough what's what down there."

They watched him descend by the flaring light of the torches. He was there one moment, wading through the water, a torch in one hand and a bucket in the other, and the next he was gone, with only a finger of light to mark his passage. And then it disappeared.

"Gone to purgatory," Peter murmured.

"We have to do something," Elizabeth said wretchedly. But it really was that *she* had to do something, that *she* had to know what Nicholas would find in those underground rooms.

"Elizabeth—let him go. The man distinctly said, no help."

"The water's almost gone." The men who were pumping at the cart.

"Someone find out if they've filled the other tank," Peter said.

"Aye." One of the men raised his hand and took off at a lope toward the house.

"Damn . . ." Peter muttered.

"Elizabeth's right, we should go down there. What if he's in trouble?" Elizabeth's father said.

"Or if the fire's out of hand and he can't control it. If the water pressure isn't enough. If he's unconscious because there's no air . . ." There was no end to the litany of disasters Elizabeth could think up, but it was Victor who voiced the ultimate one.

"What if he's *dead?*" Victor said.

"That answers the question," Peter said, waving toward the torch bearers. "Everyone—in close. We're going to proceed with Elizabeth's plan. A bucket brigade, and a circle of light, while we go down and try to help Nicholas. Here, Elizabeth—take this torch, a spare piece of wood, and some water, just in case. Victor, two buckets. And Frederick. You—stand by the steps—one of us will report back. Meantime, make sure there's enough men and enough to fill the buckets. And keep that water pouring in there. Elizabeth—let's go."

He took two buckets in hand and stepped down and she followed him, the torch held high so that he could see in front of him, and her father and Victor behind them.

The smoke still hovered, diffusing the light into an amorphous fog.

As well as she knew these steps, Elizabeth felt like she was walking down into nothingness, and that with every step, she could fall into a void.

"I'm at bottom," Peter whispered. "Be prepared to step into water. God, it's a nightmare down here. I can't see a thing, but at least the smokiness isn't dense. Elizabeth—give me the torch."

She handed it forward and took one of his buckets in exchange.

"Nicholas!" Peter shouted into the dead silence.

Nothing. Every second was like a heartbeat, pounding away in terror and fear . . .

"Here!" They could barely hear his voice.

Oh, God, he's found the room . . .

"I'm damned . . ." Peter muttered. "All right. You stay here. I'll go get him; no use everyone dying."

"But *he's* alive," Elizabeth protested. "And the smoke has dissipated appreciably. We'll all go."

Peter raked his hands through his hair. "Maybe so. Maybe so. Any objections, Frederick? Victor? No? Give me the spare torch." He lit it from Elizabeth's guttering flame. "There's but one way to go."

He turned and led the way, and they sloshed through two inches of water that was still gushing along the floor of the tunnel like a running river.

"Nicholas!"

"Almost there," he shouted back, and Elizabeth's heart dropped to her stomach. He was exactly there; he had found the room.

They weren't but thirty paces from it, and coming closer and closer to her having to giving up the lie.

And then suddenly, she tripped and fell over—against Peter?—and both torches went out—scrambling and grunting . . . she floundered in the several inches of water on her knees, scraping at the walls with her fingers, cursing so close to her ear—

". . . damn it to hell . . ." Nicholas, not that far away from her. And the water, dank and cold, and the fuzzy drifts of smoke—she felt dizzy; she felt hands clawing at her, a husky voice—her father? "Elizabeth—" Peter?

"Damn it—where are the matches?" Nicholas, his voice curiously constricted. And then a scraping sound, and a guttering light illuminating them all flat in the water.

"What the hell?" Her father, this time, clambering to his feet to survey the tangle of arms and legs on the floor. "Nicholas . . ."

"I'm all right." But his voice sounded thick.

"Elizabeth?"

"Yes." She could barely get out the one word. Nicholas had found the room and now, by the light of his torch, he looked so grim and forbidding, she just wanted to run from the lies. He handed her one of the two torches he'd picked from the water without saying a word about what had just happened.

What had *just happened?*

"See if we can light this." He touched the flame to the tip. It sputtered and guttered, and caught. "That's fortunate. Come see what I found."

They crowded around him at the door frame of what looked like an enclosed storage room that reeked of smoke.

"What is this?" Her voice, scratchy, antagonistic. *Damn.*

"This is the locus of the fire."

"Meaning what?" Victor asked.

"It was confined to this area. Nowhere else along this tunnel is there anything charred, and there are timbers that could easily have caught fire. But only this room burned."

He let that sink in for a moment, holding the torch up high so he could see their expressions. "The fire was contained here." He swung around to illuminate the room. It was a reasonable size, perhaps eight feet by ten. Stone walls. Dirt floor that was now saturated with the water sluicing in from the tunnel. Objects burned beyond identification. Smell of smoke still purling up into the air. "Victor, Peter—dump those buckets in the corner; there are still embers."

"Is it over?" Elizabeth asked unsteadily.

The fire was contained here. The words hung in the air, pungent as smoke. What wasn't he saying? What was he *thinking?*

He turned and looked at her, slender, fragile Elizabeth, strong enough to lift a heavy bucket of dirt and a torch, strong enough to bear *him.*

"It's over," he said cryptically. "And now Victor will go back outside and get the bucket line started up. And keep that water coming. Peter, go back to the house and do what you must to secure it. Frederick, you might find some lanterns to hang down here to get in some stronger light. I'm staying here until every last ember has been put out."

*   *   *

They all gathered in the library an hour later, everyone but Nicholas, and they sat and stared at each other.

"Well," Victor said finally, "now you see—there are forces at work. This disaster should not be taken lightly. It is a warning. Enemies . . ."

"For God's sake, Victor . . ." Elizabeth's father said disgustedly. "Just because a little fire got started . . ."

"Yes," Elizabeth said slowly, "but—how?"

"A half-dozen ways," her father said. "Someone unintentionally lights a match. Or leaves a candle burning. Or—"

"But there's nothing down there; no one ever goes down there."

Her father shrugged. "So, someone went down there."

"And started a fire?" Elizabeth said skeptically.

"I didn't mean that. I just meant . . . a moment of carelessness, that's all."

"That scared us all out of our wits."

"Exactly," Victor interposed. "Someone wanted to scare some*one* in this house. A warning. Enemies . . ."

"Victor!" He did get tiresome, Elizabeth thought. But then, as always, he voiced the things they did not want to think, would never say.

"It's too late in the night to even speculate about this," Peter said. "What's important is, the fire—fires are extinguished, no one was ever in any real danger, and everyone is safe."

"So why do we all crowd together in this room if everything is so safe?" Victor demanded. "If there are no enemies . . . ?"

"Be quiet, Victor."

"You never listen." He moved to the French doors. "Enemies are here; change is in the wind . . ."

"He really needs to go back to London," Elizabeth's father said. "He doesn't have the proper audience here."

"Fools," Victor spat. "Or are you all waiting for Nicholas to come?" He paced around the room looking at them. "Ah, yes. You are all waiting. Waiting to hear it was an accident.

That there was no purpose. That a fire can light and then burn itself out without spreading, without causing destruction. Gullible fools."

"Well, I've heard enough," Elizabeth said, uncoiling herself from her chair. "This is boring. No one is waiting for Nicholas . . ." *Liar.* ". . . and I'm going to bed."

"Elizabeth—" Peter grabbed her.

"Not tonight," she murmured, aware suddenly that not three hours ago, she had been ready to melt in his arms.

"Of course not. I just wanted to . . . there's nothing to be afraid of."

"I know."

"It *was* an accident," her father said as she passed him.

"I know."

"You are a fool," Victor said as she opened the door.

She turned and gave him a long, level look. "I know."

He should have known better, Nicholas thought. He should have caught it immediately. But instead, his enemy had tiptoed in and caught him.

Goddamn.

Anyone could be an enemy, known or unknown.

Four of them, equally capable . . .

And a fire where no fire should be. All that smoke and chaos and fear—for the sole purpose of distracting and luring the victim.

And he'd been well and truly caught, playing the hero who would risk his life to save his inheritance. After that, the rest would have been easy: kill him in the cellars and relight the fire—

And the story would have been that embers flared, and the timbering caught, that the smoke was too dense, that they didn't know where he was, that he could have become confused and walked right into the fire . . .

An accidental death by an Unseen Hand.

The first gambit—the cat sneaking up on its prey.

* * *

... everything will be as it was ...

No longer, now the room was destroyed, an act of panic, and wholly unnecessary. She couldn't see the purpose, not at all. No one would ever have found it. She could have made sure of it, if she had known, cleared it of anything incrimminating.

But now ...

A fire aroused questions. Caused investigations. Someone would sift through the rubble to try to find explanations.

And that moment when she tripped ... she thought she'd felt a hand against the small of her back. But that wasn't possible; it just wasn't possible.

Then again, anything was possible these days. These *three* days since Nicholas had arrived. It was just as her father said: three days ago Shenstone had been hers and everything that went with it.

That didn't bear thinking about either.

She dragged herself slowly up the stairs. There was still the scent of smoke in the air.

The scent of fear.

And Nicholas. Unnerving as anything to see him limping along the hallway from the guest wing, followed by one of the servants carrying his bag and boots.

"What are you doing?" she demanded.

"I'm moving into William's bedroom, of course."

"What!" *Of course? William's room, with the connecting door to hers?*

"My dear Elizabeth, what did you think? That I'd be relegated to the guest wing forever?"

"I think I did," she muttered.

"You haven't been thinking at all, Elizabeth."

"Well, who expected the house to burn down tonight?" she said testily.

"Obviously the person who started the fire."

Now she knew her head was fuzzy, it had to be smoke

fever or something, and it was just a hallucination that Nicholas was there. Certainly she had to be imagining what he seemed to be saying. "The person who—*started* the fire . . . ?"

"My dear Elizabeth. Fires don't just start. And they don't just burn some things and not others. Nor do they stay in one place once started. Or stop burning for no reason."

She felt faint. She couldn't even find the words to protest his conclusion. "I see."

"Do you?" he murmured, and he turned to open William's bedroom door. "Perhaps you might wonder what *I* see," he added cryptically, as he followed the servant inside.

She froze. "What? What *do* you see?"

"Just what Victor says, Elizabeth." And he closed the door.

Enemies.

. . . If something happened to him? What would that mean? . . .

No. No. Not for that, not for her.

God, she hated her father for even putting the thought in her head.

And now the fire . . .

Besides, there was an easier way—and perhaps she had made a mistake not revealing the possiblity.

No. Maybe not, because there was no guarantee she would find any proof. Nicholas had said there wasn't any.

But then—how could Nicholas know?

And she'd been toying with the idea anyway; her father again, desperate for her to take back control.

And in truth, didn't she want to? And to be able to offer Shenstone to Peter, with all it entailed?

Three days ago, it had been hers to offer.

. . . think about when Shenstone was wholly yours—and how alluring that was to some interested parties . . .

Insidious of her father.

Perhaps it was not too late to do something about it.

She was the one who had William's papers. And though she and Mr. Giddons had gone through the obvious things, she hadn't really looked closely at anything else except what was necessary for the estate.

But now she was dealing with a host of extraordinary events: Peter's return. A stranger taking over her life. A fire that could not have started by itself. Nicholas's moving into William's room . . .

There was a dose of reality she could not escape.

So it was time, time to wield the one precious little weapon she had: the very thing that Nicholas had used against her— whether or not he had a legitimate claim to the title, the estate and her.

Chapter 9

"On second thought," her father said at breakfast, as he helped himself to herring, scrambled eggs, and freshly baked scones, "I don't think I like what Nicholas was insinuating last night."

"As opposed to what you insinuated last night?" Elizabeth asked from her seat opposite the sideboard, where she was pushing the food around on her plate.

"I? I said nothing at all that would cause you to make a comment like that." He settled himself across the table from Elizabeth and gave her a meaningful look. "We should all be grateful the house didn't burn down around our heads."

"We should be grateful it was *contained* in one place," Elizabeth said.

"Exactly my point. But for anyone to make something of that—fires burn themselves out all the time. That whole tunnel and cellar area is mostly constructed of stone and dirt floor. There's no reason to believe the fire was anything but an accident. So. Now that we've settled that question, what will you do?"

"What will I do—about what?"

"About Nicholas. You do know he's gone and moved into William's room."

"Of course, I know."

"Well, get a lock on your connecting door, my girl. He might think he has some kind of privileges—you know, *droit de seigneur.*"

That made her face burn. What a thing for a father to say

to a daughter—and what would he say if he knew that point was altogether off the table?

"You wouldn't want Peter to get wind of that, would you? How long do you think he will wait under these conditions?"

"*What* conditions?" she demanded. "You know, you made a similar statement last night. I want to know what you mean."

"I? I said nothing of the kind. I've always said I never believed he would ever offer for you; and if he even had the intention, which I don't think he did, your portion is not nearly attractive enough to make him consider it now. Let alone your age, of course."

"Father!"

"Elizabeth, I never lied to you about this. But you as a tragic widow with a great estate—ah, that's another proposition altogether. If indeed having him is your heart's desire. That is the way. A great estate, an income, a willingness to accommodate . . . a place for your father—"

And there it was, the underlying motive for everything he did.

He wanted everything as it had been. He wanted Nicholas never to have come, and everything settled on her. And with all that in her basket, Peter would marry her, and he would be able to pursue his wild schemes.

So, she thought irritably, it wasn't sex that ruled men's lives: it was money, and she'd gone about it all the wrong way.

Or rather, she hadn't gone about it at all; she had taken Nicholas's word, Nicholas's bargain, and Nicholas's money with no compunction in the least. And why? So her father could keep making those disastrous speculative investments in a country so far away, he couldn't monitor them, or even know for sure whether the money was being expended properly.

And all this on the advice of people he barely knew, including a revolutionary whose avowed purpose was to bring down the autocracy of his motherland, and who did it by indulging himself at the country estates of those aristocrats who found him dangerous and romantic.

Like herself.

What she had traded for comfort and preservation of her income . . . and yet, Nicholas had held good to the bargain; he had *educated* her and she was very well versed now in the stuff of men's fantasies.

And Peter was jealous and he wanted her, badly, just as Nicholas had predicted.

She'd gotten better advice than her father, at that. But in the end, she was but a too-young widow with a too-small income and nowhere else to go.

And not a likely marriage prospect for the uncle of a royal on the face of it.

"Yes, Father," she said finally. "We do know that is the major problem. It would have been a lot more convenient if Nicholas had never come."

"You said it," her father said. "There's nothing *I* can do about it."

"Nor I," she retorted.

"Well, my dear. It's *your* desire—to marry Peter. So don't look to me. I've got my own problems. It's up to *you* to make that dream come true."

Was it? Up to her?

She wandered out onto the terrace. It was still very early, the time of day the servants scurried around, getting everything ready for breakfast, sweeping the floors, polishing the woodwork; and in the distance, as she could see, the elderly gardener and his three or four helpers pruning bushes and scything up the lawn.

The smoke had dissipated altogether this morning, and only patches of blackened plaster in the entry hall by the cellar door showed any sign there had been a crisis last night. And even that would be gone before anyone else came down to breakfast this morning.

Her servants were efficient; she had trained them well.

Not your servants anymore.

Damnation. Moments like this brought home to her just much she had given up for far too little. But she had such a tenuous straw to clutch at to try to resurrect her fortunes: something only William was privy to, something only she knew.

And Nicholas. *Nicholas knew.*

And had dismissed it out of hand.

And yet, and yet—

—the mere mention of it had compelled him to offer her that ridiculous bargain, to tempt her with the unthinkable, the forbidden.

What if she'd never said a word?

No—never think it. That path led nowhere; it was too late to change anything, too late to repine.

All that was left was this one slim chance to regain everything.

It was such a dicey gamble on the barest of possibilities, the longest of odds: to try to find some proof that Nicholas was the product of that star-crossed affair between his father and William's first wife . . .

And to keep him suitably distracted while she tried to figure out what to look for and where to find it.

It was like the lull before a storm. Everything was too calm, and so quiet as she and Peter sat on the terrace together enjoying the late morning sun and playing a desultory game of cards.

This was how life should be, golden and leisurely, with time for talk and tea with the man she loved. This was the goal, the aim, the end.

Nothing was more important than this. Her father was off someplace; Mena was still abed; Victor was out riding; Nicholas had not yet appeared.

Or perhaps he was up and about, but he had not yet come in for breakfast, and that was just as well.

Elizabeth did not want to talk about the fire or the future. This, for the moment, was enough.

And if she could have had leave to take Peter to her bed.

... *if he fucks you, he won't want you ...*

Oh, but he wanted her, he wanted *it*. She could see it in his eyes, the way he leaned toward her, hoping to catch a glimpse of her ankle or her the swell of her breasts.

"You ought to not dress in such a businesslike way in the morning," he commented at one point. "You look like one of those mannish women off to a day at the office. Surely you can leave off strict mourning now and wear a softer dress?"

Of course he would want that; so did she. Anything to attract and sustain his interest; and he was right: a shirtwaist and skirt were not the most feminine of attire in the morning.

But she had dressed to rummage around in the attic where she had had the servants store William's things along with three boxes of papers that she meant to go through. Although when she might get to them was another question altogether.

This time with Peter was to be treasured. Quiet. Sweet. Nothing intruding on the soft spring morning, the intermittant slap of cards on the table, the goading comment which always provoked a smile from him.

The connection was still there, the yearning, the longing, the desire—if she could only give in to it ...

Soon, soon—when she found what she was looking for ...

"Oh, this is too much," Nicholas said, limping onto the terrace. "Playing cards after Rome has burned."

Peter shot her a look. *You see? Here he comes, interrupting again, and why, do you think?* "Don't be ridiculous, Nicholas," he said, slapping down a card for emphasis. "The thing is over. Why would you harp on it this beautiful morning?"

Nicholas poured himself some hot chocolate. "I'm just amazed no one is interested. Not your father, Elizabeth. Not Peter. Not you? Not even you. I can't understand it." But he could, and all too well. "You're like a bunch of cats. If you turn your back on it, the thing doesn't exist."

He sat down heavily at the card table, and Peter swiped up

the cards angrily. "Very well. The thing doesn't exist. So what else is new this beautiful morning?"

"Rudeness," Peter said bluntly. "Incivility is new this morning, and all the different ways a host can find to insinuate himself in places he is not wanted."

Nicholas looked taken aback. "Oh. Oh. Well, I wouldn't dream of interrupting—"

Elizabeth shot him a look. *Oh yes, you would.*

"I'll just leave you two alone then—"

"Do."

He limped off, and Peter turned to Elizabeth. "Elizabeth, you must do something."

"So everyone tells me," she said guardedly.

"Have you been able to—?"

She held up her hand. "I would tell you if—"

"Not that I'm encouraging anything—"

"Oh no—"

"Just for your sake. I mean, this must be intolerable."

"You have no idea."

"Oh, but I do, my dear Elizabeth. Just a little." He reached for her hands. "I'll help in any way I can."

"I knew I could count on you, dear Peter."

"Let me comfort you."

"Just being here with you is comfort enough."

"Elizabeth—you know what I mean."

She leaned forward and touched his thigh. "There's time enough, Peter. You know that."

"If you touch me—"

"Then I won't."

"I wish you would," he murmured wistfully.

"I know what that makes you feel."

"I'm feeling it now anyway, Elizabeth. Give me release."

"Peter . . . I can't—I won't. Not here, not now."

Except she could have and she wanted to, but she knew instinctively it was still too soon. But it was enough to make another man just walk away.

Instead, he threw up his hands. "I won't beg. If you won't play with *me,* well, we'll just play with the cards."

Enemies.

He watched them from afar for a few minutes. Elizabeth was keeping a tight rein on Peter; he would not get far with her, and both of them occupied with each other suited his plans this morning very well.

He had other fish to fry: that damned underground room, for one thing, and who would want to torch it—and who would want to kill him—and why.

The smoky smell still hung over everything as he entered the tunnel. There was still water underfoot that had not soaked into the dirt floor. And it was as dark and dank as a tomb.

It could have easily been *his* tomb. He took the lantern he'd hung at the foot of the steps last night, and swung it around. Not an inch of support timber was charred here or anywhere surrounding that little room. All of it was confined to the one storage area.

And all those lumps of burned-up things. He knelt down to examine them more closely, something he hadn't been able to do last night, and the objects crumbled at his touch. But in the ashes he found pieces of wood, melted wax on metal, a fragment of a cup, a basin, a length of burned cloth, a fork.

Someone had been hiding here.

Who, and for long? Why? And who was so desperate to keep the secret that burning it up was the only solution?

He never would have found this place—not soon, anyway. Months from now, probably, if indeed he would ever have used the cellars. His one foray with Elizabeth had been enough to convince him that there was nothing of interest there.

But it was enough to make someone set fire to the cellar. Why?

Because someone thought he would find that secret room?

But that begged the question of whether that someone had merely been trying to destroy some evidence, or had that someone set out to kill *him?*

Not an unlikely conclusion.

Enemies.

The four of them had insisted on coming down in the tunnel with him. The four of them were together when the torches were doused. The four of them were scrambling around and creating chaos when one of them tried to choke him.

God. He kicked at the ashes. *Vapor.*

He felt as transparent as glass.

They all had too much to gain by his death. All of them. Elizabeth, her father, Peter. And it all came down to money, and the fact there was never enough to fund anyone's dreams.

Even his.

The mission wasn't over yet; he could have cut and run, and lived like a king.

All that money . . . all those jewels—

Bait for his ruthless enemy moving in for the kill.

Yesterday, last night, this morning, Elizabeth would have given half her income to have all this unprecedented time in Peter's company. It was perfect: they talked about everything. They touched each other. He kissed her now and again. There were moments when they were silent, just looking at each other.

There were times she thought he might speak and say the thing she most longed to hear. But even then, she was impatient to leave him so she could root around in William's papers in the attic.

This afternoon, however, she was tethered to her chair. If it wasn't Victor coming to join them, it was Mena. And then it was luncheon on the terrace: cold salmon, a cheese salad, jellied chicken, gingerbread, and lentil soup. And then Victor went for a walk, and Mena to her room, and her father came to sit with them on the terrace.

And all the while Nicholas was nowhere to be found, a fact Elizabeth found disconcerting in the aftermath of the fire.

"Did you tell Peter?" her father asked idly as he pushed his salmon around his plate.

"Tell him what?"

"That Nicholas has taken over William's room."

Elizabeth glared at him. "I thought—"

Her father ignored her. "You should know these things, Peter. I think it makes everything so much easier."

"Absolutely," Peter agreed. "Right next door?"

"Connecting door," her father said.

"Ah. Elizabeth! This is the opportunity we were talking about."

"Is it?" she murmured. Or was she going insane altogether? They both had no problem with Nicholas being right next door to her, when her father had at first cautioned her not to tell?

Well, Peter had as much as given permission for her use her feminine wiles on Nicholas, but the two of them in agreement over Nicholas in William's room was just too ridiculous.

"You'll be able to come and go," her father said.

"I've come and gone, and got nothing for my trouble," she reminded him.

"Well, he's been hiding things quite obviously," her father said. "And now, he can't. Because Elizabeth will make sure of it. Won't you, Elizabeth? He has to be disinherited, it's as simple as that."

She looked at them both. Her father was keyed up; Peter winked at her as if they were conspiring together, and her father was the fool.

Well, unfortunately he was. And she would bear the burden, as always.

"And what do you think I might find that would be enough to overset his rights?"

"I'm sure I don't know, my dear. But you will know it when you see it."

She appealed to Peter. "This is utterly unrealistic."

"My dear girl, this is the *best* opportunity . . ."

Yes, and she remembered the previous *opportunity* all too well: Nicholas feasting on *her* in the dining room, which had gained her nothing at all.

". . . and we need every advantage. Shenstone should be yours."

"I should say," her father chimed in. "After all those years with William—I can't even imagine what *that* was like. And then to have this—this—*poseur* just walk in and take it away . . ."

"All right, all right." No use her father getting incensed when she had been furious enough for all of them. "It's only been four days, for heaven's sake. And his *heir* has a perfect right to use William's room. Let's be reasonable about this. Until such time as it is proved otherwise, that is."

"Exactly how we see it," her father said. "But it had better be soon. He's getting too damned comfortable at Shenstone."

She had been up to the attic with Nicholas only yesterday; it was late afternoon before she had a chance to get up there today, and even then, she had to resort to pleading a headache because Peter seemed to only want to be with her all day.

"I could bathe your forehead," he offered. "We could be together, in bed, holding each other."

She loved the images that statement evoked. The two of them, their arms and legs entwined. Naked. Lovers.

Not yet. No fucking yet.

"No. No. I need to be alone, in a darkened room," she told him. *Oh, the lies, the lies.* "An hour, two at the most, and it will be all gone."

"I'll come to you then."

"I'll be down for dinner, Peter. I'll see you then."

A man and his penis did not like to be ignored. Especially when he kept offering it and she kept refusing.

He scowled. "I'll bring your dinner to you. We'll eat . . . together."

"Let me see how I feel."

God, she had thought she would never get away. But he wanted her badly, and her withholding herself made him that much more eager to have her. That *was* the way to hold him, just as Nicholas had told her.

One thing, at least, was working out.

But where, among the boxes of papers, to look for an elusive scrap of anything to do with Nicholas's past? That was something else again.

She'd need more time than an hour to go through those boxes, for one thing. And she couldn't do it in the attic: the light was far too dim, and dust motes danced all over everything, including her sleeves and hem, and that would arouse suspicion.

The boxes would have to be brought to her room, one at a time, and heavy though they were, she was the one who would have to do it.

And without anyone seeing her.

Dear lord, what had she gotten herself into? Sneaking down from the attic, her arms burdened with one of the boxes, scuttling through the hallway, hiding behind furniture at the least sound, diving into her room when the noise quieted down.

And where to hide it now? Getting the box there had taken almost an hour. And Peter could barge in at any moment. Or her father. Or Nicholas.

Under the bed, quick . . .

Just barely, the edges scraping against the side pieces, damaging the beautiful wood. *Damn, damn, damn.*

Was that a sound? Nicholas?

Her clothes! The *headache . . .*

She tore off her skirt and shirtwaist and threw them in her closet. Bed. She needed to be in bed. No robe. Maybe at the foot. Compress. Did she have time? Pull back the covers.

What if Nicholas walked in?

No, he would knock, wouldn't he?

She found a handkerchief and dipped in the washstand pitcher. There. Now—just . . .

KNOCK KNOCK . . .

She dove into the bed, and slapped the dripping handkerchief onto her forehead.

Oh damn, the curtains . . . She leapt out of bed.

"Just a minute." She yanked the curtains closed, jumped back into the bed, and pulled up the cover. "Come in-n . . ."

Drat—she sounded way too vigorous to have a headache.

Peter poked his head in the door. "Oh, Elizabeth, you poor thing, you're still in bed. Let me join you."

"Not one step further, Peter. I'm fine. Another half hour and I'll be down."

"I'd rather stay up for one half hour."

"I appreciate your coming up," she murmured, deliberately coy.

"I know another way you could show your appreciation."

"Not with a headache, Peter."

"You know, it strikes me I'm giving in far too much to what *you* want."

"But you know eventually you will be rewarded, don't you?"

"Do I?"

"There's nothing I want more than to be with you."

"Then why do you hesitate?"

"It's not hesitation, Peter. There's so much more involved than just my giving myself to you."

"There's nothing more involved than my climbing into that bed and pumping my penis into you. And the rest will take care of itself. But that's obviously not going to happen today. Well, use your opportunities, Elizabeth my darling. *All* of them." He pull the door closed behind him. "Use them well."

That was what—a warning? advice? She let out a long deep breath and cautiously got out of bed to lock her door. Oh, and the connecting door too—

No . . .

Nicholas was standing right in the threshold, half dressed, and looking almighty amused.

"Stop laughing," she said irritably and climbed back into bed. "Go away."

"I like Peter's idea better."

"Which idea was that?"

"The *pumping-his-penis-into-you* idea. He's just tearing to rut in you."

"So are you," she muttered, averting her eyes. It was too easy all the time to focus on his groin.

Don't ignore a man's penis—

Lord in heaven; there was no earthly way to ignore his.

"All the time. Tell me his words didn't make you wet."

"Indeed, that is such a romantic proposition: just lie back and let him *pump* his penis into me. That would make any woman hot with desire."

"Your nipples are hard."

"So are yours." Barechested as he was, she still couldn't keep her eyes off his bulge. She wasn't ready for this, this afternoon. She hadn't thought she would even see Nicholas. She thought she'd have the rest of the afternoon to go through that box of papers.

Oh lord.

Now what?

Distract him . . .

"So why don't you just spread your legs and let *me* pump." He started shucking his trousers.

She didn't even have to work at it. And she was halfway there herself the minute he was naked.

Why did she have to turn everything upside down to accommodate everyone else?

But that was the bargain, and she would hold to it just to keep him from nosing around in her business.

Damn it.

She shrugged. "That's the bargain, isn't it?"

He climbed onto the bed. "That's the bargain." He nudged her legs apart, seeking her slit through the lacey overlap of her drawers, and hovering just outside her cunt lips.

154 / *Thea Devine*

She could feel him there, hard, strong, long, and all the power behind that strength that he kept in check; he held himself in his hand, sliding his penis head against the rim of her cleft, seeking the wet, the heat just at the entrance of her vulva.

How did he do that? She would have said she wasn't nearly ready for him, and just that one little movement made her wild with need. No choice now but to get it over with.

She arched against him urgently, begging for his penetration, but all she felt was the tip of his penis stroking her just inside her slit.

"And you still haven't worn my pearls," he murmured. "I'm going to let him pearl up inside you," as he stoked her mercilessly. "I'm going make you beg so you know exactly whose penis you crave inside you."

"I'm begging you now . . ."

"Not yet . . ." He gyrated his hips, keeping only his penis head moving precisely inside her.

She bore down on him, hard. "Nicholas . . ."

"No."

She shimmied to pull him in more tightly.

"Don't."

"I need it."

He shifted himself and stopped moving. "You need what, my lady hump and pump?"

"Your penis. I need . . . your penis—"

"And . . . ?"

And? And? If he didn't pump *soon, she was going to scream and bring the whole house down on every one of her plans and schemes.*

"And . . . ?"

"I'm waiting."

And he was, poised at the brink, ready to jam every thick pulsating inch of himself into her. She could feel him wrestling to keep control, fighting not to give in to her, and she almost thought to just grasp his penis and shove him in.

"And—and . . . I want . . . I want—you . . ."

"*Yes* . . ." he groaned, and he reared back, and he took the plunge, and with one mighty stroke, he rocketed into oblivion.

He hadn't even intended to take her this afternoon. He just couldn't resist mocking Peter and his oh-so-gentlemanly intentions.

There was just something about Elizabeth. She was too carnal, too wild, too willing.

And yet, Nicholas thought as he rocked himself inside her, what had it cost Elizabeth to capitulate to him? She had gotten what she needed out of it already: money, the right to remain at Shenstone as long as she wished, sex . . .

She had given up hardly anything, and somehow he had lost control of everything.

It was the most stunning thought.

He lifted her hand in his own and examined it minutely. It was a shapely hand, strong, as she curled her fingers around his.

Strong enough to kill? Desperate enough to try?

Know your enemy.

"More," she murmured languidly,

"Ummm . . ." Oh, he knew her, all right. Elizabeth the virgin who had fallen into his arms and defined her own passion.

He had *educated* her too well.

It was hell when a woman discovered sex.

And wanted back everything that was her own.

What wouldn't she do to get it?

Fuck the enemy? Screw the man she loved?

Both? Neither?

You never knew who your enemy might be.

"Nicholas . . ." she whispered in a whimper of desperation.

"I'm still here." And in that, *he* still had the power.

"That's very obvious." Tart now. Impatient. "I'm hoping you might do something obvious while you're still *there.*"

It was what it was. No regrets.

He drove into her languorous body and took her home.

Chapter 10

She didn't know if it was two minutes later or two hours later when she heard the insistent knock on her door.

Oh dear God, not Peter . . .

It was dark. Nicholas had long gone; dinner was probably well over. And while she had probably slept, she didn't think she was up to dealing with Peter at this hour.

Whatever this hour was.

She debated opening the door at all, and then she grabbed her robe, turned up the gas lamp on the wall, and opened it just a crack.

"Father?"

"Well?"

"Well, what?"

"I thought you were using that excuse of a headache to *do* something."

"I could kill him," she suggested, not without irony.

"Don't think I haven't thought of that," her father muttered.

"Father!"

"Forget I said that. Forget I said anything. You'll do what must be done."

She had done it already. Going from irritation to desire a minute after Peter closed the door. Giving herself like that to Nicholas before Peter was even down the hallway.

What kind of woman was she?

"Did I miss dinner?"

"You did. *And* Peter and Nicholas point to point. Not a

pretty picture. But they've gone their separate ways now, although I wouldn't put it past Nicholas to be eavesdropping through that damned connecting door. Do you want a tray? Shall I send Mena up to keep you company?"

"No. No. I'll ring if I want something."

"All right then."

She closed the door slowly behind him and locked it. The connecting door too, although curiously, there was no sound from within his room.

No more interruptions tonight.

Her allegiance had to be to herself, to her father. To her future, and to Peter. Whatever it was, she had to try.

She pulled the box of papers from under her bed, sat down on the floor, and began to read.

The clock struck one.

Elizabeth put down the last of a long dry boring set of housekeeping accounts from ten years before, written in William's first wife's cramped hand.

This was a bad idea on the tail end of three hours of reading meticulously kept details about all aspects of running Shenstone.

No, it was a good idea, if she just had an inkling what she was looking for. A diary of some sort? That would be the best kind of good luck.

No, more like a note perhaps, or a reference somewhere.

No. If there had been an illegitimate child, there would be no record in Exbury. William was too proud for that. He would have gone out of town with the child. Probably he would have given it over to his brother at the instant and paid him to go as far away from England as humanly possible.

Russia was that far away . . .

And now she was concocting fairy tales out of dust and desire.

She wasn't done yet. This was but the first of the boxes to be gone through, and if nothing turned up . . .

Well—she hadn't thought that far ahead.

What *would* she do if she found nothing among William's papers?

She wouldn't give up, she thought. That was the last thing she'd do.

But—she could ask questions. Rumors got to be rumors for a reason. She'd talk to people. The vicar. She'd ask Giles. He'd been here all those years ago. And Cook. William's first wife had hired Cook, according the household accounts she'd just read.

There, already she had a plan. A slight, whisper-thin plan grounded in quicksand—and desperation.

And her father and Peter goading her on.

She was wide awake now, with energy to expend and nothing to do. She wished she'd had enough time to remove another box from the attic. But it just wasn't something she was prepared to do in the dead of the night.

She shoved the box back under the bed, and climbed in.

Absolutely unable to sleep.

Damn. And not even hungry.

Why wasn't Nicholas moving around in there? *He* was probably sound asleep.

Which was so unfair.

She swung herself out of bed and hesitated for amoment; did she really want to risk *distracting* him at this hour of the morning?

She paused, her hand on the key to the connecting door. And froze.

Something was raking and scraping along the hallway, too heavy for footsteps, too eerie for words.

She flung open the connecting door—

The clumping sound came closer . . .

Nicholas wasn't there . . .

Like someone limping and dragging chains—

Dear heaven, what now?

It was the most terrifying sound; she darted back into her room to light a candle, and then she slowly eased open her bedroom door.

"What was that?" Her father at his door.

"Did you hear that?" Poor Mena.

"Ghosts—ghosts to haunt the palaces of the idle rich—" Victor, pulling the brocade dressing gown Peter had lent him around his slender body.

"Don't anyone panic—" Peter, last to open his door, but taking charge immediately. "Where's Nicholas? Does *he* know about this ungodly sound?"

"Of course he knows," Elizabeth's father said. "It sounded like a giant in heavy boots limping down the hall. And that metal sound . . ."

"Like a chain," Mena exclaimed. "Like it was dragging a chain. It was so spooky."

"Is Nicholas in his room?" Peter demanded.

Elizabeth shook her head. "It was the first place I looked."

"Well, then, we're all stirred up for no reason. It was probably Nicholas, wandering *his* house in the dead of night. Who can even guess for what resason."

"Exactly," Elizabeth's father put in. "After all, who are we—mere guests—to question the eccentricities of the newly entitled?"

"It was ghosts," Victor proclaimed.

"There's never been a hint of an otherworldly presence at Shenstone," Elizabeth said sharply. "Don't start that."

"But it was so eerie," Mena said. "And there was no one there."

"It was Nicholas, and he was probably on the stairs or in the attic, and that's why you didn't see anything," Peter said. "Everyone—just go back to sleep."

"Oh, you think we can sleep," Victor grumbled, withdrawing into his room.

"Elizabeth, do you want me to be with you?"

"More than anything, but not tonight, Peter. If it really *was* Nicholas, he'll come back and he'll hear us."

"Not that *I* would mind," Peter muttered.

"I would." They waited until her father and Mena had

closed the doors to their rooms before they continued on in whispers.

"Do you really think it was Nicholas?"

"Who else could it be? The thing was *limping*, for heaven's sake."

"Yes. Of course. He just scared us all to death. Why would he do that?"

"You know, Elizabeth, he made such a fuss this morning about the fire. You don't suppose *he* set it?"

"Are you serious? I never considered that for a moment."

"There's a lot we don't know, Elizabeth. It's imperative you find out what you can about him, any way you can. He could well have started that fire, don't ask me to define for what purpose, and then—*this?*"

She nodded. "Yes, yes. This evening . . . this is strange. He meant it to sound like a ghost was walking, didn't he?"

"Or maybe William's ghost. Then we could have a nice seance and William could speak to us from beyond the grave and approve Nicholas's succession to the title."

"That is a bedtime story beyond belief, Peter, and I think with that, I will say good night."

He held her fast for a moment. "Dear Elizabeth—truly—we all want what's best for you. And that has to be for you to somehow disprove Nicholas's claim to Shenstone."

"I know." He didn't have to keep telling her. "I'll think of something." *The attics, tomorrow.* "I know."

So now there was an unexpected heir, unexplained fire, and an unearthly ghost. And Nicholas somehow at the center of all three.

It just went beyond all reason.

Nicholas was not mad, she was absolutely certain of that. But he did have his secrets. And a life before he came to Shenstone that surely went beyond his having been here and there, and over and yon.

That was a key. And not one she would find in William's papers either.

It seemed to her that the more anxious she was to get to the attics, the harder it was to sneak up there without anyone seeing her.

Peter caught her first, after a restless night and little sleep, as she was just starting for the attic.

"You look like hell. Come have breakfast with me."

"It's a little early, Peter."

"Hell, yes. We're up with the gardeners, my darling, and no one is around to scare us on this glorious morning. Come. Your father and I thought we'd go to London this morning so he can take care of some business."

Meaning her father would write a check, Elizabeth thought as she resigned herself to accompanying him down to the family dining room. And probably a *large* check, given the balance that was in the account Nicholas had set up.

Dear heaven, none of this made sense. Why would he have done all that, and then try to scare them out of their wits last night?

"Have you seen him this morning?" Peter asked as he poured her a cup of tea.

"No. No. Nor last night. I didn't hear him come into his room at all. But I might have been asleep by then." She settled herself at the table and took a slice of toast and liberally spread some orange marmalade all over it. "And he was probably sound asleep this morning; I didn't hear any movement beyond the door."

"Good. Good. I don't pretend to understand the man, Elizabeth, I really don't. He's hostile to me, and he seems to want you very badly. Witness that he is determined to give us no time at all alone together—which is what I had hoped for when I came back to you. But then, no one expected an heir to materialize out of nowhere either. It's a strange business."

"You will come back with Father this evening?" She tried to make the question as offhanded as possible, but in her heart, she was terrified the city would lure him and she would lose him.

He had been there five days, a long visit by country house standards, and the wonder was he hadn't gotten restless with the lack of activity. A man could only do so much riding, hunting, and card playing. Especially a man like Peter, who was used to fine company and a good round of amusements wherever he went.

"We'll be back for dinner," he assured her. "That should give you some time—and the opportunity to . . . well—ah, here's your father."

"Elizabeth." Her father sat down next to her. "So Peter has told you that today I must see to my investments."

She let the fiction lie. "You won't need me to take you to the station, will you?" There was a nine o'clock morning train as well as the one at four in the afternoon. "No? Well, then, I need to go upstairs and change if I am to accomplish anything today."

It was still early—around eight o'clock; she could sneak up to the attic now without anyone accosting her.

She made her way back to the bedroom floor at a leisurely pace, and then darted down the corridor to the guest wing.

She didn't like this furtiveness at all: ducking into alcoves, waiting until servants were out of the way. Tiptoeing down the hallway. Hiding in the linen closet.

Someone grabbed her arm, and she thought she would die.

"Jesus, Elizabeth, what hell are you doing sneaking around the guest wing at this time of the morning?"

She couldn't find her voice. Her heart was somewhere in the vicinity of her belly, and pounding hard.

"I might ask you the same question," she finally managed to say.

"I stayed in my guest room last night," Nicholas said. "I needed to get some sleep. That connecting door is too much temptation."

"I'll be happy to lock it from now on, and then you won't have to go creeping around the hallway like the ghost of Christmas past."

"What are you talking about?"

"You—last night. Clumping down the hallway and making a godawful amount of noise."

"Not me."

"Yes, you—limping and dragging around some chains . . ."

"Are you crazy? *I* was stomping around the bedroom hallway rattling chains? Did anyone see me?"

"Well—no."

"I could have guessed. Whatever it was, Elizabeth, it was *not* me. And it was meant to scare the life out of you, as it obviously did."

And there it was: the voice of reason. Not him. Not that. Not the fire. Just the claim to everything else in her life.

"And so, have you come to see to the needs of your *guest?*"

Oh lord—he'd frightened her so badly, she'd almost forgotten why she was even in the guest wing. And explanations would only make things worse.

"No," she said finally. "You scared me out of my wits and I can't even remember why I came up here."

He plainly didn't believe that either, but he didn't pursue it.

"Why don't we go riding today, Elizabeth, and take a good look at the estate?"

"Fine." It was the last thing she wanted to do.

"Around ten?"

"That's fine."

"I'm not your ghost."

"I believe you."

Did she? he wondered. "And someone set that fire deliberately, much as none of you wants to hear that."

"Peter thinks it was you," she threw back at him.

"Maybe it was him," Nicholas called after her.

But she didn't hear that incendiary retort, because she was already down the stairs and gone.

They rode out at ten, taking the road from the stables and veering deep into the estate lands edged with tenant farms five miles beyond the verdant lawns and terraced gardens behind the house.

So he had a good seat, Elizabeth thought, and was quite competent too. A fact among too few to store until needed.

And he asked cogent questions about the running of the estate, the monies derived therefrom, and how taxes were paid and profit distributed.

What had he been doing all these years that he was so well schooled he knew what questions to ask?

She felt him watching her, watching her.

"You love Shenstone," he said at one point, still watching her.

"There wasn't much else," she said without thinking, and then wished she could take it back. "I do, I love it here," she amended. "I assume it's quite different from where you were raised?"

He looked away from her, and shielded his eyes from the sun. "No, quite similar actually. There was money on my mother's side. We were quite comfortable."

So that answered that. Maybe.

"And how did your parents meet, with your father being an ex-patriate?"

Nicholas didn't seem loathe to answer that question.

"He was a doctor, you know."

She hadn't known.

"He took care of her during a bad illness, when he first arrived in Moscow; he had the good fortune to have knowledge of the most current medical techniques that were not available in Russia at the time. They fell in love."

"Does she still live?"

"No. The illness recurred; she died—very recently."

"I'm sorry."

"I was with her; it's my one consolation." *That, and the fact he could fulfill her last request—that he claim the title and his inheritance and vindicate his father's name. Could she have even envisioned a place like Shenstone?*

Could she have conceived of all that lay in wait for him here when she asked that one small favor of him?

And Elizabeth, could his mother have imagined a woman like Elizabeth, with her wanton's body, and her vixen's heart?

What did it all matter after all? Everything that he could see, and miles beyond, belonged to him now. And he was standing straight in the bright light of day for all his enemies to see.

Something had changed. Something had radically changed, but Elizabeth could not quite put her finger on what it was. Nor did she have the time to figure out what it was.

She had but a half hour before lunch to get up into the attic and bring down another box of papers.

It was quiet now. Nicholas had gone to the gardens. Her father and Peter had taken the early train. Victor had walked into Exbury. And Mena was reading in the library.

Now, now . . .

Up the stairs she went, down the hallway, up to the guest wing, down the corridor . . .

"Miss Elizabeth."

Giles. Dear heaven, Giles.

"Yes, Giles." He didn't betray by the blink of an eye that he thought it was unusual she was in the guest wing at all.

"I thought you might like to know that the master spent the night in the guest wing."

"Thank you, Giles. That's very useful to know."

"I thought so, my lady."

She had no choice but to turn and go.

And now what? Back in her room, she stepped out of her morning clothes, and washed herself thoroughly. There. She ought to nap, and maybe, sometime in the afternoon, she might get up to the attic.

Whose ridiculous idea had this been anyway?

If only her father and Peter would stop hounding her like that.

She pulled out a dressing sacque and slipped it on. If she could just slip up to the attic before lunch—

She listened at the connecting door. No sound. No evidence that Nicholas had returned. She eased out into the hallway. It was quiet as a tomb. She tiptoed down the hall, up the steps, into the guest wing corridor once again, and to the attic stairwell.

Minutes, minutes, that was all it would take . . . her heart was pounding; every little sound sent her nerves skittering.

She opened the stairwell door and slipped inside. Up the steps, into the attic rooms, quick, quick—grab a box, any box, and get it down to her room.

Not easily done. A bulky box, the long sweeping hem nearly tripping her up as she edged her way down three flights of stairs. Servants' voices, as disembodied as ghosts, coming from nowhere.

Giles, summoning Mena to lunch, futilely knocking on her own door.

Herself, wedged in an alcove near the guest wing staircase, wondering why she was hiding, when she had a perfect right to take things from the attic, *William's* things . . .

And five minutes later, into her room, and collapsing on her bed.

And—

"Elizabeth, are you in there?"

Nicholas, through the connecting door.

"No, I'm not," she said crossly. "Don't you dare come in," as she hurriedly pushed the box under the bed, and shrugged out of her dusty sacque and thrust that under the bed as well.

Now what? She raked her fingers through her hair. "What do you want?" Oh, that was a leading question. "I mean, I know lunch is ready; I'll join you in fifteen minutes." No, that wasn't what she'd meant to say either.

But Nicholas didn't pick up on it the way he might have just yesterday. All he said was, "I'll see you downstairs."

Immediately that disquieting feeling she'd had earlier returned.

Something had changed. And it had to do with the ghost, the fire, or something in the air.

She came downstairs dressed in a navy blue silk dress with a narrow gored skirt and lace collar. Her golden hair was piled up into a topknot and fastened with a gold clip.

She wore very little jewelry, but still, her diamond wedding band sparkled on her finger; there was a cameo at her throat, and a gold bracelet encircling her wrist.

She didn't look like his enemy. She looked like what she was, a beautiful woman, an expensive toy.

And he had paid way too high a price to have her.

The atmosphere at the lunch table was markedly different today, as Elizabeth seated herself: calmer, quieter.

But there was only Mena to keep them company this afternoon, sitting in the corner, contentedly slicing her way through medallions of cold beef, boiled leeks, potato salad, bread pudding, and with that, tea.

There was something about Mena. She was not contentious. She never argued. She was perfectly content to be a presence, a buffer, a companion.

Every once in a while she looked at him meaningfully, as if she were still trying to identify how she knew him.

But that didn't disquiet him anymore.

It was something more than that: someone in this house was his enemy. And there were only four likely someones. And that was besides the Unseen Hand.

"Nicholas, you're looking at me strangely," Elizabeth said as she forked a slice of beef onto her plate. She knew it—she *knew* it . . . something had changed. Immediately she lost her appetite.

"Just thinking."

"I think I don't like it when you're thinking. What are you thinking about?"

"The fire."

"Oh, blast the fire. It was an accident. Nobody started it. Nobody even knew about that little room." *Lies, lies, lies. And saying it so emphatically didn't make it so.*

"Somebody knew," Nicholas said.

She felt a squeeze of cold terror around her vitals. "What do you mean, somebody knew?"

"Somebody was using it."

Her breath caught. She just barely got the words out: "How do you know?"

She tried to hide her panic. It was an unnecessary question: she already knew. He'd gone back down. He'd examined what was there, what was left in the ashes and rubble.

Why was he looking at her like that?

"I went back and looked at it."

Expected answer. She pushed down her fear. "And found what?"

"Fragments. A bit of pottery; charred wood; a melted candle."

"Oh." Oh. All the little clues that could not be destroyed in a blaze that had somehow to be contained.

"Who was hiding there, Elizabeth?"

She swallowed the lie. "I don't know."

"Who set the fire?"

She bit back the bile. "I don't know."

"And who planned to kill me down there when the torches were doused, Elizabeth? *You?*"

Chapter 11

She was still reeling as she blindly made her way back upstairs.

Someone had tried to kill him?

No, all they wanted, all she wanted was to find a way to
disinherit him. That was all, but now he'd never believe that.

"No one wants to kill you."

"There are enemies everywhere, Elizabeth. You're naive if
you don't know that."

"You sound just like Victor."

"Not when there's so much at stake. Not when you were
the one who had the most to lose and the most to gain. In the
dark, when a man is down, anyone could get his hands around
his throat and snuff out his life."

"Oh God, I won't listen to this." She'd bolted from her
seat. "I won't. I was content with the bargain; I got what I
needed, in spite of the fact I'd rather have had Shenstone to
myself. It's not like you appeared out of mists somewhere or
that no one knew you existed. It was just—they thought you
were dead. They thought you'd died in infancy. They tried to
find you, but you were never perceived as a threat—"

"Until I walked in the door."

"Even then." But that wasn't true. He had been a threat to
every one of her expectations and her desires.

"A threat to you and everything you felt belonged to you.
So you were the most likely one, Elizabeth. Someone knocked
me down in that tunnel, and tried to choke me. All that chaos
you created when you tripped and the lights went out. Who

was where, Elizabeth? Could you tell? Four people down there, all insisting they must come, and all with a vested interest in the outcome of my claim. And I wasn't a threat?"

"I don't believe it."

"You're a liar." He got up from the table, standing nose to nose with her. "Get rid of me and everything devolves back to you. Who wouldn't attempt to kill for that kind of gain."

She hauled back and swung, catching him square on his jaw. "You, Nicholas. Only you."

But that part wasn't true either. Her father had as much as admitted he'd thought about it. But thinking wasn't doing. And he did exaggerate, her father. He only wanted what she wanted, Shenstone back in *her* hands.

Damn the fates. No one ever had to have found that room. It was such an ill-considered move, to torch it. She could have removed all evidence of occupation if she'd even thought it was a threat.

She could have prevented this whole thing, if she'd only just gone and cleaned the place out after the occupant had left.

Her fault, all of this; she'd taken for granted all along that things would work out somehow, and instead her life had gone like a row of dominoes, with one thing toppling disastrously into another in a long straight unending line.

And now that Nicholas thought she was capable of murder, he would make her leave Shenstone.

Oh no, no no—there had to be a way. Nicholas had imagined it.

But hadn't she thought she felt a hand at her back moments before she went down and the torches were doused?

No—it was too horrifying to contemplate, that kind of desperation. It just didn't make sense when he'd made every effort to keep things unchanged.

All they wanted was for him to go away. It was their sole intent, their only purpose.

And now that was the thing that she must do—find the magic wand that would make him disappear.

She'd counted on having time to accomplish that. And now

she had no time at all. No time to be careful or discreet either. Or to be able to do it in secret.

She had to start this minute.

She slipped off the bed and onto her knees, and she pulled the second box of William's papers from under the bed, dumped it all on the floor, and once again began to read.

It had been an awful, doomed marriage. Here were the marriage lines, the details of the dowry, the specifics of a union arranged solely to get a son, all William ever wanted.

Why?

They hadn't been giddy with passion, or in love, William and his Dorothy. Rather, in almost the exact manner as she herself had done, Dorothy had sealed a bargain: her body for his son. Shenstone and its comforts for the wife from whom William got his heir.

It was chilling, how her own union with William exactly mirrored his first. And William hadn't been all that young then and Dorothy wasn't very old.

Notes from an assortment of doctors in London were testament to that, couching in the most general roundabout terms the fact that it was not Dorothy who could not produce the heir.

Poor poor Dorothy.

But nowhere in that cache of papers was any evidence anywhere that she'd gotten a son by another man, by other means. No diaries. No love letters. No documents or attachments mentioning anything out of the ordinary.

Just dry notes from William requesting certain things be attended to. Invitations to dinners and events. Theater. Opera. A *bal masque,* which seemed rather frivolous for someone like William.

Some photographs. Dorothy, looking older than her years, stately in a gown with overpuffed sleeves and a sweeping skirt. William, stolid, thin of hair, with a long mustache, dressed in a stiff vested suit and leaning against a column.

Some scribblings on the history of Shenstone. A sketch of

the family tree. William *was* meticulous. Everything relating to Dorothy was in this box, and Elizabeth supposed that everything relevant to her life with him was contained in the other.

It was time to get that one now.

And now she didn't care who saw her. Giles, as it happened, but she waved him away.

Fifteen minutes later, she had all the rest of the papers spread out around her. Two hours later, the task was done, and all that work and all that time had been to no avail.

There was nothing among William's papers to disprove Nicholas's claim.

"Here we are, here we are," her father sang out as he and Peter entered the house later that evening. "Elizabeth! Where are you? Ah, there you are. What a day. Come into the library, I have much to tell you."

"The only thing I want to know is, how much did you spend?"

"Oh, now—there. My daughter is a skeptic, Peter. Didn't I wager you that she would say something of the sort?"

"Indeed you did. I'm the one who underestimated Elizabeth's, shall we say, attention to detail."

"Well, we've saved the day, Elizabeth. And I met Krasnov today, and he says the company can assure us it is but a mere twenty fathoms from striking oil. A small infusion of cash today, and we'll all be millionaires tomorrow. Let's drink to that." He grabbed the bell pull and yanked it. "Giles! Brandy all around."

"Very good, sir."

She couldn't bear to put a damper on her father's celebration; he'd waited so long for all this investment and planning to produce some results. And surely Krasnov was trustworthy.

Peter had been with her father; he must know Krasnov. So it truly wasn't a lost cause the way she'd always thought.

Of course, it begged the question of what the company would do with all that oil once it was flowing. Provisions for storage and transportation came to mind, but her father never planned beyond the next moment, let alone long-term for things like that.

"Call Victor down to join us," her father said when Giles had passed the tray. "And Nicholas."

"Very good, sir." Giles set the tray down on the desk.

"God, that is a stiff man," her father murmured. "Just the sort you want as your butler. Always knows the right thing to do. Well, here we go. To the company." He lifted his snifter. "When we strike oil, we incorporate as a joint venture, and then we'll set up formal offices in London and Moscow, and contract with a shipper so we can get those reserves *here*. No, better than that, we'll start our own shipping line. Our own storage facility. Once we strike oil, there is no limit to what our partnership can do. And it is all due to my dear daughter and her generosity and faith."

He bowed to Elizabeth. "My dear girl, to you." He inhaled, he sipped, and an expression of the most sublime happiness came over his face. "This is excellent, excellent, excellent. Peter will tell you later.

"And by the way, there hasn't been another story about that madman who was randomly killing people. Can you believe it? In the space of two or threes weeks, that monster has gone to ground and there hasn't even been another attack. All that worry, all that panic, for nothing. They'll never catch him now. He's had his thrill and gone. So now, you tell us, Elizabeth, what's to do with you?"

"In short? In sum: Nicholas says he was not the ghost last night, and he thinks one of us tried to kill him in the tunnel. So maybe the madman is here."

Her father looked taken aback. "Oh. *Oh.* Never say so, Elizabeth—even in jest. Where is Nicholas, then? Why doesn't he just confront us, and then toss us all out and have done with it?"

"I'm right here," Nicholas said from the threshold. "And I'll tell you why: I'd rather have you all where I can *see* you sooner than turn my back on you."

"Oh, that's comforting," Peter murmured. "That's as good

as saying one of us *is* the madman. Well, Nicholas once again sets the standard for being a gracious host. On the other hand, *we* are all here for Elizabeth's sake so all this other nonsense just doesn't matter. The fire was an accident, and whatever we thought we heard last night, well—perhaps we all just imagined it."

"Exactly," her father chimed in. "So let's have another brandy and forget about it."

"We *imagined* it?" Elizabeth muttered in disgust as her father poured himself another tot.

"We're all such creative people," Nicholas said trenchantly. "And so that ends that fairy tale: they all lived happily ever after at Shenstone."

"Have a brandy," Elizabeth's father said, ignoring the sarcasm and handing him a snifter. "And here's Victor. Come in, my boy, we're having a toast to a most successful day."

"Which means he spent money," Elizabeth said. "He hasn't yet said how much."

"Well, there it is, the justification for everything," Nicholas reminded her, taking the snifter from her father's hand. "As we celebrate with *my* good brandy."

"William's good brandy," Elizabeth corrected him.

"Money can buy anything," Victor said to Elizabeth's father. "Loyalty, arms, governments . . . when the revolution comes, what good will your oil wells do you, here in England?"

"Don't listen to that seditious romanticism," Peter said. "The fact Victor is here and chose not to exile himself with his insurgent leaders is proof enough that he's all words and no substance. Have a brandy, my dear man, and we'll drink a toast to *your* loyalties."

"Bah. When the state takes over your oil wells and the government, we shall see who toasts whom, Peter. Your autocratic nephew will be the last of your line to ever ascend the throne, I swear to you." And he threw himself into a corner to stare broodingly out the closed French doors.

"My goodness, ghosts, and lessons in revolutionary theory—all in the space of day," Elizabeth's father said lightly.

"This has been an evening to savor indeed. Just the kind of thing that makes our visits to Shenstone so memorable. Well, I'm going to ensconce myself in the morning room with my papers. Anyone care to join me? Victor—you come along, and tell me more about how I will lose my investments when the government is overthrown."

"And what shall *we* talk about?" Peter asked as Victor followed Frederick out of the room.

"Perhaps the advantages of being a member of a royal family?" Nicholas suggested.

"There seem to be *no* advantages," Peter murmured, "if you listen to Victor. It might be that I should align myself with his philosophy and thus be liberated when the revolution comes. But liberated for what? A worker I most certainly cannot be. I've been bred to wealth and all the finer things, and if Victor thinks all of that will be handed over just because some jury-rigged provisional government will demand it, well, he's more of a romantic than Elizabeth's father with his wells. And blood will run in the streets like oil."

He turned to Elizabeth. "Forgive me, my dear. I'm more than certain Frederick will never see a return on that in his lifetime."

"You ought to have stopped him then."

"He wouldn't have listened. Krasnov sequestered him and the check was written before I was even aware."

Elizabeth looked at Nicholas, who shrugged. *An account to waste as he would* . . . And so her father had. It curdled her stomach to think of how much money he might have handed over to Krasnov today. Likely every farthing. And she'd wager he would come after her for more within the week too.

Which made her all too aware yet again how fragile her position was.

She might well be trying to discover Nicholas's secrets, but it was true she had some of her own. The balance must be kept, and tonight was the first time it became clear to her: she needed to keep the bargain intact no matter what she had to do.

178 / Thea Devine

But she wasn't ready to give up Shenstone either.

It was a fine line—serving her own ends while trying to keep Nicholas distracted. And all because of one ill-considered act of panic.

He was deeply suspicious now of all of them. And yet he hadn't leapt on her father's suggestion he just send them all packing.

And it wasn't just that he wanted to watch them. It was something more—more secrets?

Who was Nicholas, really?

"My father was ever a dreamer," she said finally in response to Peter's comment. "No one can stop him once he has his teeth in a bit."

"Then how fortunate it is that you can support such a visionary," Nicholas said blandly.

She sent him a sharp glance. "I've always been proud of my resourcefulness."

"Yes, it's true—you are amazingly adept. And adaptable," Nicholas murmured. "And all in the aid of one man's whims and desires."

"I wish someone would take *this* man's whims and desires into account," Peter interpolated testily. "Can I not have some time alone with Elizabeth?"

Nicholas threw up his hands. "You can have whatever you want, Peter. You see, I am a considerate host: I will inflict myself on you no longer. Elizabeth . . ."

She watched him limp away with mixed emotions.

"And now?" Peter said. He slipped his arms around her from behind and pulled her back against his chest

"You know the whole. He mistrusts us more than ever. And he is still master of Shenstone." She wrapped her arms around his as he held her.

"Then we have not done enough, searched deeply and widely enough, you have not used all those resources, Elizabeth." His lips brushed the side of her head. "How could you bear to hear him talk about *his* brandy? *His* house. *His* everything.

But more than that, if your father keeps on the way he is, he will drain you to a ha'penny of all you now possess."

"I know that." *More lies, more secrets. But this she could not tell him, that Nicholas was funding her father's folly.* "I've set limits. There's a point over which he cannot go."

"Tell him that after this afternoon." He nuzzled her ear.

"I wish he would just go to Siberia and oversee the thing."

"And what could he do there, except write more checks?"

She made a sound acknowledging the truth of this, and Peter went on, "You must continue with our plan, Elizabeth. It's the only thing that can save you."

. . . save us . . . was he saying?

"Not if Nicholas thinks I attempted to . . . to hurt him."

"Then you must convince him otherwise, Elizabeth." He turned her around to face him now, his hands on her shoulders.

"And how do I do that after everything that's happened?"

"Be nice to him." He brushed her lips. "Be accommodating. You'll know what to do when the time comes." He kissed her again long and lovingly before he released her and set her away from him gently.

"Go to him. It's not too late to start now. I'd much rather you stay with me, but you must act quickly to quell his suspicions. You can see that, can't you? Trust me, my darling girl, it's the only way."

She didn't think she could do what Peter was suggesting. But as she made her way up to her room, she wasn't exactly sure *what* he was suggesting.

That she talk to Nicholas?

They were too far past the point of talking, on any level.

And how do you respond anyway, when a man accused you of wanting to murder him?

There weren't too many explanations that covered it.

And every other possibility included a scenario of seduction.

That was how far she had come. To take it down to that and push everything else out of the way.

Wrap yourself in pearls and seduce him.

... our signal that you lust for my penis to service you ...

... that you want to be fucked now ...

Her breath caught.

Remind him of the bargain, and his command that you must come to him when you need a good stiff penis.

She began shucking her clothes.

—fuck him, marry Peter ... Peter was right: this was the only way. Only Peter would never know a thing about it.

She took the necklace and the pendant from her jewelry box. It was so long, so lustrous, so smooth; holding it against her naked body evoked images of a half-dozen ways she could wear it for him.

She could wrap the necklace around her neck and suspend the pendant between her breasts. She could wrap her breasts to push them close together, so he could play with her hot pointed nipples. She could wrap the necklace around her hips with the pearl pendant suspended in such a way that she could tuck it between her legs; or she could insert the pendant and the beads together, the one hard up against her clit, the other deep inside ...

Each possibility excited her more than the next as she sat on her bed, arousing her nipples by stroking the pendant across each hardening tip.

It was important to wear the pendant, she decided, because of what he deemed it signified. So she couldn't wear it inserted against her nub. But she could wind the necklace once around her neck, attaching the pendant there, and then insert the pearls as far up between her legs as they would go.

So that when they were all inserted, the pearls were taut on either side of her breasts and as they came down to the vee just at her cleft and disappeared erotically between her legs.

Perfect. Perfect. She couldn't get over the image of her body in the mirror. Her nipples were so hard, she shivered at the sight of herself wrapped in his pearls.

There. Now to just pretend that she was fully dressed. Perhaps a pair of shoes to complete the ensemble? She had a pair of ivory backless satin slippers, the color as lustrous as her pearls. She slipped her feet into them, and minced around the room.

Just the right touch that canted her body forward slightly on the heel, and enhanced the feel of the pearls against her naked crotch.

Now she was ready, every part of her shuddering with excitement as she made her way carefully to the connecting door.

A Pandora's box, that door.

Open it and unleash all the fleshly pleasures. Open it, and command his prowess and his power. Open it, but understand fully and completely what you crave and what you burn for . . .

Open it . . . and surrender your naked body wholly to his lust and desire—

OPEN IT . . .

Slowly, she opened it, pushing it into his room.

And he was standing there, naked, hot, engorged with his need to possess her, his gaze kindling as it swept her body.

"You wear the talisman."

"I dressed for you."

"You know what it means."

"That's why I came to *you.*"

"Did you? Why?"

"I crave a thick hard penis tonight."

"There are others who can service you."

"But I want *your* penis."

He almost couldn't stand looking at that body, those quivering breasts, those hard pointed nipples, and imagining the hot lush embrace of her body where those smooth hard pearls were nestled.

A man had to be a saint not to be provoked by that body. And by hell, a man could bury anything in the heat of possessing it, even an attempt on his life.

"What will you do to have it?"

"I came to you, I dressed for you, I wear your talisman. I did everything you demanded. Now I want your penis."

"It seems to me there's nowhere to put it."

"You'll find a way."

"Let me see what I find. Give me your leg."

He held out his hand; she stepped out of her slippers, lifted one leg, and he caught it.

And now he could see everything, and what he saw was breathtaking: his long lustrous string of pearls stretched taut down her body, disappearing into her thick tuft, and wedged deep in her cunt.

His.

With everything else in this house: his.

He felt a primitive urge to take her, mark her as his possession.

His body, his own.

He slid his hand up her leg, moving in on her closer and closer still. She grasped his arm for balance, and he twisted his hand under her thigh and cupped her mound.

Her gasp at his touch was just audible, just arousing. She swung her leg to the floor, and he backed her into her room, still holding her possessively between her legs.

He could feel the wet of her, the soft downy pubic hair, the hard roundness of the pearls inserted in her vagina; he could feel her need and her heat radiating from her like sin.

She was the embodiment of a wanton, from her lush naked body to her hot knowing gaze.

And when her bottom hit the edge of her bed, she braced herself against it, undulating her hips and bearing down on his fingers.

Her hands moved from his arm to his hard poking penis, and she grasped him tightly and held on like a stone.

And there they stood, her fingers wrapped around his thick length, his fingers pressing hotly into her mound as she shimmied her hips to center them.

"And so, my lady fuck-me, where do you propose I put him?"

"Put your fingers first . . . right—*th-ere* . . ." She uttered a long, satisfying groan as he found her distended clit. Her voice broke as her body convulsed hard against his questing fingers. He knew just where to touch, just how hard to plumb, and she ground herself down hard against his magic fingers, as her hands moved spasmodically all over his penis.

She felt him jerk under her frenetic touch. She felt him push her onto the bed, felt him wrench away her hands and hold them down as he rubbed himself all over her belly, her hips, and upward toward her breasts, to her nipples, to rub his penis head all over the hard hot points. First one, then the other, back and forth he stroked her, back and forth, relinquishing one hand to hold one breast so he could just rub her nipple back and forth with the underside of his shaft.

She wrapped her legs around him as his thrusts became tighter and shorter, tense and bursting. And when she arched up against him, as he felt her pearly cunt undulating against his legs, he pulled back, he positioned himself over her one nipple, and he drove himself against the tight hard point, and he came, and came, and came, erupting like lava all over her nipple, her breast, her body.

And when he could breathe again, when his body stopped convulsing and spurting, he rolled over onto his side, braced himself on one arm, and began stroking his cream into her skin.

He wanted to mark her with it, cover her with it, envelop her in it. He rubbed it into her cunt, her belly, her breasts, her chest, and was instantly erect as a pipe again as he coated her hard nipples with his thick cream.

"Put some between my legs," she sighed as he rubbed her nipples lightly.

"Oh, I'll put something between your legs, my lady stiff nipples. And you know just what it is."

"Then take out my pearls, and take *me.*"

He lifted her right leg and draped it over his hip, so that he could get a good long look at the erotic way her cunt enveloped her pearls.

"I don't know. I think I'd rather just look at you."

"I'd rather you just fucked me." She levered herself up on her elbows. "Let me watch you pull out my pearls."

He tugged gently and first one popped out from her vagina, and the next and the next, again and again, like fat little raindrops kissed by her cunt lips before she let them go.

And then, as reverently as if he were lifting the skirt of a dress to discover the treasure within, he lifted the pearls over her head and unwound them from around her neck and onto her pillow.

"And now, my lady naked . . ." He eased himself over her. "Here's something else between your legs."

"Hurry . . ."

But he was in no hurry, with her especially. He wanted her to feel his power and his strength. He wanted her to yearn for his hard thrusting length. And he wanted to pound her into the bed until she begged for mercy.

He thought he would go slowly, pushing and pressing himself into her the way he liked to do, inch by long slow hard inch. He thought he could hold himself, thought he could just insert his penis head and have the pleasure of watching her take him incrementally into her undulating body.

He thought he could hold out at least that long, until he penetrated her fully, until he was rocking his hips against hers and working to keep control.

That was what he thought. That was what he wanted. That long slow slide into her body. That shuddering moment of possession. And then the tight hot embrace of her sheath.

He was just there, just within the caress of her labia, just at the first push of possession—and she spread her legs wide, she bore down hard and tight on his penis, and pushed him inexorably to thrust himself deep inside her.

One little movement, one gyration of her hips and his body went wild, bucking and spurting, and seeking the wet and heat of her. There was no stopping him now, not after he'd coated her nipples with his cream.

All he wanted was to make more and more, to flood her body with it, drench her, drown her, soak her in it, saturate her whole body with it, spew his ejaculate so deep into her that he submerged her soul.

He stormed her body, ferocious in his need. This was not supposed to have happened, this convulsive wracking possession. She rippled and rolled against him, demanding every last spew of his seed.

And still he tried to hold on; still, in the throes of yet another wrenching climax, he tried to get control.

She fought it; she fought him. She wanted to exhaust him, sap him, and drain him dry, and she used all her naked wiles.

"You can't do it," he bit out as she stroked his buttocks and crease. "There's not a drop more."

"I'm doing it. Give me more."

"Damn you . . ." he muttered, burying his head in her shoulder and jamming himself hard up inside her.

"That's *more* . . ." she whispered suggestively.

"Shit." He spumed again, his hips grinding hard.

"Ummm . . ." She squeezed herself around his throbbing penis, and made a little sound. "Don't move. Just . . . just—" She drew a sharp breath as she contracted herself again and felt him long and strong and deep inside her. "Like that—" Another contraction. "That . . ." She felt the pleasure radiating from deep in her core. "And that . . ." Flowing outward as she contracted her body around him again, an unfurling of a wave that broke slowly and then violently on the hard rock of his penis and brought her slowly, languidly to shore.

Chapter 12

It was time to give her up to her heart's desire, Nicholas thought, as he swung himself out of bed and limped to the window where the sky was just streaked with dawn.

She was too much of a distraction, for one thing; he was in a constant state of arousal just being around her, and if he continued on with her this way, he wouldn't give her up at all.

Not that he didn't want her still. His unruly penis was emphatically ready to proceed, but that had been the case for a week now.

The real problem was, he was getting itchy. This was the most time he had ever spent in one place, and the only time he had operated under his true identity.

But the symmetrical life of a nobleman irritated him. It was too comfortable, too confining, too chaste.

He needed to get down to business, he was here for a purpose, and it was time to force his enemy's hand. He felt it in his bones, he knew it in his heart: the Unseen Hand was waiting, preparing to strike.

No attacks for several weeks, Elizabeth's father had said. One attack, as far as he was concerned: a ghost in a fire-scorched tunnel, seeking to squeeze the lifeblood out of *him*.

But leave that aside. Pretend it might have been an accident. Pretend he could stay in bed like the pampered earl he was and fuck Elizabeth the whole livelong day.

Maybe not pretend, he thought, watching her stretch languidly and come awake, her eyes widening at the sight of his bursting erection.

"I think I need some cream for breakfast," she murmured.
He couldn't give it up, not yet. "Come and get it."

"I will." She swung off the bed and sashayed over to him,
her nipples already tight and hard with anticipation.

"How do you want it, my lady cherry ripe?"

She stroked the thick ridge of his penis head, as his body
jolted under her touch, and then she looked up at him from
under her lashes.

"I'm hungry this morning." She knelt down in front of him.
"I think I want some breakfast—now." And she encircled his
hard tip with her mouth.

And he gave it to her, and gave in to her ravenous sucking,
her avid tongue, the luscious little noises she made at the back
of her throat as she took him.

How could he give it up, that hard hot pull at the very tip
of his penis that sought to suck and siphon out every drop of
pleasure from him?

And so here finally was the truth, as he pumped his bone-
crackling orgasm all over her: his real enemy was himself.

And then they went back to bed, and he rooted himself in
her—for hours, days, she didn't know; she floated in a haze of
unending orgiastic pleasure, feeding on his body and those
too-few devouring kisses, until finally, satiated, she slept.

When she awakened, she was alone, awash in the lather of
his come, the room filled with the scent of their ferocious coupling.

She just wanted to wallow in it forever. She swiped her fingers between her legs once, twice, and rubbed his ejaculate
into her breasts and coated her taut pointed nipples with it.

Something else she could wear.

Where *was* he?

She lay back against the pillows.

*No. She shouldn't be thinking this way. This was all a pre-
lude to her sensual life with Peter. All the stuff of men's fantasies, all the things she needed to know . . .*

Did she not know enough by now?

She bolted upright. This was getting dangerous; she was enjoying sex with Nicholas much too much.

This wasn't onerous, this bargain.

And it wasn't fair to make Peter wait any longer.

Nicholas was wrong about that. After he finally made love to her, Peter would only want her more.

So she needed not to be in bed this morning and thinking about Nicholas. That way lay disaster. She should be focused on what Peter needed, what Peter wanted.

What they all wanted.

And now that she had found nothing in William's papers relevant to Nicholas, she should implement the second part of her admittedly nebulous plan: talking to people.

Talking to anyone but Nicholas.

Maybe the vicar today. It wouldn't take long. No one would question what she was doing if she drove into Exbury today.

And it would get her out of the house and away from Nicholas.

Perfect.

She settled back down under the covers and rang for her maid.

So this was what they knew about Nicholas, she ruminated later, as she took a light breakfast of scones and tea. His father was a doctor, and his mother was, by William's account, Russian. And prior to his coming to claim the estate, Nicholas had been *here and there, over and yon,* while agents searched for him on two continents.

What could a man have been doing that no one could find him? she wondered idly. And was it possible he could have really been Richard's illegitimate son?

William had raised the issue on the news of yet another frustrating month in which she had failed to conceive.

I will not have my brother's bastard inheriting my estate . . .

No. She wasn't going to dwell on that. Just that one telling phrase that might, did it prove true, change her life.

She looked up from her reverie to find Mena hovering by her side.

"You're dressed to go out," Mena observed.

"I'm going to town, would you like to come?" That was inspired; no one would think anything of her driving out to entertain her guest.

"That would be lovely, dear." Mena poured some tea, and settled herself down beside Elizabeth. "I'm still feeling unsettled about that little fire."

"Don't. It *was* an accident. I believe that. Everything has been fine since and, you must admit, Nicholas has tried to make us all comfortable."

"Yes, Nicholas wears the mantle of a nobleman very well, I think."

"Oh, speaking of that—he mentioned to me that his father had been a doctor. Does that piece of information at all jar your memory?"

"Hmmm. I'll have to think about it. Meanwhile, let me just get my little cape and we can be off."

They started out around ten-thirty in the victoria, since it was a sunny warm day, and planned to drive around a bit, perhaps stop and shop at the stalls, and then visit with the vicar.

All of this was done to the accompaniment of Mena's serene and inconsequential chatter. Didn't Exbury look fine with all the trees and flowers blooming? Was that a shop newly opened? Oh, look at that young lady's hair. And here came the train, its whistle wailing, and pulling up in a blast of steam.

In the stalls, they found some cakes, some ribbon, and a length of black veiling Elizabeth thought she might use to trim a hat.

"Really, Elizabeth, you can go to half-mourning now."

"And I did plan to. Nicholas's arrival turned everything upside down."

And turned her upside over . . .

"Not to mention *Peter*," she added, hoping it didn't sound like an afterthought. "Well, here we are at the church, and I must make our apologies for being so remiss about attending services."

It was as good an excuse as any to visit; they had missed one service by her count, and she ought to have been on her knees every week praying for William's soul.

But it was the vicar who apologized to her, for not having come to Shenstone and formally welcomed William's heir.

"A shock to all of you, I'm sure, after all this time," he added, as he escorted them into his sitting room. "But perhaps not unwelcome to have someone to take up the reins of running a manor house like Shenstone."

"A shock certainly," Elizabeth agreed, "although we knew that William's brother had had a child. It was just thought he'd died in infancy, as nothing had ever been heard from him. And then to have him suddenly appear . . ."

The housekeeper brought in tea, and Vicar Bristowe poured while Elizabeth's words hung in the air. He handed her a cup. "Yes, I can see that might be unnerving."

"Indeed. And I'm fearful it will give rise to all that old speculation about William's first wife."

"I'm sure you have nothing to fear from that," the Vicar said. "There was nothing ever to it. It was just that Richard was such a handsome man. Dashing, adventurous, everything William was not, I'm afraid. So Richard's sojourn to Russia was the very thing for him. And he was young enough to make a life there, to get a family. It was just unfortunate that Dorothy died, and that there was no issue—from either of William's marriages."

"No," Elizabeth said. "No issue. From either union. Although—wasn't there talk when Richard left?"

"Talk? About Richard? No, there was nothing," the vicar said gently. "Only that William grieved after he said good-bye."

And that was that; she could not pursue it further without having to explain why she wanted to know or defaming William's good name.

They bid the vicar good afternoon and drove some more around the town.

"I've lived here seven years," Elizabeth mused as their carriage passed by this landmark and that, "and I can safely say I know no one except my minister. What does that tell you about me? Or William for that matter? We rarely entertained. We did go up to London quite a bit, and stay at the townhouse, but William did not enjoy it as much as I. I don't know there was much *I* cared about in those seven years we were together."

"You cared about yourself," Mena said. "The circumstances cannot have been the most romantic for you. You were too young."

"No, it was my choice."

"And sometimes young girls choose so unwisely. And I'm certain your father had a hand in that match as well. But now that Nicholas is here, you can make a fresh start."

"Would that I could."

"There is nothing to stop you," Mena pointed out. "A year of half-mourning, and then you can go about. You need not immure yourself at Shenstone or anywhere else."

"But what will I have in the end?" Elizabeth whispered.

Nothing was assured, not her income, not Peter, not a life beyond Shenstone. Or a life without her father picking at her means.

"You'll have more, so much more," Mena said. "Because in the end, you'll be free."

He went back down into the tunnel.

He didn't think it was his intention when he went out in the gardens.

But he found himself making his way to the far end and veering left toward the field.

It was the brightest of sunshiny days, the clearest of skies. Spring had burst all over Shenstone, a sight for his jaded eyes.

Never in his life had he been attached to anyone or anything. But he could feel the urge in him to succumb to the lure of Shenstone. The temptation of *her*.

That mouth, that body for all the days of his life . . .

A man could get trapped if he wasn't looking for the snare.

He walked out in a wide semicircle and then traced the path of the torch-bearers that night. He had been sweeping to the right, Elizabeth and her father to the left.

And wasn't it Elizabeth who found it? The entrance she claimed to know nothing about?

Something very unpleasant jangled along his nerves.

He limped over to that side of the field and tracked her steps.

Back this way, forward that, until he had a clear vision of how she had moved that night. And there was only one way she could have gone. Because if she had been but two meters off, someone else would have found the entrance.

Oh God, Elizabeth . . .

The doors of entrance, flush to the ground once more, opened easily enough this time, and he left them propped up as he descended into the darkness.

The lantern was still hanging at the foot of the steps; he scratched a match and lit it.

Twenty steps more and he was at the storeroom.

And a sweep of his light revealed the thing he dreaded to see: that the storeroom had been swept clean of the ashes and rubble, and cleared of all the debris.

The Unseen Hand reached everywhere.

He had put himself in the line of fire, and his enemy just reached around him and contaminated every other thing.

The only conclusion he could draw was that one of the five at Shenstone was his enemy.

Victor, Peter, Elizabeth's father, Mena . . . and Elizabeth.

It was just as he had thought: she who had the most to gain had the most to lose. The strongest motive—the strongest hands.

It jarred him to the bone that he had ignored every instinct, every warning sign.

Hell, he'd gotten distracted.

Or had his enemy plotted that too?

And now—?

And now . . . He understood what it was all about. It was a war of nerves and guile. A total comprehension of the methods of his opponent.

The kind of contest they both understood.

And Nicholas knew more about his enemy than even his enemy would allow.

He knew his enemy was bold as brass and just a little mad. Someone who fit in. Someone who stood out. Who needed attention and was desperate to hide. Someone who wanted to be acknowledged and preferred to be alone.

And most of all, someone no one would ever think it would be.

One of the five.

Or all of them.

And the game they would play was wait-and-see . . .

There had to be something else, there *had* to be. Maybe she had dismissed too quickly out of hand what else might be in the attic. There was old furniture up there, and old trunks full of clothes. Who knew but something might be tucked in the pocket of one of William's frock coats?

Or was she truly that desperate?

"I heard you went to town today," her father said, strolling into the morning room where she sat jabbing a needle into a piece of embroidery in which she had no interest at all. "I hope it profited you?"

"It was a morning out, Father, for Mena and me to get out of this house. Nothing more, nothing less."

"You went to see the vicar."

"Do you have spies in town or something?" she asked crossly. "I went to apologize for our lack of attendance these past Sundays."

"Oh. I was hoping for something else."

"Like what? And why don't you have a seat, Father? Since you're so eager to keep hounding me."

He sat down opposite. "Now, Elizabeth. I'm not hounding. I'm *prodding*. You know there's hardly enough money to skin a cat, so tell me how are we both to survive when Nicholas's generosity, such as it is, runs out, and he asks us to leave?"

"I hadn't thought that far ahead."

"Peter will not come up to scratch."

"For true? And how do you know this?"

"Would he not have asked you already? He's completely on my side in this: you must get Shenstone back, and then perhaps . . . perhaps—"

She threw down her hoop. "Perhaps he's misread my maidenly protestations."

"No. I think your modesty becomes you, and ten thousand a year and Shenstone would add nicely to that package. Of course, *I* don't get ten thousand year—"

"And neither do I at this point, as well you know. And then, of course, there are three dozen heiresses who would snap Peter up at the instant."

"Did he want them. But for some reason, he wants Shenstone and he wants you. I can't understand it. I never thought it would come to that—but it seems as if it's true. You have but to find the way."

She picked the hoop again and drew the needle through the daisy stitch she had started. "What if there *were* a way?" She didn't know she'd intended to say that, but indeed, if she were to commence an even deeper search for the proof, she'd need help, wouldn't she?

And wouldn't her father, and Peter, be the likely ones to aid her?

"What do you mean?" He leaned forward, excitement bubbling in his question. "Have you been holding out on me, my dear girl? There's a *way*? Do you know what this could mean? It could mean—*everything*. Shenstone, and all *that* money at our command. *Elizabeth!* Tell me, quickly—"

"There's nothing certain. It's just something—"

"Nothing—something, what are you talking about? *Tell me!*"

"Frederick, are you talking about money again?" Peter asked lightly as he entered the room on the tail end of that urgent command. "He *never* stops talking about money. It's a very sore subject. It gets rather tiresome, actually. What are you doing, Elizabeth?"

Waiting for you, she wanted to say. She held up her embroidery hoop. "This, and a morning sojourn into Exbury."

"It's time for you to have day in London, my dear. Surely you can go into half-mourning now and go out and about a bit more. We could arrange a little visit with Mrs. Farley. She'll be glad to take you in."

Oh, she didn't like the sound of that. That a *parvenu* like Mrs. Farley would be glad . . . *to take you in* . . . when once she had been a most welcome guest in a dozen homes. She could never show her face in London again on those terms.

"Thank you, Peter," she said instead. "That might be a very nice change."

Never—until she woke up from this nightmare . . .

"And here's Nicholas," Peter said. "What have you been about?"

"I had a most interesting morning," he said, leaning up against the door frame. Three of the five were here together. And that was interesting too. "I went down to the tunnel."

"Whyever would you do that?" Peter asked. "I thought that was taken care of. Over. Done."

"Well, *someone* took care of it within the last day," Nicholas said. "I gave no orders for the storage room to be cleaned. But someone took it upon himself or herself to clear out all the rubble and ash. Any of you know who? Elizabeth? No?"

"What difference does it make?" Peter again. "You'd have had it done anyway."

"Perhaps that's true. But there was still a lot to be examined. And there could have been a clue . . ."

"A clue?" Elizabeth's father scoffed. "To what?"

"To whoever had a reason for setting fire to that room."
That put a damper on everything.

"It was an accident, plain and simple," Elizabeth's father
was still protesting as they sat down to dinner, "and you're
making more of it gives it much more importance than should
be attached to it. Honestly, Nicholas. A little thing like that . . .
what did you expect to find in that storage room anyway?"

"Everything was burned beyond being able to tell what it
was," Peter said. "It's like milking a ram. And one of the servants probably took care of it anyway."

"Victor—would you like to essay an opinion? Evil forces
perhaps, an enemy at the gates?"

"As if there are no such things?" Victor spat. "Pah. There
is no deception here. A fire is made when someone wants to
destroy something. All that smoke and no flame. You,
Nicholas, are quite fortunate that thing was not Shenstone."

"So what was it?" Peter asked belligerently. "What was the
thing that someone wanted destroyed?"

"Evidence," Nicholas said. How odd it was to posit this
over lamb cutlets and potato croquettes. "Of something someone wanted to hide."

There was no getting to sleep early tonight.

"He thinks it's one of us," Elizabeth's father said as they
gathered in the library without Nicholas. "God, I need a
brandy."

"And we were celebrating your canny investment strategies
only yesterday," Peter said. "What a difference a day makes.
Now suddenly, we have mystery in our midst."

"I don't want to talk about it anymore," Elizabeth said.

"It is too nerve-wracking," Mena added. "To think . . . oh,
to think there was a *purpose* to that fire, and that it could well
have spread . . ." She shuddered delicately.

"I think we should all go back to London," Elizabeth's father said. "Enough is enough. This isn't hospitality. This is

like a Yard investigation. Well, I won't have it. Not in my own home. I mean, what used to be my own home." He shot a meaningful look at Elizabeth.

"Good luck finding a home of your own in the season," she muttered.

"We'll all go, agreed?" he went on. "Elizabeth?"

"Father—" she answered in kind.

"*That man* is outside of enough," her father fumed.

"Exactly, and so it will serve him right if we just up and leave him," Elizabeth said.

"It will serve him right if we leave him high and dry," her father retorted. "You especially, still handling all the servants and making sure the house gets cleaned and the meals are served."

"I'm going to bed," Elizabeth said. "This is all a lot of ball-bluster, and I'm tired."

"Fine. We'll all go up together. Who knows what might be lurking in the halls," her father gibed. "Probably Nicholas waiting to scare us all," he added in a low voice, as they went up the stairs in a huddle.

Peter escorted everyone to his room, Elizabeth last. "Don't be afraid—of anything. Not your father, not Nicholas."

"I know," Elizabeth said.

"Everything will be fine."

"Is that a promise?"

"As close as I can come." He brushed her lips. "Everyone is so unsettled tonight. So I'll just say good night."

She backed into her room and closed the door lightly, her fingers still touching her lips where he kissed her.

Everything will be fine . . .

. . . as close as I can come—

She was dreaming, of course. There was music and laughter, and the house was ablaze with light, the sound of footsteps everywhere, thump, thump, thump . . . up and down the steps, running along the hallway, liaisons behind the curtains—th-thump, th-thump, th-thump . . .

. . . everybody happy . . .

. . . th-thump, th-thump, th-thump . . .

Wait a minute, wait . . . *wait for me—*

She was racing down the hallway following a peculiar clinking sound . . . wait a minute—wait!

Smoke? Did she smell smoke?

The house ablaze with light, th-thump, th-thump, th-thump . . .

She bolted upright in her bed, her hands shaking, her heart pounding. She grabbed for her robe, fumbled her arms into the sleeves . . . God, she would never sleep without a light in the room again.

Where *was* that candle?

She struck the match with shaking hands and lifted the candlestick.

Nothing amiss in her room. The connecting door was closed and locked on her side. Then what?

. . . th-thump, th-thump, th-thump . . .

Oh God, it was real. The thumping sound was real, coming closer and closer . . .

She pounded on the connecting door. "Nicholas!" She rattled the key, got it turned, got the door open . . . "Nicholas!" a fierce whisper into the dark, not even knowing if he were there . . .

She jumped as she heard the heavy sounds from beyond the door. Bodies hitting the floor? With shaking hands, she set down the candle and opened her bedroom door.

Dark. It was dark out there in the hallway; someone had doused the lights. Shadows in the dark wrestling, tussling . . . body over body—voices—*stop it stop it stop it!*

The harrowing sound of something falling down the stairs.

Someone—Victor?—with the presence of mind to retrieve his candle. Mena shaking in her doorway. And Peter? Her father?

She wrapped her arms around Mena and the two of them just stood there trembling violently. "What happened? What happened?"

"We don't know," Victor said, holding his candlestick up high to look in their faces. "Just the noise, the sounds. Don't move. Let me turn up the sconces. Just one or two. Just so there is some more light. There . . ."

"Where's Peter? Where's my father?"

"I don't know. Something—somebody—fell down the stairs."

"Oh God, oh God . . . Mena, can you walk with me?" And at the shake of her head, "Victor, you go look."

"I'll be right back." He peered over the banister just as Peter came running down the hallway from the opposite direction.

"Oh my God, Elizabeth! Mena! What happened here?"

"Sounds. A fight. Someone down the steps. Where's my father?"

"I don't know. Let me—let me help Victor."

Victor was already halfway down the stairs. "Oh damn— Peter! It's Nicholas."

"Hell." Peter raced down the steps. "Elizabeth! Ring for Giles. Hurry."

She scuttled into her room with Mena close behind, and yanked on the bell-pull a half-dozen times. Then she settled Mena in a chair, and lit several more candles and the wall lamps.

"I've got to see to my father. You understand." Mena nodded, but Elizabeth wasn't at all sure how much she comprehended. "I'll be back in three minutes, I promise."

Mena nodded again, and Elizabeth slipped out the door before she could be detained still more.

The servants were on the steps already, hoisting Nicholas up the steps in a makeshift stretcher. She went ahead of them, opened his bedroom door, and turned up the gaslights on the wall.

And there was her father, yawning and stretching in the door.

"What's all this?"

"Nicholas—down the steps," she said tersely, as Giles,

Peter, Victor, and two other servants gently placed him on his bed.

"He's not unconscious," Victor said. "Just dazed and injured, we don't know how bad."

"How did that happen?" her father demanded.

"Oh, God—Mena!" Elizabeth turned and flew out of the room.

"Oh, Mena—" Poor Mena, sitting huddled up in a chair, frightened out of her wits, in her room. "Dear Mena—" Elizabeth pulled her up and guided her into Nicholas's room. "You see—Nicholas had an accident. He's going to be fine, isn't he? Victor?"

Victor, who was examining Nicholas's limp body, checking for broken bones and blood. "Nothing seems broken. But I can't tell if there are any internal injuries. You'll send for a doctor?"

"Giles has already done," Peter said.

"Grmmmph . . ."

"He's wakening—" Mena cried. "Thank God, thank God . . ."

They all moved in closer. His face was almost too bruised to look at, his lip split, and blood oozing from his forehead. But when he opened his eyes, his gaze was direct and clear, and pinned them all, one by one.

"Well, by God, you're all here, and somebody in this room wants me dead . . . really bad."

Chapter 13

"You are delusional," Peter snapped. "This is an insult beyond anything permissable—even if you did just fall down a flight of steps. Unforgivable to say such a thing out loud. Elizabeth . . . everyone—let's just leave him alone."

"Besides," Elizabeth said, "we all heard you walking down the hallway. So you must just have missed the top step and gone down."

Nicholas turned his unnerving gaze on her. "You really think so?"

"I think he should be quiet until the doctor comes," Mena put in timidly.

"And I want to go back to bed." Elizabeth's father, stifling a yawn. "A lot of uproar over nothing. A man gets careless and suddenly everyone wants him dead. A fine thing to accuse your guests. Well, maybe if you'd have stayed away, none of this would have happened."

"Oh, there's an interesting thought," Nicholas murmured. "I should have considered the ramifications of coming to Shenstone. Like accidents and murder attempts. Yes, indeed."

"Father—that's *enough*." Elizabeth took his arm and tried to shepherd him out of the room, but Nicholas intervened.

"Hell, no—all of you, stay at the party. Surely you want to know the doctor's prognosis."

"Don't be so cheeky," Elizabeth's father muttered. "It was a damned accident, for God's sake."

"You really need to get back to bed," Elizabeth said to him.

"I'm staying *now*," her father decided. "Damn impertinent bastard . . ."

"Well. Let's get some chairs in here and keep a death watch," Peter said. "Victor?"

There was a bench at the foot of Nicholas's bed, and a chair in the corner by the window. They brought in two other chairs from each of their rooms. Then Mena took the one by the window. Elizabeth settled into the one placed by Nicholas's bed. Her father was given the third upholstered chair, and Peter and Victor sat on the bench.

"Let's ring for refreshments," Nicholas suggested, but his voice was cracked and his tone not quite as impudent as before.

"The doctor should be here soon," Victor said. "And you should just stop all those barbed comments. You had a damned accident."

". . . no accident . . ." Nicholas murmured. ". . . not walking . . ." He drifted off and they all looked at each other.

"Well, *I* didn't hear him," Elizabeth's father said.

"I can't believe that," Peter said. "He was thumping and clumping all up and down the hallway."

"I heard it." Mena.

"And I." Elizabeth.

Victor nodded his head. "But this is curious. This is now the second time so obviously. Nicholas has been here—a week?—and never such noise."

"Well, then, he just never went out and about at night until recently," Elizabeth's father said, and Elizabeth ducked her head. No, he hadn't. And she knew why. But that didn't answer the question of what happened this night.

"He missed the step," Peter said definitively.

"But I heard scuffling," Mena contradicted him, her voice tentative.

"You heard a man trying to save himself from falling down the stairs."

"We're talking about him like he's *dead*," Elizabeth said irritably. "Be assured he is hearing every word."

"... didn't fall ..." Nicholas whispered as a punctuation to her words.

"I think we should keep our theories to ourselves," Peter said. "The doctor will give us a full report."

It was another half hour before he arrived. "This isn't a wake," he said brusquely, and he shunted them all out into the hallway.

"Well, that's that," Elizabeth's father said. "The man is an ox; he'll have some bruises, maybe he broke a rib or two, but he'll survive. *I'm* going back to bed."

"I think I will, too," Mena added.

"My father has gone off the deep end," Elizabeth muttered.

"He's worried about his investments and all that money," Peter said, touching her arm. "And he always needs more, you know that. So ..."

"What a time to talk about *that*. You mean, if Nicholas were incapacitated, then—"

"No. No one means that. We just want him not to have the legal right to the title. But this is hardly the time to continue that conversation. Ah, here is the good doctor."

He was Dr. Pemble, a brisk and no-nonsense man. "Who is in charge here?"

Victor and Peter looked at Elizabeth, who immediately felt like a fraud. "What do I need to know?" she managed, after swallowing what she really wanted to say.

"Rest. Fluids. Just for several days. He took some hard shocks to his body, black and blue in places. No blood loss, except the cuts; a broken rib I bound up. He took a very hard blow to the head on the way down. Reinjured his bad leg too. There is some risk of him slipping into unconsciousness but the fact he's been so awake and aware lessens that probability. No one is to upset him. He's told me he believes this was no accident. Nevertheless, it doesn't seem likely. I've given him some laudanum for the pain. So your job is to keep him on an even keel, and send for me if anything changes."

"There you go," Peter said with some satisfaction as they

watched Giles escort him away. "Even the doctor thinks Nicholas imagined this attack nonsense."

"I think that is enough of that for tonight," Victor said stringently. "I, too, am going to bed."

"Yes, it is time; it's very late." Peter waited until Victor closed his door. "Well, Elizabeth, you are just going to have to see to Nicholas. You and Mena, I mean. And I suppose that really works out for the best—and the not-so-best, come to think of it. He won't be able to help wanting you even more, the more he is in your company. That goes almost without saying. But *you* will have an unprecedented opportunity to . . . be . . . among his things when he hasn't had a chance to take precautions. So take this as a stroke of luck, and use it well. I suppose you'll want to stay with him tonight?"

"I could ask the housekeeper, but that would set the wrong tone, don't you think?" Elizabeth said pungently. "We'll see how he is in the morning."

"Well, he's been dosed, my dear girl. Things will be very quiet for the rest of the night." He kissed her cheek. "Take good care of him. That will be our best revenge."

Two attacks . . . possibly three if you count the night his "ghost" supposedly walked. Or had that been a rehearsal for tonight?

He struggled up from a sea of haziness to try to find something solid to hang on to. He was in his bed; the room was dark but not blacked out—there was a low light set far in a corner where it wouldn't be obtrusive.

He had no sense of any presences in the room, but surely they hadn't left him alone?

Or had they?

Helpless, wounded, alone—so his enemy could knock him up once and for all?

No, wait—a movement in the corner . . .

Worse and worse . . . a woman . . .

Strong presence . . . not Mena—

His most potent adversary of all . . .

He felt himself sliding downward . . . *just what she wanted, take him down, down, down . . . backwash of pleasure . . . down . . .*

No, NO!

He shouted it—NO! He wouldn't give over—not to them, not to his enemy, not to those hands quietly stroking him, not to the voice as seductive as sin . . .

". . . NO! . . ." His only grasp on sanity, his will to deny where his body wanted to go . . . "NO!"

"Shhhh . . ."

"NO!"

He felt himself floating upward, through sheer determination. Felt himself *there*, through sheer force of will . . . *did not fall did not fall—*

. . . heard the thumping steps . . . the chinking of chain—

. . . so obvious, take care of it in a minute—see who among them is so desperate that this child's trick must be played . . .

Lights out! Enemy hovering in the darkness . . .

Jump attack . . . got him down, beating on him, beating on him, crawling away, can't get leverage—

On his feet finally near the steps—and over and away . . .

. . . every instinct gone to hell and dammit . . .

Oh, God—every bone hurt . . .

". . . didn't fall"—the hoarsest of whispers—"didn't damn fall . . ."

And he drifted away again.

The housekeeper, Mrs. Gates, had brought the broth.

Mena was fluttering around the bed, straightening the cover, plumping pillows. And Elizabeth was trying to get him to eat. "Come on now, Nicholas. It's been two days now, and you have to build up your strength. Doctor says everything is healing nicely, except your temper. And I won't let you read the paper which Peter so kindly went and got for you, if you don't take this broth."

"You taste it first."

"You are carrying this whole attack business to the extreme." She lifted the spoon to her mouth, blew on on the broth, and sipped. And waited for a good three or four minutes. "There, I'm not dead. Now, eat."

"I didn't fall."

"Yes, you've said it three dozen times or more and we all believe you. Come on. Take the spoon."

"Hell." He took the spoon because it was the first time in these two days he'd actually felt hungry. And broth tasted good. Too good. And Elizabeth looked too good as well.

. . . his most potent enemy . . .

He ate the broth grudgingly, hungrily. "There. I'm getting up."

"Nicholas! You can't. The doctor said—"

"The doctor doesn't have to worry about . . ." he caught himself. He couldn't afford that kind of talk. It was him against them, and he was damned outnumbered, and with him flat on his back, they could do anything they wanted.

And Elizabeth's father especially was just desperate enough to try *something*.

". . . doesn't have to worry about the running of Shenstone," he amended. "There are things I have to do. Tenants I have to see. I've had a week to acclimate myself, and now it's time to take over."

"Yes. Of course," Elizabeth said faintly. "Time to take over."

"I'll want to look at William's accounts."

"Oh." *Oh! . . . All those papers that were crammed back into the boxes that were still under her bed?* "All right." *And how did she fix it so he couldn't tell she had been snooping in them?* "I'll have Giles bring them to you. Later. Here, in bed. You can go through them while you're resting. I'm fairly sure there will be nothing in them to upset your digestion."

"I'm getting up."

"Well, fine. But you can go over them later, in bed."

"Now."

"I'll have Giles send up your man."

"Thank you."

"Are you sure you're up to it?"

He felt a stirring in his loins and he quashed it ruthlessly.

"Yes, Elizabeth, you can rest assured. I'm up to it."

"So where do we stand?" Elizabeth's father demanded as she entered the dining room an hour later.

"Honestly, Frederick, can't you leave it alone for five minutes?" Peter said disgustedly. "You'll spoil lunch."

"He's coming down for lunch," Elizabeth said. "Just to show he can do it, and that even we notorious five can do nothing to stop him."

"He believes there are enemies now," Victor said.

"Then you believe him?" Peter.

"I believe that we heard someone limping down the hallway, that he is a strong man, that the lights somehow went out, and that we do not know what happened."

"But Nicholas does."

"Perception is everything," Elizabeth's father said. "It's obvious to me, and I'm much more objective than you all can be: I didn't hear a thing. And I woke up to find everyone in the darkened hallway, and a man toppled down a flight of steps. Anyone would make the same deduction: he lost his way, he lost his balance, and he fell down the steps."

Peter bowed, as if he were presenting Frederick to a jury. "There you have it, one reliable witness. We rest our case."

"So an eyewitness's account isn't admissable?" Nicholas asked, his voice laced with pain, as he limped in to join them.

"You are on record as to exactly what you believe," Elizabeth's father said. "We don't want to hear any further account from you."

"Judged and hung by the skin of the evidence," Nicholas murmured.

"Well, you've done the same to us," Elizabeth's father pointed out. "Judged us and hung one awful accusation on the lot of us."

"There isn't a one of you here who wouldn't be happy to see me go."

"Exactly. Go. Go away," Elizabeth's father said virulently. "Let us go back to the way we were before."

"And how was that? With your hands in Elizabeth's pockets? Victor—how much money has she contributed to *your* cause? Madame Mena, living off her generosity. And Peter—but of course, you have everything *you* could want."

"Except Elizabeth," he said stiffly.

"Take her. She no longer has the responsibilities of managing a great estate. Her year of mourning is over. What's to stop you now?"

"Two years is more proper," Peter said. "I could not in good conscience do anything before then."

Nicholas eyed Elizabeth, who was flushed and fuming. "Have the ceremony at Shenstone when you make up your mind. Elizabeth would look lovely coming down that ornate front hallway staircase ... but I digress. And luncheon is served. Gentlemen, ladies."

They had bouillion, a choice of baked fish or chicken croquettes, marinated cucumbers, beans with mayonnaise sauce, and bread pudding.

Elizabeth felt like she was choking on it. She could have murdered him herself, right now.

Giving her to Peter! Backing him into a corner like that! Accusing them all of wanting to do away with him and then inviting them for a meal!

He either had a fever or he *was* deranged, and her father was right: either way, he was too incapacitated to run Shenstone. This was proof; they'd all heard him, and it wanted only for Dr. Pemble to sign his consent to put him away.

Peter shook his head, warning her not to say anything or to carry the discussion further. They all understood what had to be done, he seemed to say. No one in his right mind would have attacked them like that.

Exactly. Exactly.

She still felt a tremor of sympathy as she looked at Nicholas's bruised face. He was not at all recovered. And he

looked pale and grim, and not someone they wanted to do
battle with right now.

This idyll was over, she thought suddenly. It was a moment
she had thought would never come. She had been so sure she
could overset his claim somehow. So sure that Shenstone
would eventually be hers, along with everything that would
accrue from that.

Peter . . .

Maybe he wasn't insane, maybe *they* were, trying to chip
and chop something out of this disaster of a legacy for themselves, and now it was over, and they were the ones who had
to come to terms with the fact that the only thing they could
do was get out of Nicholas's way.

The papers were a mess. She had thrust them back into the
boxes haphazardly in her rush to get through them fast and
thoroughly. The only saving grace was she had not mixed the
contents of the boxes.

Well, Nicholas would have to make do. He had days of re-
covery time ahead of him, as evidenced by the difficulty he
had moving around after lunch. Probably he was running a
fever. He could barely get back up the steps to his room.

And that only with Peter's and Victor's help.

Deadly lunch. The food had tasted like sawdust after
everything Nicholas had said. And she would not excuse it on
account of a fever. The words were too ugly, too hideous.

They should all just leave.

What use was her stupid bargain with him now? The solution was at hand: she would just give her father all that she
had. And then they could all walk away.

She finished packing the papers into the first box, the one
that had everything relevant to estate business. Now at least it
didn't look like someone was rummaging through it in desperation. But nothing was in order either, and that, if Nicholas were even cogent, would arouse some questions.

He probably wouldn't notice.

212 / *Thea Devine*

She went out to the hallway to enter his room rather than bring the box through the connecting door.

He was propped up in bed, and Mena was fluttering around him again while he grumbled and groused.

"How are you feeling?"

"Nasty."

"You're more than nasty, you blackguard: you're black hearted, evil minded, ill-tempered and vile."

"Hell, why? Because I thought it was time Peter asked you to marry him?"

"Damn you." She threw the box down on the bed, to Mena's shock.

"You could have injured him," Mena cried.

"Look—Mena defends me, in spite of the fact I was so *vile*."

"Well, you had to have been delirious, Nicholas. Why else would you have said such vicious things?"

Nicholas shook his head. "I swear, you people live in a world all your own. *Mena*—I meant what I said."

"I think you think you did," Mena said comfortingly, "but you're hot as a boiler, so that can't possibly be true. Did you want a minute with him, Elizabeth dear?"

Elizabeth was gazing at him uncertainly. "I don't think so. I think he's gone over Dartmoor, and I don't even want to be near him."

"Oh, that's a new story," Nicholas muttered.

"Which story are we talking about, Nicholas?"

"This whole new fairy tale about near and far."

"You just *gave* me away to Peter."

"That was the point, wasn't it?"

"Not *my* point."

"Not to bring him to point, Elizabeth?" He suddenly became aware that Mena was listening avidly. "Sometimes you just have to throw it into a man's face."

"I'd like to throw something in yours," Elizabeth ground out. "Now I must wait still another year because of you."

Waiting, waiting, waiting—

And nothing would ever again be as it was . . .

No, no, no—she had buried that promise deep deep away, never to be resurrected again.

Damn it, damn it, damn it . . .

"Damn it, damn you . . . there"—she picked up the box she had thrown on the bed and dumped the contents all over his legs—"there are all the accounts. I don't guarantee what state they are in. I don't even care."

And she stalked out of the room to Mena's gentle tones, mollifying and soothing under Nicholas's outraged roar.

Peter called a meeting, a gathering, he said, for them to try to decide what to do. Given Nicholas's unpredictable frame of mind, of course.

They settled in the library late that afternoon. Giles brought tea and some pudding and cakes. It seemed a little indulgent, but Elizabeth felt very comforted for some reason. Perhaps because, for a moment, it was as if nothing had changed.

"So this is what we're dealing with," Peter finally said. "A stranger, who has no connection to Shenstone whatsoever, coming in and taking the reins. A little fire, an accident in an unusual place. Mysterious footsteps in the hallway. And now this accidental tumble down the steps.

"Small things, with no explanations, I grant you. But still—for that Nicholas has accused us *all* of wanting to kill him. Anyone would consider that a misapprehension at best, or an unforgivable insult at most.

"I think it's the ravings of a man who is coming unhinged, and for the good of Shenstone and for Elizabeth's protection, we ought not yield to the first instinct, which—in my case—is to just leave the man to his illness."

"Hear, hear," Elizabeth's father said.

"Victor?" Peter asked.

"The enemy is at the gates; we must all fight him with every resource at our command."

Peter lifted his brows at that. "Victor's rhetoric always

sounds so meaningful. And then the question becomes what *does* it mean. Mena?"

"The poor dear hardly knows what he's doing or saying. Of course, I'll stay."

"Elizabeth?"

"He can go to hell," she said.

"*Elizabeth*. Well, we outvoted you anyway. And I know you yourself have very good reasons for wanting to stay."

"I'm rethinking them," she retorted grittily.

"Don't," Peter cautioned. "This is the way. What kind of people would we be if we left Nicholas in such dire straits?"

"People who have regained their sanity?" Elizabeth suggested.

"It might turn out that he's not responsible for his actions," her father put in, "and then where would Shenstone be? In some other stranger's hands, I'm sure, and no one will think to come looking for Elizabeth. No. It makes the most sense to stay with him until he recovers and then see where we are."

"Good samaritans for greed," Victor said. "It makes sense to me."

"Good," Peter said. "We all agree—at this point in his illness, Nicholas should not be held responsible for anything he says, and we'll just forget what happened today, and proceed as if he isn't."

So here it was, in his hands, everything his father had been forced to relinquish.

The story was as old as Cain: an aging husband, a handsome younger brother, an ill-used and unloved young wife. Anyone could have seen that the chemistry was inevitable, as well as the explosive end.

Of course, Richard had to go—and Nicholas had often thought his father had started out and just kept moving. It was the only thing that could account for his winding up in Moscow.

And there he stayed, while William played custodian to a family with hundreds of years of roots in England's soil and one exiled son.

Shenstone *should* have come to his father. Had William died sooner, his father would have had the joy and absolution of returning to his native soil.

He'd mourned that loss all his life.

But when Richard died, Nicholas wasn't even there. Nicholas had been on the run, and he hadn't even cared.

Bad memories. Put them away. So much paper to be taken out, taken account of and stored away once more.

And what he found was, William had been a proper steward of his property, everything in order, everything set to his command. There was nothing Nicholas had to do, and so this had been little more than a futile attempt to exercise some control.

Hell.

He hadn't even been able to shock Peter, insult Mena, or jar Elizabeth's father from his complacency.

There was control.

He shoved aside the papers and swung his legs over the side of the bed.

Dizzy. Damn. He could still feel the sensation of toppling end over end down those steps.

Not worth much now, not to himself, to his responsiblities, to his mission, to Elizabeth . . .

Elizabeth—

Shit. He'd pretty much told her she could give herself to Peter.

God. That sanctimonious son of a bitch—dangling after her all these years, giving her hope and then disillusioning her.

Jesus. He just damn wanted Shenstone. They all did.

And Elizabeth wanted . . . ?

Only yesterday—you.

* * *

He had breakfast in bed the next morning, courtesy of Giles. Mena came in to check on him, and pat him reassuringly on the shoulder.

"You seem ever so much better this morning." She touched his forehead. "Ah, the fever has gone down. Now I know you'll be back in your right mind soon."

Who was *Mena?*

Peter poked his head in. "You'll be so happy to know you can't get rid of us all that easily."

"How about not easily?" Nicholas asked grumpily.

And Elizabeth's father: "I hear you're feeling much better this morning. You'll be happy to know we've forgiven you for your lapses yesterday."

"I haven't forgiven you."

Jesus—what was going on here? It was like the Bible society spreading the good word. Hope and forgiveness for all when a murderer lurked among them.

Victor: "Our enemies are all around us, Nicholas. I believe it."

"I'll sleep well tonight knowing that." He felt as surly as a stone.

And where the hell was Elizabeth?

"Doing my duty," she said testily when he finally summoned her, "for both you and my father."

"Oh Jesus God, don't tell me he's after you for more money."

"That's none of your business, Nicholas, what I choose to do with *my* principle. And I've paid through the nines for the rest. You need never think about it again, now you've given me over to Peter."

"Wasn't that what you wanted? Obviously, there are no seeds of forgiveness in you."

"You meant every word you said, Nicholas. I don't forgive *you.*"

So that was that.

And there were moments, as the day went on, that he started to think that he had imagined the whole thing. That his scheme to bait his enemy was the product of a life lived in hiding for far too long. That the connections he had made had no basis in reality. And that every coincidence was just that: an incidental occurrence that happened by chance.

God, he *had* been in bed too long.

Someone *had* tried to murder him.

And he hadn't imagined a thing.

Chapter 14

So now the lines were drawn, with Nicholas on one side, her father and Peter on the other, and Mena, Victor, and herself sraddling the middle.

And they were all going to act as if nothing untoward had happened.

It was an interesting strategy, considering that Nicholas held the upper hand. Why on earth didn't he just banish them all from Shenstone?

One reason, now he was injured, was he needed her.

The bargain was moot at this point; the question was whether it would remain in force now that she had duly learned her lessons, and he had almost forced Peter to set a wedding date.

Dear heaven. She still couldn't get around that. And Peter was acting as if it had never happened. It was like they all wanted to step back in time one or two days, so that everything would be as it was.

Oh, my God . . .

Everything will be as it was—

But she was still waiting . . .

But not today. Today Peter had come for her, expressly come for her so that they could have some time alone.

"*That man* thought he would throw me off the scent by trying to scare a proposal out of me," Peter said. "He thinks he's so clever. Anyone could see he's just aching to get you in his bed, Elizabeth. I mean *anyone* can see."

That startled her, breaking the perfect silence of accord as they walked.

"Oh." *Anyone?*

"Haven't you noticed? How could you help but notice? The man bulges like a bull."

Elizabeth made a sound, and Peter immediately whirled her around to face him. "Oh, I'm so sorry; that was a little crude of me. Perhaps it's a man-to-man thing. But trust me when I tell you that he's cocked to the hilt every time he sees you, every time he interrupts us. If he could fuck you . . . God, it makes my blood boil just to think of it. But of course, he can't fuck you, I'm the man you want, I'm the man you need."

He wrapped her in his arms. "Tell me, Elizabeth. Tell me you want me, tell me you need me."

"I want you, I need you." *This was not the time to ignore his penis; not on the heels of that delcaration.* She slipped one hand between his legs. "*Peter.* You're the only one I notice, ever." *Big lie.* "And you're already there for me."

"Then tell me *when*."

"When we can," she whispered.

"Now?"

"Kiss me, Peter."

He kissed her, long, slow, ravishing, bumping up against her hand as she stroked him in concert with the kiss.

"Elizabeth, you are so lovely, let me take you now . . ."

If he fucks you, he won't want you . . .

"Just keep kissing me . . ." she begged.

"Don't play with me, Elizabeth; we're far enough from the house," he murmured, dropping little kisses all over her mouth between sentences. "I can take you right up against that tree. I can tell you want me. Let me fuck you this morning, darling Elizabeth. It will be so good, and I'll make it quick."

She was so tempted. Everything Nicholas promised had come true: Peter was begging, and she was calling the tune.

But a little modesty probably wouldn't hurt. She couldn't look *too* eager. "What if somebody sees us?"

"Do you care?" He was so hot to burrow into her . . . hard and pushing tight against her.

"But if we have to stay at Shenstone, we shouldn't—"

"I'm tired of excuses, Elizabeth. I want you *now*."

"And I want you—but . . ."

"No *buts* . . . I'm going to root in you now."

He lifted her skirt. "Damned underwear. I thought you'd be naked for me."

"I wasn't thinking this morning, not after what—"

"I think about it all the time," he muttered, "and maybe that's the difference between women and men."

That wasn't strictly true either, but she wasn't about to tell him that while he pawed her skirt and underthings. This was what she had yearned for, Peter, virtually on his knees to her, with no bargains, and no second thoughts to get in the way.

"Peter," she whisperd. He was almost there, almost there— *he won't want you*—could she afford to take the chance . . . ?

And in the distance, suddenly: "Elizabeth! Elizabeth!"

"Oh *hell*. Who the damn hell is that?" Peter removed his hands from her so suddenly she almost fell. "God, if it's Nicholas, I *will* kill him, and you will bear witness."

Elizabeth shaded her eyes.

Close call? Wasn't she relieved? He hadn't taken her; he still wanted her.

"No. Not Nicholas. My father. For God's sake—my *father?*"

"Nicholas sent him," Peter said virulently. "I *know* he did."

"Hello-o . . ." Her father came trotting across the gardens to the lower field. "Eliz-a-beth . . ."

She waved as he came closer.

"I'm so glad to find the two of you alone. We *must* talk."

"There's nothing more to talk about," Peter said. "I think we took exactly the right tack with Nicholas. Ignore him, ignore his accusations, and his attempts to manage our lives, and somehow make *him* go away."

"Exactly," her father agreed. "And that makes it even more imperative that Elizabeth elaborate on what she started to tell me the other day. I hadn't forgotten, my girl. You said there *might* be a way."

She froze. Had she been that imprudent? To even mention to her father, who was like a bulldog when he got his teeth into something, that there was that one little something that might be useful?

Today, she didn't feel like sharing anything, least of all her precious time alone with Peter, and certainly not the one thing that gave her leverage over Nicholas.

"I was mistaken."

Peter pricked up. "Oh? What's this?"

"She said there was a way to get at Nicholas . . ."

"Elizabeth? Come now, you *must* tell."

"I'm not prepared to talk about the possibility right now."

"And why is that?" her father demanded. "I thought we were all working toward this common goal."

"There's nothing to tell." But that was solely based on her conversation with the vicar. How had she gotten derailed from her purpose? The situation had not changed. There were still two people to whom she must speak before she left off this gossamer-thin prospect.

"When, then?" Peter, on her father's side now, pressing her. "When can we know?"

"Father, as usual, blew my comment all out of proportion," she said. "There's nothing to know, nothing to tell. I think we should go back to the house." She took Peter's arm and virtually forced him to start walking.

Better that than her *talking*.

"And for that, he ruined our bang-off?" Peter whispered as they followed her father back toward the gardens.

"This had better be something worth it, Elizabeth. I can't take much more cock-teasing; I can tell you know exactly what you're doing. So no more excuses. No more putting things off."

"Whatever you want, Peter," she whispered, "I want it too."

"Good. Then maybe now you'll come when I command you." He kissed her cheek, even as he was looking beyond her to the front door, and murmured, "And here's Nicholas, waiting at the front steps. Why is this no surprise? Look at his groin, Elizabeth. He's hard as a poker."

"Peter, don't . . ."

"As I am—hard, I mean; both of us, hard for *you*. What a luxury. But your father spoiled things for us this morning, didn't he? I hope you won't spoil them, too. But since Nicholas *is* here, I'll leave you to him. He's obviously waiting here for a purpose. Seize the opportunity, Elizabeth. I'll see you later."

Moodily, she watched him take the front steps two by two, and then she turned to Nicholas. "You should be in bed."

"You should be, too."

"Peter's bed," she said mutinously.

"Is that what he was whispering in your ear? He wants you in his bed, when he couldn't quite get it up enough to lop you off this morning? He *is* a fine figure of a man. But then again, he didn't buy you."

She stiffened. "Nor has he accused me of being a murderer."

"Oh, that. Didn't you hear Mena? I was out of my mind with fever."

"You're out of your mind, period, if you think anyone here wants to harm you."

He held up his hands. "Then I bow to your superior wisdom. I was in shock. It was an accident. Everybody just wishes I would go away."

"Why don't you? There's nothing for you here, really."

"Isn't there? It seems to me I *bought* something."

"You're not going to hold me to that, are you?"

"Why not, with your father spending money like a Black Sea sailor? He'll hit you up soon enough, when he's written down this month's account. And then what, Elizabeth? He can either fly or die. Your choice."

"Blackmail," she said grimly. This was not a conversation to have on the front steps of Shenstone where anyone could eavesdrop. But it didn't seem to matter to him.

"It always was blackmail. Your body for his bank account. Your sexual education for my sexual pleasure. That hasn't changed. But when the time comes, will you show Peter that little trick with the pearls between your legs? Will you show him how you arouse your nipples with the pearl pendant? *That* remains to be seen."

He turned to leave her. "Or that will remain *our* little secret pleasure. You can't deny this, my lady proper. You've gotten exactly what you wanted from this arrangement—one penis to tease and one penis to please. And if I were you, I'd make sure to keep it up."

So that was the message: she was to be held to this ridiculous bargain. It seemed to her that Nicholas had gotten more from it than she, but that was quibbling. The fact remained that while she allowed him to fund her father's bank account, she must allow him to fund *her*.

And she couldn't get righteous about it either; she was a full willing participant. And liking it far too much for her own comfort, given how she felt about Peter.

The tightrope she walked was stretching thinner and thinner.

She *had* to find a way to end this.

"Mena, dear. Had you any thought about where you've seen Nicholas before?"

Mena was curled up in the library, reading, when Elizabeth sat down beside her, gently reminding her about that conversation. "Remember, we talked about his father being a doctor?"

Mena looked up with a regretful expression. "I can't honestly say I've been thinking on it, with everything that's been going on."

"I was so hoping you'd have thought of it."

"Well, you know how that is: someone's face looks familiar and you just can't place it, no matter how hard you try. And you know it's just floating around the edges of your memory . . . How is Nicholas feeling today? I thought I just saw him downstairs."

"That you did. He's walking and talking, just like he always did."

"Dreadful accident," Mena said, picking up her book.

Elizabeth started upstairs, and then changed her mind as it dawned on her how quiet the house was.

Maybe this was the moment to approach Giles.

. . . *take your opportunities* . . .

Peter's good advice.

Giles would be in the pantry.

She had her hand on the doorknob, and she stopped in her tracks. What on earth could she say?

Do you remember when Mr. Richard was still living at Shenstone, and the dreadful scandal of his affair with Lady Dorothy?

No, that was no way to approach it.

She wandered down toward the kitchen.

Perhaps Cook? Elizabeth had already checked the menus for today, but perhaps she could make a change, just for an excuse to go there.

She had to do *something*.

"Ah, my lady." Here came Cook, wiping her floury hands on her apron. "And how is his lordship? And has he been pleased with his meals?"

"Everything is fine. I just wanted to make one change on the menu. I thought carrots tonight instead of green beans again. His lordship seems to be very pleased."

She hesitated a fraction of a second, and dove in. "As I would suppose you have been, having all this many people to cook for. The house hasn't been this full of company for years, in my memory. I assume it was so with Mr. William's first wife?"

"Oh, oh then. Well, we had Mr. Richard living with us then." Cook went back to kneading her dough. "Mr. Richard's friends came and went, you know. There was always some to-do going on every weekend, some party of his friends to cook for. I was sad sorry that he chose to go."

She felt her pulses leap. An opening!

"He *chose* to go?"

"Well, as Mr. William said . . . but that's water up the tower, my lady."

"The circumstances must have been dreadful."

"I don't know it of my own knowledge, my lady. I only know what they was saying, and it wasn't kind. Not for my lady to know."

"But I know," Elizabeth said softly. "Mr. Richard and Lady Dorothy."

"Yes."

"And Mr. William caused him to leave."

"That's how it was."

"And Lady Dorothy?"

"She went away for a bit too."

Her breath caught. *She went away after Richard left? WHY?*

"So sad," she murmured. *A clue?*

"But you, my lady, eventually helped to ease his pain."

"Thank you, Cook. I appreciate knowing that."

"My pleasure, my lady."

It was enough. It was more than she could have hoped for. It was something tangible, and now she had a place to start, and something she could *do*.

Things were coming to a head—he could feel it in the air. It wouldn't take very much to pitch things over the edge.

The screaming tension, the covert resentment, the galloping greed, all of it focused on him—the interloper who had expropriated everything.

To all of that, add their connections to his motherland; the hidden room; the fire to destroy the evidence of a presence; the attempt to choke him. And then, the eerie footsteps, and his subsequent fall down the staircase.

All of that underpinned by his high-handed bargain with Elizabeth, Peter's hostility, and her father's nefarious plans.

And one deluded revolutionary who steeped himself in luxury, and one consummate guest with an inconvenient memory.

Who *were* these people?

They all wanted something. They all had something to lose.

And they all tacitly understood he hadn't banished them from Shenstone because he wanted something too.

What was the link?

Everything was at the boiling point, except *his* scheme to lure his enemy into the open.

It was time to alter that plan. Or had it been an indulgence? To suborn his mission to trap a murderer?

Now there were five.

And his endgame was still the same: protect the mission, claim the title, catch the killer . . .

Unless or until the killer caught him first.

Dorothy . . . why had she not considered Dorothy?

Well, she had, but just as an appendage to William, not as someone in her own right.

Dorothy. A woman with intelligence, ideas, and passion all her own. She must have had some kind of independent streak to have defied William and had an affair with Nicholas's father.

God—to imagine that—a woman under William's thumb that bold, that brave, that foolhardy.

So she must have had some kind of life of her own, even within the strictured walls of Shenstone. She must have had friends; she must have written notes, letters, done her own household accounts, bought clothes.

Where was Dorothy in this house?

In William's room? That had been cleaned and scrubbed to

the floorboards on *her* own marriage to William, and some new furniture appropriated.

Not for Elizabeth, to sleep in the bed of another man's bride, even though William had protested that.

And now who slept there? The man William would have least expected, a man who was possibly his brother's illegitimate son.

Could it have gone that far?

Dorothy left after Richard was, to all intents and purposes, banished from Shenstone.

Elizabeth could just imagine how it had gone with William: he would have been withdrawn, sanctimonious, and unforgiving. He would have made Dorothy's life unbearable, first because she had not given him a child; and then, because she had had the audacity to want another man.

And he had been so much older, and therefore he must have felt that much more exposed.

Maybe he banished her too.

Maybe she hadn't died at Shenstone.

Maybe he'd just put her away somewhere to hide his shame.

And destroyed everything there was of hers in the house. Things she needed to see, to know right now.

Why had she never been curious about Dorothy?

She knew why: her life had been consumed with wanting Peter, missing Peter, and keeping her life with William on some kind of even keel.

So how different was she from Dorothy? She had married an older man, and loved someone else. William probably would have excised her from his life as well if he'd ever found out.

The parallels were spooky.

Only *she* had had a second chance. Which she was *enhancing* with Nicholas's lessons in the stuff of men's fantasies while she singlemindedly tried to find a way to have *him* disinherited.

How crazy was that?

It was jarring. And yet, in the context of Peter's return, and Nicholas's claim, it had somehow seemed sane.

*Sleeping with another man when you want Peter is sane?
No, the bargain was, there would be two men at my feet,
panting after me. And there are, so who am I to complain?*
Dorothy would never have agreed such a mad arrangement.

And possibly, she'd never had that affair with Richard.
Elizabeth had only Cook's word for all of this, after all, and
that had come secondhand to Cook from other sources.

This clue was weightless as air.

So where did one start when one was searching for air?

The answer was simple: where it seemed to have some
weight—in the crowded hot stuffy attic.

Nothing was going as he had planned, nothing, and it
made him edgy and filled with forebodings of disaster.

He needed to think. And he needed to do something to
shock his too-compacent guests out of their shoes; and he
needed to accomplish that with his enemy jabbing, goading,
circling all around him, and hiding in the plain sight.

One bold stroke would do it. Something that would grab
them where it hurt, wring them out, and galvanize his enemy
into action.

His mere presence had not done it. The lure of a fabulous
treasure had not done it. His enemy was content to wait for
the perfect moment, the perfect place, and leave nothing to
chance.

His enemy had all the time in the world.

And he had no time at all.

He was more than a month overdue to deliver the package,
a strategy he had planned to circumvent further bloodshed,
and to keep the package from falling into his enemy's hands.

In this scenario, he had no emissaries, and no one he could
trust. He must complete the mission—or no one else could.

Whom could a man trust, after all? His family? His father?
His mother? His wife?

His . . .

Wife.

Wait—
Wait . . .
. . . wait—
. . . here was the key . . .
He sat back in his chair, awed. In his power, *the key . . .*
The simplicity of it was stunning. It would cause a commotion. It would send them running off in five different directions. It would precipitate chaos. And it would jolt his enemy awake.

And he didn't even have to carry through. All he had to do make an announcement, and *look* as if he were going to take action.

They would do the rest.
Perfect.
That was all he wanted. Some movement. Some confusion. Some power.
And the rest would fall into place as night followed day.

In the far corners of the attic, it almost seemed like the stultifying air lay over everything like dust. There was little light, and too little room to maneuver.

Every piece of furniture from the time of William's forebears had been saved. Every piece of clothing for generations back had been saved. And over and above what hung from the rafters, there were trunks and trunks lined up under the dormers, and traces and tracks of little mice feet.

This was daunting. She had known exactly where William's papers had been stored. But anything relating to Dorothy was another matter altogether.

But still, some logic must apply: her things would be nearer the attic door than farther. In all probability, there were some clothes, some boxes of personal effects, perhaps a desk she had used, a trunk in which she had stored things.

All for this elusive clue . . .
For one long moment, as she surveyed the clutter, Elizabeth thought she must be mad. To be so desperate to unearth some proof of Nicholas's parentage when he had presented proofs

enough for the solicitors to have turned the estate over to him?

What did that say about her?

She shuddered to think. It wasn't greed—it wasn't. She just wanted Shenstone, by herself alone, with no mysterious stranger to share; she wanted *something* for her seven years' servitude to William.

And she wanted everything to be as it had been.

Folly. She would get nothing for her trouble but more trouble.

This was nonsense, this was insane.

Still—*as long as she was here*—

She held up the copper lantern and contemplated where to begin.

The trunk by the door perhaps, the easiest to get in.

On her knees now, having found a little wooden footstool on which to put the lantern, she brushed away the cobwebs, lifting the brass snaps.

And opened yet another Pandora's box.

It was the end of another long day of relaxing, reading, riding, and walking.

There was a card game ongoing in the library, with Victor and Mena now engaged. Peter sat reading in the corner while Elizabeth's father was by the fireplace, half asleep.

"So nice to see my guests enjoying themselves," Nicholas said. "It's truly the mark of a good host when those around him are comfortable enough to fall asleep. Now, Frederick, don't get up. Where's Elizabeth?"

"*We* haven't seen her all afternoon," Peter said. "Haven't you?"

"Actually, no. I've been attending to other things."

They all immediately looked at him suspiciously.

"It would be nice if Elizabeth were here," he said blandly. "Where do you suppose she is?"

"Taking a nap, most likely," Frederick said. "She felt weary when we came in from the field this morning."

"I don't doubt it. There is a lot about running this house that would sap anyone's energy."

"That is just the truth," Frederick said, "and it's about time you recognized it. She's taken it all on, in spite of the fact this is no longer her home."

"Oh, but it is—for as long as she wishes, Frederick. Never doubt my sincerity in that offer. To you as well, for what kind of daughter would she be if she accepted such a living and left you behind? I'm deeply grateful that she has kept things running so smoothly as I make my transition to living here. In fact, it plays on the very thing I wanted to talk to all of you about."

Again, they sent him a mistrustful look.

"I do wish Elizabeth would come," he murmured.

"I'll go find her," Peter volunteered, uncoiling himself from the window seat. "I'll be but a moment."

But that stretched to ten before they returned, with Elizabeth proceeding Peter into the library and settling herself primly in one of the wing chairs by the desk.

"Now. Nicholas. I hear you've expressed your gratitude to me."

"Indeed—how can a man's castle be his own without the attentiveness and management of a woman? I've been thinking about this in light of all you've done since I've arrived, without my even asking. And no, I haven't been properly appreciative of how you've managed everything and how beautifully the house is cared for.

"But I didn't ask you to stay on at Shenstone so that you could be its housekeeper. No, no—you and your father, and your friends, must always be dear and valued guests.

"The point is that even though my tenure here has been of short duration, I can see already what I must next do.

"My friends"—he gazed around at them all benignly—"Shenstone needs a mistress—and I need a wife . . . and I intend to find her and marry her within the month."

Chapter 15

Their shock reverberated like a gunshot.

"You've been here a *week* and you want a *wife?*" Elizabeth's father repeated, stupefied. "Whatever for?"

"My dear Frederick—isn't it obvious?"

"You just *got* here. You hardly know your way around. What on earth do you need a wife for *now?*"

"Frederick—" Nicholas said chidingly, "there are ladies present."

"Oh, for God's sake . . ."

Nicholas shrugged. "Well, apart from *that* consideration"—he looked straight at Elizabeth now, his expression bland—"I need someone to run my house and someone with whom to get an heir. And the sooner I start, the sooner it will happen—"

Frederick jumped up; it was almost as if he couldn't help himself.

"This is mad," he protested vehemently. "You see? Peter? Elizabeth? You see—it's just as I told you: the man is demented, and not capable of making a decision or running things or anything."

"I just made a decision," Nicholas interrupted him. "My dear man, get hold of yourself."

"You can't be held accountable, Nicholas. You took a most injurious blow to the head when you fell. My dear man, you shouldn't even be out of bed, let alone talking about finding a wife. We need Giles—Elizabeth, ring for Giles, and we'll get

Nicholas back to bed and call Dr. Pemble back to see to this head injury that's fuddled his brain."

"Sit *down,* Frederick."

He sat.

"Now," Nicholas said, "none of this impacts you in any way. I'm merely planning throw a house party in the next two weeks or so to meet our neighbors, and see which of the lovely ladies of Exbury are available for my consideration."

"Anyone who might be available is probably up to London by now," Elizabeth said.

"And besides, you can't just up and marry someone in a week," Frederick said.

"I could by special license," Nicholas pointed out gently.

"Oh. That."

"You all look so dismayed. Surely no one really objects?"

"How could we?" Elizabeth said, speaking past the lump in her throat. She didn't know what to make of this announcement, what he was trying to do. And she could scarcely grasp how *she* felt about it—if he were really serious. "You need not even have consulted us."

"To the contrary: you're the only family I have here," Nicholas said, working up a little emotion. "Of course, I would tell you first."

"Well, it's a big mistake, as far as I'm concerned," Frederick interjected. "It's too soon after you've come to make such a decision, and very much too soon after such a serious accident. And *that* is this family member's firm opinion."

"Maybe we should take a vote," Nicholas said consideringly. "One nay is on the board. Peter?"

"I'm hardly family by any stretch of the imagination," Peter said, "but—I'll play the game. I agree wholeheartedly with Frederick. It's too soon for you to make any decisions on that score. So post another *nay.*"

"Interesting. Well—Victor?"

"Take what you want while you still can have it," Victor said.

"That's a *yay,* I think. Mena?"

"I love a nice romance," Mena said mistily.

"Ah, now—two and two. *Very* interesting. Elizabeth?"

"Heiresses don't fall from trees, Nicholas," she said acidly. "You have to work to bring them to heel."

"Hmm, much like expatriate royals, I comprehend," Nicholas murmured.

"And so the question becomes, whom can you enlist to aid and abet you?"

"Trust a woman to bring a practical perspective to a highly romantic proposal. But you came down on neither side of the question, Elizabeth."

"You will do just as you wish, Nicholas, which has been the case since you've arrived."

"You're fudging." He leaned in toward her, forcing her to look at him. She felt positively violent toward him at that moment. She felt like striking him. She wanted to destroy him. It took her several moments to regain some equanimity, and even then, she would have denied him an answer if she could have.

"Who am I to deny you the *pleasure* of getting an heir?" she said finally.

He gave her a crooked smile. "Or to deny me pleasure altogether," he murmured in an undertone. And then, out loud, "I think we can count that as a *yay*. So, my friends, I will go ahead and plan my party, and we'll see what prospects Exbury holds."

> . . . *dearest darling—*
> . . . *are at the end . . . he knows—maybe he always*
> . . . *he'll send you away, I know it, and then I will*
> . . . *die along with all that is precious inside me . . .*

Here was a treasure.

Here was the end result of her frantic search in the attic, rummaging through trunk after trunk of Dorothy's things, most of which were the prosaic possessions of a lifetime—her books, her dresses, shoes, hats, her jewelry—until she discovered what looked like a small chest, pushed well down into the eaves, behind a wall of clothes and furniture.

She found it in a place Dorothy might have hidden it one furtive night many long years ago. She had to literally dig it out from under the eaves, through layers of dust, dirt, webs, and wadding before she saw that it was a train case with its leather trim eaten away.

With shaking hands, she pried open the rusted locks to find letters and photographs crammed to the top.

Dorothy's photographs, Dorothy's handwriting?

She dug into the case and retrieved a letter at random, and leaned toward the lantern to try to decipher the faded handwriting that wrapped around the jagged creases of a letter folded and stored for a decade.

. . . die and all that is precious inside me . . .

Here was a line that could read in two ways—Dorothy could have meant her soul or she could have meant a child.

Or was that reading too much into it altogether?

Nevertheless, for a moment before she carefully closed the lid of the case, Elizabeth felt as if she had trespassed all over Dorothy's private things, and regret washed over her for what she was about to do with them.

Ah, but had they not been intruded upon as well?

Nicholas had declared war, simple and plain, and he had just escalated the battle with his shocking announcement.

A *wife* indeed!

Her every feeling of elation drained away as she sat alone and numb in the library while the others went to dress for lunch.

Except her father came back, edging himself through the door and furtively looking over his shoulder.

"Well, you never know, Elizabeth; wasn't this morning proof of that? Nicholas could be anywhere, eavesdropping on what we say. Although he *said* he would take a tray in his room because he wanted to rest."

Oh, no . . . Elizabeth started, trying to remember if she had concealed the train case. Oh lord, she must have, because she hadn't been five minutes back in the room when Peter had come knocking on the door.

No, she had—she had thrust it under the bed, with the other boxes, though she would not have put it past Nicholas to come searching her room, down to crawling on the floor.

"Listen, Elizabeth—"

"What now?

"What we've been talking about *always*—you *have* to do something. Do you remember you scoffed when I said some-day he's going to bring home a bride? Well, the time has come, and if he does, where will *we* be? There will be no reversion to you if he marries and dies. Elizabeth! Do you even understand how serious this is?"

Did she? When had she not understood the prime motivating force of everything her father wanted her to do?

"Oh yes, it's all about the money."

"Now what kind of father would *I* be if it were *all* about the money? What about your needs, your rights, your well-being? Have you found anything?"

She looked at him, aghast; he couldn't possibly know about the cache of letters in her room. "What do you mean?"

"I mean your stupid *might-be-a-way* possibility to make him go away."

She swallowed yet another lie. "No."

"God, what are we going to do? He needs only to show interest in any woman and he can have her. What then, Elizabeth? You tell me, what then?"

"You give up your speculative investments, Father. And I live within my means."

"Elizabeth, you are not seeing the whole picture. Your means will not attract the kind of money *we* need to pursue our dreams."

"Well, then thank the fates that William wanted a virgin bride."

"And you'll kindly not speak to me like that, Elizabeth.

You sound like a guttersnipe and you want to eliminate *that* sensibility at once. And what good did your marriage do us anyway? You couldn't get a child which would have secured everything, and now this—this . . . foreigner, this undesirable, this *mountebank*—can take it away for once and for all. I've been telling you and telling you—you *must* do something."

"I don't know what I can do," she said.

. . . all that is precious inside me . . .

No, she couldn't tell him about that letter, which in its unfurling of its secret was just as precious to her.

"You'll think of something. You have to, because I swear to you, if Nicholas gives this party and finds a bride, Peter will leave. And I don't think he'll be back."

"You never thought he'd be back."

"Elizabeth, *wake up*. Peter came back because you had Shenstone. If you don't have Shenstone, you have *nothing*. I have nothing. And you most assuredly won't have Peter. There it is, the hard truth, which you never wanted to hear. And all the risks as well."

He threw up his hands and stalked to the door. "It's up to you what you will do."

She felt beaten down by his harangue, more so than usual because of what she had found, what she was not yet prepared to share.

"I just don't understand what you expect," she called after him.

He barely paused on the threshold. "Elizabeth, you're a woman, for God's sake. You *know* what to do."

Photographs, some of them faded, with Dorothy's distinct script on the back, littered Elizabeth's bed.

An hour after the wedding. (She had looked so young and scared.)

My father. (She had had a father too—as underhanded and undermining as Elizabeth's own?)

Our wedding trip. (They'd gone to Scotland.)

William's hunting lodge. (In Hertfordshire, since sold.)

The parlor, newly redocorated. (In the most current mode.)

Me. (A bright young thing in tennis whites and the sweetest smile, about a year before she'd been introduced to William by the date beneath the caption.)

The State Dining Room. (Shenstone's grand dining room set up for a grand dinner.)

Here was a life. Young and energetic, she had swept into William's world, and made him totally unsure.

A tennis party with the Brocktons. (A group photo, Dorothy in the middle and William nowhere to be found.)

William and Mootsie. (A famous face, much revered.)

Hunting in Ireland. (William with shotgun, his pointer at the ready.)

William's new carriage. (A brand new curricle, spiffy as could be.)

A knock at the door. "Eliz-a-beth—" Her father, ever hopeful.

"I'm coming," she called back. "You go on down."

She couldn't move for stones. She piled up the pictures and set them aside to mine the real treasure: Dorothy's letters.

But she didn't find a trove of love letters to Richard: rather, there were pages of a journal recounting the mundane day-to-day minutae of Dorothy's life when she was first married to William; there were notes to William, a young bride trying to give her relationship some warmth and spirit.

Two letters, with no salutation—to Richard? She set them aside to read.

She found notes to and from friends, and invitations, thank-you notes, and lists, and she wondered that Dorothy had saved all of these.

More photographs. Dorothy a year or two later, looking haunted. William, in company, looking grim. Menus beneath that, notes to Cook, recipes cut out of magazines or copied, birth announcements from others of her friends.

And finally, just at the bottom of the case, she found *his* photograph.

Richard.

One sharp telling word scrawled across the back.

She stared at the image and then at his name. *Richard.*

Dashing, the vicar had said. Handsome. Everything William wasn't.

And he was, too, standing with his long strong body at a three-quarters' turn toward the camera, his arms akimbo, devil-may-care in his eyes, and that crooked smile playing over his mouth . . .

Nicholas's mouth . . .

NO! She wasn't going to look for similarities to Nicholas. That *wasn't* the point.

But had William known Dorothy even had a photograph of Richard?

She must have hidden it in this case, and taken it out in rare moments when she was alone, because underneath the picture, there were three more letters.

Elizabeth took those, and the three previous notes, and went to sit by the window.

Reverently, she unfolded the first of the notes without salutation:

> —*the first of a thousand letters I will write that you will never see, my love . . . I wish that whatever he does, he will do it quickly, to spare me the anguish and pain of seeing how he could hurt you. But William was ever like that, as you must know better than I. What is his belongs to him, whether it be his hunter, his house, his bride, and he has taken enough knocks in that quarter to warrant vengeance a hundred times over. You were just the one to get in the way . . .*

And the second:

> . . . *another note you will never see . . . I can hardly bear it. His anger is so intense. He has thrown a thousand sins at my feet. I am a jezebel. Everyone is*

his enemy. His brother wears the mark of Cain. A fitting name for a child of that union, do you not think? . . . since you have destroyed your brother's soul—

Elizabeth's heart started pounding. *A child of that union . . .* Another clue?

She picked up the next note, the first one she had retrieved, and carefully unfolded it.

. . . dearest darling—
. . . we are at the end . . . he knows—maybe he always knew. But now he'll send you away. In my heart, I know he will and then I will die, along with all that is precious inside me. What can we do? What can we do?

And now, with shaking hands, she picked up the first of three letters that were under the photograph.

This first one, from Richard:

My very dear—
Cease your worrying, and let me carry the burden of our eternal love. Our time together is so precious that I will not, from this day forward, let another word about him fall from your beautiful lips. He is but a speck in the cosmic sky of our desire. All will—must!—work out in the end. We are meant to be together. We only have to be patient and we shall soon claim our reward.

And the second, from him as well:

My very dear—
Perhaps you thought me ungrateful and unappreciative of the news you imparted today. Let us say rather that I am head over heels, top over tail,

and ready to reach for the moon. With this, my darling, we can forge ahead, we can make a life, and nothing more needs to be said. Every sign points to our being together sooner than ever.

What news? What news? It sounded like—it *could* be . . . it could be read so many ways—

The last letter, in Dorothy's handwriting:

Truly, my darling, as much as I would want to be able to touch you with my words, you are long gone, so I am writing this solely to "hear" myself say it because it is just so unbelievable: he is sending me away now. Sending me—for rest, recuperation, for my own "good," he said. Just "until," he said. And then everything will be as it was . . . But I tell you, my love, without you, nothing will ever be the same. And somehow, we still have to find the will to go on.

But Dorothy had lost the man, she had lost the battle, and in the end, she lost the war.

Elizabeth put down the letters, her whole body trembling.

. . . *everything will be as it was* . . . She had gone hunting for something abstract, and she'd found herself. Worlds away, and ten years apart, she and the lovelorn Dorothy had led the same life.

It was the most stunning thing.

Two women, forlorn and alone, their husbands and lovers abandoning them both one way or another.

And nothing after was ever the same.

So what could one, in light of that, make of the amorphous references to things unknown, things that could mean something, or nothing; things that, were they interpreted in a court of law, might mean that Nicholas could be dispossessed?

She scanned the letters once again.

*. . . for rest, recuperation, for my own "good," he
said. "Just until," he said . . .*

Until what?

. . . the news you imparted today . . .

What news would send Richard "top over tail"? She knew
what her guess woud be—

But that was pushing the inference way too far. She could
think of at least one other thing that could account for such a
joyful note.

. . . all that is precious inside me . . .

How frustrating that she'd had to couch every specific
thing in language that was as thick and unsubstantial as fog.

Poor star-crossed lovers. She picked up Richard's photograph again. Daring, dashing Richard Massey, trekking across
continents to try to forget the woman he loved.

But—alone? Or with a child? That was the question, and
here in her hands, she could read into those oblique sentences
anything she wanted to, anything she needed to.

Anything that could help oust Nicholas from Shenstone.

She felt a tremor of hope. Her father's outrageous desire to
regain Shenstone suddenly wasn't so inconceivable. And neither was the possibility of a future with Peter.

These letters and notes were the key, to be used to make
her case and win her heart's desire.

Even though they belonged to Nicholas?

Oh damn, this was no time to find a conscience. She had
committed too many sins. And by heaven, she was not going
to waste away for love, like Dorothy.

But what to do with this invaluable cache of Dorothy's
things? The obvious answer was to store it away. Make it
look as if nothing had been touched—return the train case to

the attic then, and keep the three or four relevant letters for herself. And Richard's photograph.

And then, never let any of it out of her sight.

It was almost as if she were standing outside herself, watching herself grow distrustful and suspicious as she tried to determine where to conceal four letters and a photograph where no one would find them.

And what if Nicholas came snooping around her room? Or if there was another fire? Or her father kept making demands?

What hiding place in a bedroom was not obvious?

She suddenly thought of one: under a marble-topped table. But Nicholas already knew that one.

She felt herself going around in circles. Not under the bed, or her covers, in her closet or her clothes. Or under the carpet, behind the curtains, under the chair, in her desk somewhere.

So where to hide four fragile letters and a faded photograph?

There was one possible solution: to hide the evidence on herself.

And even that—between Nicholas's desire and Peter's need—was far too risky to try.

"Elizabeth, where *are* you?'

Drat, her father again. She got the pictures and letters in the train case and under the bed just as he pushed open the door.

"Well, where were you? Nicholas is all full of plans and schemes for meeting this heiress he will marry. It fair made me lose my appetite to think of it."

"A house party will be a nice change," Elizabeth said.

"Only if you somehow effect some change," her father grumbled. "*That man* means to find a wife."

"Then we'll do all we can to help him."

"*Elizabeth*. I will not have you mock me. The situation is serious—no, it is downright disastrous."

And she knew it was; she had only to look at him, his drawn face, his bloody pushing and prodding. He would deny it to his teeth, but what could it be about but the money?

"Well, I'm tired of your hounding me. And you should tell your friend Krasnov there can be no more money, and end this chapter for once and for all."

"You've never understood the complexities of this, my dear. It's not solely Krasnov to whom I am responsible: there are other investors, other futures involved."

"Then you must uninvolve them, finally. Your life cannot depend on whether I can find a way to have Shenstone reverted to me."

"Then make ready my coffin, my dear. If I cannot make good on my commitments, it's a sure death for me."

Now she felt a faint wash of fear. Her father was obviously too deep in the hole with whatever investments he had undertaken, so how far could he be from the bankruptcy?

If he was that desperate, that scared, that much in need of more funding, he was ripe for the moneylenders.

Not that she didn't think he had already considered it. But his being in the country had made it easier for him to ignore everything.

And that one trip to the city had obviously just been a stopgap; he had plugged a hole somewhere and now the scheme had sprung another leak, and there was not enough money in his private account to save it.

So there would never be an end to it. It was a bottomless well, into which he had already dropped countless buckets of money only to pull the bucket up empty.

It was time for him to stop and cut his losses. And stop depending on her. She didn't want to reckon all the money he had thrown down the well. It probably could have kept him nicely in the Funds till his old age.

Useless to think about that on top of all the other pressure he was exerting on her. Her father was a gambler, and his solutions were always the same: pour in money and more money until he made the strike. The words *caution* and *prudence* were not in his vocabulary.

But then again, they weren't in hers either, else why was she plotting and scheming to dispossess Nicholas? She was her father's daughter after all, much as she might protest it.

She wanted her risky investment to come to fruition too.

A flurry of servants raced around, starting the process of getting the house ready for a party within the space of a week. The vicar was called in for his advice on invitations. More cleaning help was hired, and two additional cooks.

"Who would have thought Nicholas's throwing a party would engender so much excitement?" Elizabeth's father said as he, Elizabeth, and Peter gathered on the terrace after lunch. "We're all acting as if we've never been to one."

"Well, we haven't been, in months, since we came back out to Shenstone. Nicholas has only been here—oh, a week and a little, and that alone seems like a lifetime," Elizabeth pointed out. "This will be a nice change."

"*That man* has nothing appropriate to wear," her father said *sotto voce*. "You remember?"

She did: three somber black suits was all, although black must always be acceptable anywhere. But that was not her problem.

"And consider that Nicholas has some fine-tuning to do if he expects to issue invitations at this late date," Peter said. "Who among the agrarian elite is aware of the new Earl of Shenstone? Why, he only just got an invitation from Baxter Grange to hunt come the fall. But in that, I see the vicar's hand. So this will be a most interesting experiment to see how much he knows and whether Exbury will take him to its bosom. It makes me wonder just what he really intends to accomplish."

"You have a most suspicious mind," Elizabeth's father said. "What are you thinking?"

"There will be many setbacks to his immediately finding a wife."

"Well, now I'm reassured," Elizabeth's father muttered. "As if anything was certain about *anything*."

"Frederick, you are the most skeptical person alive. You let Nicholas scare us all half to death with this announcement. But if you think about it, you see that it will take time for him to effect any such plan, especially starting at the beginning as he must do. So nothing is to hand immediately to hinder your plans."

"I have no plans. Elizabeth has rejected every one of my suggestions that she do something."

"So wise," Peter murmured. "Anything your father proposed could only end in calamity."

"So glad you believe that." She believed it too. They must not instigate any kind of scheme against Nicholas. She would save them, and save Shenstone, with Dorothy's letters, and she would have no hesitation about using them if Nicholas formed any kind of liaison.

And until then, *they* didn't have to know a thing about it. Surprise was everything. Knowledge was power.

"So," Peter went on, "here is what you must do."

"*You* have a plan too?"

"It's nothing you haven't heard me say all along, dear girl. But now it becomes rather imperative, with Nicholas's ridiculous notion that he must find a wife."

And there it was again: it was for *her* to do. "And what is it that I can do that you and my father cannot?"

"Why, seduce the man, Elizabeth, and take all he's got."

Chapter 16

Nothing had ever jarred her so much. She stared at Peter, dumbstruck, and then she looked at her father, who just shrugged.

. . . You're a woman, for God's sake. You know what to do . . .

If that was what he meant, then by heaven, she had already done it. And how naive of her not to know it.

And now for sure she was clothing herself in lies and deceit.

"This is rich," she murmured, shaking her head. "This is—unspeakable." Was that self-righteous enough? Indignant enough? How did Peter and her father think they were going to talk her into this? "This isn't about anything but getting your hands on Shenstone," she added irritably. Was that the right note?

"No, Elizabeth," Peter said coolly. "This is about *your* getting Shenstone back. Who would suggest such a thing otherwise? This shocking turn of events—*that man* suddenly looking for a wife—changes everything. And you have to admit, there is no way Frederick or I can compete on that battleground.

"And as much as I believe that it won't happen immediately, we—all three of us—can't take the chance that it won't. We need a plan to combat any incursion by a likely candidate.

"Not that I think there will be many. Every mama worth her salt took her daughter up to London this Season to try to catch the eye of a dozen American millionaires casting about for a wife.

"But that doesn't mean there aren't a half-dozen eligible and comely virgins within twenty-five miles of here who *didn't* go up to Town. He doesn't need to marry an heiress, Elizabeth. He just needs someone to breed."

She clapped her hands over her ears. "I won't listen to another word of this."

"Who can do this but you, Elizabeth? You could turn him topside up if you wanted to. *I* know you could. He wants you. I've seen it, and I've said it to you time and again. We can use that to our advantage. All we want you to do is *distract* him. The longer we keep him from choosing a wife, the more time we'll have to find a way to wrest Shenstone away from him. That's the plan, pure and simple. And frankly, I wouldn't think you'd have to do much more than you're doing right now."

If only he knew what she was doing now . . .

The stuff of men's fantasies—how had she gotten so wrapped up in that little lie?

"I'm to be *nice* to Nicholas," she said dryly.

"If you can. Just to gain time. It's obvious neither you nor your father have come up with any other sensible plan."

He called that sensible?

And now what? She could end this farce right here by producing Dorothy's letters. They would be a better delaying tactic than her offering herself to Nicholas.

But on the other hand, it would serve Peter right if she agreed to his plan. He didn't know what he was asking; he couldn't know what she had already done.

Nor could he possibly think that seducing Nicholas would merely involve some heavy flirtation and some harmless kisses. And he was already ridiculously jealous of Nicholas's never-ending intrusions.

How would he feel watching her pursue him?

More jealousy—and more, wondering what they might be saying, doing, feeling—alone, together.

Was this a bad thing?

Maybe it was a good thing, and maybe it would be the thing that would push Peter to propose.

And meanwhile, it would postpone things. *Things.* Courtship and marriage. She knew all about the postponing of *those* things.

But they'd never find anything like Dorothy's letters no matter how long they delayed Nicholas's search for a wife.

She wanted to tell them, she did, but something held her back.

"Elizabeth." Peter again, now with his hands on her shoulders. Compelling hands. "You are so dear to me. We all want the same thing."

Oh, she was so tired of hearing that.

"So you keep telling me," she murmured. "But no one's really asked me what *I* want."

"*I* know what you want," he whispered, bending over her. "And it's just within your reach. We just have this one little hurdle to overcome, and then you will have everything you want."

"Truly?"

"Truly."

"And with all your feelings about him and his supposed desire for me, you have *no* problem with this plan?"

Peter got down on his knees and took her hands. "But you see, my lovely Elizabeth, the best part is, you don't want *him.* So in the end, we multiply his misery—we deny him his birthright, and *you* will deny him."

And she had thought her father was deep into lies and deception.

The real truth was, *she* was the one who was steeped in sin.

And so once again, he had made himself a target.

The die was cast. And they had all scrambled to toss it back out of the ring. His announcement had turned them all upside down. It was most amusing, and so telling.

His instincts were rarely wrong. They were all a little leery of him since he had accused them of engineering his accident, and there was an air of restraint and caution whenever they were around him.

So a house party was the least likely thing to unleash on them. And the possibility of a wife.

"Such a lovely idea, a little spring house party," the vicar had approved during his visit to discuss invitations. " So generous. Such a nice way to get acquainted with everyone."

That wasn't quite the idea, but Nicholas forbore to mention that. Besides which, his house staff would be attending to all the details—all the details but one: the invitations.

He *needed* Elizabeth.

Well, he needed Elizabeth.

And he needed her not to be walking about in the fields with Peter. Goddamned anything could happen in the fields, and Peter's patience had to be at a slow burn by now. A week was more than enough time to hold a man down. And more than enough to juice him up. And he had to be more than ready for his pound of Elizabeth's flesh—and soon.

And she was probably more than ripe and ready for him. He'd educated her well.

Maybe too well?

So perhaps his reminder that their bargain was still in force had come at a timely moment.

If she wished to comply . . .

It was true—since the accident down the steps, she'd been watchful, guarded, busy. And with his announcement he was looking for a wife—wary.

The tension in the house was as thick as syrup and just as fluid. At any given moment, any one of them could be an ally or an adversary.

And Elizabeth?

Elizabeth—where *was* Elizabeth?

Hell, just where he might have guessed: with Peter and her father, cooking up secrets, concocting schemes.

He limped out onto the terrace where they were seated.

"And so plans go forward," Peter surmised.

"Rolling like a wheel," Nicholas said cheerfully. "The vicar approves, and Elizabeth is far enough out of mourning that she can participate in such an entertainment. It is the ideal thing."

"Finding a wife is an *entertainment?*" Elizabeth's father asked in disbelief. "I cannot believe that you are going about this in such a heedless way, as if a wife were to found on the sideboard with the pickles."

"And yet," Nicholas said, "she very well could be. Well, next to the sideboard, at any rate. Elizabeth, I wonder if you might help with the invitations."

Seduce the man . . .

Now there was an invitation wrapped in pearls.

She ignored her father's gestures, swallowed her irritation, and responded, "If you wish."

"Now, if you have some time?"

Now Peter was sending her meaningful looks.

Her lips thinned. "If you wish."

"In the library then."

She followed him from the terrace and settled herself in one of the wing chairs while he rustled papers on the desk. Out of the corner of her eye she could see her father nodding vigorously and making hand signs.

. . . yes yes . . . go on, go on—

And Peter, motioning with his head—*multiply his misery . . .*

And then they both disappeared.

"Here is the vicar's list," Nicholas was saying, handing over a piece of paper. "Elizabeth?"

She turned. "Oh, yes." She scanned the names. "That many of our neighbors?"

"I didn't expect so many either," Nicholas admitted, "but invite one and you must invite them all. And there are a fair number of eligible ladies among them, though, of course, only one has to do."

"You mean only one has to . . ." She caught herself. This was no place to be vulgar. He was dead serious, or seemed to be and the truth was that once a wife was in place, there was no room for the widow of Shenstone.

Seduce the man . . .

The irony of it.

There was no end to the deceits. She must pretend she had never capitulated to him, and she must overcome her aversion to the fact he thought her capable of violence toward him.

She, who had the most to gain, the most to lose did he find a wife.

So if she seduced him all over again, it would be with the sole intention of gaining time to seek that irrefutable proof, and therefore, lying to him too.

The whole thing was so sticky, she could barely keep her attention on that list of names, except insofar as she could determine which of the local ladies would be available for Nicholas's inspection.

. . . he doesn't need an heiress, he only needs to breed . . .

A too damned promising lot, she thought irritably as she scanned the list. All too young, nubile, and pure.

She sent him a covert glance. And his weasel was all too ready to pop.

"If we could send Patrick around by tomorrow tea, that would be excellent timing for the following Saturday, don't you think?"

Timing? He had a timetable? As if he meant to take care of this matter of a wife as soon as possible and check it off his list of things To Be Done.

And yet, it had barely been more than a week since his arrival.

"As you wish," Elizabeth said, furiously thinking ahead. She had no time at all to effect any kind of plan. This was it. The invitations would go and be accepted by the end of the weekend, and a dance card full of eligible virgins would arrive on his doorstep the following week.

She had just that much time to decide what she wanted to do.

And if she wanted to do it.

"Let us decide exactly what you want the invitation to say."

"Oh merely that I request their presence at an informal

gathering at the manor house to acquaint myself with my new neighbors. There will be dancing, cards, and light supper and libations will be served. How's that?"

"To the point." And he was to the point, planning for it, damn him. "And the time?" she continued.

"Six o'clock?"

"All right. And everything else is taken care of?"

"I have discovered that is why one has servants. And of course, why one needs a wife."

She bit her lip and dove into it. "There is a nice selection of untried ladies among the guests here."

"Do tell?" Nicholas murmured. "You know the ladies? Which of them do *you* think would suit me?"

Me.

She bit her tongue. "I daresay that must be your choice, Nicholas. They each have things about them you can admire, but no one of them will be perfect in every way. But then, who is?"

She bent over the list to make a note. Damn it—there was Selena Thigpen, as sweet and docile a virgin as a man could want. And Ursula Samwick, with her sultry eyes and curvy body.

Yes, they would come. They would all come, just to ogle the new Earl of Shenstone, and try to catch his eye.

The viper.

Seduce him.

She had caught more than his eye . . .

She must *stop thinking like this—*

. . . caught the most naked part of him right in her mouth . . .

She drew in a deep hissing breath. *Must stop that, MUST—*

"Tomorrow tea, you said." Yes, her voice was steady.

Seduce him.

And it wasn't as if she didn't have some recourse at hand.

. . . your hands . . .

"Tomorrow tea."

She still had a week.

* * *

The pearl—ah, the pearl . . .

She held it up to the light, turning the pendant this way and that. The shimmer was positively seductive. The body remembered, too long denied.

Secrets.

She was drowning in secrets. A secret life. Secret letters. Secret schemes.

Secret pleasures.

All she had to do was tuck the pearl in a place where no one could tell.

Secrets.

A pleasure ride on a pearl . . . the most secret thing of all.

And then, with her body convulsing, and reaching for something more, she finally knew what she had to do.

The pearl. She wound the necklace around her neck and attached the pendant. The bargain was in place. The pearl was the talisman, the signal that she needed servicing then and there.

. . . seduce the man . . .

Nothing must stand in the way, not her scruples, his accusations, his plans, her father's schemes. Nothing.

He was still a man, after all, and all this talk of virgins and conjugal bliss had primed him like a pump.

She would test him. She would see how serious he was about bargains and symbols and finding a wife.

She invited Mena to help her finish the invitations, and the two of them settled on the terrace after breakfast to commence the task.

"Isn't this nice?" Mena murmured as she bent over the sheets of vellum on which they were printing the invitations. "Isn't Nicholas generous? But so much work! Have you been watching the staff? Even now, that old gardener—Watton? Look, he's right at work on your roses. And housecleaning involved! Rubbing every last piece of furniture with linseed oil, and lemon juice on the carpets after they've beaten them to a faretheewell. My heaven. And the brass and silver! Well, I'm more than happy to help with the invitations, my dear. I wouldn't want to be polishing the silver."

"Nor should you be, Mena darling. Here, check your list; it should comprise the names of five families in Exbury."

"Exactly so. And this is the guide to what to write? Let me begin then." She angled the sample invitation to one side, and bent over her first page, while Elizabeth studied her own remaining list for a moment.

There were twenty-five names in all, with her having written ten of the invitations yesterday, and with ten more to finish today.

And how precise did the handlettering have to be? she wondered, as she carefully wrote ... *The Earl of Shenstone requests the pleasure of your presence* ... once, twice, three times, and then three times again, before she heard a telltale step on the terrace.

Her breath bunched up inside her chest, the moment was at hand, and she looked up expectantly to find—her father.

"What do *you* want?"

"Busy with the invitations, I see. I don't understand why you want to give any kind of aid to *that man,*" her father said grumpily. "I have an idea—send them all astray, so that when Saturday comes, there won't be a single virgin within ten miles of here."

She wished that herself, but she only said calmly, "And what did you want, Father?"

"Where did you get that pearl necklace? I never saw that before."

She could see him calculating every last pound of the cost. "Not a ha'penny of my jewelry, Father. That is sacrosanct. I told you."

"Don't tempt a person then. That looks like a fairly expensive piece."

Well, I am.

"And if it is? What is that to you?" Now she was being ungracious, but he was wholly unreasonable. Things would take their course—if only he would get out of the way.

"Another solution," he said bluntly. "But then, I think you know what you have to do."

Well, that was a warning if ever she heard one. She bent her head over the vellum so Mena wouldn't see her heat-washed face.

"Frederick is out of sorts this morning," Mena commented, unaware of all the undercurrents between them, as he angrily stamped away.

He certainly had set the stage for seduction, Elizabeth thought irritably. She felt tighter than a cross-stitch sampler, all knotted up and at loose ends.

She touched the pendant, and her body tightened tellingly.
. . . *the body remembered* . . .
Invitation number seven.

The widow of the erstwhile Earl of Shenstone re-
quests that you pleasure her . . .

Lord, she'd actually written that . . . ending the sentence in a big splotch of ink as she realized what she had done. She folded the page and ripped it to shreds.

This business of getting him a wife was getting on her nerves.

Well, she had it in her power to end it all here. All she had to do was give them Dorothy's letters. Show them the revealing phrases.

It wasn't conclusive, but it was something, and surely enough to delay Nicholas's actively seeking a wife.

Why was she hesitating?

She closed her eyes wearily.

Even Nicholas would say: because it wasn't incontrovert-
ible. Because every disputed sentence could be read two ways.

Was that why she was so reluctant?

She bent over the invitations in a frenzy.

Three hours later, they were done, given to Patrick, one of the footmen, to be delivered, and she and Mena were relaxing over a cup of tea.

"Nicholas seems to be recuperating from that fall very well," Mena remarked. "His constitution must be powerfully strong, and his mind seems to be sharp again. He must regret all those things he said in the heat of the accident."

"Do you think so? But you always think well of everyone, even if they don't deserve it."

"Barring that little nastiness after the fall, Nicholas has been nothing but kind to me. Even allowing me—us—to stay on as we will. So generous, Elizabeth. Even you have to credit that."

She shaded her eyes to look out toward the garden. Everything was bursting in bloom on this hotter-than-usual day. Far far away, Watton and his helpers were cutting the grass along the drive. Closer to the house, one of the maids was picking flowers, as was the custom every afternoon, for the drawing and dining rooms. And then she used to come in to arrange the flowers and supervise the table setting for dinner.

Imagine her feeling of nostalgia for the things she had done as William's wife.

But these concerns were not hers anymore. The housekeeper oversaw them now, and soon, they would be the purview of the new mistress of Shenstone.

Elizabeth shuddered. Lord, she had never thought it would come this soon.

She had thought Nicholas would take a good six months to acclimate himself to being the new Earl, and all that entailed.

She had envisioned that she and her father would stay on at Shenstone, oh, perhaps till the end of the year so that she could retrench and he could have time to wind down his scurrilous affairs.

And by that time, she had thought, Nicholas would have tired of the bargain, and perhaps would be ready to find a wife.

That was a much better timetable for his concerns. But oh

no. Apparently he didn't think so at all, and *his* scheme had
knocked her ideas and plans into a cocked hat.

So . . . *seduce the man* . . .

Hadn't she thought she was enjoying that part of the bargain just a little too much?

And then suddenly Peter had handed her *carte blanche?*

Where was he when she needed him anyway? Probably off
with Victor somewhere amusing themselves, and likely Nicholas was resting his *superb constitution* so he could torment
them all at dinner about his search for a bride-to-be.

Was there ever such a tangle?

"Nicholas, generous?" she repeated in response to Mena's
comment. "I suppose I must credit this: that he did not toss a
poor useless widow to the wolves. And for that, I am tolerably
grateful."

Ah, Elizabeth, fair Elizabeth, sitting at his dinner table dangling her pearls. What possibly could Elizabeth want?

And did it matter?

Things had been too quiet. Nothing had happened since his
announcement. His nemesis lay in wait, biding time, giving
him the chance to make the next move.

It had been a genius idea, the perfect ploy.

None of them liked the idea of him finding a mate.

They all hated it. They all reviled it.

And now here came Elizabeth blatantly wearing his pearls.

What did Elizabeth want?

How far would she go to get it?

As far as a bargain to support her father's disastrous finances,
at the least. And now perhaps as far as he would take her.

If he would take her.

What man wouldn't take her?

And since he *had* defined the terms of the bargain, and he
had let her know it was still on the table, she knew exactly what
she was telling him by wearing his pearls.

Fuck me.

He had set the terms; she was daring him to back down.

In her glittering eyes as he caught her glance.

Now.

Deliberate, calculating, purposeful . . . he didn't care.

I need it.

Clothed in black velvet–trimmed navy serge, she was the epitome of the tragic widow . . . and he didn't care.

I want it.

Her eyes said it all, and the glow of his smooth, hard, round pendant pearl.

Service me now.

He threw down his napkin. "Are we done? You gentlemen go ahead with your brandy. Mena, excuse us. Elizabeth, I need you."

Loaded words, but he didn't care.

No words; this was going to be hot, hard, and fast in the first private place available. He thrust open the cellar door under the staircase and pulled her inside.

Clandestine perfection. Dark. Private. Forbidden. People waiting, curious, wondering.

Her skirt up above her hips, naked below.

His penis boring into her, hot, thick, shoving up tight into her cunt.

Not a word, not a sigh; his hips rocketing against her, pushing her up hard against the wall.

"Now," he growled. "Now."

Now . . .

She contracted her muscles and he spurted.

Now . . . he pounded into her . . . *now, now, now, now, now—*

He felt the strength of his body, the give within hers, and his drive to possess her eased.

He covered her mouth in a long probing kiss to prolong it, and he pinned her against the wall.

He felt every inch of his power as he contained her by just the carnal connection between them. He held her there with just his naked might.

He wanted her to prostrate herself to it, to make her beg

for it. To keep her in sexual thrall to it the whole livelong night.

"This is what you want," he whispered against her lips. "This is what you can't live without. This . . ." He thrust into her. "And this." And again.

"Tell me when it's enough," he whispered, driving into her again. "Tell when you've had enough." And again. "Tell me if you *ever* have enough . . ." And again.

Because her body could take every last inch of him and more, and he could live in her cunt, spend a lifetime in her cunt, and still know she could take more.

And now he felt the fury. In darkness, where words took shape and feelings were defined, in the dark, he could not control his gut-wrenching fury to fuck her.

To find the point where enough meant enough.

Maybe that point was never. In the dark, a person couldn't see the beginning or ending of anything.

All one could do was feel—feel the heat, the wet, the hard and soft, the merging and the giving, the relentless thrust and pull of his penis as he drove into her very core.

Enough, enough, enough, enough—like a silent chant, a challenge to her endless capacity to take him and take him endlessly and deep into her cunt.

Now, now, now, now, now—

He spurted, he felt her body twinge. "Enough?"

"Never enough," she breathed.

He knew it, he knew it. There wasn't a woman alive who didn't try to sap a man's penis. And by heaven, he wouldn't cave in now.

"Good. I've got more."

And more, and more. Until they were both lathered with sweat, and determined, each of them, never to give in.

He couldn't get enough of her mouth either, and her soft luscious tongue. He gentled against her for one long moment, pulling and sucking at it.

He heard in the distance Mena's soft little voice. They were looking for them now, and for him, which added a rare edge to their coupling.

‚"Oh, lord, we have to—" she breathed.

"Let them look."

"Someone will think to look here."

"Not until we're done . . . if we're ever done—" He rocked his hips against her. "Are you ready?"

"Yes-s-s-s-s," she gasped.

"Good," he growled, and he pumped himself up high on her, and rammed himself home.

Five minutes later, he came upon Peter, looking frantically for Elizabeth.

"Where the hell were you?" Peter demanded.

"I was up with Elizabeth for a little while," Nicholas said calmly. "I assume *she* is now up in her room. I can't imagine why you couldn't find her," he called after him as Peter took the steps two at a time.

He had found her good and well.

What did Elizabeth want?

The easiest answer: a man between her legs every hour of every day. Lord in heaven, she could take it. And she wanted it. Like a bitch in heat, she wanted it.

He had trained her well.

But for a daily fucking, any man would do. *Peter* would do, though he would never marry her once he'd breached her.

Elizabeth, however, had come after him, well after his accusing her of wanting to kill him. She'd been furious then, reserved and wary since, but she wanted something now.

And she wasn't above using her body to get it.

He wasn't above taking everything she offered.

The balance was shifting.

They were desperate now, sending Elizabeth to do what only a woman could do.

He had given Peter enough time. Elizabeth should have gotten rid of him by now, and she would wait for *him*.

But anticipation was the cornerstone of raw hot sex.

And even though he was rock ready to root between her legs once again, he would let her wait a little longer.

Just a little longer.

And then, slowly, he started up the stairs.

Chapter 17

Waiting for him. Hot for him, panting for him. Breathless with need for his penis poling inside her.

So much so, she could barely contain herself until he slipped into her room to find her waiting, naked, on the bed, her body wrapped in his pearls.

This she hadn't expected after two days' temperance and one hard bang in the dark. Nor that his contempt and her insolence would add such fire to their coupling.

"All I care about is *this*." She slipped off the bed to grasp his penis tightly in both hands.

"And all I care about is jamming it up your cunt any way I can as often as I can."

"Good. We understand each other. That's all I want from you. One hard penis as often as you can get it into me."

"Get over here then and sink yourself onto it, my lady bitch."

He was seated on her chair, naked, the potentate of power, his penis at rigid full staff. She would have to climb over him, and poise on her haunches in order to get the height she needed to take him in.

She could feel the heat radiating from his body as she levered herself onto the chair, bracing her one foot beside his massive thigh, and her opposite arm against his shoulder, and then lifting herself up and over his jutting penis, spreading her legs wide, canting her body, and positioning his penis head right at her cleft.

And then slowly, slowly, slowly, she watched her cunt take his penis as she gyrated her hips and sank her body down.

Breathtaking. Breathless. With her breasts just at the right height for him to suck her nipples. With her hands braced against his shoulders while he fed, and her body rippling all over his root. His hands at her buttocks, caressing her crease.

A half-dozen sensations bombarded her: the heat, the power, and the fill of him in this reverse position; the feel of his tongue and lips lapping and pulling at her nipples; his fingers sliding all over her bottom, exploring her crease; and the unfurling of her own body, in hot undulating waves all around him.

He felt it too; his penis pulsated with an intense throbbing that her body contained. She wouldn't let him move, wouldn't. Wanted him to keep sucking her nipples forever. Feeling her crease.

She bore down on him, wanting him tighter and tighter inside her. Didn't want him to thrust, to drive, to move. Wanted all that force, all that power wholly contained.

By her. Her body. Her cunt lips. Her hole.

He compressed one nipple between his lips. "Let me move."

"No. I like it like this."

He sucked her, hard. "Let me move."

"No. I want your penis right where I have it. Maybe for the next two weeks."

Interesting. He thumbed her other nipple, and her body contracted.

He thrust himself upward. A little room for movement. Interesting. He would have thought he was stuffed as deep into her as he could go.

He pushed her breasts together so that he could lick-lap her nipples one after the other. "Yours are the hardest, pointiest nipples I've ever sucked," he murmured, and took the left one hard into his mouth.

She felt the bolting sensations all the way down between her legs, and she shimmied her body against them. The harder she bore down on him, the harder he sucked her nipples, one after the other, so that the pleasure jolts came roiling down inside her, one after the other, down down down, hot, wet, mesmerizing, two parts of her body liquefying into one molten pleasure point primed to explode.

She had his penis, he had her nipples, she heard his voice, rough, hoarse—"I can't get enough of these nipples"—and he pulled on the left one again, and hot gold skeined through her body and hardened and tightened, and blasted into a thousand glistening shards of pleasure.

All of them caught in the backwash of his shuddering, bone-cracking come.

She wore the pearls all the time, every day. And suddenly the terms of the bargain became even more serious—there weren't that many places in the house they could copulate at the instant.

The cellar steps were the best—quick, accessible, fast. Hot forbidden sex in the dark. Sometimes against the wall, sometimes on the floor, sometimes with her braced against the steps and him penetrating from the rear.

Deep in the night, in her bed, sinking himself into her. In any one of the unoccupied guest rooms, sneaking a half hour when they thought no one was around. In a carriage in the stables, with the stablehands mucking the stalls.

Sometimes, the pearl pendant was missing, and he knew just what she had done with it.

"Well, what do you expect? When a woman has something hard and pleasurable at her disposal, she ought to do something with it."

"*I* have something hard and pleasurable, and I know what to do with it."

"Then I'm the lucky one," she would whisper, sliding her hand between his legs. "I can have both."

God, he had trained her well.

Peter pulled her aside a day later. "I've been watching you two together. By God, Elizabeth, you have him dangling after you."

"Do I? I guess I have." She decided to tweak him a little. "But I don't know how much longer I can keep this up, Peter. Are you any further along in our quest to disinherit him?"

"There isn't a damned iota of anything anywhere around the house. I think I may have to go up to London to check some things out."

"That sounds like a reasonable next step."

"Probably the late train this afternoon and we'll come back tomorrow. Victor's coming with me, so I'm afraid you're stuck with your father and Mena again."

"Mena is no problem. My father . . . well—I wish you would determine if these investments of his have any value on any market anywhere."

"I'll try, my dear Elizabeth. I'm not sure how much information will be given out to a third party, but perhaps I can find something out. Meantime, all you need do is keep him enthralled. Nothing more than that, Elizabeth."

"Oh, *no,*" she murmured, feigning horror at the thought. "It seems very easy to do."

"Well, after all, how many women has he been around recently?"

Yours are the hardest, pointiest nipples I've ever sucked . . .
She made a sound.

He picked it up instantly. "Do you know something, Elizabeth?"

"Only that there must be something somewhere we can find out about him."

"You might work on that as well," Peter pointed out.

"I have. Every time I ask a personal question, he veers off to another topic. And of course, he's consumed with preparations for the party. I am dreading this, you know. All those innocent young things parading around my house—I mean, the house, parading themselves like cows at a county fair."

"Keep him occupied, Elizabeth. Young, lackluster females will bore him to tears after his time with you. Trust me on that."

"I do trust you, Peter, in all things."

"There, my darling." He held her shoulders and brushed her forehead with a kiss. "Now go find him and keep doing whatever you're doing to keep him in thrall."

Yes. In thrall.

But who was in thrall to whom?

Thank heaven, this time, she hadn't been wearing the pearl. How would she have felt, wearing it for another man?

This afternoon, after Peter left, she would insert the pearl.

"Has anyone seen Nicholas?" she asked each house servant she came across as she searched the house for him.

Mena knew. "I think he's up in the ballroom, trying to determine if that's where we should serve the dinner."

She raced up to the ballroom, halting at the door to catch her breath and compose herself. She was playing with fire now, coming to Nicholas like this, in a place someone knew where he was, but she couldn't wait, she was so aroused by the thought of the pearl.

She wanted Nicholas to insert it. And she almost didn't care if Peter caught them.

Nicholas was standing by the farthest window, staring out at a vista that overlooked the driveway and the woods beyond.

She walked toward him slowly, her excitement escalating at the thought of him fingering her as he slipped in the pearl. Her nipples tightened, her body creamed.

And then she saw the hot hard bulge between his legs as he turned toward her, and her knees went weak.

"Well, well, well," he murmured. "Well, well . . ."

She could have his penis now, she knew, in one riveting swoop behind the curtains. But that wouldn't have the erotic impact of the pearl or engender the kind of bone-crackling anticipation at the thought of where she wore it.

She unfastened the necklace as she walked, removed the pearl, and held it out toward him.

"I want this."

"You want the *pearl?*"

"I want you to insert the pearl," she whispered.

"Here? You want the pearl."

"Now. You."

"Take a chair then," he said dispassionately.

There was one nearby and she sank onto it.

"Lift your skirt."

She pulled it up over her breasts to reveal her nakedness.

"Spread your legs."

She parted her legs wide over the sides of the chair.

"Thrust your hips upward—hold it there . . ." His fingers rooted around in her cleft, spreading her labia, feeling for her clit.

And then she felt it, felt him slipping the round hardness of the pearl into her, felt him pressing it up against her clit. Felt him twisting its smoothness into her. Felt her body deftly containing it.

"You are wearing the pearl."

She let him look at her cunt, now enveloping the pearl, and then she deliberately pressed her legs together, let the skirt hem drop, sent him a provocative glance, and rose from the chair.

Oh there, the first twinge of pleasure between her legs.

She moved toward him, reveling in the sensation of that hard ball of pearl inserted so tightly against her clit.

She loved the feel of it, and how hard and fast it aroused her.

"And now, hard as you are for me, you will think about the pearl, and where I'm wearing it, and you'll get harder for me still." She cupped his balls, and ran her hand up the rigid length of his bulging penis appreciatively. "And then perhaps when you're so stiff you can't move, I'll let you fuck me."

"When I'm that stiff, my lady flat back, I won't let you out of bed for the next two days."

"I can't wait," she murmured. "Come and get me when your penis is that stiff and that hot. And remember where I'm wearing your pearl."

She didn't know how she left him there, but she had to. Peter would be leaving soon, would expect that she would see him off to the station.

And now she was wearing the pearl, and she felt no sense of betrayal, only an escalating excitement that he was going and night was coming and she could be alone.

No, not alone—

She had the pleasures of the pearl and Nicholas's humping pumping penis to look forward to.

Seduce the man . . .

How much more rigid could a penis get? It *was* a question for the ages, and one too delicious to contemplate while she was bidding good-bye to Peter.

One of the stableboys drove a carriage around to the front of the house while she and Mena waited with him and Victor.

"Keep him occupied as best you can," Peter whispered in her ear as he took her hands. "We don't have much more time."

Wednesday today, Thursday evening when he would return. Saturday, the house party, and everything in an uproar in between.

Oh, yes. She would keep him very occupied. She squeezed her thighs together.

"He is such an impossible man," she said, her voice low.

Whom was she betraying?

"Don't let your father get into trouble."

"Only when he talks."

"Don't let him talk, he may let something slip."

"You're right. I won't." She contracted her body. *Yes.* Why didn't he just go?

"We're ready to leave then." He joined Victor in the carriage. The driver snapped the whip, the horses leapt forward, and Peter's voice floated back to her: "Until tomorrow."

Many hours to go until tomorrow . . .

She started back into the house with languid undulating steps.

Oh yes.

And many hours still to go today.

The bitch. The complete and utter bitch, demanding he insert the pearl and then leaving him hanging like that. Letting him finger her cunt and then hiding herself away. Leaving him bulging and ready to cream.

Hell.

Walking around wearing the pearl.

Shit. That silky smooth round enfolded in her cunt. Coated with her juices. Slipping and sliding against her clit with every movement to pleasure her.

He would not succumb. Not to the thought, not to the call of his penis, not to the pearl.

He had other things to think about, other things to do.

But—he had given her the pearl. And he had made up the rules.

Damn.

And those nipples . . .

And the pearl—deep in her feminine core, pressing against her pleasure point until *she* couldn't stand it . . .

Hell, she could come get him.

She could come period.

Damned waste of good penis power if wearing the pearl released her orgasm. Just thinking about it made him cream.

Just as she had commanded him.

Damn. He couldn't afford to lose himself in her or over her. He couldn't lose sight of the endgame.

A few more days and something would break.

Him.

If he didn't get to her, if he didn't embed himself in her soon . . .

Oh, bloody damn hell—

He burst through the door connecting their rooms.

And now she loved being naked. Just sitting there in her bed in the middle of the afternoon, wearing the pearl, and her hot pointed nipples, naked.

"I've been waiting," she said insolently. "I need my pearls." She tossed him the necklace. "Dress me."

"For this, you come to me."

She gazed at him steadily for a long moment, and then she

languidly rose from the bed and came across the room, knowing he was very aware of what pleasured her between her legs.

It wasn't his penis.

"Put one foot on my thigh."

She lifted one foot and rubbed the flat of it against his penis, gave him a glimmering glance, and braced it against his thigh, and her hands against his shoulders, as he reached between her legs.

"And now . . ."

She could feel him probing for her hole with his fingers. And then sliding them up into her, at least three.

"And then . . ."

Somehow, he manipulated the string of pearls so that he was pressing them, one at a time, into her cunt. Crowding them into her cunt until she had enveloped more than half of them.

"That's enough. Leave the rest to hang between my legs." She removed her foot from his thigh and sashayed back across the room, turning this way and that, to entice him with her pearls.

When she reached the bed, she climbed in on her hands and knees, giving him an excellent view of her bottom and the eager way her body clasped the pearls.

"*Now* you can come and get me."

"Now I just want to look at you dressed in my pearls." She wriggled her bottom.

"You can wear pearls with anything," she said impudently, keeping her body canted so that her shoulders were down on the bed, and buttocks up.

"They go especially well with a naked cunt, don't you think?"

Shit and hell . . .

How was he going to relinquish this?

But that was a decision he didn't have to make today.

He made a move toward her, reining himself to a rigid tight control.

He would take the pearls, and then he would take her until she begged for mercy.

It was the only way when a woman teased a man's cock like that.

He grabbed hold of the necklace, and he began to pull it slowly, deliciously from her body so that she felt each pearl individually as it popped from her cunt.

He prolonged the pull, as she wriggled and shimmied with each pearl removed, each one hot and moist with her essence.

And when he held them all in his hands, he inhaled each one.

And then he stripped off his clothes as she watched, and climbed on the bed and mounted her.

"You know the pendant is still *there.*" And positioned so the bail dangled away from him.

"Yes." He could barely hold himself back as he rocked against the curve of her buttocks. He grasped her hips tightly and shoved himself even more deeply inside.

"You like the pearl."

"Yes."

"You like the way I wear it."

She was getting him. It was too easy; he was too susceptible to her.

"Yes."

"I love having you insert it between my legs."

"Yes." Gutteral response, barely able to keep from unleashing himself.

"I love how it feels . . ." She shimmied her buttocks against him. "It's so hard, so smooth, so tight . . ."

"Yes." Not even coherent now, jammed so tightly into her hole.

"And I rub myself against it, and . . ."

His body seized—

". . . I lose control . . ."

—and lost control in one long convulsive blast of cream.

* * *

Something had changed. But he had no time to analyze it with all the ongoing preparations for the party. That, and the intensive amount of time he spent between Elizabeth's legs.

That *was* the bargain. And soon again, the estate would be funding her father's account so he could go off and squander it all again.

That was the understanding they did not talk about. That, and the fact that with this house party, he was actively seeking a mistress for Shenstone. And not one as an adjunct to his life.

He was rocking against her in a swamp of hot ejaculate, absolutely drained of every last drop, he thought, when he came to life again.

"Elizabeth . . ."

"Yes?" she murmured dreamily. "Don't move."

But he needed to move. Need to drive into her. Needed that naked hot possession of her in every way. This was becoming obsessive, he thought fuzzily. He could not go a half a day without wanting—no, needing—to fuck her.

Other things were happening. He couldn't spend every hour of the day in Elizabeth's body.

Yes, he could. Hell, he wanted to.

He cupped her breasts and covered one of her nipples with his mouth.

Now she came awake; now she came wanting.

"Don't you love when I suck your nipples." He swirled his tongue around the stiff point. He pulled on it with his lips, and her body jolted upward.

"Ready again, my lady hard nipples?"

She gave him a knowing smile that just set him boiling. He felt himself elongating still more, felt all of his juices flow, and he reared back and took her, fast and hard and low.

"And so where is Elizabeth?" Peter demanded of Elizabeth's father as he and Victor entered the house early the next evening.

"I haven't seen a lick of her," Frederick said. "Mena and I

have been playing endless games of cards these last twenty-four hours, and barring our meals together, Nicholas seems to have been off tending to the party, and I must assume Elizabeth is helping him. We've already had a half-dozen responses."

"Damn and blast. Well, this trip was no help. No damned help. I couldn't get a thing out of that solicitor, Giddons, and I swear to you, Frederick, none of my connections has ever heard anything of the man. Oh, they knew his father and mother, of course. She was a Countess, a great friend of the Empress, and William's brother was a doctor who treated her for an illness which caused them to fall in love. And it is known they had a child. But after that, all traces of Nicholas cease to exist. His mother died not long ago. And that is all anyone knows. Such a waste of time, pursuing that end. Damn it all."

"Then that must be the end of it," Frederick said, ever the fatalist. "What more can we do?"

"I don't know, but I will think of something, I promise you. I will not let *that man* bring a new mistress to Shenstone and displace Elizabeth from her home."

"And Victor—what did Victor accomplish?" Frederick asked curiously.

"Oh, he made a speech; he delivered a pamphlet to his printer; he caroused with friends. What *do* revolutionaries do, after all, except drink and talk?"

"And ferret out and take care of our enemies," Victor put in ominously. "And having done so, I am now in the mood for a party."

"You're in the mood to drink, you mean," Elizabeth said, coming down the stairs. "Peter! You're back. And what's the news?"

"There is no news. And you?"

She shrugged. "It's been very easy to lead him on." She almost choked on that lie. "We have just decided that we will open the drawing room for the assembly. The ballroom is really too large. And a cold collation in the dining room, informal but sit-down."

"Major decisions being made here, I see."

"Two more days, Peter, until his prospects parade before him."

"He won't want any of them, Elizabeth. I promise you, not after being with you."

Being with her . . . what exactly did he mean by that? Could he know she had taken his advice as far as it could go, and long before his carte blanche to seduce the man?

Did she reek of the scent of betrayal?

"Well, let me tell you, we are going to strip the garden tomorrow and festoon the room with flowers. Fair warning to poor Watton, who has spent years cultivating them. And we have pulled out every last piece of lace and linen we could find, and a set of dinnerware for a hundred that not even I was aware William had, and all in all, we are turning the house upside down for this party."

"And I hear the responses are coming in."

"A half-dozen already and Nicholas is certain everyone will accept."

"All the ladies."

"Especially all the ladies," Elizabeth said. "And we are to have a string quartet, and perhaps some dancing after. Nicholas means to start out well with his neighbors, which was something William never cared about."

"Well, they may come to like him well enough, but he will soon be out," Peter said confidently.

She looked at him doubtfully. *Tell him now.*

She took a breath, and swallowed the words. It wasn't the right time, the right place. Perhaps after the party, after all the butterflies had fluttered their wings in Nicholas's direction, and he wasn't attracted to anyone.

Maybe then. *Maybe.*

"This seems like so much wind over water by now," she said uncertainly.

"That remains to be seen, sweet Elizabeth. The game is not over yet."

By no means, she thought. The game had hardly begun.

* * *

And now the menu was set. To begin: oysters on ice and smoked salmon; the meats: roast beef, ham, and pork *en croute*; and in chafing dishes, the accompanying sauces and vegetables; and potato croquettes; baked tomatoes; olives and pickles; a choice of salads: lettuce, cucumber, or fruit; a selection of pies and tarts; cheeses; fresh fruit; coffee; tea; chocolate. Wines and other libations.

"Enough to feed an army," Frederick grumbled.

"And an army is in the kitchen right now, roasting those meats," Mena said. "I just went down to check how things are going. It's going to be a lovely party, isn't it?" She looked around at all the glum faces. "Well, isn't it?"

Sweet ingenuous Mena, Elizabeth thought, as they carried an armful of newly washed and pressed linens into the drawing room to dress a table here, the piano, which had been taken from storage, there. Move the chairs all to the side. Have the servants remove any seating that couldn't be set against the wall. Take away the breakables on the tables and replace them with something lovely made of brass or pewter. Make sure the carpet was well scrubbed, and every speck of dust was gone.

Because in this room, Nicholas might well find a wife.

Elizabeth almost couldn't stand the thought.

A prospect, she amended. A candidate. Any word that was not so unforgiving as *wife*.

Why on earth had Mena never been able to remember how she knew him? It was almost too late now. No, it wasn't too late, because *she* had the letters, and the minute a butterfly landed on his shoulder, she would flick it off.

What? What was this? Was she jealous?

No no no. She wanted her home back, her life. That was all she had ever wanted. And the wherewithal to keep her feckless father in funds.

All right now. No use thinking about that. That wasn't going to change, or it wouldn't until she made a decision about the letters.

So she must focus on what was to come.

Tomorrow morning the housekeeper would bring in the flowers. In the afternoon, they would lay out all the plates and cutlery in the grand dining room and cover it with cloth.

Early evening, Nicholas would decant the wine to let it breathe, and they all would go upstairs to change.

At five o'clock, the musicians would arrive. Five-thirty, the servants would begin setting out the food.

She should be downstairs to supervise all that.

No, the housekeeper . . .

Oh God—it was all coming to fast, too near.

"Mena, darling, are you certain you can't remember where it was you ever saw Nicholas outside of this house?"

"I feel like such a fool," Mena whispered. "I can't remember."

Or won't?

Now where did that insidious little thought come from? Because Mena had made such a definitive statement that first night upon seeing Nicholas, and then subsequently denied remembering anything about him at all?

Was she looking for enemies around every corner too?

Mena?

She'd known Mena for years, the perennial little guest, expatriate Russian noblewoman with no family and nowhere to go, and a story just romantic enough to gain her sympathetic patrons who issued enough long-term invitations to keep her housed and fed.

Mena. A friend of the fiery Victor, who both derided the aristocracy and had adopted it. Who espoused revolution and lived luxuriously on the fringes of the society he wanted to pull down.

Who were these people really?

And Peter. Peter with his checkered life, his many loves, his ongoing pull and tug with his royal family now in power. How hard it must be for him to be the uncle of the autocrat of all Russias and be subject to his will and whim.

Peter had never been good with authority. Peter had been

too good, staying with her, fighting her fight to retain her right to Shenstone.

It was almost over. She would either use the letters or not. And even then, they proved nothing. It was one small thing to hold over Nicholas's head, as amorphous as the reference to the rumor about his legitimacy that had kept her at Shenstone, and brought her this far.

She couldn't begin to imagine what tomorrow would bring. Probably the end of everything.

Chapter 18

He came at her this time from the foot of the bed, grasping her legs and easing them up over his shoulders.

The room was dark, deep in shadow. All she could feel was her shuddering excitement for whatever he would do.

He lifted her higher, so that only her shoulders touched the bed, and all of her nakedness was splayed out before him. He pulled her closer still until he could touch her labia with his tongue. And closer still so that he could furrow deep within.

Closer and closer he came with his expert tongue lapping at her, tasting her, sipping the essence of her, burrowing out her pearl, flipping it from her secret center, and replacing it with his tongue.

Now *this* . . . this was ecstasy—his hot roweling tongue just plowing into her, and licking and sucking at her clit.

He wouldn't stop, he wouldn't stop. She dug her fingers into his hair, into his shoulders. She undulated her hips, seeking his tongue. Tighter, she wanted it tighter; she couldn't get him hard enough within.

More . . . more . . . and more . . . She pushed down on his tongue. *Eat me. Suck me . . . give me more*— Her body seized and stiffened, and skyrocketed high and hard into a long spangling slide down to completion.

Slowly, he eased her churning body down, and cupped her against him as she shuddered in a backwash of sensation that eddied all over her body in soft waves of pleasure.

So much pleasure. Such an intense response.

Only when she was wholly coherent, and wholly there, did he claim her, sliding himself softly into her hot and pliant core.

This was the last time.

He was a man after a wife, and he couldn't in good conscience keep fucking her when he was on the hunt.

So this was the last time.

He enfolded her against his body for the last time.

She moved against him, seeking him, knowing in her heart, it was the last time. After this night, after the butterflies, there would be no more time with him, no more incandescent pleasure.

Lord, how would she live without it?

The house party was tonight, and she waited with bated breath until he left her. He left her early, thinking it was kinder that she was still alseep.

She shivered, and it wasn't because she was cold. Already she could hear the bustling of the servants outside her door.

It was so early in the morning, and she was so cold and alone.

Something had changed.

And when she finally brought herself to look, the pearls were gone.

Men were different. It was quite obvious. And she, who had thought she had remained so detached, suddenly found herself too much involved.

It was the thought of the butterflies. Their innocence. Their purity. Their ability to breed.

Oh damn Peter for putting that idea into her head.

. . . they don't have to be heiresses . . .

No, they only needed to be the sweet virginal daughters of any one of a hundred country squires. As long as they could breed.

She felt a fury she had never known. Why had Nicholas done this when they were going along perfectly fine?

But then, what did anyone know about Nicholas or his life or his motives for anything?

She knew one thing, and one thing only, and it was now time to get on with it. Tacitly, without saying it, Nicholas had given her over to Peter, and in that she had absolutely no say.

Men were so different. He had probably just put the whole episode with her aside in some pocket of his mind. To him it was a sidebar, an amusement, something to keep the Earl of Shenstone entertained while he entrenched himself and decided when he would look for a wife.

Oh damn damn damn—Nicholas in bed with another woman, doing all those incredible things . . .

"Well, here we all are," Elizabeth's father said cheerfully as they met at the breakfast table.

"And where is Nicholas?" Peter wondered. "He's never where you expect him to be."

"He wanted to make sure there was light enough along the drive," Mena said. "I believe he's going to station some of the servants along the way."

"Ever the thoughtful host," Peter said, helping himself to herring fillets. "Well, tonight will tell the tale."

"And what tale is that?" Victor asked caustically.

"The story of a man who comes out of nowhere, claims a great estate, and like a fairy tale prince, seeks a wife among the common folk of his village to secure his inheritance. It brings a tear to the eye, does it not?"

"But," Elizabeth's father said, "everything has been legitimized. Nothing has been found to his detriment. There's nothing more we can do."

One thing more . . . Elizabeth thought. *But not yet, not yet.*

"We could kill him," Peter said. "Just get him out of the way."

"You jest," Victor protested.

There was a long pause and then Peter said, "I jest. I'm solely concerned about Elizabeth and what will happen to her when Nicholas finds and takes a wife."

"Look," she said brusquely, needing to foreshorten this rehash of all their protestations, "what will happen will happen.

You had the right of it, Peter. This taking-of-a-wife thing is not a one-day affair. He will not throw us out. He will give us ample notice and time to make other arrangements. And when that happens, we will go."

"But still," Peter said obliquely, "certain plans are still in effect."

"As much they can be, today," she said, edging around the truth that Nicholas was done with her.

"Good. Then it's not over."

No, it was only beginning. All the preparations started full bore right after breakfast.

Every piece of furniture was inspected and dusted again. The carpets were swept by sweepers who followed the servants as they worked around the house.

In the drawing room, the dais was set up for the musicians, the furniture placed against the wall, with small tables scattered here and there for those would sit and have a conversation.

Everything was at the ready by midday, the point at which masses of flowers were cut and brought into the house.

Elizabeth supervised the arrangement at Nicholas's request. Bowls of cut flowers on the dining room table, accentuating the golden table garniture, and the elegant ivory table cover. Tall vases on the sideboard, and scattered around the drawing room.

A large arrangement in the entry hall.

And then nosegays in the swag of the curtains, beside each table setting, in the sconces on the walls, anywhere she could find a place to tuck a small handful of flowers so that their sweet melting fragrance permeated each room.

It was now four o'clock and the servants began toting hot water up to the bedrooms to give everyone time for a long luxurious bath.

Outside, the various groundskeepers were cutting and sweeping up all around the driveway.

At five o'clock, the china, which had been thoroughly washed by place setting was brought out onto the grand dining room sideboard; the cutlery, arranged by implement, side by side; the napkins, folded and banded with ornate golden napkin rings; and candles were placed everywhere around the public rooms.

Soon, Elizabeth thought, soon, I'll know what to do.

But she didn't know what to do when she found the connecting door between the bedrooms was locked, an emphatic statement of Nicholas's renunciation.

She felt as if she had turned to stone.

Automatically, she dressed in a dove gray dinner gown made of crape and trimmed with velvet banding accented with dull jet beading at the sleeves, neck, and hem.

It was more than enough for her, for this night. There wasn't much she could do with her hair: she pulled it into a loose topknot, and pinned it with a black comb.

She looked every inch the weary widow, she thought, surveying herself in the mirror. And in no way ready to receive guests at a party.

And certainly not ready to deal with Nicholas.

But the thing must be done.

At ten minutes of six, she started down the stairway. At five of six, the servants lit the candles and then set out the food.

At six, everyone was downstairs in the entry hall, including Nicholas, looking so tall, so strong, so powerful in the muted light of the chandelier, Elizabeth didn't know how she was going to stand it.

How had she thought she could agree to a liaison with him and not be affected?

Peter turned and gave her his hand, his reassuring smile.

This was the man she wanted, the man she loved.

Was it?

She stepped down beside him.

"So glad to see you out of black," he whispered.

"We all look so elegant," Mena said, brushing a speck of dirt from her black lace gown.

At six fifteen, they heard the sound of a carriage rumbling up the drive.

The footman announced the Paxton-Whitbys, who swept haughtily into the entrance hall, and so the party began.

There were fifty to seventy-five personages crowded into the drawing room. Under the muted conversation of the assembly room, the string quartet played. Wait staff walked among the guests offering champagne and wine.

The butterflies flitted around: sweet innocent Selena Thigpen, Ursula Samwick with her greedy knowing eyes. Phoebe Paxton-Whitby, weedy and horse-faced. Elinor Raynesford, elegant and serene.

And with them, a half-dozen others, who would never stand out in a crowd. They were negligible. Ursula Samwick was not.

There was a girl who had had some experience of men. She knew just what to do with her eyes, just how to move her body to attract attention.

Even Peter wasn't immune, but Elizabeth didn't want to know that, didn't want to see it.

She moved through the crowd, accepting belated condolences and warm greetings. Introducing Nicholas here and there. Spending some time with Vicar Bristowe and his wife. Taking a glass of wine. Introducing herself to those she'd not previously met.

Out of the corner of her eye, she could see her father, discoursing vigorously with several gentlemen. This was not a good sign. Frederick was always on the prowl for another rich investor, always trying to weasel some money from somewhere.

"Father dear—" She hooked her arm into his. "I need to speak with you."

"E-*liz*-abeth . . ." he protested as she led him off. "You just interrupted a possible deal. Prime prospects, our neighbors. I never thought—"

"And you may kill that thought. You will not swindle the neighbors."

Frederick squared his shoulders. "I am offering them a good solid investment prospect."

"Solid on sand. Just this once, Father, keep you fingers in your pockets, and let us just enjoy the party."

"But there's money to be made."

"I'm going to lock you up, I swear."

"How now? Is Frederick misbehaving again?" Peter, coming up to them with Ursula on his arm. "Where's Nicholas? I'm doing my duty and effecting an introduction. Ursula, this is Elizabeth Massey and her father. Elizabeth, Frederick: Ursula Samwick."

"So pleased," she murmured in plummy tones. "And now, please, Peter—"

Peter bowed and left them alone.

"Well!" Frederick said.

"One glimpse, one introduction to Nicholas, and she will sink her hooks in as far as she can get them," Elizabeth said moodily.

"Well, there you see. Maybe he'll want her at first sight. And then what?"

Elizabeth hadn't thought it was possible. She had been living on that thin skein of hope that Peter had promulgated: that it would take time for Nicholas to find someone to wed. Time to establish a relationship. Time to clear obstacles that would surely come his way.

And now there was Ursula. Sensual curvaceous Ursula with her dark glittery eyes.

Ursula would entice him. And he would want her, instantly, completely, fully. He would marry her.

The thought made her sick. Enough so that she turned in the opposite direction from where she knew Nicholas to be. She couldn't bear to watch the meeting, the attraction, the flash of sexual awareness.

And she ran right into Peter.

"This is worse than we ever could have imagined," he told her. "She took one look at him and flared up like tinder. No pallid innocent, she."

"I don't want to know. This was the worst idea."

"Don't flag now, Elizabeth. You're one of the most beautiful women here. So elegant and tragic. Just keep moving, speak to whomever you can and find out about this hummingbird. We have to nip this in the bud."

"All right."

Not all right. With this and her father . . . and everything that had happened in between? She was fit for nothing but a sanitorium for the chronically insane.

The sounding of a gong signified that dinner was served. Nicholas led the way, with Ursula on his arm, and the butterflies swarmed around them, followed by the other guests. Elizabeth and her father brought up the rear.

"Damned greedy gargoyles," her father grumbled. "Look at them—as if they'd never had a meal in their lives."

"Get your plate, Father. You're as hungry as the rest of them. More so, come to that."

"You just never stop making references to my failures. What kind of daughter are you?"

This wasn't the time to pursue that. She left him to take her plate, take a morsel of roast and a bit of potatoes, and join Peter at the table.

She was perfect. He couldn't have invented anyone more perfect than Ursula of the hot and heavy eyes, hanging on his arm, and on his every word.

Ursula looked like just the kind of woman a man desperate for an heir would fall for. She looked like a woman on the prowl for all she could get.

God, if he'd had to try to convince anyone a man could want horsy Phoebe Paxton-Whitby, or that insignificant Selena Thigpen . . .

But fate had handed him Ursula, exactly the kind of woman he needed to convince them that he was serious about his plan.

He couldn't bear to look at Elizabeth's stricken face. This part must be done, and in the most believable way.

He turned all his attention to the shameless Ursula, tucking her hand firmly into the crook of his arm as they made their way to adjoining places at the table.

He smiled when she said something amusing. He leaned into her as she whispered in his ear. He kept his hand on her arm as they talked. He let servants bring their food.

The whole night long, she flittered and fluttered to his side, fodder for the gossips who watched, and the enemy who bided his time.

They were talking about her already as the guests finished dessert and made their way in small groups back into the drawing room.

The glorious Persian rug was now pulled back from the floor. A musician was sitting at the piano, and the violins and cello were at the ready so that when the first guests appeared, they entered the room to the strains of a lively popular tune which quickly transmogrified into a stately waltz.

Nicholas held out his arms. Ursula came into them willingly, eagerly, and he swung her into the dance.

Don't look at Elizabeth—don't . . .

One more day perhaps, no more than one more week and the thing would be over. Finally, irrevocably over, and his enemy vanquished once and for all.

Don't even glance at Elizabeth, or her tired beautiful face reflecting the strain of it all.

Don't . . .

He smiled at Ursula, who hardly needed even that much encouragement to move closer in his arms.

Dear, perfect Ursula.

And anyway, Elizabeth couldn't yet dance.

No, Elizabeth danced—on his tongue and with his body. No one moved in his arms like Elizabeth.

Soon—soon . . .

He swung Ursula around the room into the crowd of dancers at the party that was such a success.

But he also must dance with Selena and Phoebe and Elinor too. Ladies, all of them, who would never throw themselves around the room the way Ursula did.

That done, he moved through the crowd, speaking with the vicar, with the Baxters who had so kindly invited him to hunt. An appreciative word to Mena doing all she could to be helpful. A warning to Frederick whose deceits and schemes were getting out of hand.

Victor, sitting morosely out in the hall, well on his way to becoming drunk. Peter, ever vigilant by Elizabeth's side.

"It's a grand party," Peter had to admit. "And a good idea. Everyone to whom you extended an invitation came. You are to be congratulated on your ability to pull such a response from strangers."

"Yes," Elizabeth said acidly. "Nicholas is very good at pulling responses from strangers."

"Now, now," he chided. "Tell me what you think of Ursula."

"A sorceress," Peter said.

"A witch," Elizabeth put in.

"Perfect," Nicholas said, and off he went.

"God almighty, he's smitten," Peter muttered. "Now what the hell are we going to do?"

"Kill him," Elizabeth's father interjected, coming up behind them. "Heavens, haven't we talked about this enough?"

"We are not going to take such drastic measures," Peter said, injecting a little sanity into the situation. "For God's sake, all he did was dance with her. He hasn't asked her to marry him."

"Not yet," Frederick said. "There has got to be a way to forestall him. He has paid her too much marked attention for this thing to go away. Elizabeth, what are you doing to help the cause?"

Dying.

"I've done everything I can."

Except Dorothy's letters. Dorothy's sad, vague letters. Not yet, not yet . . .

"Well, the contingency plan didn't seem to work either," Peter said disgustedly. "He won't think twice about Elizabeth now that Ursula's got her hands on him."

"And how far did you get with that anyway?" Frederick demanded of her. "Obviously not far enough."

She stared at them. "Do you two hear yourselves? You're pretending that this is all about *my* rights, my well-being? Peter . . . ?"

"We were just trying to help, Elizabeth."

And she had fallen for every one of their traps and schemes just to stay ahead of their demands and stay in Nicholas's bed.

How easy it was to find someone to take her place.

She watched Nicholas passing hands with Ursula in a quadrille at the far side of the drawing room.

He had found her, his possible probable mate, and that was all she needed to see.

She wasn't going to stay until the guests might leave.

But there were some who were milling in the hallway already, calling for their carriages, and making it an early night.

Nicholas came to speed them on their way, ushering them out to their carriages which were parked at the bottom of the steps.

Three families, comprising three or four guests each, waiting to leave, with all good wishes for Nicholas and his success at Shenstone. Twelve or so people moving slowly down the steps, still talking, still expressing their appreciation for the lovely party.

Conversing with each other, making plans to meet on the morrow in church, and plans for the upcoming week. Jostling each other a little.

Laughing. Shaking hands. A push, no, a misstep, was it? Suddenly, irrevocably, Nicholas went tumbling down.

Down the steps, down, nothing to grasp, nowhere to hide. Four guests racing down the steps after him, grabbing him, stopping his slide.

"Dear heaven . . ."

"Is he all right?"

"Is he hurt?"

A gabble of voices came at him, from a haze of pain.

"Get Dr. Pemble," someone called, and the doctor came running.

"My God, Nicholas . . ."

"Yes." Nicholas was barely able to speak.

"Don't talk then. Get the servants. Everyone on his way home, the best you can do is go now. Anyone else, I need your help."

"Jesus, Nicholas." Victor, hovering above him.

"Enemies," Nicholas whispered.

"Yes, I know."

And then Victor was pushed aside, so they could take Nicholas in.

They put him on the couch in the morning room, and all the guests were told to leave.

And then it was just the doctor, Elizabeth, Ursula, and Victor.

"Someone pushed," Nicholas told them in a constricted voice as Ursula fell to her knees by his side and grasped his hand.

"Who?" Victor demanded.

"Too many people."

"Get this girl out of the way," Dr. Pemble said irritably. "This man is in pain. This is serious, Nicholas. You could have reinjured everything."

"Not head," he whispered. "Not . . ."

"Oh God, oh Nicholas, not when I've just found you," Ursula moaned.

"Shhh! Elizabeth—take her *out* of here."

Elizabeth girded herself, and touched Ursula's shoulders, took her arm, helped her to her feet, and across the hall to the library.

"Oh my God," Ursula cried, sinking into a wing chair, "is he going to die? He can't die, Elizabeth. He's so wonderful. And I didn't even know he was here."

"Well, you know now," Elizabeth said dryly. "So dry your tears. He'll be fine. I'm sure he'll be fine."

"Elizabeth?"

"Victor. Could you stay with Miss Ursula while she composes herself?"

He looked at her strained expression. "Whatever you need, Elizabeth. Who could have done such a thing?"

"He had to have lost his footing," Peter said, coming into the room. "There were a dozen people crowded up on those steps. The wonder is, more of his guests didn't fall."

"Peter!" Ursula cried.

"I'll take care of you," he promised. "I think I should see her home."

"I won't go until I know Nicholas is all right."

"Then we'll wait. Elizabeth?"

She nodded. "I'm going back to see what the doctor has determined." She couldn't wait to get out of that room, with those two men fawning over the melodramatic Ursula.

God, Ursula.

"Doctor?" She closed the door behind her. "What do you think?"

"He took another damned hard fall is what I think. What's going on here, Elizabeth?"

"I don't know. It has to be another accident."

"He says someone pushed him. His ribs are badly bruised, he twisted his bad leg again, and his back is banged up. Bed and more bed. And laudanum and not much more. I bandaged his chest. And I know he's going to be up and about in another day or so."

"Oh, you know . . . ?" Nicholas echoed in a wheezing voice.

"Just stay in bed for a few days, my man. It was a nice gathering, Nicholas, but these accidents have to stop."

"Right."

"Can he walk?"

"Just about. In about an hour, I'd try to get him upstairs."

"We'll manage."

"Good. You know where I'll be."

She saw him out and then she turned to Nicholas. God, she hated seeing him like that, his features twisted in pain.

"Nicholas?"

"Is Ursula still here?"

"She's still here; I'll get her." But her vitals twisted in pain. Ursula was so young, so fresh, so marriageable. She couldn't bear to go in with her.

She left Ursula at the door.

Nicholas spent the night on the couch in the morning room, waiting for his enemy's next strike.

His enemy was here, and his enemy was now desperate.

Did he marry, everything would change.

Who among them needed to prevent that change?

Elizabeth, Elizabeth, Elizabeth.

Damn it.

Elizabeth.

Anyone else was subsidiary to the cause. It was all about Elizabeth.

He rubbed his hand over his eyes. *Elizabeth.*

He had no choice but to proceed with his plan.

"Who could have predicted this complication?" Elizabeth's father said the next morning at breakfast. It was just the two of them, and Giles had made sure that Nicholas was brought a tray concurrently.

But he didn't want to see any of them.

"What, his accident or Ursula?" Elizabeth asked mordantly.

"Both, neither, *her.* She is to visit this morning, according to Giles. And when Nicholas is well enough, he intends to go courting her. It is a mess beyond redemption."

"And how do you know all this?"

"I make it my business," Frederick said loftily. "I'm the only one concerned with the larger ramifications."

"He was *that* taken," Elizabeth murmured. "And he will move quickly once he is well enough. The accident, however, troubles me."

"Don't make it more than it was, Elizabeth. There were too many people crowded together on one step. Pure and simple.

And now, of course, he has everyone's sympathy, and Ursula praying for him, and somehow, he has turned this tragedy into something completely else."

Then it was only a matter of time. The neighbors had accepted him, and welcomed him now.

There was hardly anything she could do to compete with all that.

Except—Dorothy's letters . . .

Not yet, not yet—

She took Nicholas his tea and found him sitting up, and strong and focused.

"Would you mind—?" He handed her a note.

"You've been busy. I thought you were supposed to rest."

"How can I rest?" he murmured in a tone that made her glance at the envelope.

Deliver to Ursula.

Her hands froze.

Not yet, not yet . . .

Ursula came to visit that afternoon. She swept up the steps and into Shenstone as if she already owned it. She looked Elizabeth up and down as if no one could ever own *her.*

"Where is Nicholas?" she demanded, handing Giles her wrap.

"Still in the morning room," Elizabeth said stiffly, "but able to receive guests. You remember the way?"

"I remember *everything,*" Ursula said and swooped down the hallway to the morning room.

She was so sharp, you could cut yourself on her, Elizabeth thought, so secure and certain in her entitlement to anything she wanted.

Even Nicholas.

And if Nicholas really wanted Ursula, she just didn't know what she would do.

Dorothy's letters . . .

Not yet, not yet.

"Elizabeth . . ."

"What now, Father?"

"I had the most incredible idea."

"I sincerely doubt it. You've not had one good idea yet."

"But this . . . *that girl* is with him, isn't she? She's begun her campaign."

She nodded. "But it's nothing more than he wants."

Her father brushed off her statement. "Nicholas doesn't know what he wants. He only knows he wants an heir."

"That's good, Father. He only bludgeoned us with *that* revelation."

"And he needs—what for that?"

"A wife, for God's sake."

"Elizabeth, Elizabeth—think for a moment. He needs an heir, he wants a wife—he needs a woman—any woman, and my darling girl, here is the genius part—*any woman* could be *you.*"

Chapter 19

Her.

In her wildest fantasies, she had never ever considered that. Her.

She stared at her father.

"My dear girl, everyone knows that it was William's failing that there was no heir. There's nothing to say you couldn't produce one. Nor anything to prevent you from marrying Nicholas. It is the utmost solution, so elegant and pure, and to top it all off, we get *everything* we want!"

She bumped right back down to earth. "What? You're suggesting *I* marry Nicholas so *you* can get everything you want?"

"Elizabeth—look at it this way. If you were his wife, did anything happen to him, the estate would revert to you. And this time, we would tie up every loose end nice and tight so this could never happen to you again."

"Oh, I see. This whole scheme is to revert the estate. You *are* planning to kill him, just as you always said."

"No need. No need. Everything becomes yours again. It's incredible. I don't know why I didn't think of it sooner."

"Because you're insane," Elizabeth snapped. "And it's out of the realm of possibility."

"Is it?" her father asked slyly. "Or did you take Peter's suggestion further than he meant for you to go?"

She clenched her fists, and said calmly, "I have no idea what you mean—as usual."

"You know what I mean, Elizabeth. You're a grown woman, he's a virile man. That's all I will say, except that—you have the advantage. A dolly-pot like Miss Ursula is no match for you. Think about it, my dear. The best scientist in the world couldn't devise a more perfect solution."

She thought about it.

Marry him.

What about Peter? What about her years of longing for Peter, and the way he had just stepped back into her life? What about all this time he had invested in her, and how he had stood by her?

What about that?

What about everything *she* had invested in him, and in her faith that someday they would be together?

What about secrets and lies and things left unsaid?

No, her father had pretty well said all the things that Peter probably wouldn't. He had stayed with her because of Shenstone, and he'd never marry her without her getting it back.

He'd never said a word about it in all the time he'd been here. Instead, he'd sent his emissary, her father. His intermediary. A royal, as peripheral as he was, wouldn't marry a commoner without *some* value added to the whole.

Her father had said so, flat out, blunt as a rock. Without Shenstone, there would no offer. He could marry an heiress off the block. He could have any woman he wanted, as Nicholas had taken great pains to point out; what need did he have of an *English rose?*

Why then had Peter come back?

For one thing, to disappear. And for the other, resurrection. And fool that she was, she had offered absolution.

And now she would be the one repenting in sackcloth and ashes.

How seductive it had been, to offer herself up for a cause. His cause, him, anything he wanted, because it was Peter, it was eight years later, and William was dead.

And Peter hadn't forgotten her.

That was the whole of it. Her fragile hope, his flagrant need, and this gossamer link—he hadn't forgotten her.

And now this. The unexpected heir wanted a wife, and she

could be *it*. Like the child's game: round the garden he goes, and anyone around his house could be *it*.

Just the fact he'd made such a deliberate announcement so soon after he'd arrived was proof enough he had in mind some kind of plan.

But then, Nicholas knew as well as anyone that the implications of his getting an heir would be stunning. For herself, for her father, for Peter, it would be the end of the road, with no hope ever of reclaiming Shenstone through her.

Even she couldn't quite grasp the magnitude of that.

Gone forever, Shenstone.

And all their puny efforts to discredit Nicholas were just so much tilting at the Thames.

Except for Dorothy's letters.

But how? How?

God, her father was crazy.

. . . *another woman could be* you . . .

Oh no. She had been far too easy for Nicholas. Too easy to gull, too easy to lead astray, and way too easy to please.

What man would take such a strumpet as his wife?

A man who had no choice . . . ?

But Nicholas had a choice; he'd had a half-dozen choices and more last night, and had come up aces with Ursula Samwick, candidate for wife.

Stop it.

Her father's suggestion was so far over the wall, it was suicidal.

You couldn't coerce a man to marry you, at any rate.

Well, yes—you could.

. . . *blackmail* . . .

Her heart started pounding.

Nicholas had done it, why couldn't she?

With Dorothy's letters.

Now. Now.

Nicholas remained in the morning room, rather than retreating to his bed, and maybe that was a message too. There, on the first floor, he could receive visitors, as many as he wanted or cared to see.

Ursula, daily, ever vigilant, who read to him and played cards and cribbage. The butterflies who came and flittered around him, patting his pillow, stroking his hair.

And Elizabeth and Mena, who changed the sheets, plumped the pillows, brought him his broth and tea.

Peter was getting edgy. "Has he said anything?"

"Anything about—?"

"His intentions, if any, toward Ursula. Hell, I think he's enjoying the attention. What man wouldn't?"

"Fall down a flight of steps then, Peter, and some sweet young thing will come and succor you."

"He always does seem to land on his feet. And meanwhile, who oversees the day-to-day work at Shenstone, I ask you? Elizabeth, you cannot be so kind when in the end, he'll disown you."

"We must solely focus on his regaining his health," she said primly.

"While you ruin yours."

She thought of a way he could mitigate that. He could carry her off to the Côte d'Azure. But that kind of extravagance had never been Peter's province, at least so far as it had concerned her.

Any other woman—all those years?

Any woman could be you . . .

Why hadn't it been her?

Why was it her?

Or maybe it had nothing to do with her at all.

"And," Peter added virulently, "give him all the time in the world to pursue that brazen piece of bedbait."

"Peter!"

"Well, dammit, you're spoiling him, letting him lie about that like. And taking care of business as well."

She looked into his restless eyes and saw the truth. *And it was nothing to do with her at all.*

* * *

Even Nicholas couldn't stand the enforced inactivity, and besides that, Ursula was getting on his nerves.

Late that afternoon, he attempted to get off his makeshift bed. How could a man implement his plans if he couldn't even get out of bed?

It was dicey at best, his balance weighed against his pain, and in the end, all he could do was sink back into bed again.

"Ursula is here to see you," Elizabeth sang out, something else that was getting on his nerves.

It couldn't be that she wanted to encourage this, he thought. And God knew, as perfect for his purposes as the blatant, bland, and obvious Ursula was, he really was tempted to end the farce.

But not yet. There was still one more scene to be played out.

He invited them all to have dinner with him in the morning room.

"Well, on this unfortunate accident I can't repine, because it brought to my bedside the amazing Ursula," he said at one point when they were deep into their suet dumplings and medallions of beef.

Elizabeth's father choked.

"Was there ever *such* a woman?" Nicholas went on. "She will be the perfect mistress for Shenstone. Raised right here in Exbury, you know. Schooled abroad. I *knew* I was on the right track when I thought to look for a wife right here at home."

"Oh, indeed," Frederick agreed, shooting Elizabeth a meaningful look, "*right* here at home."

"I'm glad you all approve," Nicholas said. "I think I may approach her on the matter sooner than later."

There was a stone dead silence around the table that Giles had pushed up to Nicholas's makeshift bed.

"Oh? You still all think it's too soon? Well, after these several days at the mercy of her tender minstrations, I am confident that Ursula is the one for me."

"And so she may be," Peter said, "but surely after two days in the sickroom, no one could tell."

"Have some pie," Nicholas invited. "Pie solves everything."

But even Cook's excellent pie and the most enthusiastic endorsement of Ursula's many fine qualities could not sway them.

It was far too soon. She was way too young.

Or worse than that, no one believed he was serious about Ursula. Or maybe it was even too soon for that, and he had overplayed his hand.

No matter. The important thing was, his enemy had attacked again, provoked solely because of his expressed desire to find a wife.

He was as certain of it as he was his name.

If he were injured, or died, the estate would revert. And the person who had the most to gain was Elizabeth.

God almighty, Elizabeth. Again.

Bed was good for one thing. No, two. When a man was incapacitated, he had a lot of time to think.

And to think calmly, without being in the heat of battle. To make connections he would not have otherwise seen.

And it came to him very very slowly that things were not exactly as they seemed. Things of which he had taken passing note, but never really thought about. Every circumstance, odd as it was. The whole history of his past three weeks here.

He had made himself a target, and his enemy had taken aim. Soft, subtle things. The murder of the priest. His coming to Shenstone.

The fire. The presence. The attack in the cellar. The ghostly footsteps. The fall. The second fall.

Incidents as light as air. Which of them had weight and meaning?

And why was it that he, an emissary of the empress of all the Russias, found himself among a hotbed of Russian expatriates?

What was the connection?

Elizabeth?

They'd all rallied around Elizabeth. Elizabeth, who had her own secrets, who told her own lies.

Silky soft luscious sweet Elizabeth. She would kill him as soon as cure him to gain possession of Shenstone.

Who needed it, wanted it more than she?

Her father? That feckless gambler?

Peter? He had no purpose, none, except insofar as Shenstone would be Elizabeth's dowry if she ever married him.

But he would never marry Elizabeth.

He still couldn't quite grasp it. There was something more here. His enemy was willing to sit and wait him out for a fortune in Imperial jewels.

That he expected; that he understood.

But someone living in that burned-out cellar room? Someone stalking *him*, patiently, coolly, with all the time in the world?

Victor?

Mena?

Who needed the money the jewels could represent?

All of them, every one.

Back to square one.

He'd stayed too long at the fair. He'd been so intent on smoking out his enemy, he'd gotten lost in the forest.

This was the thing that struck him all at once: suddenly it didn't matter. And that he'd played out this hand for far too long.

He could go to London now and complete his mission. They wouldn't be looking for him after all this time, and no one would recognize him anyway.

And the rest didn't matter. He'd go to London—soon, and then he would keep on going. He would give over Shenstone to Elizabeth.

And the rest would fall into place.

*   *   *

"You've been thinking about what I said."

"Indeed I have, Father. It's so ludicrous, it makes me laugh whenever I think of it."

"And I want to cry every time I remember last night's dinner and Nicholas's vow to commence his courting of the bold-faced Ursula."

"I see. And you think I can just walk up, tap him on the shoulder, and say, *Excuse me, but I want to marry you*"?

"That's a pretty fair representation of what I was thinking."

"You were ever a dreamer, Father."

"And you are too much the pragmatist."

But she wasn't; she was wholly and solely a product of all of her dreams, every one of which had dissipated into thin air.

What was one more dream to be trampled on?

"What happened to all your and Peter's plans?"

"Poof—gone. It rested on one thing—one of us finding something to dispute Nicholas's claim. So now, all that is left, all that stands between him and marrying Ursula, my dear girl, is *you*—if you want Shenstone enough. If you are even bold enough to act on such a shameless plan."

"But there's one thing missing here, Father—Peter. If I married Nicholas, there would nothing for Peter."

"You know—that's true," her father said. "And it doesn't bother me in the least."

And there it was, her father at his most outrageous, and out for the main chance, whichever way he could come by it. One way or another, he would hook her back up to Shenstone and he would reap the benefits, just as he always had done.

He was the one who always landed on his feet, she thought, and all problems and complications rolled off his back like water off duck feathers.

Witness the fact he was hiding in the country these past three weeks to avoid whatever unpleasantness awaited him in London.

And if he could promote a liaison that would accrue to his

advantage during that time, so much the better. He could go back to his partners and make still more promises.

And then hold out his hand and, as always, make *her* pay.

"Why did no one tell me Nicholas was out and about today?" Ursula demanded as she stormed out of the morning room and into the library. "I am here every day at this time, and no one met me at the door to apprise me of his whereabouts. Where is he, Elizabeth? We were to have finished reading our book."

"I believe he went out for a ride, actually."

"Oh, the poor dear man, he'll rattle his bones." She darted out of the library and out the front door, heading toward the stables.

"Is she gone?" Nicholas eased out from behind the door. "Like a whirlwind."

"I don't think I could have taken another day of Dickens."

"And yet imagine how it will be if you court her," Elizabeth pointed out. "Countless literary works that you will explore together. It does my heart good to even think on it."

"She has many excellent merits," Nicholas said. "And yet, I'm thinking perhaps she is a little more forward than I would like."

"Than *you* would like?" Elizabeth echoed, clamping down on her urge to either laugh or cry. If that indeed was among the merits he sought, *she* would fail abysmally. But then, she wasn't *really* thinking of offering herself, was she? "Are you looking for a nun, perhaps?"

"Maybe I'm just still looking," he said evasively.

"You're *looking* that much better," she surmised.

"I can walk on my own. That's all I need. And an end to Ursula's enthusiastic sick room manner."

"You must tell her then. She thinks you're on the verge of proposing."

"Damn and hell." There went all the finesse of his plans and schemes. "Now what the hell do I do?"

The words lingered in the air, soaking up all her breathing space. It was the time, the moment, if only she could get a breath to force out *her* words.

"Propose to someone else." Oh, dear lord, she actually said them. Or whispered them, or gasped them. She didn't even know, she was so petrified that she had even uttered them.

He whirled on her. "Propose to whom?"

And now, now the sticking point. Could she do it?

Another woman could be you . . .

She took a deep hard breath and expelled the word. "Me."

He went very still. *Damn it all to hell.*

"You?" he said finally, furiously. "Why the hell you?"

Worse than she could ever have imagined.

"Why not?" she answered past the clog in her throat. "It solves your problems, and it solves mine. You get your wife; you get your heir . . ."

"And I get your father too," he interjected nastily. *Damn, damn, damn.* Why had she done this? *Damn it all to hell.* This was the last thing he wanted right now, and the thing he wanted most in the world. And for that, he had to knock her down and cut her out. "No, Elizabeth. No."

Just . . . *damn it all* . . . *no.*

"I thought you'd say that," she murmured. "I thought you'd say I'm old and very well used, is what I thought you'd say. So I thought you'd like to see these."

She tossed some papers across the desk, and he picked them up curiously. "What's this? Jesus—my father?"

"Your father. And copies of some letters he wrote and that were written for him, if not to him. I have the originals. But I think you can see, even with reading them quickly, that there are some questionable references to consider. Things that might be interpreted in one of several ways, were other minds brought to bear on those phrases."

He went very still again. "Yes? Meaning what?"

"I'll pursue it. In court. Whether any of that meant that your mother was really William's wife."

"I told you she wasn't."

"No—Dorothy's words told me she could be. Could be interpreted that way, at any rate, and maybe that makes it the same thing."

He closed his eys. "God."

"No. Blackmail."

"Oh, yes—that." He could have walked away from everything. Was planning to. And now she'd forced him to stay, and that complicated things in a whole new way. "All right, Elizabeth. We'll do it your way."

She hadn't expected such a quick capitulation. Now what? Make a committment; do it fast. "Tonight then," she said, not even knowing if it could be done.

"Tonight?" He sounded a little dazed.

"The vicar will perform the ceremony tonight." But she didn't know that yet; that was taking a huge leap from actually forcing the issue to accomplishing it. But to all intents and purposes, the thing was done.

And everything else could be arranged.

"You were awfully sure of yourself."

She was sure of nothing, not even what she had just put in motion, but she said coolly, "By special license—I believe you yourself mentioned that possibility," as she folded up her copies of Dorothy's letters.

"Did I? How farsighted of me. And then what?"

"I believe he serves sherry and tea cakes in the rectory."

"Elizabeth."

"If you mean, will this *family* attend us, my answer is no. I don't want any of them to know."

And she knew why too, because suddenly she understood why she never could tell her father about the letters.

It was because the whole thing would then be about her. Not about him, not about his problems and finances and wants and whims. No, using the letters to get what she wanted was solely about her, and that was why she had kept them to herself.

And why she wanted none of them there.

The idea of Nicholas's taking a wife had scared them badly.

And now it would be *her*. Never had any of them thought it could possibly be *her*, or what that might mean to all of them.

Especially Peter. And not even her father.

But more than that, *she* hadn't even considered what it might mean to her.

It wasn't easy sneaking out of the house to go to a wedding. For one thing, she couldn't wear a fancy dress. And for another, her father was continually nipping at her heels.

So how she had gotten it all together in the space of eight hours, she would never know, except that it involved sending the servants, on the sly, back and forth to the vicarage with notes and instructions of how she wanted everything to be, and to make sure that somehow the vicar could procure the rings.

Sometime after seven o'clock she managed to make the excuse that Nicholas must go to bed, and the two of them limped down the servant's staircase and out the back door.

There, a gig was waiting, all prearranged, and within ten minutes, they had cleared the grounds of Shenstone, and within twenty, were at the church door.

Vicar Bristowe was there to welcome them. "My children."

He helped Nicholas, obviously still in pain, from the gig. "Come."

He led them into the parish house, where his wife awaited.

"Oh dear, Nicholas doesn't look quite the thing."

"Are the papers prepared?" Elizabeth asked, brushing the vicar's concerns away.

"Yes, of course. Come, sit down. We'll have some tea. You'll sign here and here and here. Here now, Nicholas. It's the same for you. Ah, here's the tea."

His wife set a tray before Nicholas, and the vicar poured. "There, that should make you feel better. Let me see. Now after the ceremony, we'll witness it all, right and proper. Do you feel well enough to stand? Do you want to go into the church?"

"No. This room will do nicely," Nicholas said, looking

around at the whitewashed walls, the ancient timbering, and the vicar's comfortable furniture. "This will be fine."

"Then stand together if you will," the vicar said, and they stood before him, Nicholas dressed in his usual severe black, and Elizabeth in a velvet trimmed black dress that she might wear for walking, and he began the marriage ceremony.

Elizabeth grasped Nicholas's hand as the vicar asked them to repeat the hallowed words after him: "I take you, Nicholas . . ." She slipped his ring on his finger with those words.

"I take you, Elizabeth . . ." He did the same.

". . . till death us do part . . ."

". . . till . . . death us do part."

"And now I pronounce you . . ."

And Mrs. Vicar Bristowe said, "You may kiss the bride."

Nicholas took her shoulders and looked deeply into her shadowed eyes.

Elizabeth again.

This time getting exactly what she wanted by exerting the same gentle blackmail that he had deflected before.

He brushed her lips gently. Her lovely lying lips.

And then the papers were signed, with the vicar's wife to witness, their names entered into the registry, more tea was poured, and then the vicar's wife brought in a platter of tea cakes and sherry, just as Elizabeth had said she would.

"Congratulations," the vicar said, toasting them with a thimbleful of sherry. "Nothing could be more delightful. Except, of course, a family wedding, but there's hardly anyone left between you, is there? Your father, Elizabeth?"

"Oh. Oh, he went up to London for a while," she said, the lie falling glibly off her tongue.

"I had the pleasure of knowing *your* father," the vicar said to Nicholas.

"Did you?"

"A dear, somewhat reckless young man. Went over to Russia, did he not? We lost a village doctor, you know. But— you were born there?"

"I was." Nicholas looked distinctly uncomfortable.

"I always thought it was a shame that William and Richard became estranged."

"Those things happen," Nicholas said.

"And yet, here it has come full circle, you're back where you belong, at Shenstone. And with God's great good wisdom, Elizabeth is now by your side."

"I appreciate the thought," Nicholas said, sending Elizabeth a guarded look. "And your kindness in arranging this ceremony on such short notice."

"Elizabeth made me understand that the ceremony must take place as soon as possible, and I acceded to her wishes, and, I hope, yours."

"Always mine," Nicholas murmured, his gaze still burning Elizabeth's. "I believe it is time for us to leave. Elizabeth?"

"Yes, Nicholas." She had never sounded so meek.

The vicar's stableboy brought round the gig and they climbed in.

The vicar squeezed her hand. "Good luck, my dear. God-speed."

"And exactly what did you tell the vicar to make him think our marriage must be so precipitous?" Nicholas asked. "Or should I take a guess?"

"I suppose you could guess," she said defensively, "but I didn't couch it in any kind of definitive terms."

"I see." He didn't see anything except that Elizabeth's little blackmail had just thrown everything over the wall, and his enemy now had two targets instead of one. "And how do you expect they will react when we tell them?"

"I can't wait to see. After all your huffing and puffing about taking a wife . . ."

"I scared them all to death."

"Only my father."

"He will get nothing now," Nicholas said, the controlled tone of his voice belying his fury. "We will rewrite the bargain in light of this turn of events."

Oh, she hadn't considered his anger over this. She hadn't really thought through what it would mean to coerce him into a marriage he didn't want.

She had refused to see this: she had been a convenience for him, nothing more, nothing less. There would be no more spectacular couplings with him. That wasn't what a man like him wanted from a wife.

And he had been correct in wanting to seek someone pure and innocent from among the gentry.

What he had gotten was his own well-used whore, and that was the top and bottom of it. She had no innocence, no purity, no goodness left if, without a moment's compunction, she could use deceit, lies, and blackmail to get what she wanted.

She had done that, and more; and it was now very clear that she was truly her father's daughter in all mercenary things.

"Whatever you wish," she said stiffly. It was time anyway; her father couldn't pick her purse forever.

"We're almost there."

"Do you suppose they've discovered we're gone?"

"Someone will know. The servants always know in any event," Nicholas said as he guided the gig around the final curve to the front steps of the house.

Lights were blazing everywhere.

Nicholas helped her out of the gig and stood looking up at the steps down which he had fallen not three days ago.

They heard distant voices as they started up. Nicholas slanted a glance at her. "You have only to trip me, and everything would be yours."

Her heart turned stone cold. He meant it. He saw nothing but her deceits, and her voracious desire to claim Shenstone again.

And then Frederick came rushing out of the front doors, followed by Peter, Mena, and Victor. "They're here, they're here—oh thank God, thank God. *Where* have you been?"

"To London, to see the Queen?" Nicholas said. "Are we all here? Well, we might as well tell them now, Elizabeth. Mena, gentlemen—Elizabeth and I are married."

Chapter 20

Her father was fairly hopping up and down with glee.

"My darling girl, I *never* thought you'd take my suggestion seriously," he said to her *sotto voce* as they all settled themselves in the library. "You *are* a credit to me, after all."

"That wasn't quite why I married him, Father."

He waved her statement away. "But you did, and that's all that matters."

"And of course," Peter said, voicing out loud what they were all thinking, "you owe us no explanation whatsoever, but after that whole business about seeking a wife, I truly think we deserve one."

Elizabeth looked helplessly at Nicholas.

Nicholas looked around the room. *The enemy was here.* Frederick, who looked way too happy. Mena, always confused. Victor, a drink in hand as usual. And Peter, stone-faced by the fireplace.

"It's a perfectly reasonable decision, my friends. You had only to look around at the ladies we entertained the other night. Young, innocent, pallid. And the one among them with some personality had just started to bore me to tears. And here was Elizabeth. Young, beautiful, elegant, discreet, witty, wise. Still able to bear a child. Someone I know and get along with tolerably well."

"Tolerably," she agreed tartly.

"This afternoon, I was *hiding* from Ursula, and here was Elizabeth armed as always with wise counsel that showed me the error of my ways. What could I do but marry her?"

"Yes!" Frederick exclaimed delightedly.

"And so you popped off to the vicar on the spur of the moment." Peter was definitely not delighted.

"Well, with much to-ing and fro-ing of the servants, as Giles will tell you," Elizabeth put in.

"And none of us there."

"No just impediments," Nicholas said. "And now . . . I'm tired, and still not recovered from the accident. I may just spend my wedding night in my sick bed."

He limped out of the room, and Mena came over to squeeze Elizabeth's hands and kiss her cheek. "Such a wise thing, to marry Nicholas."

"I drink to you," Victor said, lifting his glass.

"So smart," Peter said, coming to sit down beside her. "Elizabeth, do you understand what you have done?"

She couldn't decide exactly what he meant by that: that she had killed their great love, or that she had finally secured Shenstone for herself and her children?

"Yes," she said, waiting for him to elaborate.

"You seduced him so well and truly that all he could do was marry you? Did you have to follow my advice to the letter?"

"No, Peter. Only to the altar."

But could she have propositioned Nicholas at all if she had *really* loved Peter? At this fraught moment, when she herself had turned all her hopes and dreams inside out by this marriage, she really didn't know.

"Well, it is as you wanted it to be," Peter said. "Now I know there's no hope for me."

But that, too, was so easy to say in the aftermath. Nothing but death could put her marriage asunder. Forcing Nicholas to marry her had conferred on her the power to give and the power to destroy.

And here it was, firsthand. This man, whom she had loved so futilely and for long, and who had come back to her like a dream, was now a man *without* a dream.

"And don't say we must be friends," he added. "We've always been friends. And we *were* finally at a place where we might have been more. If only . . ."

If only she could have gotten Shestone for herself.

That was the crux. That was the barter.

So the fact really was there had never been any hope of a union with him, except insofar as she would give herself with no strings attached.

. . . fuck him and he'll never marry you . . .

That seemed so long ago . . .

Be a widow with income and the possibility of inheriting a great estate, and he might marry you.

And probably within a year, gone and strayed.

So this gone-and-done marriage that she had engineered might have been the best thing she ever did for herself.

"There are no if-only's," she said. "There never was anything I could use to get Shenstone back."

If only—

If only he knew . . .

But she would never tell.

"So," she continued, "why don't you just stay on for a day or two, and have your country weekend before you go back to London?"

"Do you think that's possible now?"

"Nothing has changed, Peter."

"Everything has changed."

"Well, you'll do as you will. You're always welcome here."

"Dear, dear Elizabeth. Definitely queen of the manor house again. You might not have been born to it, but you do it well."

"I always thought so."

"I wish you good luck in dealing with Ursula tomorrow. You know she'll be back."

She smiled at him. "I don't suppose you'd consider taking her riding or something."

"My dear Elizabeth, she'd probably read me a book." And he dropped a kiss on her forehead as he left.

* * *

The die was cast now. The thing that would have been so simple, finally transporting the royal jewels to London, had now become a maze of torturous planning in which he must protect his mission, and simultaneously protect and defend himself against Elizabeth.

Even now, he wasn't certain why he had allowed her to push him into this hasty marriage. He supposed it was the thought of a long protracted and expensive court battle over his father's and Dorothy's letters. He supposed, too, that he couldn't take the chance that some high court wouldn't define those fuzzy phrases to project some doubt on his parentage.

None of this could he afford right now. It seemed easier to just marry her. Hell, he hadn't stopped wanting her, and his well-conceived scheme of finding a wife had turned inside out in every way possible anyway.

His enemy hadn't taken the bait.

Yet.

But tonight—oh, there had been something hard and harsh in the air as he made the announcement of their marriage. No one had expected it, a prime goal when one wanted to counterattack the enemy. And they all were shocked by it, which gave him still another advantage.

But had he thought about it, he would have realized there was one detrimental component to it: that Elizabeth was another body between his enemy and his enemy's goal.

And Elizabeth was either in the line of fire, or the one who wielded the weapon. And even he didn't know which.

Something had to give. His enemy was truly the Unseen Hand—there to push, guide, counsel, and console, and everything that had happened was a function of those covert things.

He just wished to hell he felt more up to the mark. The accident was still telling on him: his ribs still ached, and his leg even more so, and he still couldn't sleep for the pain in his back.

But the die was cast. He would get what sleep he could, because tomorrow nothing would be the same.

* * *

When he came downstairs the next morning, he found the household in an uproar.

"Now what?" he asked resignedly. "Can't I at least get some tea?"

"Tea? Tea at a time like this?" Mena cried, wringing her hands.

"Where is everybody?"

"Where is everybody? They're out; they're all over the countryside, all over town," Mena whimpered. "Elizabeth didn't want to bother you. She didn't think it was anything. And it turned out it was. She didn't know, not at first. And I can't be of any help whatsoever."

"Out, why?" God, it was hard to be patient with her. "What's happened? What's missing?"

"Who's missing, you mean? Elizabeth's father. He wasn't down to breakfast today."

"Oh shit . . ." Nicholas muttered. *The first strike?*

"Nobody thought a thing of it," Mena went on in that agitated way. "I mean, we all know Frederick never likes to miss a meal. But he wasn't down to breakfast this morning, and when Elizabeth sent up to waken him—his bed hadn't been slept in, even though we all saw him go upstairs last night—and he wasn't there."

"So they're all out looking."

"Well, yes. Except nobody can think where he could be."

"Did anyone think to check the railroad station?"

"Peter probably did. Or Victor. And there's a whole sea of servants going top to bottom through the house and grounds."

Hell and damn. He hadn't expected this so soon.

"Where's Elizabeth?"

"I think she's gone to town."

"Then Victor or Peter must have gone up to the train station and maybe tried to track him to London. It's the most logical explanation. Where haven't the servants been?"

318 / *Thea Devine*

"They've been everywhere, Nicholas. Oh God, I just don't know what to do."

"Give me a minute to check his room." He took the steps two at a time, to the detriment of his bruised body.

Frederick's room was closer to the staircase than his, and the door had been closed this morning when he'd made his way downstairs.

He pushed it open, and it was just as Mena said. The bed was made, nothing was touched. The windows hadn't been closed for the night, and a slight breeze billowed out the curtains.

Hell.

If he didn't want to examine it too closely, the explanation that Frederick had gone to London was the most reasonable one. He'd probably gotten himself in such a deep stew financially that there was no getting out, and he needed to reassure them, and tell them the good news that his daughter had married an Earl and all the money they needed would come through.

Well, by God, there would be no more rescuing of Frederick. Elizabeth's father could sink in his own juices. It was folly enough Elizabeth had supported her father this whole year on virtually no income of her own.

But that was not the problem.

He went back downstairs to Mena.

"He must have gone to London on the sly; he just didn't want anyone to know how much trouble he was in. It's the only explanation."

"And now he's causing trouble instead," Mena said. "That man was born to trouble. And all we can do is sit and wait."

But Nicholas couldn't sit still. It was the thought of the Unseen Hand, and the atmosphere. And Frederick's haring off to London without telling anyone made no sense.

He couldn't walk or ride, but he rigged up the gig, and he drove out onto the back roads toward the tenant farms where he saw a couple stableboys checking at every farm.

Back around he came in a wide circle that reminded him

too much of the way the searchers narrowed into the gardens the night of the fire.

Oh God, the night of the fire . . .

Had anybody thought to look there?

Hell and damn . . .

He raced the gig down into the lower field, risking his breaking another couple of bones as he toppled out of the carriage on a run.

Another minute, two, and he was at the metal doors that were still almost invisibly flush in the grass. Hell. Closed down And nothing to pry them up. His damned hands, if he had to.

Wait. In the gig . . . a shoe pick . . .

God, he couldn't do this alone—he felt a tearing pain in his side as he inserted the point. It was like chopping a tree with a dinner knife.

Goddamn it. *Just give—a little . . .*

And Mena waiting, Elizabeth probably back to the house by now.

Give—dammit!

Another ferocious jolt to his body—and then suddenly, the thing gave, just enough for him to get his fingers under the flat and lift the metal door.

And enough, probably, to put him in hospital, too, he thought mordantly as, breathing hard from the pain, he eased his way down the steps.

But the lantern wasn't there.

Not there? Hell and damn. How?

Now what? *Go back to the house and lie down.*

He braced his hands on either side of the tunnel walls.

Twenty steps. He counted each and every one.

Twenty steps. Still the faint odor of smoke lingering in the air.

Twenty steps, and he was at the storage area—and his boot connected with something solid as he felt his way into the room.

* * *

They brought Elizabeth's father back to the house at sundown, and laid the body out in his bedroom until Dr. Pemble could arrive.

By that time, Elizabeth was long home, and Peter—it had been Peter who'd gone—was back from London, and they were all gathered in the morning room, with Mena dissolved in tears.

"Nobody would tell me anything," Peter told her under Mena's quiet sobbing. "Krasnov—that Machiavelli—I swear that man was bleeding your father dry. I'm almost certain there weren't even any oil wells."

"I don't want to know that," Elizabeth said stonily. "Why would I want to know he was such a failure?"

"He wasn't a failure," Peter murmured consolingly. "He had a good heart, but he was too trusting. And he had you."

But he had never had her, Elizabeth thought. She had been his worst detractor. She had never believed in any of his highflying schemes. And then she had showed her faith by selling herself to obtain the money he so desperately wanted.

What kind of sacrifices had she made? A marriage of convenience? Two? A bargain in sin? She thought she had been so clever to have outwitted him that way. She'd thought he'd go on forever, trying to siphon her money and encroaching on her life.

How had a man like that died—in a place of safety and home?

Damn it all. Damn it. And for Nicholas to have been the one to find him! And *where* he had found him . . . in a most obvious place where no one had thought to look?

She still couldn't believe it; she still couldn't cry. "When will Dr. Pemble be here?" she asked in a constricted voice.

"Soon," Peter said. "Soon."

No, soon her father would come bounding into the room, demanding to know where she'd been, when she'd come home, and how much money she could give him to cover over this week.

Oh damn. Damn damn damn . . . and he'd been so top over tails about his ingenious suggestion she marry Nicholas, and the fact she'd actually managed to do so.

How was it that Nicholas had found him? Nicholas, who had accused them all of conspiring to kill him?

"*How* did he die?"

She had asked that querstion at least ten times. Nicholas didn't know, nor did Peter. Mena was useless, and Victor just stared out the window.

Oh God, I miss him so much!

The hour dragged on. No one was hungry. Giles brought tea and biscuits and murmurings of "I'm sorry, madam, so so sorry."

The clock struck six before Dr. Pemble appeared. Peter and Nicholas took him up to Frederick's room.

Elizabeth retreated to the sofa resentfully. "I don't understand this, I don't. Why did my father die?"

"Enemies," Victor said emphatically. "All around you."

"God, Victor, that is so tiresome."

"Then believe what you will, Elizabeth. Somehow he died."

"In the tunnel," Elizabeth said as if she were reciting a litany. "He just went to the tunnel and dropped dead?"

"Stop it!" Victor commanded. "It is useless to speculate. You'll only upset yourself more."

"I couldn't possibly be more devastated."

"Then cry," Victor said callously. "All you do is sit and make up stories and pretend he could still walk into this room."

"I *hate* you, Victor."

He shrugged. "I really don't care."

"God, what are they doing up there? Shouldn't the doctor have made his judgment by now?"

"It's only been a half hour, dear," Mena told her through her tears. "I'm sure he wants to be thorough."

"*I* want him to be *wrong.*"

"We all do, dear."

The clock kept ticking. The wonder was that time went on

322 / Thea Devine

as if nothing had happened. As if her father's time on earth had not stopped dead.

Dead. Such a . . . *dead* word to describe it.

She felt the tears finally stinging her eyes just as they heard the sound of footsteps finally coming down the stairs.

She couldn't move. Tears flooded her eyes.

Peter came first, then Nicholas, then Dr. Pemble, who came and sat down next to her on the couch.

He cleared his throat. "Well, this is the story. He fell and hit his head."

She swallowed hard. "In the tunnel."

"It appears so, my lady. My lord here tells us that there was no lantern when he went there today. We must assume that the situation was the same for your father, that he decided to go into the tunnel anyway, and tripped and fell somehow. A tragic accident, my lady. Nothing more, nothing less."

"Yes," she whispered, while every instinct in her screamed NOOOO.

"I notified the church. The ladies will come to lay him out properly, and the vicar will discuss the service tomorrow morning, if that suits you."

"Yes. Of course." NOOOOOOOOOO . . . *How would she even find tomorrow?*

"It was an accident," Peter said, correctly reading her stunned expression. "Nothing could have been done. An *accident.*"

She gave the doctor her hand in a daze. "But why did he go down there?"

"I'm afraid, my lady, we'll never know."

His enemy was waiting, and now, with this bold stroke, had entered the game. The death of Frederick was a chess move, Royal to pawn. What had Frederick been, after all, but a drain on the castle?

Who could have wanted Frederick dead?

Elizabeth again.

He was so debilitated by all the exertion and by Frederick's death, he could do little more than station himself in the morning room and let Mena and Elizabeth handle the arrangements.

Elizabeth was so very good at handling arrangements.

Maybe it was better that he was among a crowd.

His instincts prickled tellingly.

Why had Frederick gone to the tunnel?

He could think of four explanations: someone had lured him; he was meeting someone; he was hiding something; he had followed someone . . .

Ah . . .

Last night? But they'd all been bowled down by the announcement last night. He didn't think the Unseen Hand would have had time to plan anything last night.

But still . . . His enemy was clever and cautious, and if he were going to make a move, he would have had to have done it last night. Or very early this morning at the latest . . .

Because whatever he'd done, it had warranted his committing murder. So the obvious conclusion must be that Frederick had seen something, and for that he'd been killed.

He got up and limped around the room. That made sense. But there was something . . . something he was missing perhaps . . .

He heard Elizabeth in the entry hall, composed now, but her voice laced with tears.

"Oh dear, Ursula. I don't suppose anyone's told you. We've had two monumental events today: a death and a marriage. Oh yes, Nicholas and myself. Yes, quite a surprise. But you're still welcome to stay."

She appeared in the doorway a moment later. "You won't be surprised to hear she chose not to keep you company today."

"Nothing would surprise me today." He saw her face crumple, he held out his arms, and she walked into them.

He felt so strong, so safe, so *there*.

324 / Thea Devine

"Why did Father have to die?"

Nicholas held her; he didn't have the heart to tell her—Frederick had just gotten in the way.

He went back down to the tunnel with Victor and made a thorough search of the area around the storage room.

"Nothing to see. But isn't that always the way," Victor said. "Whatever it was that lured Frederick here, it is not in the tunnel now."

Nicholas thought about it for a moment. "He may have seen someone *removing* something from the tunnel." And in fact, that was the likeliest supposition.

It fit the scenario perfectly.

Frederick might well have been out for a walk that morning, had seen someone working around the tunnel, hidden himself nearby, and finally confronted that person, a foolhardy act which precipitated his death.

When he limped around to the thicket of bushes about three yards away, he saw evidence that Frederick had been there in the trampled branches, and the scuffed footprints.

Frederick had been murdered and the lines were narrowing down.

"What do we do?" Victor asked him.

"Hell, I don't know. Maybe we just wait."

That was hardly a line of defense, however, and Nicholas was keenly aware of that fact.

He could just close things up and take Elizabeth away, he thought. But there was still the funeral to be gotten through. The undertaker had been there, Frederick was laid out, and tomorrow they would walk with the cart to the family burial plot, a half mile from the house.

The house was like a morgue. Menace hovered like fog, creeping into the air, into the rooms, into their bones.

One by one they took turns sitting with Frederick.

"Ah, Elizabeth," Peter said, drying her tears, "you did all you could."

One more day, one more night, and other decisions could

be made, she thought; they didn't have to stay at Shenstone at all right now.

They just had to bury her father and get on with it.

And because of this unexpected death, she didn't have to deal with the ramifications of her marriage of coercion.

Because of that, Nicholas could be the one on whom she leaned. She found there was comfort in that. For all the wild unbridled sensuality in him, he was a man of substance, someone in this time of trial, on whom she could count. And that was a most pleasant shock.

But even she felt unsettled by the atmosphere.

Victor, drinking too much. Mena, continually wringing her hands. Nicholas, prowling like a lion. Peter, still and quiet as a monk.

"I think, after the funeral we'll all go up to London," she said finally, just to interject something positive in the air. "Not that there's much I will be able to do, but it is just so . . . *deadly* here—"

"You've just taken a staggering blow," Peter protested. "Two such life-changing things happening within the space of two days, Elizabeth. Running away isn't going to help you cope with them. You'd be better off just staying here. And I say that with all due affection. You know I want the best for you."

And I want my father, Elizabeth thought. God, she still expected him to be hovering just outside the door, listening to everything, and finding some way to turn it to his advantage.

"Maybe. I don't know. Maybe I'll just go lie down."

She didn't even want to do that. It meant she would leave them all alone, and she couldn't trust what Peter might say, or do.

Or Nicholas for that matter.

What had she done by forcing this marriage?

If only she had left things alone . . .

But no, not she. And now, she was Nicholas's wife and her father was dead, so what had she bartered for that?

Lies and deceit. She had been running them nonstop since

Nicholas had arrived. He alone, of all of them, had been true. He was who he said he was; he'd presented the proofs, and then generously offered her and her father a home. He hadn't had to do even that much, and still she tried to bamboozle Shenstone away from him.

Even Dorothy's letters—a bluff at best, and terrible risk had he not backed down. And one she'd been willing to take, so what did that say about her?

She was the one who should be mourned—for her loss of innocence and for all the devious things she had done in the name of loving Peter.

In truth, she loved nothing but the idea of being the mistress of Shenstone.

And now she was.

The house was dead as a tomb. Not a sound anywhere. And only the faintest of lights glimmering in the hallways.

It was a night for death—the death of a life, of hopes, of dreams. The death of the spirit perhaps, as everyone tried to sleep, wanted to sleep, to shut out the nightmare.

Deep into everyone's dreams curled the scent of smoke. Light as air, vaporous as fog, drifting down the hallways, under the doors.

Different this time; not the rolling thunder of a smothered fire. Rather, a slow burn, not unlike the sentiments of the sentient presence that wandered floor to floor.

This time, only one would escape.
The one with whom the game must be played.
The one with the treasure.
The one with the most to lose.

He was dreaming of fire—or maybe the thought of it had invaded his dreams because of the way Frederick had died, and the scent of charred wood was still in his consciousness.

But fire was in his dreams. A slow insidious fire crawling up the timbers, licking at the stairs . . .

He bolted wide awake. This was not a dream. And this was

not the dense heavy smoke of a concentrated area of flame. This was something worse—it was like a smothering veil.

He leapt out of bed and crashed across the room to the connecting door. The *locked* connecting door. His side? God, he couldn't remember—and he was starting to choke up.

Which meant this damned fire, wherever its locus, had been burning far too long.

He banged on the door. "Elizabeth . . . !"

He raced to the window and bashed the glass. "*Elizabeth* . . . !"

Out into the hallway where the same fine film of smoke floated like death.

"Mena! Victor! Peter!" He ran down the hall banging on their doors. He heard them coughing, and fumbling at their locks, and then they stumbled out into the hall. "Get down, get down. On your hands and knees . . . *now*—!"

But not him. He moved back into his bedroom and frantically kicked in the connecting door.

But Elizabeth was not there. Elizabeth was not in the room. *Oh dear God, now what?*

They crawled down the hallway, and he slipped down the stairs to the first landing where the smoke was the thickest.

"Hell. It's in the cellars again. Shit. Get back, get back; we can't get out this way. Guest wing—back stairs . . . now . . ."

He didn't even have time to think, to assess, not even to calm his pounding fear as the smokiness wafted downward and settled on him with the caress of a lover.

Where was Elizabeth?

Jesus God. Crawling down the hall, up the steps, down the corridor to the guest wing, and down the servants' staircase, all the way coughing and hacking as the smoke drifted with them like a companionable lover.

They burst into the kitchen and out into the rear garden, and then turned to look at what his enemy had wrought.

Shenstone burned.

And Elizabeth was missing.

* * *

There was nothing to be done. They heard the fire bell clanging; they heard the rumble of the water carts coming up from town. All they could do was make sure that the servants were accounted for.

And Elizabeth. Dear God, where was Elizabeth?

The architect of this funeral pyre or its victim?

Nicholas felt an anguish so profound it almost crippled him.

Elizabeth . . .

Peter was watching him. Really watching him.

He felt his skin prickle.

"Everything beautiful inside burning," Peter said. "What a shame, what a loss, Nicholas."

"I'll live with it."

"It would be too bad if there were anything in there you absolutely needed to save."

"Only Elizabeth," Nicholas snapped. "Did you see Elizabeth? She wasn't in her room. I didn't have a minute to search for her." Oh God—he just couldn't give in to the pain.

"She's not in there," Peter said dreamily. "And she's the most valuable jewel of all."

"Where *is* she then? What the hell are you talking about?"

"Ah, Nicholas." And suddenly he had a pistol. "Only you and I know."

The roar of crackling flame, walls searing down, the hubbub of the crowd behind him puncutated that moment of revelation.

"You." That one word expressed it all; here he had been all along—the Enemy, the Other, the Unseen Hand.

And the object, always, had been the imperial treasure.

"So now, let us go retrieve that which we both know is in your possession."

"Then find it," Nicholas goaded him. "Or else it dies with me."

"I wouldn't mind killing you, Nicholas. You'd only be one in a long long line of murders I've committed. No. We'll deal for the jewels. You're fond of bartering. Well, here we are, a simple exchange: Elizabeth's life for the Empress's cast-offs."

"Where is she?"

"Oh, I'm performing a little rope-trick with her. She's in a place where the fire hasn't gotten to—yet. It just remains to be seen how long she will stay there, and that, my friend, is up to you."

"Why? How?"

"Don't be naive, Nicholas. Under-royals always need money. We have to keep up the lifestyle, you know. And that takes hundreds of thousands of pounds. So imagine my dismay when I heard this little whisper that Alexandra was going to have those jewels transported to England just to *sit* in a bank somewhere. As if my brothers hadn't fed enough rubles into this economy by maintaining their country homes here. Oh, no—I wanted that. That was for me. I didn't see any purpose to Alexandra's jewels sitting in a dusty vault for the next fifty years. And the rest you know."

"Frederick?"

"Saw me moving flammables into the house. No point to that man living, parasite that he was."

The roof caved in suddenly, in a shower of sparks, and a volcano of flame shot into the air.

Someone screamed, a distraction, and Peter started, and looked around.

Instantly, Nicholas rushed him and Victor jumped him from behind.

Both of them, down on the hard ground with him, as he struggled and howled, writhing like a ghost in the light of the fire, until they got him subdued.

When Nicholas looked up, Mena was standing over Peter's limp body, his pistol in her hand.

"Victor?" Nicholas said uncertainly.

"Umm?"

"Thanks."

"No thanks needed, Nicholas. That's our job, Mena and me—we were always here to be back up for you."

"Jesus." It took a moment to sink in. "How?"

"Your mother, when she was certain you would claim the title."

"Hell." His mother. His darling sainted mother watching over him from afar. "You were supposed to have been given the code," Victor amplified, watching Peter carefully. "But when Mena said she knew you, and you didn't respond, we thought it might be better that you didn't know."

"Shit." This was all coming at him too fast and there was no time to analyze any of it. And then—"Elizabeth?"

"I heard him. Where do you think?"

"Only one place: down the tunnel where her father died— if we're not too late . . ."

Chapter 21

The smoke was like a funeral shroud, rolling slowly toward her as fire ate through the wooden beams and the secret doors, licking at the dirt floor, and scorching the stone walls of the tunnel in an acrid pattern of doom.

He had tied her up against one of the wooden beams of the burned-out secret room, and she felt almost fatalistic that she would die in the place she had once thought would be the impetus of all her dreams.

Everything will be as it was . . .

Peter's promise. Peter, her golden god, whom she had trusted with all her heart, soul, and might. Peter, who when he needed help, came to her. Not one of his expatriate friends. Not his family. Not his emperor, his nephew.

Her.

Foolish gullible *her.*

How could she not have been flattered by that? And all the secrecy surrounding his need for a place to hide that his enemies could never find.

He needed a week, he said, and he didn't care if he stayed in an attic, a storeroom, or a closet. Just a week for the thing to blow over. And he needed the utmost secrecy on her part. No one must ever know.

And then, when his enemies were vanquished, he promised, he would come to her, and everything would be as it was—and they could start all over again.

He didn't tell her about the murders until later. The very ones that she and her father and Mena and Victor had dis-

cussed, the lunatic killer whom the whole of London feared—
Peter.

Peter.

She felt insensible with her own simplemindedness. To have
loved him like that—to have taken his every word about
things that on the surface any sane woman would question—
how desperate she must have seemed. And how easy then to
deceive.

Besides, what did she know of the life of expatriate royals?
It seemed perfectly plausible that enemies were all around
them. And that, at some point, a safe haven might be needed.

She had wanted to be that haven for Peter. A repository of
all his secrets, all his love.

All his vicious, malicious hate for his family and the
chronic diminished financial state in which they deliberately
kept him to curb his uncontrollable appetites.

But all of that came later too . . .

It was her secret marriage that sent him over the edge.

"You didn't understand," he told her in that ragged reasonable tone of voice that she hated as he dragged her to the tunnel, "it was all about the jewels. It's always been about the
jewels."

Jewels she had no idea existed. Jewels for which Peter had
committed a score of murders. An undertow of desperation
that pulled her along in its wake. And an international secret
agent who turned out to be an heir . . .

She heard the crackling of the fire in the distance, saw the
pall of smoke hovering like the door to heaven—

Secrets. They all had secrets.

And for all that and her foolish blind faith in him, she was
going to die.

They ran. By the light of the fire, they ran, scrambling,
stumbling across the drive, down to the gardens and out toward the lower field where the smoke already lay like a thick
gray mantle.

And the metal doors would be hot as hell. And his body felt like he'd been pummeled in a boxing match. And he didn't know how he was going to save her.

Damn and blast—they had not an implement between them, nothing of use but their hands.

Goddamn bloody bastard—

Elizabeth . . .

The son of a bitch . . . he'd been almost sure about him from the moment he arrived. But not quite. He couldn't quite see what Peter had to gain after she'd had to relinquish Shenstone.

And all that time she had been searching for something to use against him.

At Peter's behest?

Damn it. There were so many things he needed to know and the smoke was so dense here, and she was down in that tomb of a tunnel . . . goddamn him, he would kill him . . .

They pulled sharply as Nicholas stepped on one of the metal plate doors and cursed.

"Hot as hell. Don't touch those doors—" he warned Victor. "Get something around your mouth and nose. We'll need it. That bloody son of hell—all right, find a heavy branch. Shit, I can barely see. Damn him, damn him, damn him . . ."

They scrounged desperately for something heavy to lift the doors. Victor had a knife, a blessing, that they used to taper two sturdy branches, and by the smoke-diffused glow of the distant conflagration, they lay on the ground, inserted the points into the metal, and wedged their bodies hard against the wood.

The smoke was getting to them, curling under their makeshift masks. There, on the ground, it was heavy and thick and they inhaled mouthfuls of it with every breath.

And Elizabeth was down there.

And his bruised body felt like it would just snap in two as he pushed and pushed against the burning metal door.

Bloody bloody hell . . .

Elizabeth ...!

She could be unconscious—she could be ... no, he would not let himself think it because he would die too ...

Thank God for Victor, working methodically and steadily beside him.

"We'll get her," Victor promised in a thick voice. "We'll get her."

The metal plate moved. They leaned into it again, levering themselves upward against the branches—the one snapped—and the one metal plate lifted. Just an inch—just enough.

In one minute, Victor had the two doors open and smoke poured out.

"Hell and damn—"

"I'm right behind you," Victor said.

No time for anything. They tumbled down the smoke-logged stairs and on their hands and knees crawled blindly toward the secret room.

The fire hadn't reached here yet, but the intensity of the heat was critical. Peter had torched the portion of the cellar under the house, and now the flames were spreading into the tunnel.

They had minutes, perhaps not that.

"Got her—unconscious ... knife?"

Victor thrust it at him, and Nicholas cut rope wherever he touched it and inched her limp body toward Victor until she was entirely free.

Now they had to get on their feet, and by touch and memory, find their way to the steps through a dense fog of nothingness.

This was hell. There could be nothing worse than this. Coughing and sputtering, dragging Elizabeth's deadweight body between them, they felt their way down the tunnel wall, dropping every few minutes to the floor to gasp for what little air was left.

And then Victor touched the bottom step. He pushed Nicholas down on his hands and knees, and laid Elizabeth's slack body on his back.

"Up." He could barely get out the word. And he didn't know if Nicholas even had the strength to crawl up the steps carrying her.

But Nicholas nodded, moved. Slowly, and in deep shocky pain, he inched his way up the steps, with Victor crouching beside him.

VWOOMMM!

They heard a roar behind them as they reached the top step; flame had caught wood and shot into the tunnel.

They fell onto the ground and lay there coughing and gulping the smoky air.

"Got to get away from here . . ." Victor gasped. "Too close . . ."

Nicholas nodded, and got to his feet. Wobbly—light-headed. Lungs felt sore, scorched . . . no time even to check Elizabeth's condition—with Victor's help he lifted Elizabeth into his arms.

"Oh no, don't go."

Nicholas staggered and almost dropped Elizabeth as he recognized Peter's voice.

"Put her down."

He appeared out of the bushes, almost like a ghost, backing them toward the tunnel.

"Put her down, Nicholas. We still have business to attend to."

"He's got the pistol," Victor whispered. "Better put Elizabeth down."

"Is she dead?" Peter asked solicitously as Nicholas laid her on the ground.

"Why don't you come look?"

"No, there's something else I'm looking for, my man, and you know just what it is."

"We had this discussion; I have nothing you want."

"That's so amusing, Nicholas. I thought for sure if the house was burning, the jewels would be the first thing you'd save. And you just strolled out of the house like you were going for a walk. You goddamned son of a bitch—where are the jewels?"

"Where's Mena?" Victor demanded suddenly.

"Old bitch. She's out of commission now . . . Now Nicholas, I've got the gun, you've got the Empress's jewels, and you've got nowhere to run except that tunnel. God knows what you've already done for the motherland, but I must take into account you might be so altruistic you would die for her. But I wonder." He got off a shot that grazed the ground near where Elizabeth lay—"if Elizabeth would."

Nicholas took a step, and Victor pulled him back. *Not yet.*

"So you did it all," Victor said. "Just to get him to reveal where he hid the jewels."

"Aren't you the smart counterrevolutionary agent, Victor. It would have been nice if this could have ended cleanly with no more deaths."

"Oh yes, the deaths, all those mysterious deaths," Nicholas said slowly.

"And then the maniac disappeared."

"I resent that. Haven't you put it together yet? *I* was the one in the secret room. I came to my beloved Elizabeth after I killed all those people and murdered your priest, and I promised her the world. Well, what she wanted in her world. Which was me. She was the one who hid me there."

More secrets. It almost destroyed him to hear it, but Elizabeth couldn't have known. He just would not believe she had known she was harboring a killer.

He looked at Victor. *When?*

The smoke was getting thicker now, billowing up from the tunnel, and blasting almost unbearable heat behind them.

Victor mouthed, *Mena . . .*

"Elizabeth knew," Peter taunted them. "Elizabeth knew everything. I was girding myself to marry her. But instead of finding a way to disinherit you, the bitch went and married you. Did you know about that too? If she could have done it, I would have married her, and just stayed hidden in the country. Well, that's ever the way with women, Nicholas. Played us against each other and duped us both. And now I want those jewels."

Nicholas shrugged. "Go ahead and take them."

Peter got off another shot, disturbingly close to Elizabeth this time, and she actually stirred.

"Did you want to play games? Haven't we done enough? They weren't in the house; they aren't in the tunnel; there are too many to be hidden on your person—so where are they?" BAM—he punctuated the question with another shot, this time hitting close to Nicholas's boots, and Elizabeth's body jerked.

Where was Mena? It was just light enough now that Nicholas could see Peter, and the smoke-ravaged landscape behind him. Nowhere did he see Mena. And the smoke was getting thicker and the air hotter with every passing moment.

And then he saw movement on the ground behind Peter. Subtle soft movements behind, and Elizabeth, coughing and groggy at his feet.

A distraction. With a sudden sharp "Now!" he threw himself over Elizabeth and Mena bounded up, swinging a thick heavy branch at Peter's knees.

Down he went, pitching forward, aiming low. Down Mena went, with a long protracted moan.

Victor launched himself onto Peter. Nicholas rolled Elizabeth out of the way just as Peter squirmed out from under Victor and jumped to his feet. Nicholas dove as he began to run, caught Peter at his ankles, couldn't hold him, and Peter fell forward into the tunnel, hitting his head on the steps, and he toppled down into the flames and smoke.

Nicholas crawled to the edge, and Victor stopped him.

"Don't."

Nicholas looked up at him, his eyes rimmed in red, his face smeared with ash.

"Let it go," Victor said, and he held out his hand, pulled him to his feet, and they staggered away from the tunnel.

But there was no getting away from the smoke. It was everywhere, and it circled Shenstone like a halo, diffusing the glare of flames behind what was now a skeleton of a house.

"Jesus," Victor muttered as all four of them dropped to the ground a couple of hundred yards away from the tunnel, and finally saw the breadth of the devastation.

They didn't move until the sun came up. Mena was injured, though it didn't impair her ability to walk, so they slowly made their way across the lower field. It was like a death march, single file, with Victor in the lead and Elizabeth and Mena between them.

They ran into the vicar barreling up the drive in his gig. "Thank God in heaven!" he exclaimed. "My dear God, we didn't know what to think. This is the most awful thing. We've been taking your people into town, and looking everywhere for you. Are you all right—Elizabeth?"

"We're all right," she answered for them all, but her voice sounded raw.

"Then you must come and stay at the vicarage until you can determine what to do. This is a horrible, horrible tragedy."

"Thank you, we appreciate that," Nicholas said. "But I think we need to make sure all of our people are out."

"Yes, I was just coming back myself to see to that, since we didn't know where you were. I'll just go on ahead then, and meet you up near the house."

"He has everything taken care of," Victor said, shaking his head as they followed the vicar up the drive. "He lives to be useful in the throes of a disaster."

"And there's the disaster. My beautiful beautiful Shenstone," Elizabeth groaned, suddenly reaching out and grabbing Nicholas's arm because she felt as if her legs would give way.

With the morning light filtering through its broken windows, Shenstone looked like nothing so much as an ancient tomb. The roof was gone, the brick was scorched, everything flammable was black as the night, and acrid smoke still permeated the air.

The vicar came driving back slowly toward them. "There's nothing more here. Everyone's gone. I'll be glad to take Elizabeth and the other lady back to the vicarage right now, and send a carriage back for you."

"That would be perfect; Mena was grazed by a bullet—nothing serious, but perhaps Dr. Pemble should look at it," Nicholas said. "Will you both be all right?"

Elizabeth nodded, and he helped Mena up into the gig first. It was a tight fit, even as tiny as Mena was, to have three people abreast, but the vicar assured him they would manage it, and off they went.

"And now," Nicholas said, holding up his hand like he was giving a benediction, "the end of the story."

The story ended in a run-down one-room thatched roof cottage set back from the road about a half mile from the house, near where the tenant farms were situated. It was the kind of little house no one would ever give a second glance. There was nothing to distinguish it from any of the other cottages that dotted the road; there wasn't even a path to the worn wooden door or a key to the lock.

Nicholas pushed open the door, and he and Victor entered a large square room with three windows, two on the front wall, one on the far side. The floor was covered with hay, with a small carpet laid over that. In the far left corner, there was a bed and a chest. To the right, near the front window, there was a fireplace with a chair and a table set in front of it, and a shelf with some pots, utensils, crocks, jars, and two bowls covered over with cloth, and on the floor beneath, a basket of moldy bread.

"The home of Watton, the head gardener," Nicholas said, "whom William Massey hired five or so years ago. A most crotchety old man, who only likes to tend his flowers, and who admittedly has some peculiarities. But good help is hard to find these days, especially an old man who nurses each and every bloom like it was his child. Mind you, he is crippled"— and Nicholas contorted his bruised body with not a little pain—"and he does shake a lot"—his hands began to quiver—

"and he isn't the most personable of men"—speaking in the quavering tones of a perennially irritated old man—"but the missus likes him, and the master thinks he got an excellent prize in this old man who will take any seasonal gardening work for a reasonable cost per annum."

"Oh my God . . ." Victor breathed.

"And so," Nicholas went on, straightening out his body and resuming his normal voice, "here I stayed when I needed to go under deep cover."

"You chose to go in deep cover at Shenstone," Victor said, a tone of creeping disbelief in his voice.

"Know your enemy," Nicholas said. "Where better than the last place anyone would think to look?" There had been more to than that, of course, all of it tied into his father's exile, his mother's dreams for him. But that was another story.

"And then Peter went on his murder orgy," Victor said, still grappling with the idea of Nicholas's covert presence at Shenstone all these years.

"And isn't the coincidence staggering, that he was hiding in the tunnel, while I was hiding here?" Nicholas moved to the shelf wall, shaking his head. "I didn't know, and it will be hard to forgive myself for that." More so because he had come across Elizabeth more than once ambling around fields in places where she would normally not be.

"But Peter had some advantage of me," he went on. "Because of his court connections, he knew who I was; he studied how I operated. So when he got wind of this mission, on the heels of yet another refusal by his family to fund his lifestyle, it was simple for him to manipulate a place for himself among my men. And now we see the end result. Only one of us could have survived."

He picked up the basket of moldy bread, tore off one end of one loaf, and tilted it over the table. A brilliant fall of gems came tumbling out, sparkling even in the dim light.

Nicholas looked up at Victor. "The deed is done; the mission will be completed. Because the someone who survived had to be me."

London
One Week Later

Secrets. They all had secrets.

And perhaps his was the worst transgression. He had deliberately concealed himself where he could observe his family in a place where no one took notice of the servants or groundskeepers.

A stroke of genius, he thought, until he saw Elizabeth.

For five long years . . . Elizabeth. Watching her covertly every day. Wanting her insanely. But penance must be paid for that kind of forbidden yearning.

And so for want of his desire to abandon his shadow life, nearly a dozen lives had been lost, a great estate burned to the ground, and a Romanov uncle had died.

Whose life was above the price of rubies?

And whose was the greatest sin? Elizabeth, who wanted to disprove his legitimacy and marry the man she loved; or him, for insinuating himself into her way of life at Shenstone, and lying to her about everything?

And so they came, with all the servants, to set up house in London at the end of that week, at the height of the Season, at a time when every calendar was crowded, and there wasn't a dressmaker or tailor to be had.

Oh, the vicar and his parishoners made sure they had some clothes; they couldn't go up to Town without being properly outfitted. And there were some solicitous invitations to stay with neighbors until such time as they could determine what to do about Shenstone.

But the last chapter must be closed, the mission completed, and a new life charted, and that, Nicholas decided, they must commence far away from Shenstone for the time being.

The Tsarina's sister agreed to see him the morning after they arrived in Town. He was ushered into her formal reception room in Number 24 Carlton House Terrace.

It was an immense room painted over with murals of bucolic scenes. The sun poured in through two long floor-to-ceiling windows that fronted the terrace, and there was also a fireplace and ceiling-height mirror, and a parquet floor that made the room even wider than it was. The only furniture were two chairs and small table beside the fireplace, so that Victoria, Lady Battenberg, could dispense with business as efficiently as possible.

She was older than Alexandra, but it seemed to Nicholas that the Tsarina had aged more since becoming Empress and before he even left Russia on her mission.

Lady Victoria was elegantly outfitted in a dress of figured blue silk that was set off by a yoke of lace spilling over her breast, and knots of flowers sewn into the lines of the skirt. She was a most compelling figure, and she looked at him with some doubt as she entered the room.

As well she should. There he was in a made-over suit with a linen bag full of bread on his arm.

"I'm sorry," she murmured. "If you're selling something, you should go around to the servants' entrance."

Nicholas shook his head. "If you please, my lady . . ." He extended his hand; in his palm was a ring.

Lady Victoria gasped, and took it from him. Alexandra's ring, a token and a signal that this was her emissary.

Nicholas stepped over to the little table. It wasn't large enough that he could lay out the entire suite of jewels he carried with him. He tilted the loaf from which he had torn off the end, and spilled the smallest stones onto the perfectly polished little cherry table.

And there they were: small diamonds and little round opals, shooting off a radiant rainbow of color in the early morning sun.

"Oh my God, oh my God," Lady Victoria breathed. "I didn't believe, after the priest was killed, I didn't see how . . . my dear man—my dear, dear man—" She reached forward to grasp his hands.

"You have the accounting. Everything is here," Nicholas said.

"My dear man . . ." She looked close to tears. "You may have saved her life."

She had always loved the townhouse. There was something exciting about living in the midst of a fast-moving city with its endless crowded streets, and endless entertainments.

At least there would be something to do when Nicholas shunned her.

Her betrayals weighted her soul. Never had she thought it would all end like this, with her father and Peter dead, and Shenstone burned to the ground.

But in fact, she hadn't thought past the wedding ceremony, and securing Shenstone for her own.

What if Nicholas wanted to do something about that after everything that had happened?

What if he wanted a divorce?

Lies and deceit. An avalanche to bury her forever, and exclude her from everything she had ever wanted.

She saw no hope of saving anything in the aftermath of all the death and disaster.

And what had she wanted after all? Love, a home, a family. A father who wasn't a swindler. A prince charming who wasn't a murderer.

Dear God, what if Nicholas hated her?

Hated her for bringing Peter down on him. Hated her for trying her utmost to find something to disinherit him. Hated her for marrying him to get what she wanted. Hated her because Shenstone was gone.

She hated herself. She despised herself for being so credulous, so trustful, so *naive*.

One couldn't build a life on betrayals. She didn't know how she was going to live with herself. And there was no possibility Nicholas would want to stay with her.

He was the Earl of Shenstone now, and the whole world, and all its women, were open to him.

Maybe the thing for her to do was just leave.

344 / Thea Devine

Secrets . . . no more secrets, except one. He would never tell her about Watton, never reveal how close he had been, and how much he had wanted her for far too long.

So instead, he'd taken away the life she'd known, he had bartered for her and bullied her, and put her in the position of being Peter's pawn and her father's puppet, and then he'd pinned her to the bed at every turn.

Just the way to make a woman want you.

The only smart thing he'd done was marry her.

And even that was in doubt at this very moment. What if she wanted to divorce him?

Damn and hell. Now that everything was cleared up, the mission was over, their enemies were vanquished, and they could start again?

No. By God, no. The one thing he would not let happen was Elizabeth walking out that door.

The townhouse door. He stood looking up at it, wondering if she was even still there.

Only one way to know.

He walked slowly up the steps and opened the door.

In the hallway: "Elizabeth?" In the parlor: "Elizabeth?" In the drawing room: "Damn it to hell, *Elizabeth?*"

And then frantically as he ran up the stairs: "ELIZA-BETH!!!"

Elizabeth, at the door of one of the bedrooms. "I'm here, Nicholas."

"Well, thank God for that."

The words sat in the air as they stared at each other. How brave was she? Elizabeth wondered; ought she take that grumpy acknowledgment and make something definitive of it, or just pretend it all hadn't happened?

She could live with him on that basis, couldn't she?

"Do you?" she asked finally, tremulously.

"Do I what?"

"Thank God—"

"That you're here, that you didn't die down in that tunnel,

that you married me?" he interjected roughly. "Yes, I thank God, or the fates, for all that, and the hope that something good will come from this mess. It's my mess, and I *will* clean it up, and I'll make it better for you, I promise. I'll get after Krasnov and save what I can of your father's dreams. We'll rebuild Shenstone. We'll—"

"After all that? After what I did?"

"After what *I* did, Elizabeth. It's all on me. My lies. My deceptions. My betrayal. Mine. And I will have to live with it, and all the resulting tragedies I caused. But I'm not going to let it go, do you hear me? *Not*. Not the title, not my life, not you. I'm not letting it go."

It was the most incredible gift. She stood there staring at him, listening to him take the litany of her sins onto himself and absolving her from blame.

"I won't let you divorce me after forcing me to marry you."

"No," she whispered, as tears stunned her eyes. "I couldn't possibly defend that when I blackmailed you into it."

"Exactly," he said carefully. "So we'll abide by this marriage, and all the history of how it came to be. I know you don't love me . . . not yet—"

Almost, she thought. It wouldn't take that much more for her to love him.

"But I thought, I hoped I might barter these"—he dug into his pocket and brought a long string of pearls with a round lustrous pendant attached—"these, for a kiss."

"Just a kiss?" She remembered that kiss.

"Just a kiss." He draped the necklace over her shoulders, sixty inches of beautiful perfect pearls, and the pendant dangling just at the vee between her thighs.

She felt her body tightening, and little curls of pleasure spiraling downward. Her body remembered. "A kiss would be fine."

He pulled her into his arms, and slanted his mouth over hers. "Just a kiss—" he whispered against her lips, and settled himself hard against her body, and deep into her mouth

346 / *Thea Devine*

Just a kiss. Just that take-everything, deep, hot, wet kiss.

Just the tight hard clasp of his arms around her, as if he would never let her go.

Just the thought that there would be a tomorrow, and there was still the rest of today.

Just the symbol of the pearls, and everything sensual and pleasurable they had ever meant to her.

Just everything that was embodied in that seductive explosive bone-melting kiss.

And maybe, she thought as she reached for him, it wasn't too soon for a whole lot more.